Something Extraordinary

OTHER TITLES BY ALEXIS HALL

SOMETHING FABULOUS

Something Fabulous

Something Spectacular

LONDON CALLING

Boyfriend Material

Husband Material

SPIRES

Glitterland

Waiting for the Flood

For Real

Pansies

WINNER BAKES ALL

Rosaline Palmer Takes the Cake

Paris Daillencourt Is About to Crumble

KATE KANE, PARANORMAL INVESTIGATOR

Iron & Velvet

Shadows & Dreams

Fire & Water

Smoke & Ashes

ARDEN ST. IVES

How to Bang a Billionaire

How to Blow It with a Billionaire

How to Belong with a Billionaire

PROSPERITY

Prosperity

Liberty & Other Stories

There Will Be Phlogiston

Other Titles

A Lady for a Duke

The Affair of the Mysterious Letter

Looking for Group

Something Extraordinary

ALEXIS HALL

 Montlake

Published by Montlake, Seattle

www.apub.com

Amazon, the Amazon logo, and Montlake are trademarks of Amazon.com, Inc., or its affiliates.

ISBN-13: 9781662509421 (paperback)
ISBN-13: 9781662509438 (digital)

Cover design by Hang Le
Cover image: © alex74, © IDEAPOINT, © irАArt,
© YANUSHEVSKAYA VICTOR / Shutterstock; © auchara nimprositthi / Getty

Printed in the United States of America

It can never be wrong to live with someone you are fond of.

—*Jenny Lives with Eric and Martin*, Susanne Bösche

Chapter 1

He was drunker than she thought she'd ever seen anybody. Then again, she didn't have much experience of drunkenness. Her aunt and uncle were tipples-after-dinner-type people, her twin preferred other vices, and Peggy was not one to surrender control lightly. Belle had flirted a little on her own account with becoming a drunk, since it was the sort of thing that characters did in novels when they were unhappy. Unfortunately, she'd found it too unpleasant to stick to. Which was yet further evidence—as if she didn't have enough already—that characters in novels didn't know what the fuck they were about.

It was a shame that Sir Horley did not share her sterling common sense on the subject of intoxication, because he looked both miserable and dreadful. A similar sort of puffy-faced, red-eyed dreadful that usually accompanied a bout of intense weeping. Except, in Belle's experience, the body usually exhausted its tolerance for weeping. Sir Horley had clearly been drinking all night. Perhaps longer. It filled her with that half-angry, half-sad, wholly helpless feeling that often swept over her when she had to bear witness to the people she cared about making messes of themselves and their lives.

"Bonny?" Sir Horley squinted through the gloom.

"Do I look like Bonny?" demanded Belle. "In ways other than the familial, that is." Twins they might have been, but the passing years had brought, to Belle's perception at least, only an increasing sense of difference. Bonny was as sweet and round as a summer peach. Whereas she was sharp and stabby and angry, like a hatpin driven into a testicle.

Sir Horley tried again. "Belle?"

"Who else?"

He gave a low rasp she took to be if not a laugh, then the mean-spirited bastard cousin of a laugh. "Who else indeed? I mean, it was never going to be him, was it? Bonny wouldn't come for me."

"These days," Belle remarked, "he only comes for Valentine." She paused. "That . . . that did not sound as I intended."

Once upon a time, Sir Horley would have laughed and teased her. Now he seemed to be barely paying attention. Or even care that she was there at all. Which was not—if Belle was to be completely candid with herself, as she tried to be these days—surprising. Of course it was Bonny he had hoped for. Bonny, who was loving and easy to love, and who everyone preferred. She had tried, for a while, to be . . . better? Different? The sort of heroine the world would always steer towards a happy ending. But she wasn't that sort of heroine. And she didn't even know what a happy ending looked like for someone like her.

At last Sir Horley spoke, apparently oblivious to the passing seconds which had marooned Belle in awkward silence. "What are you even doing here? What time is it? How did you get in?"

"How do you think?" Belle began picking her way across the dusty carpet, through a battlefield of empty bottles.

"You knocked on the door and asked to be admitted?"

"Try again."

Scraping a lank lock of rusty-red hair back from his brow, Sir Horley seemed to be doing his best to focus. "You disguised yourself as—" He broke off, a strange weariness in his tone. "I don't care."

"Then why did you ask?"

"Habit?"

"Well, no disguise was required, although I am wearing breeches for practicality's sake. I simply waited until dark, slipped in via the back garden, and climbed through your open window."

Sir Horley brought a glass to his lips, realising quite some time after he had raised it and tilted it that it was completely empty. "Belle, my dear, is there a part of *I don't care* you're failing to comprehend?"

"The part where you mean it, I suppose?"

There was another long silence. Belle's ingress had brought with it some fresh air, but the room was still the worst-smelling room she'd ever encountered. And she had spent a moderate portion of her childhood visiting with Boudica, her uncle Wilbur's prize pig. This, however, was an unfair comparison to make, for pigs were clean and elegant animals. And Sir Horley, at this present moment, was neither clean nor elegant, and nor were his surroundings.

"You shouldn't be here," he said.

Belle's nose wrinkled. Considering the darkness, the dankness, and the . . . *pungence*, she wasn't entirely sure *anyone* should have been there. "Neither should you."

His look grew fuzzily bewildered. "It's my house."

"It's your aunt's house."

"And she's my family."

"Only by blood."

"You Tarletons." Sir Horley, who had been sitting slumped against the far wall, now slumped sideways and kept slumping, until he landed in a heap on the floor. "Don't you ever . . ."

"Ever what?"

The pile of Sir Horley somehow grew smaller, curling in upon itself like a slug in a rainstorm. "Give up."

Not for the first time in her life, Belle was beginning to suspect she might be in over her head. Her last encounter with Sir Horley had taken place nearly a year earlier, when she and Bonny had kidnapped him, along with his fiancée, in the hope that an artificially induced sense of extremis would encourage the couple to share some frank discourse about their future together—discourse that was surely necessary, given her tendencies towards religiosity and his towards sodomy. The endeavour had failed somewhat extravagantly and perhaps had always been doomed to failure, given its lack of grounding in anything even slightly resembling reality. Of course, in a story such a scheme would have come off perfectly. But that was fiction for you, thought Belle, hammering yet another nail into the coffin of her naiveté, filling one's head with false hopes of happiness, and breaking like dandelion clocks at the first rough wind.

Sir Horley had refused to speak to any of them since, which Belle had felt keenly, and Bonny had perhaps also felt keenly. Though, with his duke to distract him, perhaps he had not. Truthfully, it had been quite some time since he'd seemed to care about the same things she did or care about them to the same extent—which was to say, he cared enough to join her in misguided, if well-meant, shenanigans but not enough to deal with the mess such shenanigans inevitably left in their wake.

And yet Belle had still secretly nurtured a conviction that Sir Horley would change his mind. About what had happened. About her. That his anger would fade and with it his insistence that there lay no real affection between them.

But the months had slipped away, and now it was the eve of his wedding, and she had found him like this—drunk and bitter and distant—and it was impossible not to wonder if he'd been telling the truth all along, for not everyone thought of friendship as she did. Cherished it and clung to it. Found it worth fighting for.

Nevertheless, it would not do to falter now. It never did to falter. You could only try, and keep failing, and hope your failures did not pierce you too deeply.

"I have given up on many things," Belle announced, with a defiant little head toss. "But I will never give up on you."

Bonny, too, was small and loud and dramatic. The difference was, when he was small and loud and dramatic, people believed him. When Belle was small and loud and dramatic, they didn't. And Sir Horley was no exception. He laughed his unpleasant non-laugh. "You don't know the first fucking thing about me, my little Bellflower."

"I know you're my friend."

"You were friends with a phantasm. A pretty figment. Someone who never existed."

He had said something like this during the kidnapping. Belle had disregarded it then. But she finally allowed herself a moment to consider it. To consider him. The bedraggled, inebriated, under-washed ruin of a man she had once believed simple. As if any man was simple. As if any *person* was. "I did not feel as though I were friends with a phantasm."

"Then more fool you."

"You did fool me," she agreed. "But why would you?"

A kind of sluggish bewilderment flickered across his face. "Why what?"

"Why would you wish to? Making someone feel close to you, making them trust you and delight in you, that's an awful lot of work, when the only gain is something you claim you never wanted to begin with."

"I'm too drunk for your . . ." He also seemed too drunk to find an adequate word for what he was too drunk for. "For you."

"All I'm saying," she said, as slowly and distinctly as she could get without crossing the line into patronising, "is that the only benefit to simulating friendship is friendship itself. I don't understand why you would take such pains over something you insist was an illusion all along."

He shrugged. "I was probably bored."

"Or it was not an illusion."

"Oh, for fuck's sake, Belle." He cast his empty gaze at her wearily. "The illusion was that I am someone worth befriending. I pretended I was, for a while. To this day, I couldn't tell you why. Then reality caught up with me. And now you find me as I truly am."

"Inebriation is a passing state."

That drew a dismissive sound from him. "Not if you work at it."

Clearly, he *had* been working at it. She rather wished he hadn't. "Is that why you refused to see us?" she asked, trying to sort through what was hurt, what was spite, and what was mere drunken swagger. "Because you believed we could only care for some performance you were putting on?"

Another shrug. "Whatever I believe, it doesn't seem to have made a damn bit of difference. Because here you are. Attempting to disrupt my life all over again."

"I've been *worried*," Belle cried. "Attempting to disrupt someone's life is one of the ways Bonny and I demonstrate affection."

"It's one of the ways you demonstrate you don't have a fucking clue about how the world works."

Despite the harshness of the words, there was very little passion in his tone. Even hostility she would have welcomed. Anything but this hollow resignation. Unfortunately, she wasn't sure how to stir him from it, which meant she was obliged to fall back on being reasonable. Never her favourite role in a conversation.

"Even if we thought we were acting in your best interests," she said finally, "it was wrong of us to attempt to force a confrontation between you and your betrothed. Then again, you can hardly blame us for not understanding what you needed, or how to help you, when you apparently spent the whole relationship playing a part for us."

Sir Horley responded with a groan of displeasure. "How many times, my tenacious little Portia, must I remind you that I am currently a poor subject for your rhetoric?"

"Then simply answer me this: Are you angry with me?"

"My dear, I'm not wholly certain I can stand up. Do you really think I'm capable of complex emotional reactions?"

"I was afraid you were angry," she admitted. "I was afraid I'd made you hate me."

"Well, now you know better. Perhaps we should both continue with our lives?"

"How can I? When that leaves you convinced I would cast you aside rather than deal with the reality of who you are."

His bleary eyes sharpened momentarily. "You mean this reality? This ugly reality? After I made you think I was like you."

"Which is what precisely?"

"Joyful. Unabashed. When I have always been a coward, a liar, and a whore."

Closing what remained of the distance between them, Belle dropped to her knees before Sir Horley.

He flinched into the wall. "What are you doing?"

"I am taking you at your word."

"What the fuck does that mean?"

"It means"—Belle put her fingers beneath his chin and made him look at her—"that if this is who you are, then I will not give up on him either."

For a split second, something small—a mere flicker of light—seemed to be struggling in the depths of Sir Horley's eyes. Then he pushed her hand away, his touch careless, almost cruel. "Stop trying to save me. I've enough women in my life trying to do that."

"The others aren't trying to save you, though."

"They're offering me family. Security. In their eyes, a future without sin."

"But we love sin," protested Belle. "Sin is the best part."

This didn't even earn the barest twitch of a smile. "And my family? I'm to abandon them to—what?"

"To be with us."

"Ah yes . . ." Rising to his feet, Sir Horley staggered past her. He was in his shirtsleeves, which Belle knew was the sort of thing a lady ought to be shocked by. But she was long past the point of being shocked by male-presenting arms. "I can live in one of Valentine's innumerable bedrooms like an unmarried daughter."

"Oh, like I do?" Belle heard her own acerbity, but Sir Horley—who used to notice everything—paid it no heed whatsoever. He was preoccupied with looking for a fresh drink.

"And how much satisfaction does such an existence give you?" he asked.

"Not very much. But then I begin to question whether a satisfactory existence is to be my lot at all."

At last, accompanied by a choir of hollow clinking, Sir Horley had located what he was looking for: a half-empty bottle of . . . Belle could not tell what—wine, perhaps, or spirits. "It is the questioning that will destroy you."

"You're saying I should maintain hope?"

"The opposite, my kitten, the opposite. Accept your fate, as I have."

Belle remained on the floor, watching him with eyes she had long known were considered beautiful, and whose beauty had turned out no use whatsoever. "This is not your fate. This is a mistake you're making, for reasons I don't understand."

Having flung himself into an armchair, Sir Horley drained his bottle to the dregs. His mouth gleamed, wine-stained and wolfish, in the gloom. "What? You think that because I share the proclivities of your brother and his duke, I am entitled to what they have?"

Belle had promised Sir Horley she would take him as he was. But it was hard, in that moment, not to mourn for her friend, her wicked, laughing, irrepressible friend, who in the end had fled her—as so many had fled her—leaving this rough-voiced, hard-mouthed stranger in his stead. "I think Peggy would tell you there is more to life than *this* or *that*."

"I'm not Peggy."

"Neither am I. But we can learn from her choices."

"Leave me alone, Isabella."

He knew her name. She knew he knew her name. This was nothing but a weak attempt to hurt her. And, given that the deepest hurts she carried came from people who hadn't even been trying—who had simply been careless or oblivious—it pinged off her like a button, and she disregarded it just as easily.

Regaining her feet, Belle pursued Sir Horley across the room. "Please stop this. And please stop drinking."

"What does it matter if I drink or not?"

"I don't think it's helping you."

That made him laugh again. "My sweet child"—he reached out, catching clumsily for one of her curls, letting it twine about his finger—"people don't drink to be helped. They drink because they can't be."

"*I* am trying to help you," Belle retorted, pity and frustration and fondness swirling irreconcilably—and unpleasantly—inside her.

"Fine." Sir Horley's gaze slipped past her to the greyness beyond his window. "I have a few hours before my wedding. I can indulge you one last time. What's the plan?"

"The plan?" she repeated, taken off guard.

"Yes, you're a Tarleton. There's always a plan."

In all honesty, Belle had not thought that far ahead. She had rather been counting on Sir Horley *not* being foxed out of his skull, envisaging instead some kind of triumphant return to his senses. Perhaps a hug. "Well . . ."

"You were just passing my aunt's house in the dead of night?"

"I did not think you'd see me if I called in the usual fashion. I mostly just wanted to talk to you before you did something irrevocable." She twisted her fingers together nervously. "Find some way to repair our friendship."

"Oh, Arabella," he said, faintly chiding. "This will never do."

"I've actually gone to quite a lot of trouble," she pointed out, not best pleased by his tone.

"For mere conversation? Why, how staid. How commonplace." He put a hand to his brow in a mockery of mourning. "Am I no longer worth a wild scheme or two?"

She narrowed her eyes, once again adrift on the tides of his drunkenness, uncertain where sincerity lay. "Do you *want* there to be a wild scheme?"

"How about," he suggested, "we disguise ourselves as servants, steal my aunt's jewellery and horses, and ride away into the sunset? Or sunrise, I suppose, technically speaking."

His tone was sneering, but Belle chose to ignore it. "I would prefer that to watching you marry a woman who cares nothing for your happiness. I would prefer almost anything to that."

"We start new lives as highwaymen. We become pirates. We open a brothel that tends to the well-being of its workers." She remembered a time when Sir Horley had delighted in her outlandish ideas. Now he kicked them over like sandcastles. "We build wings like Daedalus and fly across the seas. We enchant a Spanish galleon and sail it amongst the stars. We throw ourselves off the cliffs at Dover and become sea-foam."

This was the closest Sir Horley had come to an admission that he was not fully committed to seeing things through with Miss Carswile. "Or," said Belle quietly, "you could simply leave with me tonight. Let Bonny and Valentine and me find some other future for you."

Sir Horley rolled his eyes heavily, roused at last to something other than sodden apathy. "There is no other fucking future for me. I have nothing, Belle. A meaningless knighthood that I cannot even pass to my children. No home or fortune of my own. Only what my aunt may, someday, deign to bestow."

"Is that really why you wed to her direction? For money?"

He shrugged. "It's expected of women. Egalitarian, in a way, to expect it also of me."

"Perhaps it should be expected of nobody."

"That's a fantasy more fantastical than princes who live on the moon." He was still twisting the strand of her hair that he had captured, tighter and tighter until it made her scalp sting. Not that this little pain was enough to frighten Arabella Tarleton. Or so she told herself for every pain. "Besides," he went on, "you've forgotten what it is to be poor and powerless now you live upon the largesse of a duke."

Belle sighed. What was it with gentlemen that they laid claim to such cynicism? As if the world was not set up for them. Even the ones born without wealth swam freely upon the tides of opportunity. "It's sweet you believe that," she murmured. And then, because he had as good as *asked* her for a wild scheme, she went on brightly, "Though if material security is all you seek from matrimony, then you might as well marry me."

Chapter 2

The words bounced across the room like a badly skimmed pebble, then plopped into silence. If Belle shared one trait with her brother, it was a Tarletonian tendency to do some of her thinking out loud, and she had caught herself by surprise. She had long since concluded marriage wasn't on the cards for her; she was never going to fall in love the way Bonny had, the way the books had told her she would, the way she was supposed to. And without that, it seemed pointless to become the property of a man. Even if it meant she spent the rest of her life alone, unloved, and derided for it. Marrying Sir Horley, though? He was clearly a mess. But so was she. And really, was it the worst idea she had ever had? Many would argue it barely broke the top ten.

It took Sir Horley a moment to recognise she was serious, bitterness and mirth alike drying upon his lips like the dregs of his wine. "Why, Miss Tarleton," he drawled out at last. "You have quite swept me off my feet."

"Oh, I'm sorry." Belle's burgeoning sense of frustration fully burgeoned, and she yanked herself away, uncaring of the strands of hair she left behind. "Was that not romantic enough? When we have heard nothing from you for the best part of a year, and you have already made it abundantly clear that you would prefer me to be my brother."

Sir Horley blinked at her, unperturbed by her outburst. "Well, I want to fuck your brother. That's a kind of preference."

There was something in his voice as he spoke. Something she recognised because she'd heard it in other people's voices. Seen it, too, in their eyes. It was oddly lonely, to have such familiarity with a feeling she'd probably never experience. "You want to more than fuck him."

"More than fuck him?" he repeated, with a touch of his old spirit. "I consider myself quite the connoisseur of carnality, a duke of depravity, a virtuoso of vice, but how, precisely, in detail if you please, do you *more than fuck* someone."

"You're in love with him," Belle pointed out, still slightly irritated with herself for not having noticed previously. The fact was, other people seemed to catch love like the pox, and Bonny had always been highly infectious.

Unfortunately, it was very much the wrong thing to mention. For it sent the last traces of the Sir Horley she had known, cared for, and come—in all the foolishness of hope—to rescue dwindling away, as inevitably as stars before the dawn. His fingers, her lost hair fluttering like mayday ribbons, inscribed a gesture of dismissal. "He would never love someone like me."

"For heaven's sake." It was too late. She had put her foot in her mouth, and the damage was done. But Belle tried away. She always tried anyway. "Bonny has loved all sorts of people, some of them extremely ill-advised. He does not love you because he sees nobody but Valentine. Not because he *could* not."

"And now you have kindly offered yourself as a consolation prize?"

"I hope I think a little better of myself than that." She sighed again, wondering if she did, in fact, think better of herself than that. It had been an impulsive proposal, admittedly. But she had not quite realised how this entirely-to-be-expected rejection would make her feel. "I know you would rather no wife at all. And I may well say the same of a husband. But surely with a little accommodation on both our sides, might we not deal rather well together?"

"Deal rather well together?" asked Sir Horley incredulously.

Repeated back to her, the words—the whole notion—sounded ludicrous. "I mean . . ." Belle attempted a confident, reassuring smile, but it felt small and strained, even to her. "You will never desire me. I will never fall in love with you. Does that not seem a wonderfully comfortable arrangement?"

"Certainly." There was such an upswell of enthusiasm in Sir Horley's voice that it could only have been counterfeit. "A man dreams of spending his life with someone he doesn't wish to fuck."

"Yet you're about to anyway. The difference is that you matter to me." Belle was fraying into whispers. Breaking softly and invisibly beneath what she had always, in her heart of hearts, known was a poor façade of audacity. "And we could allow each other all the freedom we wished. And . . . and be friends, just like we used to."

"My aunt would disown me, Belle." And there it was. Beneath his sharp words and studied indifference, sorrow deep enough to drown a world or two.

"Is she so worth being owned by?"

"We must all be owned by someone."

"Perhaps," said Belle. "Perhaps not. But at the very least I take care of what is mine. I do not cast it aside."

"You might. If it was worthless."

"Sir Horley." She tried to catch his eye, but he refused to let her. "To me, you are a pearl beyond price."

"You have confused what is cast with what is before."

"That saying is very rude to swine." Some part of Belle realised she had become distracted. The rest of her was too distracted to care. "In fact I would rather have a pig than a pearl, I think."

"Once again, very much the attitude of a woman of means."

"On the contrary, what would be the point of having a pearl if I lacked for means? I could sell it, I suppose. But then I'd have no pearl and, in time, no means either. A pig, however, makes for an excellent companion."

He blinked at her. "I can't decide if that says good things about pigs or poor things about your taste in companions."

"Probably both," Belle admitted. "But pigs really *are* excellent companions. They're very clean and intelligent. They keep you warm on cold nights. They can till soil for you and provide fertiliser. They can root out truffles, and they are naturally resistant to parasites. Also, they are very thorough eaters, so you can feed them your enemies in order to ensure no traces of the bodies remain."

"They're also delicious."

Righteously impassioned, Belle stamped her foot. "Do not speak of such things. I do not eat pigs. Pigs are not to be eaten."

"Tell that to my breakfast."

"You should look a pig in the eye someday."

Sir Horley tilted his head inquisitively. He was not anything close to his old self. But in the gesture, she caught the shadow of her old friend: a prisoner in a cage of flesh and blood. "Why would I want to do that?"

"Because their soul will gaze into your soul. And you will never consume bacon again."

"Belle, I . . ." His voice broke upon its rush of fondness. And then he dropped his head not into his hands but against them, pushing his knuckles hard against his eyes, as though he meant to drive all emotion, all kindness and affection, back inside him. "I'm not marrying you."

"Are you sure?" Belle aimed for teasing and backfired straight into pleading. "I'm very rich, you know. And I have a house."

"What house?"

"Well, technically it's Bonny's house. But he's not using it. And since he's unlikely to marry or have children of his own in a legal context, probably it would pass to me or at least my children. If I were to have children."

"Do you want children?"

"Do you?"

They stared at each other, Sir Horley still partially obscured, neither one of them willing to chance an answer.

"It's still no," he said finally. Lowering his hands, he focused a glare at her. "Of all the ludicrous, cloud-chasing, windmill-tilting, bubble-brained things you Tarletons have done, this one must take the prize."

"Recall, I have shot Valentine." Technically it had been years ago at this point, back when he had been determined to marry her for the good of both their families, and before he understood his tastes ran to Bonnys rather than Belles. But, to her, it still sometimes felt horribly present. Horribly close. Easier to pretend the whole thing had been a joke, a lark, typical Tarleton nonsense, instead of one of the most terrifying—the most terrifying and most regretted—experiences of her life.

Sir Horley's lips softened with the faintest suggestion of a smile.

"And frankly," Belle went on, "I don't see why marrying me is any more ludicrous than marrying Miss Carswile."

Any hint of warmth vanished from Sir Horley's face, like someone had blown out a candle. "I will not have you throw your life away on me."

"But you will throw away your own life? And Miss Carswile's."

"Saving my soul will give her something to do." Sir Horley gave an ill-coordinated shrug. "Christianity is a dull business."

Worried, exasperated, and quite at the end of her tether, Belle was reduced to stamping her foot again. "I don't understand why you're so determined upon this course of action."

"Because, my dear"—leaning forward, Sir Horley propped his elbows on his knees—"people are different to you and therefore make different. Fucking. Choices."

She bit her lip. "But this is a *bad* choice. One I think you're only making because you think you're not allowed to strive for happiness."

"And you're going to make me happy, are you?" It was not an unreasonable question on the surface. Except Belle wasn't sure she trusted what lay beneath. "With your heart that cannot love and your body that will never tempt me?"

There was little in the world that could cut as deep as the truth. And though Belle was doing her best to bear it bravely. To remember he was drunk. He was unhappy. That unhappiness, in particular, sometimes made you say and do terrible things. Wasn't she practically an expert in that herself? But—and here was another truth—she was not feeling very brave. Her bravery had fallen away, as ephemeral as Cinderella's magic finery, as soon as she'd found Sir Horley sprawled on the floor, almost insensible. She had lost her twin to one love and she had lost her best friend to another—losses she could welcome, in return for the happiness of those she cherished. But she was not sure how she could bear a loss that brought no promise of someone else's joy.

"I suppose I hoped," she said, hating how weak she sounded, "there could be more to life or relationships or the worth of people than love and sex."

Another silence. Sir Horley's gaze settled upon her again, heavy as silt, and still tarry from drunkenness. Then he reached out and re-captured her hair, a fistful of it this time, and used it to yank her towards him. She yelped more in surprise than pain and managed not to overbalance by flattening her hands upon his knees. It felt jarring, emotionally as well as physically. Sir Horley used to touch her fairly regularly, with ease and affection. This was different, not threatening exactly, but she did not think he would have cared had she fallen. If she was comfortable. If she minded the sour sweep of alcohol that was his breath against her cheek.

"You never learn," he told her, and she couldn't tell if he was angry with her, or sad, or nothing at all. "You just never learn."

That was unfair. For Belle thought she had learned rather a lot. Most of it quite negative. "What do you mean?"

"You keep trying, little Belle. Fracturing that indomitable heart over and over and over again." He gave a sharp tug upon her hair. "And for what?"

Alexis Hall

"Presumab—ow." She shifted her hand from his leg to his wrist. It did not help with her balance, but it mildly helped with being dragged about to his whim. "Presumably, I think it's worth it."

"But why? When you know they despise you?"

Belle curled her fingers into claws, and applied her nails, until he released her. She had, she was forced to acknowledge, a rather non-ideal history of enacting violence on men. On the other hand, they had a non-ideal history of frightening her, judging her, and trying to command her, to which Sir Horley was currently contributing. "Are we still talking about me?" she asked. "Because I don't believe anyone despises either of us."

"They would, though." Sir Horley examined the marks she had left on the inside of his wrist, his words too dreamy for their purport. "As should you. For I am naught but poison."

"You've certainly been *drinking* naught but poison." It was slightly disorientating for Belle to find herself in the role of *reasonable one*. Normally 100 percent of conversational naughts were perpetrated by her.

"And as for you . . . ," Sir Horley went on.

"If you dare to try and claim that I'm poison, when I came all this way on your behalf, I will poke you in the eye."

"You're not poison."

Somehow being told she wasn't poison was less reassuring than Belle had hoped it might be.

"But you'll never be like them, either, will you? These people for whom love is an easy and inevitable thing?"

"Does that matter?" Belle tried, wondering if she should poke him in the eye anyway.

Sir Horley glanced up, his attention briefly focused, his pupils pin-prick sharp in the haze of his irises. "You tell me."

She wanted to say it didn't. But she wasn't sure that was true. In fact, she'd been asking herself the same question for what felt like the

18

latter half of her life—ever since she'd realised the moment the handsome prince, or the dashing duke, or the beautiful skypirate declared his, her, or their undying love was the moment the story ended for her. No fluttering heart or teary eyes. Only a pit in her stomach. And a sense of wrongness stretching into forever.

Her silence, it turned out, was response enough. "See?" Sir Horley's lip turned up sardonically. "Oh, don't look so stricken. I'm sure they care for you. But they'll never understand you. They'll dismiss you as foolish and selfish, or shrill and wilful, or whatever other words they find for women they can't fit in a box, and all because your pain isn't the same as their pain, and the world isn't made for people like us."

"Then," Belle said desperately, "couldn't we at least have each other? You liked me once. Before you convinced yourself you shouldn't."

"Belle . . ."

"Think of the fun we could have. We would have money and freedom and whoever else we wanted. Whatever future we chose."

"Belle . . ."

"And we would make a promise to always share the best gossip. And laugh at everyone else's absurdities together. And you would help me buy shoes. And I would help you pick men. Because you have absolutely the worst taste in men."

"You have absolutely the worst taste in shoes."

"You see"—her voice swelled in triumph and the first glimmerings of real hope—"it is fair exchange."

Except then Sir Horley rose, unsteady on his feet, and abruptly enough that Belle had to scrabble back lest they collide. He was of middling height for a man, nowhere near as statuesque as Valentine, but it still felt as though he towered over her. "For the last fucking time, Miss Tarleton, no. Whoever you thought I was, I am not. And whatever you think we can have is impossible."

"More impossible than Valentine and Bonny? Than Peggy and Orfeo?"

19

"We must all, at some point, face the fate we deserve. You will find someone worthy of you. And I . . ." Sir Horley broke off. Then sank back into his chair, his face turned away from her. "I will face the consequences of my actions."

"What actions?" demanded Belle, with the tenacity that ill-endeared her to nearly everyone.

He waved a hand at her. "Go. I'm done with you. For once in your infuriating life, take a hint."

"If you are sincerely seeking redemption through suffering," Belle said tartly, "I think you will find redemption has already been provided generally to humanity courtesy of the suffering of Jesus Christ. Thus rendering"—she flicked her fingers at him—"*this* at once hubristic and unnecessary."

Sir Horley gave her a scornful look. "I feel like a married man already."

"I'm not sure that's a perspective on the virtue, or lack thereof, of anguish that your fiancée is likely to have considered."

"When are you going to get out of my house?"

"When you have told me why you feel you owe the world your misery."

"It will make my aunt happy."

"She does not seem like a very good aunt."

"Well"—Sir Horley gazed at her, his face stripped as bare as winter trees in the gloom—"I'm not a very good nephew."

"Because you desire men?"

"Because I killed her husband."

Belle opened her mouth. Then closed it again.

"Nothing to say, little Bellflower?"

"Did he . . ." Her mouth had gone dry. "Was he cruel to you?"

"No. He loved me very much. And I him."

"Was there some kind of accident?"

He shook his head. "His death was quite intentional. To be fair," he went on, mildly, "he is not the only man whose life I have ended.

But the others I murdered at Wellington's side. So those deaths were glorious, patriotic, and just."

This had gone in an unexpected and mildly startling direction. But from Belle's perspective, there was only a kind of sadness in such a transparent attempt to shock her. "I don't believe you."

"How treasonous."

"Not about the war," she said impatiently. "About your uncle."

"Ask my aunt, if you wish."

Belle folded her arms. "What a splendid notion. When I meet her, I shall be sure to say 'Why, hello, Sir Horley's aunt, do let us discuss his history of murder.'"

"Be my guest."

"For heaven's sake"—she made an exasperated gesture—"I have read too many gothic novels for your nonsense. I will not countenance for a moment the notion that you killed your uncle. And you cannot let a sense of complicity in his death dictate your life."

"God damn you, Arabella." There was little rancour left in Sir Horley's voice. Just a sick and endless weariness. "Are you in love with pain?"

"As we have comprehensively established, I am in love with nothing and no-one."

"I'm not worth this. Are you truly so desperate that you would throw yourself away on a man who . . . who . . ."

"Who showed me care and kindness?" she suggested, when it became clear he did not know how to continue. "Understanding when, as you have pointed out, few people do?" She risked a smile. "Yes."

"Even though I was never who you thought I was?" He offered her the bleakest smile she thought she had ever seen. "Even though *friend* was a mask I wore because I cannot bear who I am?"

This was another point of divergence for her with Bonny: he took it for granted that what he wanted, the world would deliver, perhaps because, when you were with a duke, it did. In Belle's case, things had always been more complicated, but she had been trying, of late, to worry less about what she sought for herself and focus, instead, on what she could do for the people she cared about. There was even a kind of comfort in being able to offer freely to Sir Horley everything she most yearned for and feared would never be hers.

"I can bear you," she said. "I can bear you easily. And I've already told you, I'll take you exactly as you are."

He stared at her, his face such a mask of scepticism that she half expected to be dismissed. But then something inside him seemed to give way, as though he'd lost a fight his heart had never been in to begin with, and he stood, coming close enough that his shadow fell across her and she had to steel herself against the scent of stale alcohol.

"Well." She arched her neck—an act that had once been little more than vanity to her—so she could see him properly. "Perhaps not *exactly*. I would dearly love it if you were to bathe a little more often."

Whatever struggle had previously occupied him, the surrender was still not easy. His eyes were distant, his expression a conflicted tangle of fears and needs. "You're a damn fool, Arabella Tarleton."

"I think you'll find bathing is eminently sensible."

"Not about that. About me."

"Oh." She was silent a moment. "Is it so terrible to be foolish about each other sometimes?"

"It's never worked out for me."

"Perhaps I've chosen a better subject."

"You can't—" He broke off, shaking his head. "You shouldn't trust me like that."

"It's my decision."

His knees buckled, and he slid slowly to the floor, Belle doing her best to steady him. His head came to rest lightly against her hip, and what an odd tableau they must have made. A knight and his lady, though Sir Horley was the most impure of chevaliers, and she an ill-chosen recipient of courtly love. His sudden closeness was slightly startling, especially after all his harsh words and the cruel, neglectful way he had pulled her hair. But he had not been wrong to call her *foolish*, for it also made her hope, just a little, that he might be coming back to her—not necessarily the man she thought she'd known, but whatever part of him had liked her once.

"Belle"—he made a damp raw sound, perilously close to a sob—"I don't think I know how to be happy."

"That is also something that has rather eluded me," Belle admitted. "Perhaps we will have more success together."

Tilting back his head, he gazed up at her—his eyes moonlit and tear-washed. "But I am to be married on the morrow. Even if—it's already too late. What are we to do?"

"Well . . ." Belle thought for a moment. "In books . . ."

"Oh God." He hid his face again. "I'm regretting this already."

"In books," she went on doggedly, "if a young lady feels obliged to marry one person when she, in fact, wishes to marry another, there is only one course of action available to her."

"Don't say it," he begged. "This is madness."

Belle said it. "Sir Horley, we must elope."

Chapter 3

The elopement of Arabella Tarleton and Sir Horley Comewithers did not get off to the most auspicious start, given it almost resulted in the immediate demise of one of the participants. Belle had always known Sir Horley's indolent manner was, to some degree, artifice, but she had not counted on his lack of sobriety. He didn't so much climb out of the window as fall out of it, landing—fortunately for his continued existence, though less fortunately for his arse—in a gorse bush below. Even without Belle's shriek of alarm at witnessing his abrupt auto-defenestration, the crash would have been household-rousing. As Belle vaulted over the balcony and began scrambling down the ivy, she heard windows opening around her and caught the gleam of lamps and candles.

"I'm too drunk to tell," remarked Sir Horley, still embedded in a gorse bush, "but I think I'm in quite a lot of pain." He paused, meditatively. "Physical pain." He paused again. "From a certain perspective, it's a pleasant change."

With no-one to help, Belle landed in a heap upon the grass. Perhaps it was just the shock of Sir Horley nearly plummeting to his death or the indignity of her own descent, but the oddest sense of loneliness surged up out of nowhere and threatened to swamp her.

She was no stranger to (mis)adventure, but this was the first time she had embarked on one alone. In the wake of their disastrous attempt to kidnap Sir Horley for his own good, Bonny had declared himself officially retired from further antics. And Peggy—once upon a time Belle's other companion in chaos—was now too in love with Orfeo to let her love for Belle embroil her in scrapes against her better judgement. Of course, Belle theoretically had Sir Horley on her side for the present endeavour. But she suspected his combination of drunkenness/hollowness/sitting-in-a-gorse-bush-ness made him a liability rather than an ally. Gritting her teeth, she went to assist him. Which mostly entailed trying to drag him out of the gorse bush.

"Ow," he said, rather plaintively.

From above them came the rattling of a window casement, and someone called out, "Horley? Is that you?"

"Come on." Trying not to think about what would happen if Sir Horley's aunt caught them eloping—barely pre-elope though they were—Belle pulled at his arm. "We have to go."

"Who's that with you?" demanded the same voice as before. And then, since it was the sort of voice that didn't seem as though it would be contented with a single demand: "Are you drunk again?"

"*Again*," declared Sir Horley, "implies a return to a previously entered state. Whereas I have not ceased to be drunk for quite some time."

"This isn't the time for a semantic debate." Belle finally managed to heave Sir Horley out of the bush, only to have him flop into her arms like . . . well. Someone larger and heavier than her who had flopped into her arms.

Gravel crunched and skittered beneath her boots as she tried to brace him. There was, however, to put it bluntly, *no fucking way*. With Belle trying to cling to Sir Horley and push him upright, they ended up staggering about on the path like a pair of exceptionally inept dancers, trapped in a cursed waltz. Their steps took them through a herbaceous border and round a piece of topiary that had probably not been intended to look like a phallus, then finally sent them tumbling backwards into a stone birdbath. It rocked beneath them but did not topple, apparently having been designed for extremely rambunctious sparrows. This, Belle thought, was a principle that seemed to underlie the whole estate. Not that the sparrows were expected to be rambunctious. But that things should be built . . . solidly. Practically. Unbeautifully. Walls to define and contain. Stone to last, unchanging.

Still, it was no more a time for architecture than it was a time for semantics. And besides, her bottom was getting wet from being partially dunked in a pool of standing water. She shoved at Sir Horley's shoulder and flailed one foot in the air by way of encouragement to get off her as a matter of urgency.

Another window opened, and at it appeared Sir Horley's fiancée—beautiful even like this, in an unflatteringly demure nightgown with her hair in a long braid. "What is happening?" she asked, all sweet silver bells and certainties. "Sir Horley, what are you doing to the birdbath?" Some of those certainties were fading rapidly. "What are you doing with that boy in the birdbath?"

Sir Horley levered himself back to his feet, Belle wrapped around him like a soggy monkey. "You have the most extravagant imagination for depravity, my dear. I can never tell if it means you're wasted as a Christian, or if it's what makes you such a good one."

"Stop disrupting the household." The initial speaker—presumably Sir Horley's aunt—had now progressed from demanding to commanding. "Go back to bed at once."

Leaning against the phallus, Sir Horley squinted upwards at the house. "You seem to be labouring under the misapprehension I was in bed to begin with."

"You are to be married tomorrow," returned his aunt, implacably.

"And," Miss Carswile added, with measurably less *plac*, "you will imbibe less after we are wed."

"Will I?" asked Sir Horley.

She gazed at him with the bewilderment of the unshakably virtuous. "You cannot *want* to be like this?"

"Indeed no." He seemed to be sober, just a little, his sudden half smile stark in the moonlight. "But I fear it is not to be changed. We have tried, have we not, Auntie?"

There was a long silence.

"You sicken me," Sir Horley's aunt said at last, the words teeth-worn, as though she had spoken them often.

Since Sir Horley offered no reply of his own, Belle called up, "I don't think I like you very much either."

"And I," returned Sir Horley's aunt with indifferent regality, "have no notion who you are."

"Mrs. Greenleaf?" Ignoring Belle's interruption, Miss Carswile leaned out of her window. "You promised you would not say such things."

Sir Horley's aunt—it struck Belle belatedly that she had never before even thought to ask her name—was not the type to lean wantonly out of windows. If anything, her spine grew even stiffer and more rigid. "The truth, you mean?"

"Surely truths," said Miss Carswile softly, "are the most deserving of compassion."

"Well, I don't want your fucking compassion." Sir Horley's words exploded across the not-particularly-quiet garden.

Belle stared at him in shock. Maybe there *was* something to be said for drunkenness.

"I just," he continued, at the same sky-cracking volume, "I just want to drink myself senseless and fuck boys. Well, not boys. Men. Like the filthy beast I am."

Mrs. Greenleaf still barely reacted. Her face was stone, framed by stone. "I always knew there was the devil in you, child."

"That wasn't the devil." Sir Horley's defiance was only mildly impeded by his staggering into the topiary phallus. "That was me. That was all me."

This time, Mrs. Greenleaf's only response was a huff of air.

"Your precious husband was mad for me, Auntie. I gave him more than your vicious tongue and your cold god ever could."

"And you killed him."

Sir Horley had already expressed the same sentiment to Belle. But she knew very well that saying terrible things about yourself, out of bravado or some other nonsense, was not the same as hearing them said about you. The boldness fell from him like a cloak from a beggar. And the way he flinched she recognised too. A kind of heartsick shiver.

"What do you expect to accomplish," Mrs. Greenleaf asked, "with your little scenes?"

"I . . . I don't know." Sir Horley put a hand dizzily to his head.

"Return to your room," his aunt told him. "Sober up. Act like a man for once."

"Oh, but"—even though she had found him in tatters, there remained in his smile a trace of the Sir Horley that Belle had once believed she knew—"that has never been a priority of mine."

Belle went to him, taking his hand in hers. "That is one of the many reasons I like you," she whispered. "May we leave?"

He glanced at her, almost as though he had forgotten she was there. "Leave?"

"Yes."

"Of course." He barked out a sudden laugh. "We're eloping, aren't we?"

"And doing an appalling job of it," Belle pointed out.

Mrs. Greenleaf took a step forward, though not enough of a step forward—unfortunately—to send her toppling into the garden. "You're what?"

"Eloping?" Sir Horley called up to her.

Belle kicked him in the ankle. "You're not supposed to tell them."

"I'm not?"

"No, we're supposed to escape discreetly in the dead of night."

"You're eloping?" repeated Miss Carswile. "With that boy? I don't think you *can* elope with a boy, can you?" Something a little wistful crept into her voice. "Can he?"

It didn't seem relevant in that moment for Belle to correct the mis-apprehensions surrounding her identity.

"No," declared Mrs. Greenleaf. "He cannot. And he shall not." Her gaze fell upon Sir Horley like an executioner's blade. "If you take another step, I am done with you."

"You've been done with me for a while, Auntie."

That Sir Horley's aunt would be a fairly unpleasant person, Belle had prepared for. That very occasionally, perhaps as some cruel trick of the uncertain light, there might be some traces of familial resemblance she had not. There in the curve of cheek and jaw, the shape of a nose, elusive as an echo. A flash of blue-green from a stranger's eyes. "I pay for you, don't I?" she was saying. "For your *lifestyle*. Your ridiculous clothes and your trips to the opera and that disgusting hunting lodge you keep. Without me, you'll have nothing and you'll *be* nothing."

"I think," said Sir Horley, resigned rather than regretful, "I already am."

Belle tugged at his hand. "Not to me."

"Arabella . . ." He offered her a strained and distant smile. "What can we possibly be to each other?"

If she had been Peggy or Bonny, she would have said something like *Whatever we want to be* and believed it. But she was not her twin, and she was not her friend, and all her pretending had never truly solidified into conviction. "We can . . . work it out?"

He lifted one shoulder in a clumsy shrug. "I've had less appealing offers."

"Please come on." She escalated from tugging to yanking. "This is already the worst elopement in history."

"The very worst?" asked Sir Horley, as he allowed Belle to lead him towards the gate, only staggering through three more herbaceous borders en route. "In the whole of human history? That feels a vain-glorious claim."

"Perhaps we could discuss it further when we are not actively fleeing?"

"Oh, so we're actively fleeing now?"

"We were meant to be actively fleeing all along." Belle indulged in a little squeak of frustration. "It's just you're very drunk and bad at it."

"Horley Rufus Grandison Comewithers." Sir Horley's aunt was not the sort of woman who had to raise her voice to be heard. It was almost admirable, Belle thought, the way she could slice through air and starlight. "If you take one step beyond my gates, you will never set foot across them again."

Sir Horley's hand was sweaty in Belle's, shaking slightly, but holding tight nonetheless. "And here I thought you didn't care."

"You are my heir, and you will act like it."

The path seemed to weave and lengthen before Belle's eyes. She had not thought the garden so large when she had infiltrated the estate. But with Mrs. Greenleaf's words raining down on them like burning pitch, and Sir Horley's stumbling at her side, she wondered if she would ever escape it.

"You owe me a child." Apparently Sir Horley's aunt had thrown a vase from her windowsill, for it shattered behind Belle—a miniature city of petals and porcelain, fallen to ruin, and partially submerged beneath brackish water. "It is the least you owe me, after what you did."

"And we are pledged to each other," added Miss Carswile, imploringly, "in the eyes of society and the eyes of the Lord. I cannot understand what you must be feeling to drive you to this, but I promise—"

Miss Carswile's promises were no match for Mrs. Greenleaf's fury. For the sort of pain that had carved itself into her, year on year, like water weakening rock. "I am your family." Another object, an ornament this time, possibly a shepherdess, or some other pastoral figure in the midst of being wooed, crashed to the ground. "Your sole remaining family since your own worthless parents were only too glad to hand you over to me. From the moment I laid eyes on you, I knew you were vermin. But I still took you in."

Sir Horley paused, half turning, though whether it was shame or pity, or anger, Belle could not tell. A piece of vase or shepherdess had opened a shallow cut upon his cheek; in the moonlight, the blood fell like slow tears.

"You recall what I said about active fleeing?" Belle yanked him back to face her and the gates and the world that lay beyond them. "Now would be an absolutely wonderful time for it."

To her surprise, he nodded. "Let's go."

And so they ran. Or rather, Belle ran. Sir Horley wobbled with greater alacrity. His determination, at least, was to be admired. Less so his tendency to collide with garden furniture and drag her into topiary.

"If you run like a cur," his aunt cried after them, "I will have you hunted down like one. I will have you dragged back and horsewhipped."

It was not, Belle thought, the sort of pronouncement one wanted to have hurled after one in the dark. "She's not actually going to do that?"

Sir Horley wheezed out a laugh. "You've met the woman. Of course she will."

Belle risked a glance back at the house. Its mistress had, indeed, abandoned the window—although the light from her candle illuminated enough of the room beyond to present the ominous tableau of Mrs. Greenleaf instructing her servants and rousing her household.

"Oh fuck," said Belle.

Chapter 4

In the distance, Belle heard the baying of hunting hounds. In front of her, Sir Horley was being spectacularly sick into a ditch. Even if it was not the worst elopement ever, it was definitely her worst adventure. Up to and including shooting Valentine. That, after all, had come with the compensation of shooting Valentine.

"So," said Sir Horley, his voice raw from retching. "I might just lie here and die."

Belle, who had been holding his hair back with one hand, patted him gently upon the shoulder with the other. "I don't think you should lie here and die."

"My stomach wants me to. And so does my head. I'm not inclined to disoblige them."

"You will disoblige me most drastically."

"You'll be fine."

"Sir Horley, I will be torn apart by dogs like Jezebel."

He paused to effortfully vomit up a few strings of yellow-green bile. Belle tried to look at the stars instead. How bright and pretty they were. How very much the opposite of strings of bile.

"No no," Sir Horley gasped out. "They'll be distracted with eating me or something."

Belle sighed. "I do not know how to deliver this truth kindly, but no canine in its right mind would voluntarily choose to consume you at the moment."

"How dare you." It was a weak protest. "I am positively succulent."

"You are drunk and smelly and look as though you have been dead for several weeks already."

"Oh, I've been dead for longer than that, my dear."

"And I'm very moved by your emotional pain. But I would really love it if we could focus on not being in a ditch right now."

Sir Horley gave a sort of miserable spasm. "I'm not sure I can go much further. Sincerely."

"The inn is ten minutes away."

"You said that ten minutes ago."

"Yes, but I hoped detouring through that river would throw the dogs off our scent."

"Fine. Fine." He pushed himself to his hands and knees, and then to his knees, and finally to his feet. His complexion had passed through green and was now somewhere on the wrong side of grey. "But what do you think is going to happen when we arrive? It's an inn, not Golan or Kedesh."

"Well, it will probably make it more difficult for your aunt to horse-whip you," Belle pointed out. "Also Bonny and Valentine are there."

Sir Horley blinked a sudden sheen of moisture from his eyes. "They . . . they are? They came to save me?"

This was the last straw. "No," Belle vociferated in a way that was not shrieking but might have been mildly shriek-adjacent. "*I* came to save you. Me. On my own. Because the truth is I care about you, I care about you very deeply, and I wish to God that just once in my life that could be enough for someone."

"It was very good of you," said Sir Horley, in a blandly pacifying way that would have made her push him back into the ditch had she not been afraid that she would be unable to get him out of it if she did. "But that doesn't explain why Bonny and Valentine are here?"

Swallowing something that was half *gah* and half *grr*, Belle moderated her tone. "For your wedding, of course. Your fiancée invited us."

Sir Horley threw up on her boots.

"She wrote us a very nice letter," Belle went on, assuming the boots were a lost cause, "explaining that she had prayed and reflected, and come to the conclusion that we had kidnapped you out of a misplaced sense of kindness. So she forgave us."

"How magnanimous." It was hard to sneer when you were wiping your mouth on your sleeve, but Sir Horley did his best.

"Actually, it *was* magnanimous, because she also apologised for being such a churlish abductee. She was concerned about you, Sir Horley, and wanted to repair the rift between us."

"I can go back and marry her, if you wish?"

"For God's sake." Belle would have stamped her foot, but it seemed inadvisable just then. "I'm simply saying I do not hold her in abhorrence. That does not mean I think she is a suitable wife for you."

"And you are?"

"You said yourself: you've had less appealing offers. And if you're quite finished disgorging your innards, I'd like us to proceed to the inn."

"Ah yes." Sir Horley rolled his eyes, then seemed to regret it, pushing the heel of his hand against his brow as he swayed. "The famous ten-minutes-away inn. Do you even know what we are to do when we get there?"

This was another issue with lone adventuring. Previously Peggy had handled the tedious business of where and when and what. "Well." Belle thought about it for a moment. "You shall have a bath. I shall get changed. And after that we can take Valentine's carriage to Gretna Green."

"Then"—Sir Horley, too, took a moment to gaze at the night sky, his expression speckled silver and unreadable—"she who hath the steerage of my course, direct my sail."

"I direct you," responded Belle tartly, "to never trust a friar, always examine a presumed corpse before taking irreversible action, and come with me to this fucking pub."

⟡

The fucking pub, which rejoiced under the sign of the Cheese and Anchor, was not another ten minutes away. Nor another ten after that, though when Sir Horley complained, Belle pointed out that he ought to be flattered she'd come all this way on foot for him. Of course, she'd taken fewer detours on her original route and, admittedly, she'd got lost quite a bit less. On the other hand, their pursuers had yet to catch up with them, which Belle decided was due to her cunning evasions and not at all the logistical complexities of arranging an impromptu cross-country nephew hunt in the early hours of the morning.

With the rose moon almost full above them—swirled the colour of Belle's favourite lip salve against the deep Prussian blue of the sky—it was a beautiful night. Had they not been sweaty and breathless, had Sir Horley not been vomiting so abundantly, and had their feelings been more of the sort that traditionally underpinned elopements, it would have been romantic. To be honest, there was a part of Belle that still wanted it to be romantic. She had, after all, spent her adolescence dreaming of such undertakings—of desperate flights and moon-drenched chases, of gothic spectacle and grand passion. Of anything, in fact, that suggested life could be more like the books she read, and less like whatever had been left after the sudden death of her parents.

They'd helped, the stories. The ones they found and the ones they made up. So had Valentine, back when he was a tender boy who listened and picked flowers, instead of a man who had to unlearn his own power. But it had also been the first time she'd truly understood herself as distinct from her twin. Until that point, they'd shared everything. Grief had turned out to be something they couldn't. It had made Bonny

35

even more in love with life. Louder, brighter, warmer. She, it had simply made smaller. Afraid of things she had not known to fear before. And feared still.

A world so full of the promise of loss.

In the end, it was a glaze of light upon the horizon that led them across the fields and back to the Cheese and Anchor. To Belle's surprise, the sleepy inn she had departed was now in uproar, with men carrying lanterns running hither and thither, and a half-dressed Bonny standing in the stable yard, waving his arms at a still dressing-gowned duke.

"—must be at least the fourth time you've lost my sister," Bonny was yelling.

"I think," Valentine returned, with the hauteur that came all too easily to him, "your sister is perfectly capable of losing herself."

Bonny stamped his foot and tossed his hair. Not, in Belle's opinion, a set of gestures that ought to be combined, because it made one look like a petulant bovine. "That's neither here nor there. This can't keep happening, Valentine." He drooped. "I can't keep . . . I can't keep worrying about her."

"Well," said Valentine, "you don't have to."

Bonny undrooped violently. "Val-EN-tine. How can you say that? She's my twin, my Belladonna. Of course I have to."

"No, I just—"

"I know you're an only child, but try to have a little understanding, maybe?"

"Bonny, I—"

"She could be anywhere right now. Trying to run away to the Americas again. Or just lost and alone and frightened in the dark."

"Bonny, *please*."

"Don't 'Bonny, *please*' me." Bonny stamped his foot again—though with so much emphasis he accidentally stubbed his toe against the cobblestones and was forced to hop around for a moment or two, muttering *ow* and *fuck* to himself. "I really thought you'd changed," he finished, dolefully. "But you're still the same man who would have left Belle to get eaten by wolves two years ago."

"I am not that man." Valentine finally managed to get a word in edgeways. "I was never that man. He was simply someone I thought I had no other choice but to be. Belle has never, in all our acquaintance, been in any danger of being eaten by wolves. And the only reason I'm telling you that you don't have to worry about her is because she's behind you."

Bonny spun round so fast he knocked a passing stable boy into the water trough.

Belle waved in what she hoped was a reassuring fashion.

"Belle," Bonny managed at last, contriving to sound both relieved and betrayed.

She risked the wariest of smiles. "Bonny."

"We promised," he said. "No more adventures."

"This is the last one. I promise that."

"But you promised *before*."

It was at this juncture that Sir Horley fainted into a puddle, putting an end to the conversation. Whether Valentine believed he had changed or not—he was certainly just as fond of baths and just as resistant to getting out of bed as he had ever been—he was, at least, considerably better in a crisis. Hurrying forward, he dragged the somewhat delirious Sir Horley upright and bore him into the inn, Bonny and Belle trailing after him like twin shadows.

"Oh God." An extremely harried-looking man in a nightshirt greeted them at the door. "What now?"

"You may call off the search," Valentine said. "The young lady has been found."

The innkeeper, for it had taken Belle a moment to recognise him, given his state of distress and undress, stared at Sir Horley. "That's the— well, I suppose it's none of my business."

"Not him. This is a friend. Who will need a bath and bed."

"At this time in the morning?" protested the innkeeper.

"You're already up"—Valentine, at his tallest and most ducal, gazed down at him—"are you not?"

"He won't need the bed," Belle put in quickly, as if this was the most effort-intensive part of the request. "We should be on the road as soon as possible."

"On the road?" asked Valentine at the same time the innkeeper said, "Who are you?"

"I'm the young lady who has been found," Belle explained. And then to Valentine, "Yes, we're being chased by Sir Horley's aunt. We're eloping."

"You're what now?" asked Valentine at the same time the innkeeper said, "Why are you in breeches?"

"They're more practical," Belle explained. "Eloping."

The innkeeper visibly reeled. "Eloping? In breeches? In my inn? You're going to be the ruin of me."

"Nobody will be ruining anyone." Once again Valentine had taken refuge in an impenetrable loftiness. "I am a duke."

Something must have caused the innkeeper to lose his mind, for he promptly seized Valentine by the sleeve of his dressing gown—an act usually sacrosanct to Bonny—and pulled him towards the taproom. "You may be a duke, but do you know who *that* is?"

Valentine did not know who *that* was. Nor from the manner of his demurral did he care to.

"That," whispered the innkeeper, undeterred, "is none other than Mr. Bogstwaddle. Mr. Roland Bogstwaddle."

"My commiserations to you both."

"*The* Mr. Roland Bogstwaddle. Of *Mr. Bogstwaddle's Advice for Persons Making Trips Including Easy-to-Reference Summations of the Quality of Hostelries Utilising a System of Stars (Patent Pending)*."

Valentine sighed. "And?"

Manhandling his ducal visitor back out of the taproom, the innkeeper released him and produced, from somewhere about his person, a crumpled pamphlet. "This is the last edition. The new one promises to be even more comprehensive."

"Comprehensive of what?" asked Valentine.

"Oh." Sir Horley came briefly awake, which at least reassured Belle that he hadn't died as he had several times now threatened to. "This Bogstwaddle travels about interviewing the people at the places he stays. Then he publishes the results and—"

"And I shall be ruined," re-iterated the innkeeper, who had perhaps missed his calling on the stage. "Instead of a lovely paragraph where Mrs. Withers of Walthamstow explains how 'there was only a small vermin infestation' and she 'felt right at home (four stars),' I shall be blighted with 'was woken by a loud elopement (one star)' or 'witnessed the thighs of a woman at three in the morning (one star).'"

"Sorry," said Valentine. "What was that about a small vermin infestation?"

The innkeeper cast himself to his knees. "My reputation. My livelihood. My hopes. My dreams. My sense of self-respect."

"For heaven's sake." Valentine put a hand to his brow. It was a gesture he indulged occasionally at home and often when confronted by the world at large. "The situation cannot be nearly as dreadful as you claim." Opening *Mr. Bogstwaddle's Advice for Persons Making Trips Including Easy-to-Reference Summations of the Quality of Hostelries Utilising a System of Stars (Patent Pending)*, he began flipping through it. "On second thoughts, many of these do seem unreasonable."

"You see?" cried the innkeeper, now fully prostrate, and close to tears.

"'Jamaica Inn,'" read Valentine, "'is a quaint hostelry, conveniently located between Bodmin and Launceston, deep in the heart of Cornwall. Although the hoped-for sea views did not materialise, the lonely vista of the moors has a majesty of its own, likely appealing to travellers seeking respite from the tumult of the modern world. While visiting, I solicited comment from one Mr. A. Timms of Shrewsbury, who said, *Sign needs fixing. One star.*'"

The innkeeper gave a soft howl. And even Belle—who had many other things to concern her at the present moment—winced in sympathy. She was rather glad her own life was not subject to review, for she could not imagine the reactions were likely to be favourable.

"I bet I'd get five stars," said Bonny cheerfully.

"You're not an inn," retorted Belle.

He grinned. "But if I was an inn, I would be capacious and welcoming, and everyone would love me."

"I am sure"—Valentine was rapidly turning the pages of *Mr. Bogstwaddle's Advice for Persons Making Trips Including Easy-to-Reference Summations of the Quality of Hostelries Utilising a System of Stars (Patent Pending)*—"I have merely stumbled upon an unfortunate selection of entries." He cleared his throat. "'The Tabard Inn, Southwark. Respected coaching inn established circa 1300, etc., etc. Here I solicited comment from one Mrs. L. Blott of Lower Swell, who said, *Party of twenty-nine travellers kept me up all night telling lewd stories. One star.*'"

Sir Horley stirred again. "You'd think that would be worth five stars, not one."

"Wouldn't you?" agreed the innkeeper, fervently.

"You do recall"—as it happened, Belle wasn't sure anyone *did* recall—"we are eloping as a matter of urgency?"

But Valentine was still lost amidst *Mr. Bogstwaddle's Advice for Persons Making Trips Including Easy-to-Reference Summations of the Quality of Hostelries Utilising a System of Stars (Patent Pending)*: "'The Boar's Head Tavern, located in Eastcheap, is a fine Tudor building with a lively clientele and a capacity for hosting large parties. While visiting, I solicited comment from one Mr. P. Cholmondeley of Hunstanton, who said, *A patron spat in my face and called me a horse. One star.*'" He paused; brow furrowed. "This is most peculiar. I have never been to the Boar's Head Tavern in Eastcheap, nor do I have any knowledge of this Mr. P. Cholmondeley of Hunstanton, but I suddenly find myself quite convinced that his opinions regarding the Boar's Head Tavern in Eastcheap are correct."

"It's because they're written down." The innkeeper made a gesture of eloquent despair. "Everything becomes more convincing once it's written down."

"Surely," murmured Valentine, flicking back and forth, "*someone* must have had a good experience somewhere in England."

"Oh." Bonny bounced, as he was wont to do when struck by an idea. "Try that place we stayed at when, you know, you were trying to force Belle to marry you. The Wayward Goat, wasn't it?"

"That was a dreadful tavern. I am sure it has been soundly excoriated as it des . . ." Valentine's voice faded away. Then, he went on coldly, "'The Wayward Goat is a charmingly rustic hostelry located in Surrey en route to Dover. While visiting, I solicited comment from one Mr. V. Wellhungly of Greater Gropebuttock, who said, *Excellent service from the ostler. Four stars.*'" Flinging aside *Mr. Bogstwaddle's Advice for Persons Making Trips Including Easy-to-Reference Summations of the Quality of Hostelries Utilising a System of Stars (Patent Pending)*, he ground it beneath his slipper, which lacked for both dramatic and physical impact. But he kept grinding regardless. "This publication is nonsense. I hate it."

"I hate it too," cried the innkeeper, clearly hoping he had secured an ally. "But you have witnessed now its unholy power."

Valentine scowled. "Indeed I have."

"And can understand," persisted the innkeeper, "why I cannot have these kind of"—at a loss for words to encompass Belle, Bonny, Valentine, and Sir Horley, he flapped a frantic hand instead—"*happenings* in my inn just at present. Or, ideally, ever."

"So," Sir Horley slurred, "no bath, then?"

"It's fine," put in Belle. "That bath was by way of a . . . luxury. The most important thing is that we leave and swiftly."

The innkeeper was nodding enthusiastically. "*Leaving and swiftly* sounds good to me."

"I'm still really confused." This was Bonny, plaintiveness not so much creeping as bursting into his tone. "Why are you eloping with Sir Horley? He's getting married in the morning, and also he, and also you . . . and I think he has tuberculosis."

"Tuberculosis," shrieked the innkeeper, before clapping a hand over his mouth with a frantic glance towards the taproom, where Mr. Bogstwaddle was still scribbling away, his manner somehow inherently condemnatory.

Belle sighed. "It's not tuberculosis. It's just being extremely drunk."

"On the contrary"—Sir Horley lolled against Valentine's shoulder—"this is the beginnings of sobriety."

Valentine, meanwhile, had set his jaw in a way that betokened misfortune for someone. "There will be a bath; I insist upon it. Bonny, take Sir Horley."

Perhaps predictably, Bonny was in no way prepared to take Sir Horley. But Belle stepped forward hastily, and, between them, they just about managed to catch him. She found herself wondering what was the average frequency with which wives-to-be dropped their potential husbands on the floor before the wedding. And whether his falling out of a window counted.

"Good evening." Valentine, meanwhile, was standing before Mr. Bogstwaddle. "I understand you are the author of *Mr. Bogstwaddle's Advice for Persons Making Trips Including Easy-to-Reference Summations of the Quality of Hostelries Utilising a System of Stars (Patent Pending)*?"

Mr. Bogstwaddle looked up with an air of perhaps understandable nervousness. While not ill-favoured exactly, he had a thin face and a longish nose; the sort of features that gave him a permanent impression of being about to point something out. Probably something you wouldn't like. "I am."

"Well, I am the Duke of Malvern," returned Valentine. "And to prove it, here is my signet ri—"

"No no no no." Passing Sir Horley to Belle as though he were an unwanted parcel, Bonny dashed after Valentine. "We are not doing that again. He's the Duke of Malvern; I vouch for it, she"—he flailed a hand backwards towards Belle—"vouches for it, the innkeeper vouches for it."

Mr. Bogstwaddle blinked even more nervously. "Very well."

"I would like to comment," explained Valentine, "on the quality of the hostelry for your publication."

"I . . ." The situation seemed to be in danger of overwhelming Mr. Bogstwaddle wholesale. "I've never interviewed a duke before."

"Then you shall tonight. While visiting, you solicited comment from—are you writing this down?"

"'While visiting, I solicited comment from . . . ,'" repeated Mr. Bogstwaddle obediently, fumbling with his pen.

"The Duke of Malvern of Malvern House."

"'The Duke of Malvern of Malvern House.'"

"Who said, 'A thoroughly excellent tavern, recommended to all. The innkeeper, in particular, tended to all my needs with a—'"

"Flower," interrupted Bonny, "that makes it sound like he fucked you."

The innkeeper stuck his head into the room. "I don't mind."

Bonny stamped his foot. "I mind."

"Is that a service on offer?" asked Mr. Bogstwaddle politely.

"Why not," said the innkeeper, nodding, at the same time Bonny said, "No, never." And then, whirling on the duke: "You're mine, Valentine. I won't have the world doubt it for a second."

In the candlelight, Valentine's aristocratic cheekbones gleamed with a soft blush. Belle could tell he was pleased. That he liked to be so openly *possessed*, at least by Bonny. Abstractly, she knew this was meant to be romantic. But it just felt skin-crawlingly strange to her. She neither wanted to possess anyone nor be possessed by them.

"So"—Mr. Bogstwaddle glanced between the various parties—"what am I writing?"

"'A thoroughly excellent tavern, recommended to all,'" repeated Bonny impatiently.

"What about the bit about the innkeeper?" asked the innkeeper, who had abandoned all pretence of absence. "I liked the bit about the innkeeper."

"'A thoroughly excellent tavern'"—Bonny tried again—"'with a thoroughly excellent innkeeper. Five stars.'"

"I'm not sure I'd give it five stars," said Valentine, looking thoughtful.

"Yes, you would," said the innkeeper.

"What's the point of this exercise"—Bonny once more—"if you don't give the place five stars?"

Valentine gave a fretful huff. "But five stars implies perfection."

"Not at all." That was the innkeeper. "It just implies better than four stars."

"Within your system," demanded Valentine, turning to Mr. Bogstwaddle, "what does five stars represent?"

Mr. Bogstwaddle seemed to be, at this point, physically unable to stop blinking. "They represent . . . stars."

"But surely there must be some systematic correlation between the number of stars and the quality of the hostelry? That's what your entire guide purports to be about."

"Well," said Mr. Bogstwaddle, "no."

For a moment, Valentine seemed lost for words. Then his head drooped in some impressive commingling of exasperation and defeat that was familiar to Belle from their own history of interactions. "Fine.

Five stars it is." Turning, he gathered both his dressing gown and his dignity. "I presume that bath is possible now?"

The innkeeper bobbed obligingly and scurried away.

"Bonny?"

"Yes, Your Grace?" Bonny's look was playful, as though he was enjoying Valentine's high-handedness. Which Belle knew for a fact he was. It was another of those ever-accumulating points of divergence with her twin.

"Can you take care of Sir Horley?" Valentine asked. "Belle and I need to talk."

Chapter 5

Talking to Valentine was not one of Belle's favourite pastimes.

"This," she said, "is not one of my favourite pastimes."

Valentine gave her a tight smile. "I'm aware, Arabella."

They had withdrawn to the upstairs private room, away from listening ears, prying eyes, and the solicitousness of a newly minted five-star innkeeper. Despite having spent over a year in the same house, it was still fairly rare for them to be alone together. They didn't precisely avoid each other, but usually there were friends between them or, at least, around them. Now they kept their distance in the most literal sense possible: Belle by the window, gazing abstractedly down at the stable yard, Valentine in a chair by the smouldering ashes of the fire.

When, not being sure what she could say, Belle did not reply, he sighed. "You're never going to forgive me, are you?"

"I think," she said finally, "I find it hard to forgive the world. All the ways it is set up for you that half the time you do not even notice."

"I cannot wed the man I love. How *set up* for me, as you put it, can the world be?"

He had offered the words mildly. And, truthfully, she could not muster much irritation for them. Just a certain stale weariness. "So it does not give you one tiny piece of what you want. Boo-hoo."

"Then what is it you want, Belle?"

"That's just it. It's not simple for me."

Caught in the glass, she saw his reflection raise a brow. "Boo-hoo?"

"You know," she remarked, "for someone apparently seeking my forgiveness, you are making some bold choices."

His expression smoothed immediately. "As ever, I simply hope for peace between us."

"We are," she tried, "not *not* at peace. I am happy you make Bonny happy. And as for what has happened between us . . ." Her mind drifted to the earnest, awkward Valentine she had known as a girl. And then to the cold man who had tried to force her into matrimony. It was like looking down a well or from a great height: whatever she saw, distorted by distance. "I find I no longer care. Can that be forgiveness enough for you?"

"Is it truly the best we can manage?"

Belle shrugged. "I find ideas of forgiveness rather abstract and exalted. It seems more meaningful to me simply to grow past hurt."

"I am trying to be someone you can trust. Someone you can believe you matter to."

"If I matter to you, it is because Bonny matters to you more than anything." She smiled to soften the truth of it. "I think perhaps I would like to have something of my own for once."

"And you believe that could be Sir Horley?"

It was a question that would once have struck at Belle rather deeply, carrying as it did the implication that nobody could independently wish to be connected to her. But she'd offered Valentine not-caring for a reason. If she'd tried to bear the weight of every heedless thing he'd ever said or done to her, she'd have been crushed into dust. "I mean," she tried instead, "he *is* my friend."

Valentine frowned. "Right now, I'm not sure he's anyone's friend."

"Least of all his own," Belle agreed. "But we . . . *I* . . . cannot abandon him."

"We did not abandon him. He has refused all contact with us since we . . . *you* . . . kidnapped him."

Kidnap someone *once*, and you never heard the end of it. "I will be the first to admit kidnapping him was an error."

"And yet you have done so a second time."

"This is not a kidnapping. This is an elopement."

"An elopement to which one party barely seems capable of consenting *is* a kidnapping."

"It is so interesting," said Belle musingly, "that you have become such a proponent of consent in matrimony."

The look Valentine cast her was mostly sad. "I did learn from you, Belle. Or I tried to."

"And yet you continue to oppose me at every turn."

"I've only asked to talk."

"As ever, I find little pleasure in your conversation." Belle knew she was needling him. She also knew it wasn't entirely fair of her. It was just . . . easier. Easier than trying to trust him again. Easier than having to risk hurt. Easier than having to face for herself all the ways she, too, had changed.

Valentine's patience visibly wobbled but, surprisingly, did not crack. "I have seen to everything you've asked for. A bath for Sir Horley. My carriage, should you need it. I'm not standing in your way. I simply question why you're doing this. Whether it is right for you?"

"You seem mostly concerned about whether it's right for Sir Horley."

"I am concerned," he growled, "about both of you."

"Do you believe us so incapable of managing our own happiness?"

"Frankly"—Valentine's fingertips were pinching the bridge of his nose, his whole attitude redolent of despair—"yes. But you don't have to tell me it is none of my business. Nor remind me that until I fell in love with your brother, I was hardly a great advocate of happiness for myself."

Belle shrugged. "Oh, you did all right. With your great wealth and influence."

"I cannot change what the world has given me."

And maybe it was just because they'd had this conversation, or some version of it, what felt like a thousand times before, but Belle relented. "I know. And I know you want to help. But, for once, could you help by . . . helping instead of the opposite of that?"

"I am," Valentine protested, faintly wounded. "But will you not at least allow me to care a little?"

"I have not cared much for you caring in the past."

"You did once."

"Yes, but I am no longer that girl. I will not give my faith so lightly nor forget how readily I may be dispensed with."

A trace of the old Valentine—the one who had done the ready dispensing—flickered into being as he briefly dropped his face into his hands. "Must you always be so damnably dramatic? Nobody is dispensing with you, nor have they. That makes it sound like you are regularly murdered."

"You are with Bonny?" she asked. "And *I* am the one you find dramatic?"

"It's different when—" Aware, as ever belatedly, that he wasn't helping himself, Valentine shut his mouth with a snap.

"When he's Bonny?" Belle finished for him. "If it's a man in general?"

"If the person in question hasn't shot me."

She narrowed her eyes at him. "I'm sorry that I shot you, Valentine. Don't make me change my mind about that."

"Can I at least make you change your mind about marrying Sir Horley? For your own sake?"

"My own sake," she repeated, unable to entirely keep the contempt from her voice. "You have tried to make me do many things I have not wanted, ostensibly for my own sake. Forgive me, but I don't think your judgement in this area can be trusted."

"You are running away"—Valentine's voice, by contrast, was surprisingly gentle—"against the wishes of his family, a few hours before his wedding, with a very unhappy man who, at the present moment, thinks little of us and, as far as I understand it, has no romantic or sexual feelings for women. This does not seem like a recipe for contentment."

"Whereas Sir Horley marrying Miss Carswile *is* a recipe for contentment?"

"That is a matter for his future and hers. Not yours."

"Well, his future is important to me," Belle retorted. "And some friend you are that it is not."

Valentine rose abruptly, in a swirl of dressing gown. "Of course it is important to me. But Sir Horley has made it overwhelmingly clear that he does not welcome our interference."

"He's here now, isn't he?"

"Because he is drunk, and I have witnessed firsthand how persuasive you can be when you are set on some foolish course."

"He was sober when he banished us from his life. I think his decision-making has been suspect in several directions lately."

"Belle." Valentine made the sort of sound he often made in her presence: exasperation and resignation in unhappy harmony. Bonny would, on occasion, inspire him to make similar sounds, but then they would be leavened by affection, as things so often were where her twin was concerned. "We cannot run roughshod over people's lives just because they do things we do not believe it is in their best interests to do."

"And when Bonny—seeing how miserable you were making yourself—rode roughshod over yours and made you chase me nearly to Dover? You had to get out of bed before noon. You spent a night trapped in a cellar. You were without your valet for *days*."

These horrifying memories of mild inconvenience made Valentine shudder. "Yes, but Bonny was . . . Bonny is . . . in love with me."

"Why is that significant in this context?"

"It just is," Valentine declared unhelpfully. "Everything changes when you're in love. The rules . . . the rules aren't the same."

"So what you're saying is that you can behave in as unreasonable a fashion as you like as long as somebody feels something that can be called romantic? But it's wrong for me to try and help someone I care about?"

"How is marrying Sir Horley going to help him? It's the last thing he needs."

"I did not offer lightly," Belle protested, aware she had indeed offered lightly. "It seemed the simplest solution to our mutual difficulties."

"His difficulties being?"

"The fact he is financially dependent upon his aunt. His conviction that she is his only family."

"And your difficulties being?"

"The fact I do not know what is to become of my life. Am I to spend it as some adjunct to you and Bonny?"

"You know you are welcome in our home."

"And what of my home, Valentine?"

He looked blank. Which would have been comical had it not also been infuriating. "Your home?"

Belle ground her teeth to control her frustration. "Yes. The one I lived in until my parents died. The one you've had unofficial steward-ship over ever since you took up with my brother."

"Oh." Valentine's blankness gave way to mildly abashed apathy. "That home."

"I know it legally belongs to Bonny, and I assume we have accrued considerable debts to you, but—"

"I refuse"—Valentine cut her off loftily—"to discuss business with a woman while I am in my dressing gown."

Belle's teeth creaked in her jaw. She rather doubted it was the dress-ing gown that was truly the issue here. "I do not mean to interfere. I'm not sure I could, even if I wished to. I have not been educated in estate management."

"There is nothing to worry about in that regard. I have appointed an excellent man to take care of such matters."

Of course he had. "Even so," Belle persisted, "surely it is better for the house to be occupied than stand empty. Bonny will not mind me staying there."

"With Sir Horley?" asked Valentine.

"Why not with Sir Horley?" asked Belle back.

"Well, not to return us to the issue of legality, but once you marry him, everything you have will become his."

"And you as good as own my brother's estate."

"But . . . ," began Valentine.

"But you are in love with him," Belle finished. She put a hand to her brow and then realised Valentine would likely condemn the gesture for its theatricality—despite it being the sort of thing he did all the time. "I'm tired, Valentine."

"If you will go running around at night, breaking into other people's houses . . ."

"More tired than that. I just want to go home."

His handsome, haughty face softened. "You could have gone any time."

"I suppose," she said, "I didn't want to go alone." And promptly hated herself for admitting that to Valentine of all people.

"We would have accompanied you."

It was the sort of offer best made in the subjunctive. Bonny—who had been only too glad to leave the future of the Tarleton estate first in Belle's hands, then Valentine's—would not have thanked his lover for the reminder of the responsibilities he had been born to or the memories he had buried with their parents. Memories Belle had, instead, carried round with her like a stone in her pocket. "And how," she tried aloud, "would that have helped me feel less like an adjunct to your lives?"

"I think what you are calling an adjunct to the lives of others, we would call *part of our family*."

It did not seem the moment—or rather it did very much seem the moment, but it would not have been helpful—to remind Valentine that Bonny was very literally her family. And had been so before he had ever been Valentine's.

"Besides," Valentine went on, "if this is how you feel about us, are you not in danger of going from an adjunct of Bonny's and mine to an adjunct of Sir Horley?"

"Perhaps. But I hope he understands me well enough that we can be adjuncts to each other."

"I still think—"

Whatever Valentine thought, which was probably the same thing he had been insisting all along—that Belle was making a mistake, did not know her own mind, that Sir Horley would prefer a self-destructive marriage to a stranger than a self-destructive marriage to a friend—Belle was spared having to argue with it because Bonny entered at speed and struck a pose of consternation.

"Belle," he cried. "You must fly."

Caught by his urgency, she startled. "What? Why?"

"Because there's an angry woman and some dogs in the taproom asking for you. I mean, the angry woman is asking. The dogs are just sort of barking and snuffling."

"Oh God." Belle struck a pose of consternation of her own. "You're right. I must fly. Where is Sir Horley?"

"Asleep in our bed."

"I'm sorry," said Valentine, who, as ever, had his own set of priorities, "I thought you said Sir Horley was asleep in our bed."

"Yes, flower," returned Bonny. "That's because he is. He sort of fell into it, and now I can't get him out."

"Tell me"—Belle did her best to channel the conversation in a useful direction—"he is at least washed and dressed."

Bonny nodded. "As best could be managed. I think he's still drunk beyond the dreams of wheelbarrows."

Knowing what she did of Sir Horley's feelings towards Bonny, Belle felt a pang of shame at having abandoned him to her brother's care. Then again, the chances of his remembering any of this by tomorrow were surely slim to none. "Valentine," she said, "you must retrieve Sir Horley. Bonny, please stall the angry woman and the dogs."

"What?" they said almost in unison. "How?"

"Use your initiative. I, meanwhile, will knot some sheets together in order to form a makeshift rope which we can then use to descend from the—"

"Or," suggested Valentine mildly, "you could sneak past the visitors and out the back way through the kitchen?"

Belle stared at him.

He blushed slightly. "You told me I ought to be helpful by helping. This is me helping."

"Oh but," protested Bonny, looking quite woebegone, "a rope made of sheets is *a classic*."

"And Sir Horley, or your sister, could classically break their necks."

Normally Belle would have defended her right to throw herself out of whatever windows she damn well pleased, but one window-centric exit per night was probably more than sufficient for most reasonable people. Or, indeed, unreasonable ones. Plus, they were in a hurry, and there was the tiny matter of Sir Horley nearly plunging to his death last time to consider. "Let's try the door," she said.

Chapter 6

"We must be quiet," Valentine cautioned her, as they crept along the corridor and into the room he was sharing with Bonny.

"I really don't think Sir Horley's aunt will hear us up here."

"It's not her I'm concerned about. I will never hear the end of it if I wake Periwinkle."

Of course Valentine would be thinking of his valet. It was almost reassuring in a way. The stars could fall from the sky and the sun explode into cinders, and Valentine's main preoccupation—after Bonny's well-being—would be how to get his boots shined and who would press his neckcloths. Then again, given Bonny's tendencies towards chaos, living full-time with him probably required the intervention of a third party of unflappable temperament and orderliness, even without the dissolution of the cosmos.

This was borne out by the state of the room, which was surprisingly neat for a space Bonny at least partially occupied. The eight to ten books he insisted on travelling with—*But what if I can't find anything to read?*—were, for once, neatly stacked on the bedside table. And the sight of them, all dog-eared and stuck with bookmarks, gave Belle the oddest sense of nostalgia. If you could feel nostalgic for something that belonged to a place and a time you didn't want to go back to and reminded you of a person you no longer knew how to pretend to be.

In any case, now was not the time. She boxed up the feeling, telling herself she would return to it at a more opportune moment, but secretly suspecting she was far more likely to consign it to some dusty internal corner—along with the other tidied-up relics of hurt and disappointment and rage—and never examine it again.

Sir Horley, clad somewhat haphazardly in garments clearly borrowed from Valentine, was sprawled out on the bed, sleeping fitfully. Attempts to rouse him mostly resulted in piteous requests for five more minutes.

"Can you assist in some way?" Belle demanded of Valentine.

He started. "I'm sorry. I was just thinking how different people look when they're asleep."

"Yes yes." She tugged urgently at Sir Horley's arm. "They look younger and more vulnerable. Except Bonny, who looks smug and cherubic."

This proved a poor technique for focusing Valentine's attention. He smiled helplessly. "He does look smug and cherubic."

"For fuck's sake, Valentine. This is an emergency. How long do you think Bonny is likely to be able to stall Sir Horley's aunt?"

Valentine cast her a look from beneath his eyelashes. "Indefinitely?"

"Even so, this is not a moment to lose yourself in sentimental reveries about my twin or guilty ones about how you should have been a better friend to Sir Horley."

"I should have been a better friend to Sir Horley," said Valentine, mournfully and predictably.

Belle bit back an impatient growl. "Yes."

"I had no notion he felt this way. Alone and powerless and . . . and uncared for. He always seemed happy to the point of irritating."

"Oh, Valentine," muttered Belle. "Are you not over thirty? Surely even through your strawberry leaves you can see that the bold can be fragile, the exuberant despairing, and the obliviously arrogant capable of occasional kindness in very specific contexts."

"I suppose I am the obliviously arrogant in this schema?"

"I did also note your capacity for kindness."

"I know. It is probably the nicest thing you've ever said about me."

"Well, I do not advise growing accustomed to it."

"Arabella?" His eyes drifted to hers. "Which in your reckoning are you?"

None of them? All of them? "The one who wants your help with Sir Horley before Bonny tells Mrs. Greenleaf he has been taken up by the wild hunt and swept away to a land between here and now to dwell forever as the consort of the king of the winter fae."

It was, she thought, a sufficiently good point, sufficiently well made, that even Valentine would heed her. He was not a man disposed to physical activity—another very specific context involving Bonny notwithstanding—but he had height and, when he chose to employ it, a kind of languid strength. Thankfully he chose to employ it now because if the evening had taught Belle anything, it was that her attempts to hoist Sir Horley about on her own rarely ended well. Supporting him between them, they managed to half push, half drag him towards the door.

"Wait," said Belle, just as they reached it. "Let us throw one of your coats over his head."

"Alternatively," suggested Valentine, "we do *not* throw one of my coats over his head?"

"It may soothe him."

"How will having a coat over his head be soothing?"

"Is it not soothing to parrots? Having something over their cage, I mean?"

Valentine made a noise like a troubled stallion. "And the next time Sir Horley is a parrot, we can bear that in mind."

"But," Belle protested, "what if he is recognised?"

"I think anyone capable of recognising Sir Horley is capable of recognising him with a coat over his head."

"I still feel we will draw less attention."

"How will two people smuggling a man out of an inn draw less attention if the man in question has a coat over his head?"

"Well, we would not be arguing, for starters."

"Fine." Valentine's attempt at a dramatic gesture was hindered by the fact that, in order to be truly dramatic, he would have been required to let go of Sir Horley. Which, since he was bearing most of Sir Horley's weight, would likely have gone badly for everyone. "Take whatever coat you require. But I don't want to hear another word—*ever*—about how I don't support you."

"You're certainly supporting Sir Horley."

It was the sort of thing Bonny would have said. The sort of thing that, had Bonny been the one to say it, Valentine would have smiled at. But because it was Belle, he barely glanced at her. Even when she tried, she would never be anything to him but an obligation. An obstacle or an irritant. Some combination of the grieving child he had abandoned and the confused woman who had fled him. No wonder she got so bitter every time he encouraged her to view him with *nuance*. Certainly, you had no right to ask other people for things when you had neither intent nor capacity to provide them in return.

Holding on to petty—or not so petty—resentment was not, Belle knew, supposed to be admirable. Indeed, she did not admire herself for it. But the reality was it could sometimes be terribly useful. Strengthening, both metaphorically and literally. When you had to, for example, smuggle your friend/fiancé out of an inn, and the person assisting you in the process was only moderately committed to it. Still, the lateness (or, more accurately, earliness) of the hour was helpful, and they managed to get down the corridor and then down the stairs, not quietly exactly, but without either encountering or rousing any of the other guests.

Things became a little more complicated as they approached the taproom. Within, Belle could see the gaunt and ominous silhouette of Sir Horley's aunt as she stood with her back to the mostly dwindled fire. A woman of her word, she was accompanied by a couple of hunting dogs as well as three slightly dishevelled-looking servants, and Miss Carswile, who had probably been nothing less than fully shevelled her entire life.

"So you're telling me," Mrs. Greenleaf was saying, this apparently addressed to Bonny, "you don't know anything?"

"Excuse me," Bonny protested. "I know plenty of things. Like the square root of sixty-four is eight. And Lord Byron's middle name is Gordon. Which isn't very Byronic, is it?"

"About my nephew. And this meretricious flibbertigibbet he's run off with."

"You mean, my sister?"

"What else am I to call a young woman who cavorts about the countryside in breeches?"

"Arabella Tarleton?" suggested Bonny.

Mrs. Greenleaf turned to one of the servants. "This is a waste of time. Search the premises."

With the instinct of a twin, Bonny barely turned his head towards the doorway. Belle made frantic "Do something" gestures at him. His eyes blinked "Like what?" and she hand signalled an emphatic "Anything." Then an even more emphatic "Now." Because Sir Horley's aunt was already in motion. And they were trapped in the corridor with nowhere to hide, and she could feel Valentine beginning to panic the same way you could sometimes feel a rainstorm approaching.

There came the tap of Mrs. Greenleaf's shoes against the flagstones. The whine-click of a dog yawning extensively. Belle's heart squeezed and her mind whirled. What was she going to *do*?

"Oh my God," Bonny shrieked. "Look over there." The slightest pause. "*There.* Outside."

"What?" asked Miss Carswile, alarmed.

"I saw something. In the window."

"Your own reflection?" That was Mrs. Greenleaf, her tone dripping condescension. Though she did, at least, seem to have paused.

"No," Bonny protested. "Not my own reflection. Something . . . else. Something *extraordinary*."

Miss Carswile had crossed the room. "There's a tree."

"Not a tree."

"The branches are quite sinister."

"It's. Not." Bonny punctuated each word with a foot stamp. "The. Tree. It was . . . *under* the tree. Ghostly figures. But"—he was gathering steam—"strangely beautiful. And riding on spectral milk-white steeds." He gasped. "It was probably the wild hunt. Sir Horley and Belle have been seized by the wild hunt."

"You," declared Sir Horley's aunt, "are as bad as your sister. Possibly worse."

"Oh, I'm definitely worse." This had clearly brought out Bonny's competitive side.

In any case, irritating Mrs. Greenleaf turned out to be an effective way of distracting her. Nudging Valentine into action, Belle hustled him and Sir Horley past the taproom and along yet another corridor towards the kitchen.

Where they collided with Mr. Bogstwaddle, coming the other way. He was in a stripy nightshirt, complete with matching cap, and was holding a sizeable slice of the game pie that had been served at supper. Everyone took a moment to flinch guiltily.

"I was awoken"—Mr. Bogstwaddle was the first to gather himself—"by a commotion."

Belle did not have time for this. "No, you weren't. You were already up and sneaking pie."

"I was not. What pie?"

"The pie in your hand."

Mr. Bogstwaddle stared at both hand and pie in consternation, as if the one had spontaneously materialised in the other. "I have no notion—oh goodness. The truth is I . . . I have an affliction."

"An affliction," repeated Belle, not quite as a question.

"Y-yes. You have heard, of course, of those who ambulate in slumber. Well, I masticate."

"You sleep eat?"

"Yes," returned Mr. Bogstwaddle defiantly. "And anyway, what are you doing with a man with a coat over his head?"

There would be no assistance from Valentine. He had all the problem-solving initiative of a squashed teacake. "We're helping him," Belle explained.

"How is it helpful for him to have a coat over his head?"

"Um," said Belle.

"Could he by any chance be the lady's runaway nephew?"

"No," said Belle, at the same time Valentine—clearly caught off guard—said, "Yes." And then, in response to Belle kicking him in the ankle, "That is, I mean. Technically."

"How," asked Mr. Bogstwaddle, showing surprising tenacity for a man with gravy dripping between his fingers, "is he not and also technically her nephew?"

Belle shot Valentine a furious look. "Yes, Valentine. How is he not and also technically Mrs. Greenleaf's nephew?"

"He *is* her nephew," he said slowly, his voice tinged with the desperation of someone who has no idea what his next words ought to be, "but he's also not because he's . . ."

"Yes?" said Belle.

"Because he's . . ."

"Yes," said Mr. Bogstwaddle.

"Dead," finished Valentine.

There was nothing for Belle to do at this point but to stare at him. Mr. Bogstwaddle blinked. There was something very obnoxious about his blinking. "That still doesn't explain the coat."

"No." Valentine was speaking like he was a grandfather clock winding down. "It does explain the coat. Because the coat . . ."

"Yes?" said Belle.

"The coat . . ."

"Yes," said Mr. Bogstwaddle.

"Is a gesture of respect. You see"—Valentine appeared to have found his footing—"he was killed in a particularly bloody and brutal fashion. And his face was left . . . unrecognisable."

Belle was still staring. "Do you truly think this is helping?"

A vein was pulsing at Valentine's temple. "You try explaining it then."

"Why do I have to explain it? This is your fault."

Mr. Bogstwaddle's eyes were flicking between them as though he were chasing ants. "If he's dead, where are you taking him?"

"Where are we taking him, Valentine?" asked Belle sweetly.

Valentine's mouth opened and closed a few times. "I don't know. I just . . . I don't know."

"It's because the Duke of Malvern murdered him," Belle offered, "and has forced me to aid him in hiding the corpse."

"What?" The pie was beginning to slide slowly between Mr. Bogstwaddle's fingers, gravy splatting onto the floor like blood drops.

"Oh yes. He's a very dangerous man. Beneath his façade of"— Belle's eyes slid sideways to Valentine—"not being dangerous at all."

Mr. Bogstwaddle swallowed with an audible *gulp*. "I should probably . . . probably . . . be going to bed."

"Yes," said Belle. "Yes, you should."

He slithered awkwardly past them in the narrow corridor, trying not to jostle them or drop his pie, and then walked away with the rigid calm of a man who believes he may have turned his back on a bear in the woods.

"He's going to summon a magistrate, isn't he?" asked Valentine, with an air of resignation rather than distress.

Belle nodded. "Most likely."

"Devil take it."

"You were the one who—"

"I'm aware."

She took a moment to assess the situation. "Consider the positives. Your being arrested could well provide Sir Horley and me with a useful diversion."

"And my being hanged?" Valentine's tone remained unexpectedly mild. Either he had discovered a deep well of personal resilience, or his mind had buckled under the stress of the evening.

"They can hardly hang you for the murder of a still-living man," Belle pointed out.

"Who is in Scotland."

"I believe people in Scotland are generally understood to be alive."

"I was thinking more of the distance."

"Oh, don't worry about that. We will make our return just in the nick of time to save you from the gallows."

"Will you?"

"Of course. It's the trope."

This did not seem to reassure Valentine as it would have reassured Bonny. But, in the midst of an extremely spontaneous elopement, it was the best Belle could manage. At the very least, it allowed her to hurry Valentine—and along with him Sir Horley—through the abandoned, though recently pie-denuded kitchen, and out into a well-kept herb garden that was quickly rendered simply a herb garden by their passage. Pressing tight to the wall of the inn, they crept towards the stable yard, where Valentine's carriage was waiting. Unfortunately, this also brought them close to the taproom, where Bonny was doggedly performing amateur theatrics in front of the very window they were needing to pass.

"Get down." Belle dropped to the ground, pulling Valentine and Sir Horley with her and hopefully out of view.

"I'm not sure this is mud," whispered Valentine.

"Right now, the least of my concerns," Belle whispered back.

"But I'm quite concerned," he insisted.

"Live with it," she insisted back.

Reaching a hand carefully above her, she felt through the moss and a stray cobweb until she was able to crook a finger beneath the frame. Thankfully, in the excitement of the evening, the window had not yet been latched, and she was able to ease it partially open.

"—clearly not well," Miss Carswile was saying, her voice falling on Belle's ears with impossible sweetness after that long, dark, and emotional night.

"There's clearly something not right with him," Sir Horley's aunt agreed, albeit without sweetness.

"Excuse me." Bonny sounded genuinely outraged. "There are lots of things not right with me."

"This is a waste of time." That was Mrs. Greenleaf again.

"Is it not," asked Miss Carswile, "our moral duty to help him in some way? His sister is missing too. And he seems"—she broke off, clearly at a loss—"delirious?"

While they were distracted, Belle took the opportunity to distract Bonny in return. "Psst," she tried.

Bonny twitched. Then half turned. Then jumped. Then tried to pretend he had done none of those things. "What are you doing?" he mouthed. As best as one could mouth without moving one's mouth.

Belle flicked her fingers in a "Do something" gesture.

"Like what?"

"Anything."

"Are you talking to yourself?" demanded Mrs. Greenleaf.

"What?" Bonny at least sounded plausibly startled, if not plausibly like he hadn't been mumbling out of a cracked-open window. "No. No, I'm—*look over there.*"

Risking a peep over the sill, Belle discovered neither Mrs. Greenleaf nor Miss Carswile looking over there. They were, in fact, still looking directly at Bonny, Mrs. Greenleaf with an expression of unmitigated disgust, and Miss Carswile bewildered pity.

With a muted squeak, Belle huddled down again. "I think we're fucked."

"My dear Belle," murmured Valentine, "we are long-standing recipients of fuckery. It began early, continued vigorously, and has yet to cease. This has been one of the most protracted fuckings of my life."

It was at that moment that Mr. Bogstwaddle burst into the taproom with such ferocity, and at such velocity, that the door slammed into the wall with a glassware-rattling crash. "Help," he cried. "Murder! Pie thievery! Kidnapping!"

At any other time, Belle would have enjoyed the chaos. For there was much of it: raised voices, barking dogs, rapid footsteps, and the clatter of furniture being knocked over or pushed aside. As it was, however, she merely took the opportunity to make a run for the carriage, clambering into it while Valentine hoisted Sir Horley in after.

The inn, meanwhile, had gone full hue and cry. Although some of the cries were the innkeeper, wanting to know if five stars from a duke still counted if the duke was a known criminal.

"Belle." Valentine caught her wrist and held it, admittedly somewhat muddily, but there was warmth there too. "Are you sure this is what you want?"

Exhausted, she lifted a shoulder in the barest approximation of a shrug. "If it isn't, it's too late now."

The moonlight had transformed his eyes to silver. And they gazed up at her, earnest and uncomprehending. "Don't do this. Stay. I can find the life that fits you."

"Maybe you can." Leaning forward, she pressed her lips briefly to his brow. "With all your wealth and power, education and intellect, I'm sure there's little you could not accomplish."

"Then let me."

She shook her head. "I would rather a life I chose."

"Even if it makes you unhappy?"

"As long as it is mine."

It seemed as though he wanted to argue with her. But either he thought better of it, or there was no opportunity. Instead, he stepped away from the carriage, while Belle folded up the steps and pulled the door closed.

"I can't believe I'm about to say this," Valentine told the coachman. "But . . . to Gretna Green? As fast as you can."

Chapter 7

Sir Horley, who had taken to waking only reluctantly, awoke with even more reluctance than usual. He felt, despite some stiff competition, worse than he had ever felt in his life before.

The whole world was rocking monstrously.

And it was his wedding day.

Oh fuck, his wedding day.

He knew—had known all along—it was a terrible idea. Unfair to Miss Carswile, for all she believed otherwise. But the alternative was what? To be cast aside by the only person who had not done so? A woman who knew him, and hated him, and yet had stuck by him. When her husband had professed such love, supposedly the opposite of hate, and fled him into oblivion. Not everyone, of course, had fled quite so fast, nor quite so far, but he had lost them nonetheless: to respectability, to God, to a bigger dick and a prettier face. What did it matter, really, what he lost them to?

He had thought, at first, it was the consequence of his nature. The price for desires that did not run as they ought. Except no; his aunt had the right of it as, in her own dreary fashion, she tended to. It was him. There was something about him. He was not worth staying for. His own parents had set the pattern.

These, though, were old thoughts. Blunted by time, by repetition, by familiarity.

Sir Horley's head throbbed and his gut churned and still came that ceaseless, soul-tilting swaying. The light that swam behind his eyelids felt ominous somehow. Shark fins upon the ocean. He would have to face it at some point. The light, like his marriage, was not something that could be avoided, hidden from, or even drowned a thousand bottles deep. But it could wait. The whole fucking world could wait. He would hold it at bay, for a few more moments at least, in this private grey nowhere. Neither sleep nor wakefulness, and not devoid of pain, but peaceful in its own way.

He had long envied Valentine his talent for slumber. Lazy mornings that lingered past midday, afternoon naps that spilled into evening, endless nights in his lover's arms. The man had the soul of a cat. An endless capacity for contentment. Whereas Sir Horley preferred not to contemplate the state of his soul and spent his nights accordingly, fretful as the devil, or finding rest at the sword's point of exhaustion. Yielding to it in desperation and defeat.

Last night, his dreams had been strange and vivid. The drink did that sometimes. It had brought him Tarletons, unbearable in their compassion, flaunting the love he had won from them under false pretences. Love for a man they thought they knew. Who had always been a serpent, whose smile was a mask, and all his laughing lies.

Miss Carswile could not save him. No more than her God could or Bonny's heart could, even if that had not belonged irredeemably to Valentine. But his had been a life of parts, some cast upon him, others adopted for expediency or desire. Disregarded son, burdensome child, traitor and thief, soldier and whore, dandy and jester. He had even played at friend for a while. And so he could, he supposed, be a good husband. Well, an adequate husband. At least, he could imagine worse husbands. There were duties he would not want from his wife once he had an heir. He had no wish to control her, financially or otherwise. He would allow her all the freedom he knew how to give, even if she squandered it on piety and good works. As futures went—and, really, what others were there—he told himself that his was not so dire. Marriage would give him a home, family, fortune, security. Some shreds, perhaps, of self-respect in having, for once, done his duty. Been a man. Given, instead of taking away. As for the cost? Well. He could drink at home. And what could sodomy provide that his own tight fist did not? There was even a kind of freedom in it. The future. Not the tight fist. Though he supposed they both had him by the tender parts. In any case, freedom. This could be freedom. The freedom of choosing one's cage.

He opened his eyes, wincing as the light seemed to pierce his pupils, through aqueous and vitreous humours alike, and straight into his brain. His surroundings smeared in and out of focus.

And he did not recognise them in the slightest.

"So," said Arabella Tarleton, "you may be somewhat alarmed. But there's nothing to—"

Sir Horley lurched violently from the spine-bending, neck-twisting slump in which he'd been sleeping. A couple of his joints crackled like gunfire, feeling, in that moment, almost as painful. "Where the fuck am I?"

"I would say somewhere to the north of Leamington Spa?"

"Why"—his throat was as raw as if he'd spent the night servicing sailors—"am I somewhere to the north of Leamington Spa?"

Arabella Tarleton looked about as abashed as it was possible for a Tarleton to look. Which, by normal person standards, was not very. "Because you're on your way to Gretna Green."

The world reeled afresh. Sir Horley's brain and stomach both felt worryingly liquid. And not a pleasant liquid: a kind of grey sludge that sloshed back and forth with the carriage. "I can't be on my way to Gretna Green. I'm getting married today."

"You *were* getting married today," Arabella corrected him, less than helpfully.

It was slowly beginning to dawn on him that he wasn't surprised. His emotions were mostly buried beneath a pervading sense of absolute physical disintegration, but, on excavating them, he discovered mostly exhaustion—the kind that had nothing to do with how much you'd slept—and resignation. "Take me back. Take me back *at once*."

"It's a little late."

"Take me back anyway. This . . . whatever this is, it can be undone."

"I do not think it can, Sir Horley." Arabella's abashedness level reached an all-time Tarleton high. Or low. Depending upon what scale abashment was measured. "Our departure left an impression."

"*Our* departure?" he repeated. "What is that saying? 'Kidnap me once, shame on you; kidnap me twice, shame on . . . still you'?"

"I didn't kidnap you. You agreed to come with me."

He stared at her in pure incomprehension. Into eyes that were the same blue as her brother's eyes, but still, strangely, her own. Bonny was summer skies, long days and warm nights, and the hope of dreams come true. Belle was a glacial lake, full of depths and secrets, and too-clear reflections. "Why in God's name did I do that?"

"It's a longish story, but what it came down to was that I told you I cared for you, that I could offer you the same security of future and fortune you would gain from marrying at your aunt's direction, that I believed we could be happy together, and"—she paused, gathering that Tarletonian intensity the way most people paused for breath—"that you deserved to be happy."

"I was obliteratingly drunk," he retorted, trying not to wonder how he'd responded to her last night. If it had been needy and shameful. "I would have to have been to accept such childish, sentimental pap."

Her lips pulled into a censorious little bow. "Being obliteratingly drunk is clearly not good for you."

"Is that so? Because I was saturating myself in ethanol for the health benefits."

"The fact you could only countenance marriage to Miss Carswile by saturating yourself in ethanol, as you put it, does not, to me, speak strongly in favour of the match."

"And the fact you had to drag me into an elopement against my will says nothing but good things about our current predicament? Fucking hell." Sir Horley pressed a hand to his head, partly as an expression of distress, and partly because he thought his skull might be about to split down the middle. "What am I saying? Five minutes in your company, and I'm carrying on like a character in a badly written melodrama."

"Oh, Sir Horley." Belle's voice was deadly sweet. "You don't need my help with that."

He stifled a groan. "Touché, little cat." Then he tried to stifle a second groan and failed because the groan appeared to be his entire body. "Stop the carriage."

"I told you, it's too late. You missed the wedding hours ago."

"Stop the carriage," he said, with terrible precision, "or I cast my accounts into your lap. Your choice."

Belle knocked with gratifying haste upon the roof. And Sir Horley, barely waiting until they had come to a standstill, thrust open the door, not so much climbing out as tumbling down. He couldn't tell if this was emotional upheaval running riot through weakened flesh or weakened flesh surrendering to the inevitable. Either way, it felt like dying. All viscerality and human mess. A battlefield he'd created from himself. Or of himself.

Fresh air should have helped. But it barely registered upon his senses, his throat seizing as he tried to breathe. He took a few staggering steps forward, anticipating both the shame and the release of the drunkard. His stomach was a bed of snakes. His mouth an abattoir. Dropping to his hands and knees, he braced for the imminent abandonment of dignity and control and other rudiments of grace. An inescapable erosion of the line between higher being and helpless beast.

Except even this was beyond him. Denied him. There was just a racking, wretched, impotent nausea that rose up from his guts and found no relief at all beyond what spit remained upon his tongue and some unsightly fluids that he disgorged into a patch of otherwise blameless wildflowers. And still his body struggled until his temples pulsed with fire and his mind was blank with weakness.

He had not realised there could be something worse than vomiting. How naive. There was always something worse. Always lower to fall.

A hand touched his shoulder, cool even through the fabric of what was blatantly a borrowed coat. "I am increasingly concerned," said Belle, "at the destruction our escape has wrought upon the local flora."

Sir Horley choked on air, his muscles spasming helplessly, sweat dripping from his brow, sticky sweet and pungent. "Leave me alone, dammit."

"Never."

For something comprised almost entirely of gasps and shudders, whatever ailed him took a miserably long time to run its course. He did not want to be grateful for her touch—for the way she scraped the hair from his eyes, or how tethering it felt when her palm moved to the back of his neck—but he was, and mortifyingly so. Because he had always been easy to comfort. He took to it like a starving dog, cringing and desperate, only too glad to call scraps a banquet. All it needed was a look, or a word, or the hint of a smile, and he was anyone's. For anything. Just for the moment when bodies met, or occasionally—rarely—mouths, or afterwards in the dark, listening to a stranger's heartbeat.

This was not that, though. It was not the shadow of some stolen thing. He hardly knew what it was, the pattern of Belle's breath upon the air, the velveteen of her fingertips. Only that it—that she—asked for nothing. Simply gave.

Chapter 8

Eventually exhaustion proved the victor. What was left of Sir Horley's strength gave out, and he collapsed onto the grassy verge that ran along-side the road. Throwing up, or failing to throw up, should not have felt so familiar. But he remembered fragments of moonlight. Fingers curling uselessly into dirt. Sheets that smelled of Bonny. Belle leaning over him, her hair the impossible gold of a hobgoblin's promises as it spilled over his wrist.

Then you might as well marry me.

"Here." In the present—assuming that, too, was actually happening—Belle was kneeling at his side, offering him a flask.

Too defeated even to question, he took it shakily from her and drank. It was just water, a little brackish, a little warm. But in his mouth it was the sweetest thing he had ever tasted. He had to force himself to sip, rather than consume it in great ugly gulps.

"Did you say something?" asked Belle.

He hadn't intended to. But apparently he was now vomiting out his thoughts as well as his innards. "'Purge me with hyssop.'"

"I don't think I'm into that."

"It's a psalm."

"Which improves the situation how?"

Inexplicably and against all reason, his lips pulled upwards, tempted towards a smile. "'Purge me with hyssop, and I shall be clean: wash me, and I shall be whiter than snow.'"

"In my experience, and I do have some because Bonny ate a bad oyster once, those who have undergone purgation of any kind are rarely whiter than snow."

"I understand it's meant to be more of a light sprinkling."

"You don't need any hyssop, Sir Horley."

"I am well beyond its power."

Belle seemed unimpressed, even by the standards of a woman who was not overly inclined to pressedness. "If David had been more like you, at least Bathsheba would have been able to bathe in peace."

"Ah." Despite feeling slightly better, Sir Horley was still not capable of gestures beyond mild twitching. But he twitched emphatically now. "The good Lord had a plan for my ilk all along. We exist that ladies may perform their ablutions undisturbed."

"You mock," Belle pointed out, "but given how your desirous counterparts have historically interacted with ladies performing their ablutions, I see nothing but positives for everyone in this arrangement."

There was no reasonable answer he could give to this, although being Belle, she would likely have accepted an unreasonable one just as readily. Possibly even preferred it. So, they lingered in silence by the roadside, Sir Horley progressing from prone to partially upright with all the elan of a slug upon a windowpane, while the coachman and under-coachman stretched their legs at a discreet distance. Whatever Valentine paid them, they were probably beginning to feel it wasn't enough.

It would have been quite a nice day to get married. It was even a fairly decent day for dry heaving into hedgerows. Not too hot, not too breezy, the sky marbled by pale wisps of cloud to break the monotony of blue. Some part of him was expecting to wake up. Find himself back in his aunt's house. A dark room. Too many bottles. Events still waiting to play out as they were meant to.

The previous evening was still mostly moments, vivid but disconnected, raindrops caught upon a broken spider's web. But it was easy enough to imagine what had happened. The way he might have responded, when his defences were down, to words he knew better than to believe. Wasn't this exactly the kind of nonsense he'd wanted to avoid when he'd pushed his friends out of his life? Or was it, in some pathetic, barely acknowledged way, what he had secretly been hoping for? Someone to do something foolish, unnecessary, ridiculous for him. To prove he was worthy of it. That he mattered. Even the possibility of the thought was beyond humiliating. It made him nauseous all over again, but this time it had nothing to do with his body. Nausea of the soul. Was that something?

Oh, why could those damn Tarletons never leave anything alone? Well. Tarleton on this occasion. Just the one. Just Belle. Had her brother even spared him a thought? Probably not. Bonny was too busy being happy. And wasn't that what Sir Horley had tried to give him? It was too late now to resent it.

"You should try a little of this too," Belle said at last, producing another flask.

"What is it? Arsenic?" He took a whiff, and it almost set his eyes to watering. "Hair of the dog. Why, Arabella, I thought you didn't approve of my drinking."

"I don't. I have no idea what you see in it—"

"I see nothing in it. That's the appeal."

"You know"—she slanted a sharp look at him—"I rather enjoy you like this."

He arched a dubious brow, wary of where this might be going. "Like what exactly?"

"So cynical and self-destructive. It's very gothic."

"It's not gothic," he snapped, riled, despite his best intentions, by her insouciance. "It's who I am." And then, recalling a time when he had been insouciant, too, and they had been insouciant together, he scraped up the dregs of a smile. "Fine, I'm absurd. But I'm also a rather unpleasant person who has lived a rather unpleasant life and been not wholly undeservedly unhappy for a great deal of it."

"Of that sentence, the only part of it I believe is that you've been unhappy."

"How very lovely of you, then, to make sport of it."

"Well, I'm rather unpleasant too," Belle said, unruffled. "Besides, would you have accepted solace?"

"Probably not," he conceded.

She nudged her shoulder lightly against his. It was the sort of thing she might have done back when they'd been friends, but it felt different now they weren't. Or rather, now she knew too many truths about him. It made him shiver with the same strange longing as her fingers against his brow and upon his neck. Except he hardly knew what it was he longed for. Certainly nothing he had ever sought before. Or expected to receive.

Distracted, half-dismayed, he swigged from Belle's second offering. For strong liquor it went down far too easily. He could likely have downed the whole flask. Part of him wanted to. Quite a lot of him wanted to. But he wasn't sure he could allow himself to in front of Belle, and so he handed it back.

"Keeping an eye on me?" he drawled. "It's like we're married already."

She shrugged. "Not really. I was just thinking how very good you are at consuming alcohol. I can hardly make it through half a glass of whisky without spluttering."

"Practice, my dear."

The slightest of pauses. Then, "I think . . ." She sounded oddly hesitant for Belle. "I think I read somewhere that it can help. To take a little alcohol, I mean. If you have been used to taking a lot."

"Is this your way of telling me to moderate my intake?"

She drew her knees up beneath her dress and hugged them. "I'd rather not be wed to someone who is drinking himself to death. But I'd also rather not be wed to someone I am obliged to command or who expects to command me."

And there it was. Point non plus.

"Miss Tarleton," he said, as gently as he could. "You must see we cannot marry."

Somewhat predictably, as was the way of a Tarleton crossed, she pouted. "We've already had this conversation."

"When I was drunk."

"If it's any consolation, you were still difficult to persuade."

"And that didn't give you pause?"

"Sir Horley, you've met me."

He blinked, not sure whether he was exasperated or secretly—in some foolish, unbroken corner of his heart—charmed. "Good point, well made."

"Besides, we can't go back. Your aunt made it clear she would not forgive you, and, frankly, I don't believe you should forgive her either."

"What do I have to forgive her for?"

"Oh." Belle's voice cracked with some emotion that bewildered him. "Many, many things. But setting the dogs on you last night might be a start?"

"Wait. What?"

"She set the—"

"No, no, I heard. I'm simply surprised I'm surprised."

"She was also extremely rude."

"That I'm even less surprised about."

"And you destroyed her topiary."

That drew a half laugh from him, though it was bitter enough to sting his own tongue. "Ah yes. I always take a stand against the things that really matter."

"I'm afraid it was the lack of standing that did for the topiary."

This time, his laugh was softer and sounded faintly startled, even to his own ears. Yet another reason to bring an end to this. "Forgiveness has never been on the cards as far as Aunt Ruth is concerned. But I believe with time and patience we can probably work our way back to a relationship where she doesn't want me torn apart by dogs."

"Mm," said Belle. "Aspirational indeed."

"And Miss Carswile is sure to forgive me. She's too grotesquely Christian not to. The wedding can be rescheduled. Which, in turn, will please my aunt. Or at least make her less inclined to murder me in cold blood."

Belle hugged her knees tighter. "It is not right of you to marry Miss Carswile. Let's not pretend otherwise."

If she had sounded condemnatory, he would have been able to defend himself. Unfortunately, she just sounded sad. And that made sadness—sadness and even a touch of guilt—prickle at him in return. "She knows what I am."

"Knowing something is not the same as understanding it."

There. This, exactly this, was what he had needed to avoid. It was complicated enough to go through with something against your personal inclinations without also having to defend your right to do so. "For someone who feels as you do about romance, you seem to have extraordinarily romantic ideas about marriage."

"I'm aware it's a matter of duty for you."

"Duty," he agreed, "and a mild disinclination to starve on the street."

"But if that's truly all you care about: wealth, security, a place in society, atoning for some wrong you erroneously believe you did your aunt—"

"I fucked her husband. There is no *erroneously* about it."

Belle cast herself back into the wildflowers—not the ones her companion had vomited over—her forearm pressed to her brow. "I am a simple woman, Sir Horley. I can only argue with you upon one subject at a time."

"You cannot argue me into marriage," he retorted.

"I only wish," she retorted back, incorrigibly, "to understand why you will accept this compromise of your personal happiness with Miss Carswile but not with me when it might not be so much of a compromise?"

"For fuck's sake"—the words escaped him in a moment of frustration—"because I like you."

He wished he had not spoken. But he had also achieved the impossible: rendered a Tarleton speechless. Belle's mouth opened and closed several times. "That was very much not the impression you gave last night."

So he'd hurt her, then? Probably in some nebulous attempt to do right by her. As he was trying to do now. Except it felt execrable. A novel new flavour of thinking little of himself. "Of course I like you. Who could not?"

"Oh." She gave a pretty little laugh he knew was practiced. As hollow as all his careless ways. "Lots of people—haven't you noticed?"

"Well, they're wrong."

"I'm not sure they are. I'm *quite* annoying."

"Belle, don't you see?" Unable to bear these glimpses of her pain, he let out a slow, surrendering breath. He might as well be honest about one thing. "You're everything I pretended to be when I claimed I was your friend."

"Which is what exactly?"

"Brave. Kind. Generous. Fun to be around."

"I'm mean, Sir Horley. Everyone knows I'm mean."

He gave her a reluctant smile. "Mean is fun."

"And we *did* have fun." Her tone turned ruthlessly coaxing.

"I was happier than I've ever been in my life. And I was still profoundly miserable." More honesty, though probably less comforting to her than his previous admission. He finished the water in a couple of deep swallows and pushed himself to his feet. "You cannot help me, Belle."

She squinted up at him, the sun threading glitter through the strands of her hair, spread wide across the grassy verge. "You could try helping yourself. Just a suggestion."

"I won't marry you. I can't do that to you."

"But you will to Miss Carswile?"

"She won't care. She's a sanctimonious pill."

Belle's eyes flashed ice. "She's not a pill. She . . . she's misguided. Which you've done nothing to remedy."

"Come." It was difficult to take decisive action upon legs that felt like daisy stalks. But he wobble-strode over to the carriage as best he could. "We're going back to my aunt's."

"No," Belle cried. "Wait."

What followed was a jumble. Disordered impressions—the rapid pitter-patter of boots upon the road, the stirred air of someone else's motion, a hand closing around his elbow—partially submerged beneath the rush of instinct. It was only when he heard Belle's startled yip that he realised he had her pinned against the side of the carriage, his forearm pressed to her throat.

"My God." He pulled away quickly. "I'm sorry. I'm so sorry."

She only glared at him, far angrier than she was afraid. "Don't be sorry. Stop being nonsense."

"This isn't nonsense."

"It *is* nonsense. You can't marry a woman because you don't care if you hurt her."

"I can *only* marry a woman I don't care if I hurt."

"No." She shook her head rapidly. "No. You are not that man."

"You have no idea what kind of man I am," he reminded her.

Her finger caught him hard in the chest. It was the most brutal poke he had ever experienced. "Wrong. *You* have no idea what kind of man you are."

For a moment they just stared at each other, both breathing heavily, Sir Horley trembling slightly. The confrontation had shaken him with its unexpectedness. And he had shaken himself with his own actions. It had been a kind of animal panic, a relic of battlefields past, drawn to the surface by all the other ways he felt trapped, helpless, and under attack. But it still horrified him, that spectre of violence, lurking in his skin.

"I am a gentleman," he said softly. "I 'toil not, neither do I spin.' To live I must wed. And when I do . . ."

He only realised he had stopped speaking when Belle prompted him with an equally soft "What?"

He hardly knew how to continue. There was honesty. And then there were truths like these. The terrible nakedness of them. "I'm not fit for what Bonny and Valentine have. God knows, I would sell my soul for it, if my soul was worth a clipped copper. I don't know if I ever truly let myself seek it or if I always recognised it would be futile. But I do know that when I marry, I give up even the hope of it."

"You are fit for whatever you need," Belle told him, with that unbearable, impossible, Tarletonian ferocity. "And I would stand in the way of no love you wanted to share."

"I'm sure." He raised his hand, intending to brush her cheek as he might once have done, then dropped it again, fearing she might flinch from him. "But it wouldn't be the same. It would always feel like a compromise. A poor simulacrum of what I truly wanted."

"And so," she asked, "you seek misery?"

He shrugged. "Better that than letting someone I care for take my last dream of happiness. That would be too much even for me to lose."

Silence fell between them and lingered for long, heavy moments. Belle's gaze was distant, her teeth digging abstractedly into her lower lip. "For the record," she said at last, "I agree with none of this. Absolutely none of this. Do you understand?"

A pained kind of fondness rolled through him. "I understand you agree with absolutely none of this."

"But it's your life and your decision."

"You mean"—he could not keep the shock from his voice—"you'll take me back?"

She rolled her eyes. "I was sincerely not attempting to abduct you." Pushing past him, as though he was not stronger and taller than she was, and had never thrown her against her carriage, she waved a readiness to depart to the coachman, then pulled open the door and climbed aboard. At his hesitation, she made an impatient gesture. "Are you coming?"

Was this the first time in history a Tarleton had ever changed their mind about anything? He should have been triumphant. Or relieved. Relieved would have done. But he felt almost nothing. "Yes," he said quickly. "Yes."

As she reached down a hand to help him, he caught again the dance of the sun in her hair—mellow light that spun the evening through her curls, turning the gold tawny.

The evening? Oh no.

"Belle?"

"Sir Horley?"

"How long have we been travelling?"

She peered over his shoulder at the sky. "Some of the night, and nearly all of the day. Why?"

"Did anyone see us?"

"Travelling?"

"Travelling. Departing. At any point."

"Well, your aunt made rather a scene at the inn."

"Fuck." Whatever little strength remained fled Sir Horley's limbs, and he crumpled into a sitting position in the carriage doorway. "Fuck."

Belle regarded him with growing concern. "Whatever is the matter now?"

"Your reputation."

"I don't care a fig about that."

"You should. This will be a scandal, assuming it isn't one already."

"So?"

"So," he snapped, "you'll never be able to do anything in society again."

"Possibly not. But to be honest, I was intending to go home anyway. I . . . I don't think London has anything to offer me."

He ran his hands through his hair, then pulled at it hard, hoping the sting of pain would . . . help somehow? Provide him with some miraculous solution to his current quandary. Instead, he started to laugh and then found himself unable to stop.

"You're being very strange," Belle said.

"I've ruined you." Sir Horley's voice wavered with too much mirth and not enough breath. "I've never so much as touched a woman in a sexual way, and I've ruined one. I've not even lifted a skirt or bared a breast. How has this happened?"

Belle huffed out an aggrieved sigh. "You haven't ruined me."

But now Sir Horley's laughter had become something else, and tears were spilling over his fingers as he tried to cover his eyes. "Belle, my sweet Bellflower, don't you see? I've ruined us both."

Chapter 9

"You realise," said Belle mutinously, "you have gone from objecting to my alleged abduction of you to abducting me back?"

Sir Horley had his head turned away, his gaze fixed upon a darkening horizon he barely heeded. "You started this."

"That does not mean you should finish it."

"Well, I am."

Belle kicked the edge of his seat. "But I don't *want* to marry you."

Sir Horley ignored Belle kicking the edge of his seat. "For someone who doesn't want to marry me, you've certainly tried very hard to marry me."

"That was before I understood what it meant to you. What you felt you would lose."

"Oh, so now that you see the pit of crocodiles you've thrown yourself into, you wish to trade places with Miss Carswile after all?"

He would not have blamed her, but—far from regretful, resentful, or aggrieved—Belle simply seemed startled. "What? No. I don't think you should marry anyone. I think if you sincerely believe that marriage, even to an understanding partner, would destroy the possibility of the kind of relationship you're looking for, then you should . . . get a job. In a shop."

He did not, at present, require more reminders of his selfishness. "I doubt there are many shops who would have me, either, my dear."

For forty-seven blissful seconds, Belle was silent and not kicking anything, though rage was rising from her like steam from damp clothes. Then, "The last time a man tried to force me into matrimony, it did not go well for him."

"From a certain point of view," said Sir Horley mildly, "it went very well for him. But"—and here he seized her ankle before she could recommence her assault upon his seat—"*you* would do well to remember I am not Valentine."

Belle gave a low and ominous growl, attempting, without success, to extricate her foot. "Indeed you're not," she concluded at last. "You're *worse*."

This, also, was not new information. "I've told you several times now who I am. You should have believed me."

To his bewilderment, Belle briefly stopped glowering at him. "You've told me who you think you are. I consider your judgement impaired."

"Have you forgotten I'm abducting you?" Probably it was better—fairer—that she remained angry with him, rather than trying to reassure him. Her anger, at least, he had earned. Her compassion he had not.

"Yes but . . ." She ground her teeth resentfully. "For what you perceive as my own good. Albeit without regard for my actual wishes."

He shot her a look he knew to be infuriating. "I consider your judgement impaired."

Somehow she did not slap his face. "In what way is my judgement impaired?"

"Putting aside your peculiar, and entirely incorrect, convictions about me, there's the fact we live in the same damn world, Belle. You know what reputation means to a woman of your station."

"But we only die from the loss of it in Richardson."

"So your plan," Sir Horley asked, exasperated and taking refuge in scorn, "is to be a fallen woman?"

"My plan," she returned haughtily, "is to be a rich one, or at least a moderately well-off one, and to live in my family's home, where nobody will care what they say about me in London."

Was this naiveté or obstinacy? Actually, knowing Belle, it was probably both. "They always care. About everything. But especially indiscretions."

"*I* will not care. And since it's my life, that's all that matters."

"You say that now. God knows what you'll want in two days' time."

Belle did not have quite the same repertoire of disdain as Sir Horley. She gave it a go, though, curling her pretty lip at him. "I can take care of my own future, thank you very much."

"Less than an hour ago, you were dead set on marrying me. Now you're dead set on not. Forgive me if I entertain some doubts as to the constancy of your decision-making."

"Well, what about yours?" She started ticking his inconsistencies and hypocrisies off on her fingers. "You don't want to get married because of some perfect fantasy you're clinging to. But you also insist you *must* get married to earn the goodwill of someone who is very much not worth your goodwill. *And* that it should be Miss Carswile. Except now it must be me."

He let his gaze drift back to the window. Above the flat grey-and-brown fields, the sky was blooming purple like a bruise. "I haven't exactly lived a life to be proud of, Arabella. But I draw the line at causing you harm."

"What about the harm you caused when you vanished from our lives in pursuit of wedded unbliss?"

That surprised him, when it probably should not have done. The Tarletons were shamelessly manipulative and disastrously open-hearted. It was, if he was honest, part of what made them so entrancing. "At worst, I mildly hurt you. You would be long over it if you weren't so bloody stubborn."

"I do not, as a general rule, *get over* losing people I care about."

"Then consider this a lesson in taking more care where you place your care."

She offered a bright and brittle smile. "What a reassuring sentiment to hear from my future husband."

Sir Horley was far too tired and physically compromised to be capable of much by way of emotion at the moment. But there was guilt aplenty. And, somewhere in the dusty recesses of his soul, a crumb or two of anger to sustain him. Was his life to be permanently derailed by Tarletons? First the brother, with his melting eyes and fuckable arse? And now the sister, who deserved infinitely better. "I'm not marrying you to reassure you," he snapped. "I'm marrying you because you've left me no other bloody choice."

The sister who deserved infinitely better drew her teeth back in an actual snarl. "You have plenty of choices."

He tried to think, but the wheels of his mind were mired to the axles. Maybe Belle was right. Maybe with Valentine on their side, they could smooth this over somehow. Maybe he didn't have to marry anyone. He could rejoin the army. Become a goat herder. Jump off a cliff. "Right now, my choice is to sit in silence for a while because my stomach feels like it wants to eat my brain."

"And my choice," declared Belle, "is to vengefully not let you."

"Belle . . ."

"Think of it as a preview of married life."

"For heaven's sake, will—"

"'Early one mor-or-ning, just as the sun was ri-i-sing'"—Belle's voice was not terrible, but what quality it possessed was presently given over solely to volume—"'I heard a maid si-i-ing in the vaaaa-al-ley below.'"

With a groan, Sir Horley folded his arms over his head and hoped to die.

"'Oh, don't decei-ei-ve me, oh, never lea-ee-ve me. Ho-ow-ow could you u-ooh-oose a poor maiden so.'"

"This is an assault on human dignity."

"'Remember the something something that you something tru-oo-leeeey.'"

"Jesus wept, you don't even know the words."

"'Remember how you something something—'"

"Arabella Tarleton, I will gag you with my cravat."

The look she cast him was pure steel. "I'd like to see you try."

He tried. She bit him. Not hard enough to draw blood, but hard enough to make him rethink his actions. Including having threatened to gag a woman with his cravat in the first place.

"Now I've forgotten where I was." Belle sighed tragically. "Oh well, I'll just have to start again. 'Early one mor-or-ning, just as the sun was ri-i-sing—'"

"Please," he said desperately. "Bonny and Valentine will not let this go."

"Bonny and Valentine?" Belle's eyes went wide in mock surprise. "Those people you don't give a damn about? Who never truly knew you? Who would despise you if they did?"

"Do you think they'd stand idly by and let me run off with you, then jilt you and leave you to suffer the consequences?"

For a second so fleeting Sir Horley half wondered if he'd imagined it, Belle hesitated. "I hope," she said finally, "they would agree I shouldn't be obliged to wed you on account of having shared a coach with you for a day."

"They would never say that *you* were obliged to wed *me*, but they will certainly feel that *I* am obliged to wed *you*."

"Isn't marriage rather a reciprocal arrangement?"

"What I mean, Bellflower—"

"Abductors don't get to use pet names for their abductees."

He pressed his temple to the side of the carriage. It did not help. Although how he'd thought it might, he wasn't sure. Not unless when he looked up again he found himself in a completely different set of circumstances, which he didn't. Not even his headache had lessened. "What I mean, *Miss Tarleton*, is that even if you are correct, even if scandal does not follow you, even if you never want anything more from life than to live quietly in . . . in wherever it is."

"Warwickshire."

"Fine. In Warwickshire. Even if all of that is true, your prospects will be lessened, your horizons narrowed, your choices stripped to near nothing. And in your brother's eyes, and in Valentine's, and, frankly, in mine, it would be my fault. It would be a thing that I had done to you."

"And my eyes are immaterial in this scenario?" Belle had gone still and icy. He much preferred her tempestuous, but she did—finally— seem to be listening. Or rather, not just listening, but heeding.

"I am afraid so." He tried to ignore another surge of guilt. "There are certain injuries to which one cannot consent. If I leave you unwed after all that has happened between us, all that has been *seen* to happen between us, the consequences will be irreversible."

"Whereas marriage is famously impermanent?"

He offered a consoling smile. "Married, you will at least have the hope of one day being a happy widow."

"That," said Belle, in a strange, tight voice, "is not amusing."

"I merely thought you'd appreciate a silver lining." It was hard to see in the shadows of the carriage interior, but she'd gone quite pale. "Oh, come on, everybody dies."

"Given that one day I went to bed in possession of two parents and woke up possessing none, I am well aware of that, Sir Horley."

He flinched. "I simply—"

"I do not care what you *simply*. I do not need you, or anyone, to lecture me about loss."

She had turned slightly away from him. He did not doubt she was genuinely upset, but he also knew how her mind worked. "I apologise. But if you think I'm distracted enough to let you jump out of a moving vehicle, you are profoundly incorrect."

"Could you stop me?" she asked, somewhere between sullen and curious.

He pondered. While he was not exactly in the best physical (or emotional) shape, the space was small, and so was Arabella Tarleton. "Yes," he concluded.

Her eyes flicked between him and the door and back again.

"Try it," he warned her, "and I'll tie your hands together."

"This is going to be a *delightful* journey."

"Perhaps you'll feel better about it after food and rest. I think I see an inn ahead."

At first, it seemed like she would not deign to reply. Then, in her most deadly and dulcet tones, "Sir Horley?"

"What?"

"Do you have some proclivities I should know about?"

"I beg your pardon?"

"In the space of a single evening, you have threatened to gag me and bind me." She tilted her head, her expression carefully guileless. "I am not judging. But given your *other* proclivities, towards men, I mean, you probably should not be sublimating such desires upon me."

There was, he was sure, a suitable response. By which he meant, devastating. Unfortunately, l'esprit was waiting for him on some future escalier, and he could think of nothing whatsoever. He was therefore reduced to "Oh, fuck off, Belle," and her resultant laughter contained a note of fully deserved derision.

Chapter 10

As soon as they drew to a halt outside the Hungry Boar, Belle dived out of the carriage and ran away, surprising Sir Horley not at all. Having left the horses in the care of the coachman and the ostler—a very nice man but not likely to Bonny's tastes—he gave pursuit. If strolling after someone into an inn could, strictly speaking, be termed *pursuit*.

She was in the taproom, looking quite the part, with her cloak and hair streaming, and her hands clasped to her bosom.

"—for I am being abducted," she was saying, "spirited away from the protection of my friends and family, by a wicked man who wants my fortune."

"Good evening." Sir Horley gave a slight bow to the assembled guests. "Did my fiancée mention I am a knight of the realm?"

The only answer was a nervous murmur.

"Well," he went on, "I am. I also happen to be well connected and influential. So while I am not myself wealthy, I know many wealthy men. Many titled men. Many men who have seats both in Parliament and in the countryside. I take tea with the gentlemen to whom the whole country pays homage and to whom, more pertinently, you all pay rent. The most powerful of my friends are dukes, the least powerful are magistrates. Propriety, society, and the law give me let and license to do what I like, when I like, to whom I like, and permit no common tavern-goer to stop me. Now, I have an abduction to carry out. I trust that meets with nobody's disapproval?"

Not a soul stirred. A lot of beers were being stared deeply into. Walls gazed fixedly at.

"I know a duke too," Belle tried, rather piteously. "The same duke. He's practically family to me."

Once again, the room was still.

Sir Horley smiled. An easy untroubled smile that felt like a crack upon his face. "I see we all understand each other." He turned to the innkeeper. "We'll take your best room, and a bath, and dinner, to be served in a private parlour, if you have one."

After the slightest of pauses, the innkeeper nodded. "Right this way, m'lord."

"Come along, dear."

Not trusting, entirely reasonably, that she wouldn't bolt, Sir Horley caught Belle's arm and steered her firmly after the innkeeper. He felt the tension in her, but clearly she was not of a mind to fight him in the middle of a pub, although perhaps only because she recognised she would lose. She did, however, mutter "One star" quite viciously as they made their way upstairs.

The parlour, with its unfussy furniture, wood panelling, and open fire, would actually have been a pleasant room. Unfortunately, Sir Horley was not given much opportunity to appreciate it.

"I hate you," Belle announced, two seconds after the innkeeper had left them. "What you did downstairs? That was *horrible*."

Sir Horley, unsure whether hours upon hours spent in a carriage meant he needed to sit down or definitely didn't, shrugged. "I warned you I wasn't Valentine."

"Is that truly how you see the world?"

"It's how the world works."

"Perhaps," Belle conceded, looking unexpectedly shaken. "But there is no need to *contribute* to it."

The day was catching up with Sir Horley hard and fast. Very few of the experiences it had offered had been experiences he would have described himself as needing. But crowning them with a discussion of power, fear, and injustice was perilously close to the last straw in an already straw-limited situation. "I would not say I contributed. So much as took advantage."

"That's the same thing, and you know it."

"Do I? Very well. Let us assume I do. But like the man who pisses in the ocean, I remain safe in the knowledge that my contribution is utterly meaningless. Given that, what can *you* do in return?"

"I can . . ."

"Make a scene?" he asked. "Be terribly, terribly spirited? Valentine was comfortable with his power over you, Arabella. That's why he never felt the need to use it to the fullest. But I, my dear, am a small man. And small men are dangerous."

Stalking over to a chair, Belle sank into it contemptuously. It was, frankly, a wonder she still had the energy for stalking and contempt. "So dangerous you cannot even liberate yourself from your own aunt?"

"My aunt has taught me nothing but shame my entire life, and that is precisely why you have no hope of defeating me. All your theatrics and your dramas and your tantrums are effective only against someone who has pride that you can injure. I have none." The words came so easily, when once, he was sure, he would have hated even the thought of uttering them. "You will never embarrass me into acceding to your wishes, so you must accede to mine."

"I shall do no such thing." It was the expected rejoinder. But Belle offered it with fading conviction. And Sir Horley wasn't sure if he was wearing her down or if she was as tired as he was.

"You have no choice," he said, pressing the advantage regardless. "Besides, it's for your own good."

Belle's eyes were dark in her pale face. "Even if it is, you're not doing it for me. You're doing it for you."

"I am not—"

"Yes you are," Belle insisted. He would have preferred the words to be thrown at him with typical Tarletonian passion. Instead, they came with a dull certainty he told himself it was not reasonable to be hurt by. "You can pretend that you're protecting me or teaching me harsh truths about a cruel world, but really you're just . . . you're sad and lonely and afraid and—"

A knock on the door interrupted what could have become a well-nigh endless litany of Sir Horley's failings. It was a recitation he was extremely familiar with, but it felt different—sharper, truer—offered in a new voice. In any case, given the events of the previous day and a half, he was fully expecting to find yet another complication waiting for him in the hallway. Valentine and Bonny, perhaps. His aunt, with or without dogs. A Bow Street Runner. Wellington himself. Thankfully, it was only the innkeeper and his wife, who had come to serve dinner. A process that, between the number of dishes brought up and the fact they both gave Sir Horley a wide berth, took a while and felt unnecessarily cumbersome.

At last they departed, leaving Belle at the head of an impressive spread and Sir Horley lingering uncomfortably before the fire. For all his bluster downstairs, it seemed rather gauche to be dining with a woman you were also abducting. Even if she had abducted you first.

"Belle," he tried, not sure if he was coaxing, commanding, or pleading. "Can we call a truce? If you think about it, nothing has materially changed."

She glared at him across the plates and dishes. "What do you mean, *nothing has materially changed?*"

"Well, you started the day with the intent of marrying me. And you're ending the day in very much the same position."

"I started the day," Belle clarified furiously, "under the impression that if we were to be married, it would . . . help. Perhaps help us both. I have ended the day having been convinced that you will always see our union—and me—not as giving you something you might need but taking away something that you want. That is not the future I wish for you, and certainly not the future I wish for myself."

"We can—" he began.

"And moreover"—now Belle was back on her feet—"I have once again made the mistake of thinking better than I ought of a man who, the moment a lady defies his will or fails to accede to his wishes, brandishes his authority like he's displaying his member as he pisses up a tavern wall."

"That is not—"

"God," Belle cried, half-distraught, half-incensed. "Why are you all like this? Why can't you . . . why can't you ever . . ."

She seemed to run out of verbal capacity. Which was, perhaps, why she seized up a roast chicken and hurled it at Sir Horley in a shower of its own trimmings. It was confusion, rather than any especially developed poultry-catching skills, that allowed Sir Horley to grab the bird before it struck him.

"What the fuck are you doing?" he asked.

"I'm throwing a chicken at you. What does it look like?"

It did, indeed, look very much like Belle had thrown a chicken at him. A chicken that had left a chicken-shaped splodge upon his shirt and waistcoat. "I mean, why."

"I don't know."

He placed the somewhat-worse-for-wear chicken back on the table. "Are you sincerely claiming that you threw a chicken for no reason whatsoever?" A potato sailed over his head. Followed by a second. "Can you please stop throwing food at me?"

"I'm annoyed," Belle said.

"That"—Sir Horley ducked another potato—"I can work out for myself."

"And hurt."

"I'm truly sorry I hurt—"

She dug a spoon into the mustard pot and used it as a makeshift catapult to impel mustard in Sir Horley's general direction.

"Though"—he managed to catch the glutinous yellow missile on the outside of his wrist—"I'm getting less sorry by the second."

"I'm just so tired of being made powerless. Of having my feelings discarded and my choices deemed irrelevant."

"I understand this is difficult, but . . ." A carrot arced into the air and then nosedived to the floor. "This isn't the way."

"What is the way, then?" She cast about listlessly for something else to throw, her gaze finally settling upon a rack of lamb. "I have tried theatrics. I have tried reason. I have tried sincerity. Each and every one of them has proven broadly pointless."

"If you so much as touch that rack of lamb, I shall empty the gravy boat over your head."

Her hand hovered. "You would not."

"I absolutely would. I warned you not to fuck with me, Arabella."

As soon as he'd spoken, he knew he'd overstated his case. At best, he was fifty-fifty on pouring gravy over another human being, irrespective of how tired he was and how infuriating they were. Unfortunately, it did not do to show weakness before a Tarleton. And so, to prove his point, he was obliged to snatch up the gravy boat and advance with it.

Belle darted to the other side of the table. "Remember, I have grown up with a twin brother. You should not fuck with me either."

"Did you often get into food fights?"

She blinked. "How else were disagreements to be settled?"

"Consideration? Discussion? Negotiation?"

"You're the one holding a gravy boat."

"I will put the gravy boat down the moment you return first to adulthood and, secondarily, to your chair."

"And if I don't?"

Sir Horley didn't, in all honesty, have an answer for that. But he made the mistake of taking a decisive step forward. Which drew a shriek of mingled fury and alarm from Belle and led to her hurling an entire bowl of trifle directly into his face.

He had never had an entire bowl of trifle hurled directly into his face before. Abstractly, he rather admired the technique. It required speed, skill, and commitment. There were so many ways it could have gone wrong. The layers of jelly, cream, and custard separating mid-flight, for example, and plopping harmlessly to the floor. Or, worse, rebounding upon the hurler. In less abstract terms, however, the trifle had connected with a kind of cold, wet force and was now dripping off his eyelashes and down his nose.

The mostly empty dish fell, with a clunk, from Belle's fingers. "I . . . I panicked," she said. "I may have overreacted."

"Sit down," he told her.

She sat down.

"Give me your hand."

She gave him her hand.

Dragging the somewhat dessert-splattered cravat from his neck, he secured one of Belle's wrists to the leg of the chair, low enough down that she couldn't just reach over and untie herself. "I'm going for a bath."

"That's . . ." Some trifle had slid from his hair and landed in her lap. "That's probably for the best."

"And when I come back, if I find you climbing out the window, or roping some poor fool into some outrageous shenanigan, I swear to G—"

"When you come back, I'll be right here."

"I mean it, Belle."

"I mean it too."

He didn't trust her, because how could you trust someone you were abducting? But he had passed the point of caring for much beyond the fact he was covered in trifle. It was an oddly clarifying situation. By the time he came back, not covered in trifle, Belle would likely have fled. And then he would—

Actually, he didn't care about that either.

Chapter 11

The door closed with a cold little click. Belle blinked hard. She was not going to cry. She was not going to cry. She was not—

A tear slipped traitorously from the corner of her eye, and she dashed it away with her free hand. It would not do for Sir Horley to find her weeping. This was, after all, entirely her own fault. And she suspected people who threw trifles had as much right to shed tears as people in glass houses had to throw stones.

She had learned to cry back when she thought she was going to be a heroine. It had seemed like an essential skill, to shed perfect, crystal tears in a quantity that did not mar the complexion. Real crying, she knew, was ugly, and she did not trust it. At least not when she was the one crying. With heroine tears, she did not have to worry what people would think of them, other than that they were pretty. If they saw her truly crying, truly distressed, what if it came across as manipulative somehow? Especially when, sometimes, in darker moods, she half feared it was herself she was trying to manipulate.

After all, what cause had she for self-pity? Most of her problems, she would be the first to admit, were of her own making. There were so many things she *could* have done, had she just been a little braver, or a little less proud, or quite a bit less wilful. Then again, if she'd married Valentine as he had demanded, he wouldn't now be with Bonny. And if she'd lied to Peggy about loving her . . . well, Peggy would have seen through that, and left her for Orfeo regardless. And when it came to Sir Horley, all she'd really done was adjust the woman he was unhappily married to. So perhaps he was right. Nothing had materially changed, and she had always been—would always be—irrelevant.

Her gaze wandered to the splatter of jelly and custard that she, or technically, if you wanted to split hairs, Sir Horley, had left upon the rug like the remains of a murder. She tried to console herself with the thought that the last time a man had frightened her, she had shot him. From a certain point of view, this was an improvement. It was still not ideal. Probably you should not, as a general rule, throw desserts at people when you felt angry and hurt and overwhelmed. Of course, she *was* being abducted. Although it likely said something about the world as a whole that not being sufficiently ladylike during an abduction would be deemed of greater concern than abducting someone in the first place.

She gave her bound wrist a little tug. It was impressively secure. Provocative remarks aside, this was not so very surprising. When he was not obliterating himself with alcohol, Sir Horley had a capability that, between Bonny's commitment to the fantastical and Valentine's commitment to doing as little as possible, Belle had always found rather reassuring. Besides, there was a knife within easy reach—she could have been free in seconds. Through the door or out the window and . . . and . . .

So why wasn't she?

Sheer exhaustion? Not wanting to break her word to Sir Horley, even under the current circumstances? Or was it something even more banal than that? The realisation that she didn't have anywhere to go. Yes, she'd talked up a storm to Valentine and Sir Horley both about her desire to return home (that, at least, was no lie), but what would she do when she got there? She had no education in either estate or domestic management. Not that she really needed any. Valentine had dug them out of debt and hired people on Bonny's behalf—probably she would find the place pristine, profitable, and better run than it had ever been. Which left her what, exactly? A fallen woman, as Sir Horley had said?

An eccentric? A haunting? And stranded, yet again, somewhere she didn't quite belong.

Maybe it was right, after all, that she and Sir Horley wed. They had unhappiness in common. The only difference was that she would not hold him responsible for hers. *That* she had long since feared was entirely her own business. Her own doing. Much like her present circumstances.

With a sigh, she picked up a fork and speared one of the roast potatoes she had not previously used as a missile. It was a perfectly reasonable roast potato, but in that moment it seemed like a wearisome roast potato. While she was conscious of a distant sense of hunger from her body, the thought of eating did not please her.

Very annoying, because she would have loved to have been the sort of woman who addressed her emotional turmoil by tucking into a plate of food the size of her head. It was how her twin would have addressed *his* emotional turmoil. It was probably a residual problem of heroism. Having determined as a teenager that being a heroine was likely her only path to happiness, Belle had trained herself to discipline in ways Bonny hadn't needed or wanted to, and now she was stuck trying to undiscipline herself. To be someone who lived fully in her body rather than fashioning it for others.

By the time Sir Horley returned from his bath, looking better in general, not just better for a man who was no longer covered in custard, she had managed a halfhearted repast. Silence hung between them like laundry forgotten upon a line. It was hard to know what to say to a man you had thrown a trifle at, after which he had tied you to a chair. Although, as husbands who blamed you for the ruin of all their hopes and dreams went, she supposed she could have done worse.

She had always enjoyed looking at Sir Horley, in the comfortable, purely theoretical way you could look at someone when there was no question of desire. And she had enjoyed, in return, a relief from the burdens of beauty. As her friend—back when he had been her friend, instead of whoever he thought he was now—he had made her feel admired but not desired. Liked but not loved. And it had been a gift as sweet as spring water. A fresh breeze in a too-small room.

He was not beautiful like Valentine was beautiful—pristine and impossible—or dazzling like Bonny, which, honestly, was mostly about Bonny and had little to do with his actual appearance. But there was something complicated about Sir Horley that Belle found compelling: brazen hair and distant eyes, and a curling cat smile that rarely reached them. That was supposed to be a bad thing, she knew from every book she had ever read. Your eyes were supposed to light up with the sincerity of your joy. And yet, she wondered, why be so indiscriminate with your joy? Why keep it somewhere for anyone to witness and anyone to take? She trusted Sir Horley's wariness, if only because it was familiar.

"I've sent for more water," he said, at last.

"How kind," she returned, not intending sarcasm but finding sarcasm thrust upon her by merit of her situation. "Do you think you could perhaps see your way to releasing me?"

"I . . ." Sir Horley was radiating discomfort. "I suppose I should not have tied you to a chair."

"I suppose I should not have thrown a trifle at you."

"Or a chicken."

Her eyes widened in outrage. "Sir Horley, that is against the rules."

"What is?"

"During an acknowledgement of fault on both sides, it is dishonourable to pile on additional faults."

"Where is this legally codified?"

"It does not need to be codified. It is *known*."

"Well, I did not know it."

"And now you do."

They considered each other, eyes far more wary than they were joyful.

"So," Sir Horley asked, "I am not permitted to seek verbal redress for both the chicken and the trifle? And, for that matter, the potatoes."

"The aim is to reach a state of equity. If you must include the chicken and the potatoes, I shall have to remind you of the fact that you are abducting me."

"And I shall have to remind *you* of the fact that you abducted me first."

"I did not abduct you. You agreed to come with me."

"Because I was drunk and desperate. I did not ask you to interfere in my life."

Belle opened her mouth to point out . . . oh, all manner of things. That perhaps he should have. That he clearly needed her to. But then she realised she was far too sad and tired. "This is not equity," she said instead. "It is continuing to argue." Picking up a dinner knife, she sawed none too carefully through Sir Horley's cravat and laid its remains upon the table. "I am going to bathe."

Ideally, bathwater would have had less cream and custard bobbing on the surface of it. But this was not a situation for idealism. It was a situation for . . .

Well. Belle was still working that out.

She was unsurprised, either because it was not surprising or because she was fully out of emotions, when—her ablutions complete—Sir Horley insisted she take the bed. He was, after all, insisting on marrying her. And the prospect of a marriage filled with nothing but insistence made what was left of her spirit quail.

Creeping between the covers in the semi-darkness was at least a little soothing. And the bath—even including the remains of a trifle— had been welcome too. Perhaps after a good night's rest she could . . . she could . . .

Oh, she could what?

Run away yet again? Cause some mayhem yet again? Drag some strangers into her apparently infinite nonsense? Even Belle's interior voice sounded just about done with her. *This is your bed*—her metaphorical bed, that is; the literal bed belonged to the inn—it wanted to tell her. It was probably about time she lay in it. Her life, she reflected, was becoming, or perhaps had always been, brutally cyclic. She had grown up knowing it was her duty to marry, for Bonny could not, and she was as good as promised to Valentine. Though in the end it was Bonny who had saved her from that fate and Valentine who had offered her independence. And yet here she was, being impelled into matrimony all over again, and this time she had only herself to blame.

She knew she should have used her freedom better, but reality was a cruel mistress. With piracy and highway robbery off the table, or any of the other sorts of things that seemed to come about so easily in novels, she'd been forced to confront the fact that she had neither the genius nor the education to change the world. She would never be the first woman to land on the moon or discover a river or demand admittance to the Royal Society. And perhaps none of that would have mattered if she'd been able to fall in love like Bonny, or like Peggy, or like every other damn person she'd ever met, for whom it seemed as natural as breathing. As inevitable as sunrise.

At the advanced age of two and twenty, she could no longer pretend that she was simply waiting for the right moment or the right person. Love was not going to *just happen* to her like her monthly menses. Moreover, she did not want it to happen. Even the thought sat strangely upon her. A puzzle piece with nowhere to fit. And yet she felt no lack without it.

In some ways, was that not worse? Should she not have been aware of some . . . hollow or unwholeness? Certainly Bonny thought there was something terribly wrong with her. And perhaps there was. But she also understood, with some deep personal instinct, that this . . . wrongness, this inescapable truth, hadn't been imposed upon her. It wasn't distress or mistrust or fear. It was part of her. More than that, it belonged to her. The same way her heart belonged to her.

She stared unseeing into the darkness, not quite defiant, and wondering, not for the first time, if she was a monster. What it meant for her if she was. Would marriage to Sir Horley, another man who would see her as a burden, be worse or better than marriage to Valentine would have been? He was not a duke, but she liked him more. Then again, how much would he like her after a lifetime's conviction that she had taken something vital from him? Did the vital things—independence, many of her legal rights—such a union would take from her not count?

Perhaps not. That was the problem with love. Its supremacy went unspoken and unchallenged. If you could not abide it, all that was left was to be powerless. And it was past time she accepted that. These were not the sort of thoughts likely to bring her much solace. But there was something peaceful in resignation. And she was, in any case, very tired.

⚜

When she next stirred—*tiredness* and *capacity to actually sleep* on this occasion acting in harmony—the room was greyish with predawn light. Sir Horley was slumped upon the window seat, his brow resting against the glass, and a bottle swinging from between listless fingers.

"You look like a portrait," said Belle, drawing herself into a sitting position. "*Gentleman in Despair*."

He half turned. "Fitting. Because I *am* a gentleman in despair."

"On account of having to marry me?"

"On account of everything, Belle."

They were silent for a few long moments that somehow seemed even longer. Of all the times to be awake, this, Belle had always thought, was the worst. It made one feel so utterly alone. "Are you intending to drink that?" she asked at last.

"Hmm?" Sir Horley stirred, apparently having forgotten what he grasped. "Oh . . . no, I suppose not."

"Then why do you have it?"

He sighed heavily. "I had not yet decided whether I needed it, wanted it, or simply intended to prove to myself I could not have it."

"And what was your conclusion?"

"As you see." The bottle made a definite-sounding clunk as he placed it upon the floor. "I am endeavouring to be a better man for you, my dear."

She hugged her knees beneath the covers. "I do not recall asking you to be any man but yourself."

Another silence. Belle wasn't sure if she could sleep with Sir Horley brooding so emphatically in a corner of the room.

But then he spoke again. "How . . . how is equity generally attained?"

"Pardon?"

"You said earlier that our aim should have been to reach a state of equity. Recall, if you will, that I am an only child. In my household, there was no such concept. Just authority and submission, rebellion and catastrophic mistakes."

He spoke so lightly that it made Belle shiver. But she did not think he was likely to accept sympathy from her just then. "Well"—she did her best to match his lightness—"when Bonny and I are—*were*—not in accord, we would admit our part in what had gone awry and then apologise to each other."

"An apology did not seem in the air at supper."

She opened her mouth, ready to defend herself on principle, then closed it again. Because she had only just realised something. "Bonny was always the one to initiate," she admitted.

Sir Horley's silhouette contrived to project a sardonic air.

"But," she went on quickly, "as a gesture of good faith, I can begin on this occasion."

"Can you?"

Theoretically. "You are not helping."

"Am I supposed to?"

She took a deep breath, idly chastising her past self for having obliviously taken advantage of her twin's more conciliatory nature. "I am sorry for convincing you to run away with me at a time when your . . . when frankly most of your faculties were compromised."

"This is making me feel so much better."

"I'm not finished," she snapped.

"Then pray continue."

His haughtiness reminded her a little of Valentine. But it was a reflection glimpsed through cracked glass. A wounded, brittle thing, like her own pride. "While I maintain I had only your best interests at heart, and a sincere desire to help, I do understand how . . . how painful and . . . and demeaning it is when someone acts for you instead of with you and—"

"Belle . . ." His tone was softer now.

"I'm still not finished," she snapped. "You are very bad at this, Sir Horley."

"You are surprisingly good. Do you mean a word of it?"

"Would I be saying words I did not mean?"

"No, I"—the softness lingered in his voice, and something that almost sounded like surprise—"I don't believe you would."

Having started, Belle was going to damn well finish. "Nevertheless," she persisted, "I have trapped you in a situation that you feel honour bound to see through. Also, I have thrown a roast chicken, several potatoes, and a trifle at you. I should have done none of those things."

"You have introduced me to several new experiences," he offered, sounding painfully, tantalisingly like the Sir Horley she thought she knew. "I have never had a trifle thrown at me before. Or, for that matter, a roast chicken."

"What about the potatoes?"

"Nor potatoes. Nor"—he hesitated for a bare second—"so graceful an apology."

She cleared her throat loudly.

"And for what it's worth, I'm sorry too."

Ideally an apology should not have been delivered alongside a quiver of amusement, but Belle was pleased to hear Sir Horley laugh. Or almost. "Sorry for what?"

"Threatening you with a gravy jug?"

"As you should be."

"Acting the boor downstairs."

Rising, he crossed the room and stood by the bed, looking down at her with a complicated expression. While Belle was fairly used to people looking at her with complicated expressions, this one eluded her. Tiredness she could easily identify. And perhaps a trace of fondness too. Resignation also? Old sorrows. Fresh pain.

"And," he went on softly, "for your being stuck with me now."

"That does not require apology."

"Generous. But erroneous."

She gave a faint hiss of frustration. "Must we be stuck with each other?"

"Don't let's start that fight again."

"I wasn't. I just meant—" She broke off. "Are you aware that you're looming?"

"I'll let you rest."

"No, I'm awake now, and so are you. Sit down. Or better yet, come in."

His eyes flew wide. "Do what?"

"Come in with me?" She drew back the covers helpfully.

"I can't do that." Sir Horley was actually blushing. "It wouldn't be proper."

"We're going to be married."

"When we are married, we will have separate rooms like everyone else."

"And yet right now," said Belle firmly, "we have only one bed. Surely you aren't intending to spend what remains of the night on the window seat."

"That is exactly what I'm intending."

"Your intention is stupid. Besides, talking in bed is the best way to talk."

Sir Horley twitched, neither withdrawing nor coming forward. "Usually"—he seemed to be striving for cynicism but only came across as flustered—"when I am in bed, I am unconscious or otherwise occupied."

"Then you have been doing bed wrong. Here." Shifting over a little, she flapped the covers again.

"I hope you don't think . . ."

"Think what?" Realisation struck her, and she almost laughed aloud. "That I could seduce you? That I wish to seduce you? That I would go about seducing someone in such a fashion?"

He seemed to recognise how absurd he was being. But he was still not out of protests. "You can't want this," he muttered, as he climbed gingerly into bed with her.

"Why? Do you steal the blankets?"

"Not that I'm aware of."

"Squirm like an eel all night long?"

"Indeed no."

"Snore?"

"Certainly not."

His outrage had been cresting with each question, and she could no longer contain her amusement.

"What is this in aid of, Belle?" he asked, with mingled resignation and impatience. "Other than mockery?"

"I'm not mocking. People don't invite people into bed to mock them."

"Don't they?"

"Well, I don't. I respect my bed too much."

"Good for you."

She wriggled back under the covers herself, turning onto her side so she could watch him comfortably. Not that it turned out to be a particularly comfortable view, for Sir Horley was lying on his back, rigid as a corpse.

"You look cosy," she observed.

He threw his hands in the air—impressive, considering he was lying down. "God. We're not even fucking, and you're critiquing my performance."

"You used to be so at ease with me." The hurt in her own voice had snuck up on her. She'd done her best not to dwell on how much she missed Sir Horley—if you drove people away by kidnapping them, that was, after all, your own fault—but she felt it especially keenly, almost as though she was being taunted, in this moment of closeness that was not closeness. The kind of closeness she had lost and lost and lost again, so many times before, and had begun to think could never truly be hers, in a world that saw it as a way station, when, for her, it was journey's end.

"I know," he said wearily. "But that was a different time. I was a different person."

"And the person you are now cannot accept touch in comfort or companionship?"

"The person I am now . . ." His voice broke on some aching sound that tried to pass itself off as laughter. "The person I am now clearly has no damn clue. Have you forgotten I'm abducting you, Belle? You should not be offering either comfort or companionship."

"That's my whole point, though. We need not be *stuck*, as you put it before. We could still choose each other."

"I cannot make you happy."

"You could try. That's more than anyone else has done. And I would try back. If you will allow yourself to think beyond a future that looks like Bonny and Valentine's."

"I have never believed that would be my future."

"You've already told me it's what you yearn for."

"Doesn't everyone?"

"Well, no." Belle gestured at herself. "Clearly not."

He made a vaguely apologetic noise but did not actually apologise. "Have you ever considered that it may be easy for you to reject love because you live with an abundance of it?"

It should, perhaps, have occurred to Belle before now that a man who was not sure how to reach equity might not understand the rules of talking in bed, the most important of which was not to verbally strike at your interlocutor, no matter what you were feeling. But was that how people thought of her? As *rejecting* love? Surely it was the other way round? That love had rejected her. "For what it's worth," she said quietly, "it is not so easy."

This time there wasn't even an apologetic noise. "You've always had a family, Belle. You've always had Bonny. Even the aunt and uncle you take for granted because they're boring have always been there for you."

"I do not deny that I'm fortunate in many ways."

"At the risk of sounding repulsively self-pitying, I have never had anyone. My own parents did not want me. My uncle died because of me. Now even my aunt will have none of me."

"And," asked Belle, trying to strike a balance between consoling and interrogating, "are uncles and aunts and parents the only people one may be loved by?"

"They are the *first* people one should be loved by." Sir Horley shifted uncomfortably, and his discomfort vibrated into Belle through the magic of proximity and mattresses. "What does it say about me that they didn't?"

"What does it say about *them*?"

"That they found me unfit to love. And that others have been finding me so ever since."

The pain in his voice was real, for all the sentiment was profoundly incorrect, which was why Belle delivered her conclusion of "You realise that's *complete* hogwash?" as gently as she could.

"A lifetime's experience suggests otherwise."

"You do not know," she pointed out, "that it was for lack of love that your parents gave you up."

"You're right," he returned too easily. "But as expressions of affection go, you must admit it was an anomalous one."

"And"—it was the most nonchalant voice she could muster—"you have made no attempt to contact them?"

"Why should I, when they have made none to contact me?"

"Has your aunt ever—"

"Whatever you are about to ask, the answer is no. Stop scheming, Arabella."

"Scheming?" Belle was not good at sounding innocent, even at the best of times, and this was far from the best of times.

"Yes, I know you, and I know your nonsense."

"What do you mean?"

He sighed, rather in the fashion of the governess who had been employed to teach Belle the rudiments of being a lady and lasted less than three days. "You are wondering if you can find my wastrel parents and uncover some terrible misunderstanding, proving that I was loved all along and am therefore free to be happy in whatever unconventional form is available to me."

"I am not," said Belle vehemently and untruthfully.

"Not every question has an answer. Not every story has an ending, let alone a happy one."

She was not, despite some people's conviction to the contrary, immune to hints. It was just that she tended to ignore them, sometimes to her own detriment. "Do you not wonder, though?"

"Fuck me," he growled, very much done with her. "Yes, I fucking wonder. But I prefer that to the alternative, which is offering people who have already cast me aside opportunity to cast me just a little bit further." His hand came up to partially shield his eyes—not that the gloom offered her much of his expression to begin with. "I know," he went on, more moderately, "that I should stand defiant, reject what rejects me, find meaning in bonds I forge for myself, but I am . . . I am too tired and too"—whatever word nearly slipped from his tongue, he abruptly swallowed—"tired. Just once I would like to have—or have at least the possibility of having—what other people have in the form that they have it, simple and uncompromised."

Belle had, of course, entertained such thoughts on her own account. After all, who did not, occasionally, wish to be the same as everyone else? To be able to take more of life for granted. Ask fewer questions. But it was hard to hear them from someone else, especially when you were both a complication and a compromise. "Then I should suit you down to the ground," she said lightly. "For I can think of little more commonplace than an unhappy marriage."

A deep, rich, familiar-yet-half-forgotten chuckle rippled from beneath Sir Horley's arm. He may have had an instinct for Belle's she-nanigans, but she knew his sense of humour. They had laughed together too often for her not to. It had meant a lot to her, at the beginning of their friendship, to find someone who would meet her sharp-to-sharp and follow her fearless into the dark. And now . . . now she was not sure if she relished the reminder or if it was merely something else that hurt.

"Oh, Bellflower," he whispered, half turning to her. "What a bore I am these days. I'm sorry not to be what you hoped for when you came so valiantly to my rescue on my wedding eve."

"Have I said that?"

"No. But you must be thinking it."

She shook her head. "I would always rather your honesty. It was wrong of you to play games with me in London."

"I know. Does it help that I wasn't intending to? I thought I was playing games only with myself."

Shifting onto her side, she folded a hand beneath her cheek and mirrored his posture. She was not sure what had inspired it, or if it was conscious on his part, but she could feel something changing between them. A softening. Perhaps it was the magic of talking in bed blessing them at last. "How so?"

"My aunt has been threatening me with marriage for years. I suppose I saw that time with you as a bit of a last hurrah: pretending I had no cares and little shame let me believe it for a while." He reached out, playing with one of her curls as he had been wont to do before, his touch gentle and idle and easy. Nothing like his drunken carelessness. "It was fun."

She lay very still, barely daring to breathe lest she break the enchantment of the moment, this tentative offering of trust. "You can have fun as yourself."

"With you?"

"Why not with me?"

"Because it's not real, Belle."

So much for enchantment. "You mean," she said, "*we're* not real. Because we aren't family as the world defines it and we aren't lovers because we don't fuck."

"Please"—his voice roughened, though not with anger—"don't ask me to give up my dreams for yours."

"Recall that you are the one insisting on this marriage, not I."

"For the sake of—"

"My reputation, yes, yes. But I'm a little offended you think this situation is somehow a dream of mine."

"Then we are to *both* give up our dreams?"

"I do not think the kind of dream I am built for is the kind of dream this world will permit to exist, so perhaps, in that regard, I am asking you to give up more than I am giving up myself." She paused.

And then continued more lightly, "Although I am pretty and companionable and sober and therefore probably also the better bargain."

Another laugh from Sir Horley. "To my credit, I am currently sober. But you *are* the better bargain."

"And you will claim ownership of my property and fortune, while keeping your name and legal identity."

"I would not take advantage of you."

"I know that. I would still rather it was not mandatory to give you the opportunity."

"Your point is well taken, Belle." He let her hair slip from his fingers. "I am selfish and ungrateful."

"That was only my point a little bit," she told him.

"Generous." There was irony in his tone, but a trace of sincerity too.

"My *wider* point," she went on, "is that since dreams have not thus far proven much use to either of us, would it be so terrible to try for something else instead?"

"And what would that something else be?"

"Whatever we choose to make it?" Belle tried. "Whatever we build for ourselves? On our own terms. Might that not be better than a lifetime of hoping for miracles?"

"Frankly"—he gave an odd, wry laugh—"I've no idea anymore. I'm not even sure who's trying to talk who into what. Why are you making such a passionate case for a marriage that we've clearly established neither of us want?"

Belle shut her eyes and tried to gather her fragmented thoughts. "Because," she said, carefully, "I am willing for us to go our separate ways and live with the consequences, and I am willing to marry you and try to make the best of what we have. What I am *not* willing to do is to spend the rest of my life as a sacrifice you made or a price you were forced to pay."

"When you put it that way, it does seem a rather bad deal from your end."

"Doesn't it?"

He sighed. "I cannot allow you to be ruined."

"I know."

"And"—he seemed to be choosing his words as she had done, as though they were volatile and untrustworthy, in need of delicate placement—"I cannot promise that I will never . . . wonder. Or have regrets. Or feel on some days or on some nights or in some moments—and as you have seen, I can have some *very* bad moments—that we should have chosen differently."

It was strange, Belle reflected, for a woman who had once rejected a duke for not proposing correctly to now be lying in the half light waiting for a man who had just explained why their life together would be miserable to say *but*.

"But," he went on, "I will try. If that is what you want, and if you will try also, then perhaps we can make—I don't know—something out of the wreckage of all this. And I will never reproach you for what I could never have, and I will never make my fancies and my follies and my disappointments your concern. Can that be acceptable to you?"

It should not have been. It should have been desultory. Piecemeal. Wholly not enough. Except perhaps that was fitting because *she* was not enough. She would never be someone who someone else chose, and none of the things she cared about would ever matter as much as the one thing she didn't. Once, and it was mind-boggling that it had only been a handful of years ago, she had let herself believe there could be an alternative. The friend, the partner, the lover who might stay. As a teenager, she had written stories with Bonny, thousands of stories, stories where she was a pirate, a princess, a space traveller, a sky monster, an explorer. In growing up, it had been necessary to accept that such adventures were not to be hers. But she was beginning to realise that she had not fully let go of the hope in them. The possibility of a life lived, in its own small way, uncharted. Yet as complete as any other.

"I suppose," she whispered, "it will have to be."

They said no more after that. And as Belle lay there trying to work out if this was the beginning of something or the end of it, if she was building a future or burning one, if she was the heroine, the villain, or—most lamentably of all—just another supporting character, she felt a subtle movement beside her. She heard the edges of Sir Horley's breath grow ragged. Then the creak of bedsprings and the rustle of the sheet as he turned onto his side. He made no other sound, but Belle recognised the particular quality of the silence that followed. She had lain in such silences herself, and she wondered where his thoughts had taken him. If they had followed paths as intricate and unanswerable as her own. If he, too, was scared and uncertain and alone.

After a moment, she put a hand gently upon his shoulder. He was trembling—in that tight, tears-repressing way—even before she touched him. Beneath her palm he was fearfully alive, deep shudders running through him like fractures. Drawing closer, she tucked her body around his, neat as a crescent moon, her arm curled across his hip.

"What are you doing?" he asked, in a rather stifled voice.

"I thought you might need this."

"I most certainly do not."

But the fingers he had clasped about her wrist did not push her away.

It had been long enough since Belle had held anyone that it was odd—odd but not undesirable—to be learning a new person. Sir Horley was not snuggly, the way Bonny was snuggly, or restless like Peggy. He had his own strength, for all he pretended otherwise, and his stillness was a wild animal stillness, full of mistrust and tension. She felt a little like Tam Lin's Janet clinging to snakes and lions and fire. If he had not retained his grip upon her, she would have withdrawn, uncertain of welcome.

Minutes passed. Yet Sir Horley did not grow impatient or shake her off. Instead came something almost like surrender. A barely perceptible softening, a quiescence of body and mind that eased him into sleep, still in her arms.

Sadly, slumber did not come so readily in return.

This is my husband, she thought to herself. This man who shied from comfort, cried unseen in the dark, and would forever mourn something he believed he was unworthy to seek. She wondered if she could convince him that marriage to her need not preclude him from finding whatever he needed. But she didn't think he'd believe her. It was far easier to put your faith in a beautiful possibility than risk a messy reality. Dwell in the sweetness of *could have been* instead of amongst the bitter reeds of *tried and failed* or *not what you wanted after all.*

Dawn had crept upon them as they talked. The bloody freshness of the light found threads of scarlet-gold in Sir Horley's hair. Truthfully, Belle ached for his hurts but also knew she was unequal to them. Books were so insistent on the power of love to heal, to redeem. What was left if you couldn't give that?

"Keep your dreams," she whispered. "And blame me, if you must, that you never had a chance to live them. Nor be disappointed by them."

In some ways, she almost envied him that he could still harbour hopes so specific. Over the years, hers had mostly faded into nebulous, contradictory longings, for freedom and companionship both, that increasingly felt as ridiculous as her younger self's determination to be a pirate.

A princess.

A heroine.

Happy.

Chapter 12

Sir Horley awoke with a splitting headache and without Belle. The former he did not think he deserved, and the latter felt as inevitable as the tides. He wasn't sure why he was even surprised. Belle had been running, in one way or another, as long as he'd known her. Why would she have stayed for him when no-one else had? Why would he even want her to, beyond preferring not to ruin her reputation beyond rescue? Why was he always such an irredeemable fool? He remembered, with a quiver of self-disgust, sinking into Belle's embrace. How it had taken every particle of pride he possessed not to beg for more. *Come closer. Hold me tighter. Let me feel your breath and your heartbeat and all the devastating warmth of you.*

The thought drifted across his mind that someday someone might make him a promise they considered worth keeping. But that was quickly followed by the recollection that Belle hadn't actually promised him anything beyond staying put while he divested himself of trifle. And this she had done. Afterwards she had offered . . . well, he still wasn't quite sure what she'd offered. Something she'd evidently regretted—found him unworthy of—come morning. And how could he blame her for that when she'd been nothing but generous, and he'd been . . . himself? Resistant and mistrustful, brutalising her in the name of honesty, so hopelessly enmeshed in the fear of having someone else turn from him or let him down that he'd hardly noticed he was the one drawing back and pushing away. The one thinking only of himself.

Her departure, then, should not have hurt in return. It wasn't as though he had truly trusted her or given her any reason to stay. From a certain perspective, he might even have found the situation reassuring. Those who he invited into his bed tended to vanish like stars before the dawn. Why would it be any different for Arabella Tarleton? Although from another, he had perhaps come to a pretty pass that it was no longer even necessary to fuck him in order to fuck him over.

Because—and here was the rub—he *did* feel fucked over. More fucked over than he had any right to. More fucked over than any departing liaison had left him for a very long time. Because those men had, at least, had the decency to use him, and be used, and be done. They had not held him stalwart in the dark, then left him to the cold.

Rolling onto his stomach, he pressed his face into the pillow and found that it still smelled faintly of Belle—sweet and taunting, a whisper of safety that had turned out to be illusion after all. Rolling back, he discovered there was a man with a knife sitting on the edge of the bed.

"Jesus Christ." He sat up as abruptly as could be expected under the circumstances.

The man with a knife smiled in a manner Sir Horley disinclined to find genial. "Good morning, sunshine."

"What the—my travelling companion, where's Belle? What have you done with her?"

"The young miss?"

"Yes. By God, if you've hurt her—"

"Why would I want to hurt a nice lady like that?"

"Why would you want to breach my bedroom with a blade?"

"Oh." The man, who was not displeasing in a dark-haired, dark-eyed, blatantly feral kind of way, took a moment to think about it. "Well. The thing is, sunshine. We like the nice young lady, and we don't like—"

"I'm sorry to interrupt," said Sir Horley, not at all sorry, "but who is *we* in this context? *We*, the royal we? *We*, you and your knife?"

The man stared at him. "*We* as in me and the missus. The knife's from the kitchen."

This was at least mildly reassuring. Sir Horley suspected that men who had personal relationships with kitchenware were likely to be more difficult to deal with than men who did not. Although, in an ideal world, he would not have had to deal with any men and their kitchenware, irrespective of their level of intimacy.

"She's called Betsy," offered the man.

"The missus?"

"The knife."

"How about," suggested Sir Horley, since this line of enquiry was getting him precisely nowhere and there was still an armed stranger in his bed, "we return to the issue of what you and the missus and your sharp friend over there don't like?"

The man seemed only too happy to oblige. "Right. Yeah. Basically, it's your sort. We don't like your sort."

"My sort?" Sir Horley had received such comments before, though not usually when he was accompanied by a woman.

"Yeah," said the man again. A dull light flared in the depths of his eyes. "Hoity-toity rich fucker aristos what think just because they've got a prick, they can push anyone around and nobody'll stop 'em."

Between the knife and the headache, it was difficult to think. But this was clearly a moment for thinking. For swift and useful thinking. "And, ah, that's how you perceive me?"

"You said it yourself, sunshine. Last night in the taproom, bold as brass, proud as you like over abducting that poor little lady."

"One would really think," Sir Horley murmured, mostly to himself, "I would have learned the value of keeping my mouth shut by now."

The man shrugged. "Reckon you really thought you was going to get away with it."

"Except you've nobly taken it upon yourself to prevent me?"

"I wouldn't say 'noble.'" The man ducked his head in a parody of modesty. "But I wouldn't *not* say 'noble.' See, the missus and I talked it over last night. 'What an arsehole,' I said to her. And she said to me, she said, 'I've known some mighty fine arseholes in my time—you're giving that posh bastard far too much credit.'"

"For the record," Sir Horley put in mildly, "my parentage has never been in question. They had no use for me, but I was assuredly their issue."

The man—the innkeeper, in fact, he now realised—spun the knife between his fingers with disconcerting expertise. "Is that why you go about abducting women? Mummy and Daddy didn't love you enough?"

"What? No. Also, I wasn't abducting anyone."

"Then why," asked the innkeeper, not unreasonably, "did you tell everyone you was?"

It was a question Sir Horley had been asking himself since it had happened. And the only answer he could find was "I thought it was a good idea at the time?"

"To abduct someone? What is wrong with you, mate?"

"How long have you got?"

"Not that long, actually. Got an inn to run."

"Then why not put the knife down, explain what's happened to my fiancée, and we can all go about our lives as usual?"

"Well, I am explaining, aren't I?"

"Are you?"

"Yes"—the innkeeper nodded with conviction—"it's like I said to the missus last night. 'We can't be doing with this,' I said to her. And she said to me, 'Benjamin,' she said, 'you're right, we can't be doing with this.' So her and me, we hatched a plan, didn't we?"

"And"—Sir Horley eyed Betsy—"this is the plan?"

"Naw. The plan was to knock you out with nitrous in order to help the young lady on her way."

Sir Horley sighed. No wonder it felt as though someone had been playing tennis with his skull. "And Belle has suffered no ill effects? You've let her go?"

"We weren't the ones trying to hold her against her will, was we?"

He sighed again. "No, that's a fair point. But she wasn't frightened or distressed in any way?"

"She was a bit startled when we first came in. We didn't want to wake you, see, so the missus had to put a hand over her mouth while I took care of you. Once she understood what was happening, though, she was very obliging."

"I'm sure she was."

"We can see why you'd want to abduct her if that wasn't a fucked-in-the-head thing to do." Benjamin shook his own head sadly. "Haven't you ever heard of consent, mate?"

"Clearly," said Sir Horley, "I have fallen short of the standards I set for myself. Thank you for showing me the error of my ways and holding me to account. I acknowledge the hurt I have caused and I am grateful for this opportunity to grow. Now will you please put the fucking knife down?"

Benjamin did not put the fucking knife down. "I could do that," he conceded. "But the fact of the matter is, you're presenting something of a wossname for the missus and me."

"A wossname? What manner of wossname?"

"A quandary. That kind of wossname." He shrugged. "Way of the world being what it is, I don't suppose a high-in-the-instep fancy-pantsy noblefucker like you is likely to take kindly to being knocked out and held up while the woman he's trying to abduct does a runner."

"You should know," said Sir Horley quickly, "I'm exceptionally kind."

Benjamin narrowed his eyes.

Dread had temporarily—perhaps very temporarily—gained ascendancy from within the tumult of Sir Horley's emotions. He swallowed. "And forgiving."

"Mm-hmm."

"And forgetful." This did not seem to be helping. As if from a great distance, Sir Horley contemplated the possibility of a death neither fast, blown apart upon a battlefield, nor slow, measured out in mouthfuls, just sudden and inarguable, at the hands of a stranger. Afraid to take it for himself, he had been half looking for destruction. Now it had found him, he would have rather remained unfound. "Look," he tried instead. "It's really not a good idea to murder me with a knife."

A spark of curiosity lit Benjamin's features. "What should I murder you with, then?"

"You shouldn't murder me at all."

"I think it's probably for the best, sunshine. The young miss wasn't a fan of the notion. But I can't have this—have you—coming back on any of us."

It said sorry things about Sir Horley's state of mind that he was actually quite encouraged that Belle had not intentionally left him to die. "Surely you can't believe my abrupt disappearance won't come with consequences of its own."

Benjamin shrugged. "Not really, 'cos you'll have disappeared."

"You can't disappear a body."

"Oh, you can. Wouldn't want you to go to waste or nothing."

"Go to . . . go to waste?" asked Sir Horley, in spite of feeling very strongly this was not a good thing to ask.

Betsy glinted. Benjamin nodded. "In these hard times. Lean times, you could say, for an honest innkeeper and his missus."

It had definitely not been a good thing to ask. "I very much doubt that putting me on the menu, if that's what you're implying, will improve business."

"I don't know. Lots of hungry travellers passing through."

"There must be something better to serve them."

"Well"—Benjamin had that contemplative look again—"it's a misuse of a horse, and a kitty's too small for more than a pie or two."

"And something like, I don't know, cow is too boring for you?"

"Have you seen the price of meat these days?"

"I'm a gentleman," Sir Horley admitted. "I'm not aware of the price of anything."

"See, that's being part of the problem. This way you'll be part of the solution."

"But I'll be too dead to appreciate it."

By way of answer, Benjamin only shrugged.

This was going . . . Sir Horley cast about for a suitable phrase . . . absolutely fucking catastrophically. He stole another glance at Betsy, wondering if he could somehow take her companion by surprise. While he was not inexperienced when it came to combat, an important facet of staying alive—in war and in general—involved not rushing unarmed at someone with a knife. "It can be quite difficult," he said finally, "stabbing someone. Lots of bones to get in the way."

Another shrug from Benjamin. "Lots of squishy bits, too, though."

"Isn't this your best room?" Sir Horley tried a different tack. "I'm going to bleed everywhere. Especially if you hit an artery."

"Ehhhh. A bit of blood here and there adds character. Ask anyone."

"I can see you've thought this through." Casting around for a way to prove himself at least as worthy as a horse, Sir Horley discovered he could not. It had not always been easy to live in the world on his own account. Persuading someone else of the matter felt impossible. So he put aside questions of personal merit, along with the moral, economic, and legal implications of anthropophagism, snatched up a pillow, and threw it directly into the innkeeper's face.

Betsy made short work of it, filling the room with feathers and cotton ribbons. But Sir Horley, having paused only to grab his boots, was already at the door. Thankfully, Benjamin had not thought to lock it—which spoke either well or badly of him, depending on whether you wished to categorise a lack of homicidal forethought as evidence of being a decent person or an inadequate murderer. It was not, however, something Sir Horley had time to assess. Mostly he was just relieved.

Boots under his arm, he raced down the stairs. A hasty glance behind confirmed that the innkeeper had decided chasing a patron through his establishment while wielding a knife was probably bad for business. Even so, Sir Horley thought it best to depart at speed, which he did, positively flying past the taproom and out through the front door. An unexpected sense of exhilaration carried him some way along the road before reality, and the need to put his boots on, caught up with him.

Sitting down on a nearby tree stump, he considered his situation. While it was somewhat better than it had been a few minutes ago, given he was no longer in danger of becoming part of tomorrow's carvery, it was still far from good. He was . . . he had no idea where he was, with neither money, nor a coat, nor anything—not even a signet ring—he could sell or barter. Himself, he supposed, but he was not Bonny, dispensing sunshine and strawberries, and it was hard to imagine any takers. And Belle, of course, could have been anywhere by now. The Americas. The moon. Whatever home was waiting for her in Warwickshire.

Which meant he was probably going to have to return to his aunt. And yet, having spent the last two days insisting he ought to, he discovered himself abruptly reluctant. Blame it on sobriety, or the morning light, pearly and pristine about him, or having recently escaped a socially minded man with a knife, but maybe . . . maybe he did not owe her obedience in this. She had thought little of him all his life, even before she knew what he was, even before he had taken anything from her. Who would it serve, truly, to let her marry him off to a woman of her choosing for the sake of her pride or her God, or in recompense for an old and unchangeable ill?

And, yes, she would disown him, as she had been saying she would for years. But once the deed was done, what more could she hold over him? The thought was even . . . freeing. Presumably Damocles, in the aftermath of the sword, had lived happy. Well, unless being the subject of myth, or at least mythologised history, he had not gone on to be turned into a mushroom or fucked by a goat. Neither of which were *probably* going to happen to Sir Horley. And, in spite of his many protests to the contrary, he could, indeed, sell cabbages or suck cock, or find some other way to live without his aunt's money. Because it had never truly been about the money. He had wanted from her what he always wanted, what his parents had been unable to give him, what he had spent so many years hopelessly seeking in the bodies of strangers.

Once upon a time, he would have called it *love* and asked no questions. But the word seemed bigger and smaller than he remembered— differently shaped and less perfectly fitting. No wonder, then, he thought ruefully, that he had been unable to find what he was looking for, if he hadn't understood what it was. Perhaps that was why he'd always clung to those who did not want him—willing to do almost anything to ensure they didn't become someone else who wouldn't stay—when he should have paid more attention to those he'd let go.

Like Belle?

He pondered what he could do to find her again. If Bonny and Valentine would help, assuming they did not blame him for her latest flight, which they likely—and rightfully—would. But what would he say to her now? That he was sorry? That he had spoken too impulsively and too harshly? That he wished she had not left him to wake alone in the company of a gentleman with a knife? Or more pertinently, that some of what she said had more merit than he had been able to immediately acknowledge. That he still did not know how to reconcile a life with her with what he'd always taken for granted he lacked and hoped would make him happy. But that when he said he'd try, he meant it.

In daylight he could even admit a part of him wanted to. The same part that was half-relieved his aunt was done with him, as though letting a door close released you from the burden of holding it open. Had Belle been right that the things he had always told himself would last, be real, prove him loveable were standing in the way of other things, things he could actually have? Or had she just got into his head, as Tarletons were apt to do, like poetry or fairy tales, stirring up a different set of daydreams. A different flavour of impossible nonsense.

Then again, with Miss Carswile he wouldn't even have had the option. It wouldn't have occurred to him it *was* an option.

To be married as friends.

To decide what that meant.

To even allow himself to contemplate such possibilities felt audacious. A too-high bet upon a card that had no right to go your way. It filled him with the intriguing terror of high places or deep water: those moments when insignificance became invincibility, emptiness could be freedom, and hope was as sharp as the teeth of the wind.

This should have been a crisis—and perhaps it would be once the catharsis had dissipated—for the worst had very much come to pass. His first engagement was in shambles, his second little better, especially considering the bride was absent, the closest approximation to friends he possessed he had chosen to push away, and he was prepared to call it quits on his aunt in the unlikely event she had not already called it quits on him. He was alone in the world, quite literally alone, unless you counted the tree stump, and yet he was surprisingly uncrushed. He was hoping that Belle had not got herself into some sort of trouble. Which, being a Tarleton, she surely had.

Wishing he'd managed things better yesterday.

Wondering if she'd be inclined to give him a second chance.

Because that was the strange thing about having lived so long in the shadow of other people's choices: his own were turning out to be different than he thought they would.

Having shoved his feet firmly into his boots, he rose. With nothing behind him, unless you counted the innkeeper, and no other direction that called to him, he decided to go on. He would find a town eventually. Once there, he might catch word of his former fiancée, that was, his latest former fiancée, since he seemed to be accumulating them. Or, should all else fail, embark upon his cabbage-selling/cock-sucking career.

As it turned out, however, Sir Horley's future in vegetable vending and pleasure dispensing was not to be. For about thirty minutes later he found Arabella Tarleton sitting by the carriage with a picnic spread out by the roadside.

"What took you so long?" she asked.

Chapter 13

For a moment—having been so convinced she was as good as lost to him—Sir Horley could only stare. "I was held up," he said at last, "by a man trying to kill and eat me."

Belle looked genuinely startled. "Oh no, I told Benjamin and his wife most explicitly that they should under no circumstances kill and eat you."

"Well"—he strove for his best approximation of nonchalance—"they went off message."

"Why would they do that?"

He continued to regard the mini-idyll Belle had established, the coachmen having established one of their own some distance away, where they were already tucking into their repast, and then dropped to his knees beside her on the grass. "I don't know, Belle. I expect because once killing someone and eating them is on the table, it's very hard to put away the silverware."

"You may be right," she conceded. "Would you like some breakfast?"

"Would I like some breakfast?" he repeated, uncertain if she was being deliberately callous, though that would not have been like her.

"Do you object to breakfast?"

"No, it's just . . ."

He broke off, not knowing what came after the *just*. Because a mild brush with death and a couple of hair-breadth 'scapes followed by a repast was probably an average Thursday for a Tarleton. Any emotional revelations he had personally experienced upon a tree stump were neither her doing nor her responsibility. As far as he could tell, she wasn't angry or disappointed in him, they still seemed to be engaged, and were still upon the road to Gretna Green. Typical, really, that while he'd been searching his soul and wrangling his heart and falling apart over an empty space in a previously shared bed, Belle had been laying out a picnic. It was a lesson in humility and absurdity both, and probably sorely needed.

"Actually," he said, "breakfast would be perfect. Being nearly killed and eaten does, paradoxically, give one an appetite. I am, however, apprehensive of the pie."

"I'm beginning to share that apprehension. What do you think it contains?"

"If we're fortunate, cat."

"And if we're unfortunate?"

"Priest."

"Priest?"

"Fop. Grocer. Royal marine. I'd really rather not speculate."

"That's probably for the best," said Belle faintly. Then she rallied. "I'm sure the bread and cheese will be safe. As well as delicious."

For several minutes, they devoted themselves to the business of eating. The bread was freshly baked, and the cheese was potent, and there were fresh strawberries to follow. It was a far superior repast to the hard biscuit and salted meat provided for soldiers, but being reckless, outdoors, and recently endangered reminded Sir Horley of his army days. They were not memories he usually cared to dwell upon. Still, he had rarely tasted food he appreciated more. Or he would have if not . . .

"Belle?" He had spoken before fully realising he was going to, and the uncertain note in his voice made him feel foolish.

She glanced up, in the process of stuffing an enormous slice of cheese directly into her mouth. "Mmmrffsorry. I'm not being very ladylike."

"That's nothing you need to apologise for."

"I just . . ." She paused to chew, then swallowed heavily. "I just like cheese so very *very* much."

This was not where Sir Horley needed or wanted the conversation to go. But it was a reprieve of sorts. "I had no notion."

"Well, no. Nobody has any notion. I was too busy being a heroine, you see."

"I'm not sure I do see."

"Have you ever heard of a heroine who likes cheese?"

"I'm sure there must be some."

Belle shook her head emphatically. "Not at all. Heroines must be thinking grand thoughts of love and marriage or proving their virtue in the face of blandishments or other menaces. They have no time for cheese."

"That is to their loss."

"It is to their loss," Belle declared. "It has certainly been to mine, but I intend to make up for it starting"—she pulled out an imaginary pocket watch—"ten minutes ago. Now, what were you going to ask me?"

"Oh." Having raised the issue, then avoided it, Sir Horley abruptly found himself dissembling. "Nothing of any significance."

"You are going to be a very annoying husband if you keep saying things and then insisting upon their unimportance."

A fair point. "I suppose I happened to be wondering why it was that you left me behind at an inn with a man who had floated the idea of . . . not to belabour the point . . . killing and eating me?"

"Good heavens." Belle dropped her cheese. "I would consider that *quite* significant."

"Perhaps," admitted Sir Horley.

"It would certainly bother me in your position," Belle went on. "But, you see, I very much did *not* do that."

"You didn't?"

"Not at all. I truly thought I had comprehensively dissuaded them from killing and eating you. I would not have gone otherwise."

"And why"—Sir Horley may have been underdressed, but he felt naked—"why did you leave at all?"

"Would it not have seemed very peculiar to the innkeeper and his wife if I had refused to flee from the man who was abducting me?"

That did make a kind of Tarletonian sense. "And you couldn't have told them we had settled our differences?"

"I could. But they had already gone to so much trouble, readying the carriage, preparing an escape route, sneaking into the room, and knocking you out with nitrous. I didn't want to be impolite."

"Bellflower, are you seriously telling me that you left me with an economically inclined pie-maker because you didn't want to be impolite?"

Her eyes had grown wide. They were a different shade to Bonny's, but there was still something entrancing about the blueness of them— like a corner of sky, glimpsed from between bars. "I truly did not believe you were in danger. I thought you would catch me up, and we could continue our journey. Indeed, I have been waiting here for quite some time. Surely that would be a strange thing to do, if I thought you were providing a rich, delicious filling."

That made sense, even by the standards of non-Tarletons. But it offered little consolation. Not that Sir Horley expected any.

"Next time," said Belle, "I shall be impolite. No, I shall be downright rude."

"Must there be a next time?"

Her brows lifted. "I mean . . . you've met us."

Consoled after all, a smile tugged at the corner of his lips.

"It would probably help," Belle went on, "if we both refrain in future from telling people we are abducting the other. But you have proven yourself catastrophically susceptible to drama, and I cannot be answerable for the consequences of that."

"I beg your pardon." He couldn't tell if he was amused or appalled. "I am *not* catastrophically susceptible to drama."

"But you are," Belle returned placidly. "It is one of the many things I enjoy about you."

"If anyone is catastrophically susceptible to drama, it is you."

"Am I denying it? I am noting it as a quality we have in common."

"No, no, no. You *create* drama. I am merely in the vicinity of drama perpetuated by others."

"Yes. Because you like drama. Why else did you put all that effort into befriending Valentine?"

"Actually that was guilt."

"But you've been nothing but kind to him."

"Again, it wasn't kindness, it was guilt."

"For what?"

"Well, I tortured him for years."

Belle, who had been sitting cross-legged by the cheese, propped a chin onto her hand and leaned forward, her expression rapt. "Please do tell me all about torturing Valentine."

"Perhaps *torture* is slightly too strong a word."

"Oh, you think?"

"It . . . I . . . I knew he was . . . as I am. And I thought he believed himself above it. Above me. So I went out of my way to make him uncomfortable."

"You monster."

"I had no idea he was wholly oblivious. Nor that he was hurting from it." Sir Horley sighed, the truth springing free with surprising ease. "And then when I saw him with Bonny, when I understood how it was between them, and how close he was to throwing away something that most of us spend our whole lives seeking, I . . . don't know. I felt bad.

Because Valentine is so many things that I am not. Better things. But I also think I probably just wanted someone to be happy."

"That is very tragic," said Belle. "But it is also very drama."

"No," protested Sir Horley, stirred afresh. "Not at all. Drama would have been, to take an example at random, shooting Valentine? Or trying to take Bonny for myself by kidnapping him, or seducing him, or engineering a situation where I rescued him from lions."

"From lions?"

"Or wolves. Or antelopes. These are just suggestions, Belle."

Belle was silent for a moment or two—or at least as silent as possible for someone who had returned to vigorously inserting cheese into her mouth as though both cheese and mouths were going out of fashion. Then she said, "I hope this will not be taken as a lack of affection towards my brother, but I am concerned you are harbouring a too-generous impression of Bonny."

"Is that not what love is?" asked Sir Horley, with a faint smile. "An excess of generosity?"

"I suppose"—her mouth curled with that hint of irony he had always found charming—"I am the wrong person to be speculating. But my own deepest *level*, shall we say, of esteem comes when I can see a person fully, including their faults, and suffer no diminution of that esteem."

"Perhaps that speaks more to the irrelevance of the faults, rather than the nature of esteem. My own would not be so easily dismissed."

"But Sir Horley, you have shown me nothing but your faults for two days solid, as well as insisted upon some I do not believe you possess, and I am still with you."

"Had we not ridden roughshod over your reputation, I would encourage you to question that decision. And what does this have to do with Bonny? Do you think Valentine sees him as anything other than perfect?"

"No," Belle admitted. "Bonny would not be with anyone who considered him less than an angel on loan from heaven. But you must have noticed that he is extremely vain, to say nothing of shallow, bossy, and fundamentally incapable of accepting a world different from his experiences in it."

"These qualities matter no more to me than they do to Valentine."

"I am not speaking of what matters. I am speaking of what is seen."

"How enjoyable I am finding it"—Sir Horley felt he was permitted a little tartness, given the conversation—"to be reminded of my unsuitability for your brother."

"All I'm asking," Belle returned placidly, as she began to pack up what remained of the picnic, "is whether you've at any point given consideration to the notion that *he* might be unsuitable for *you*?"

In all honesty, Sir Horley had *not* considered it. "And, by contrast, are we so compatible as a couple?"

"We are friends. Is that not a kind of compatibility?"

He sighed. "Belle, you cannot talk someone out of love."

"I understand that, Sir Horley. But I don't believe you are in love with Bonny."

"Oh?"

"I believe you love what you think he represents. And what you hate in yourself."

Sir Horley opened his mouth. Then closed it again. "I think I might at this point prefer to return to the man with the knife." Or his tree stump.

"Please don't do that. I have over-stepped, I can see that now."

The worst of it was, she wasn't wrong. He had rather a history of loving what he couldn't have or perhaps just expecting not to have what he loved. "How about, in the spirit of marital negotiation, we never speak again about my feelings for your brother?"

"As you prefer."

"And . . ." He abruptly ran out of emotional momentum.

"Yes?"

"I . . . I did not . . . Belle, I . . ."

She made a heroic attempt to save him from himself. "I will never again trust in the good intentions of a murderous cannibal, irrespective of their kindness in the moment."

"No, I . . . I mean, that's probably wise, in general. But"—how to admit it was not, ultimately, the murderous cannibal that had dismayed him—"I found . . . I found I did not like to wake alone this morning. After we. Even though we—even though I—we did not—even though it is—"

He got no further because Belle put the basket aside and dived into his arms at such speed, and with such conviction, that it knocked him onto his back, one of his elbows going straight through the suspect pie.

Chapter 14

"I've just had the most terrible thought."

Sir Horley gazed across the carriage at his companion. "After so many days stuck in an undulating box, I am having many terrible thoughts."

"No, but"—Belle's eyes were stricken—"I've had a truly terrible thought."

"Tell me?"

"Am I going to have to spend the rest of my life as Lady Comewithers?"

"I'm afraid so."

Casting her head against the squabs, Belle gave vent to a piteous moan.

"Do your best not to predecease me," Sir Horley offered, attempting consolation. "And then remarry someone of superior rank."

"That is quite the long game."

"You should probably have taken that into consideration before eloping with me."

Belle smiled a little shyly. "I'm glad we're eloping instead of taking turns to abduct each other."

"As am I. Although you must admit, as elopements go, we have put in rather a poor showing."

"Do you think?"

"I think we are probably one of the worst elopements in history."

"When I made that claim, you said I was being vainglorious."

"Then let us be vainglorious together. We are one of the worst elopements in history."

"Emotionally or logistically?"

"Both."

It took a special kind of contrariness to argue against something you yourself had previously argued, but Belle rose to the occasion. "What about Lydia and Mr. Wickham?"

"They are disqualified, my dear, on grounds of being fictional."

"The Earl of Rochester and Elizabeth Malet?"

Sir Horley shrugged. "He wrote her some pretty letters, did he not?"

"Yes, but he also spent two years in the tower, fell in love with another woman, and then died of the pox."

"I suppose I can guarantee at least one of those will not happen."

"I would ideally like you to guarantee all three."

"In which case"—he smiled teasingly at her across the carriage—"I shall do my best to avoid treason also."

"And you can avoid the pox with a little care. There are protective sheaths one can wear. And stay clear of any partners with open sores or lesions."

"Well, that's disappointing." It was Sir Horley's driest voice. "I choose partners almost exclusively on the basis of their open sores or lesions."

"Also," Belle went on helpfully, "if you squeeze the tip of the member, and find the discharge unpleasant, either in texture or aroma—"

"Belle?"

"Yes?"

"It is a long way to Scotland. Please stop talking about unpleasant discharge."

She looked chastened. "It's taking my mind off being Lady Comewithers."

"Comewithers is an ancient and noble name. It alludes to the unshakeable bond betwixt a knight and his loyal steed, such that the pair become as one—"

"That doesn't sound legal."

"As one," finished Sir Horley huffily, "on the field of battle."

There was a pause. "Is any of that true?"

"Probably not. Who gives a fuck?"

Another pause. "You have been struck by notable misfortune in the field of nomenclature, Sir Horley."

"What are you insinuating, Little Miss Belligerent?"

Belle's eyes slid away from his. "Nothing."

"Are you taking issue with Horley now? It's from the Old English, meaning *horny wood*. Nothing more respectable. Although now I'm saying that out loud, I'm beginning to see your point."

"Oh my God," cried Belle. "You've made it *worse*. I previously thought it was mildly regrettable. Now it is positively cursed. I cannot spend our life together addressing you as *Sir Horley*."

"Well, no, that would be absurd. Why don't we begin with *Horley*."

"It sounds wrong without the *Sir*, though. Unbalanced."

He made a noise that strongly implied she was being unreasonable. "It's just my name, Belle. My aunt insisted upon it."

"Your aunt hates you."

"I'm sure she didn't at the time. I was, after all, a baby. Nobody can hate a baby."

Belle wrinkled her nose sceptically. "She strikes me as a woman with a keenly honed sense of loathing. You don't even have a diminutive."

"You're being absurd. Of course I do. You can just call me Hor—oh dear God, no you can't."

"*See.*"

"Lee, then?" he suggested, with the air of someone discovering lampreys in their garden pond. "Lee is a diminutive."

"Lee sounds like someone selling potatoes."

"That is a very specific impression, Belle, and probably quite unfair to Lees."

"Even so," she said firmly, "you are not a Lee."

"Would it help if I sold more potatoes?"

The carriage kept rolling. Travel like this was such a strange combination of discomfort and tedium, each of them conspiring to prevent the alleviation of the other. Sir Horley glanced idly at the scenery, which was quite beautiful—middle England being a little more rugged than the south, its rise and fall brushed purple here and there with heather—and continued to feel both tedium and discomfort.

"Could I call you something else?" Belle asked, abruptly. "If that does not feel presumptuous or rejecting?"

"Something else?"

"Another name."

"Another name?" he repeated, bemused. "What, like Fuckface or Beryl?"

She nodded. "Exactly like Fuckface or Beryl. They were just the names I was thinking of. 'It is either Fuckface or Beryl,' I said to myself."

"I take it you do not wish to call me either Fuckface or Beryl?"

"No. And I am beginning to think I have grossly over-stepped as usual. Of course I will call you Sir—I will call you Horley, if you are attached to it."

"I used to be fairly neutral about it," Sir Horley murmured. "But now you've lain into it for the best part of a mile, I've rather changed my mind. Shall we consider Fuckface or Beryl?"

Which was when Belle saw fit to blurt out, "May I call you Rufus?"

It was a good job he was sitting because otherwise Sir Horley would have fallen. He had not heard the name in years, nor really thought of it. And yet it struck him now with a peculiar force—like seeing a stranger across the road, having dreamed of them once. "Where . . ." His mouth was desert dry. "That's . . . that's my father's name."

"I did not know that."

"God knows why he bothered. When he gave me fuck all else a father should."

Belle was getting that keen-eyed Tarleton look again. "Do you not think it means something that he did, though?"

"No" was the only answer he felt able to return. Because, for a while, especially when he was young, he had thought it might. Had clung to the possibility, in fact, until nothing had piled upon nothing and too many years had passed.

"I'm sorry," said Belle quickly and, for once, not pushing. "I . . . I just thought it suited you. Because of the red hair and everything. Is that a family trait also?"

"If so, it is one that long faded into abeyance. No"—he shrugged—"the hair is an aberrance, the name a relic, and it's rather odd you produced it out of nowhere."

"Oh, I didn't. Your aunt bellowed it at you while you were attempting to flee her in a drunken stupor."

He half smiled, pretending amusement, something he had once been better at. "Well, doesn't that sound just like us?"

"Perhaps it's best I learn to call you Horley."

"No," he said swiftly, surprising himself. "Call me Rufus."

"I do under—" Belle began. "Wait. Really?"

"No, I'm toying with your emotions. Yes. Why not?"

She squeezed her clenched fists together gleefully. "Oh, I'm so happy. I like it for you so much better than Sir Horley."

"Who knows." Rufus shrugged. "Perhaps I may like myself a little better too."

He did not like himself better. He verily despised himself for this entire enterprise.

"How much further?" he ask-groan-wailed.

"The same as last time, minus ten minutes."

"Ten minutes? Whose godforsaken idea was it"—he twisted his neck, until it cracked like it was snapping off his shoulders—"to put Scotland so far fucking north?"

"The Scots?" suggested Belle. "The Romans? William the Conqueror?"

"This is no judgement on your company, my dear, but if I have to spend another day, nay another minute, in this carriage, I am going to kill myself with my shoe."

Belle blinked. "I am so glad we are such calm, reasonable people with no tendencies towards unnecessary theatricality."

"Belle, I'm *dying*. My entire body feels like Satan's own cravat."

"There will be an inn we can stop at in an hour or two."

"It used to bring me comfort," said Rufus mournfully, "when we stopped at inns. But I've since realised that they are merely a taunting delay in the inevitable return to a carriage."

"Think what adventures may await us, though. This next one might have a bath. Or only a moderate quantity of bedbugs."

He sighed. "Are you never daunted?"

"All the time. But on the last occasion I was truly daunted, I shot someone, so it is probably best I continue to moderate it."

"You did not throw a trifle at me because you were daunted?"

"I was a little daunted," Belle conceded. "But I think I was mostly frustrated."

"It does not reflect well on Valentine that he, ah, daunted you so severely."

"Most people believe it does not reflect well on me that I shot him."

"It can reflect poorly on both of you."

That made her laugh. "How very egalitarian of you."

She was giving every impression of being amused, but there was also something strained about it. And this was not, he realised, the first time she had spoken of the incident with that kind of brittle lightness. Not even the first time on this trip. "I hope you don't blame yourself overmuch for what happened?"

"What is *overmuch* in the context of a pistol discharged into someone else?"

"I'm not sure Valentine has given it a thought since."

Her lips pressed into a hard line. "I still wish I hadn't done it. I know it is what spirited heroines do in books, but I did not feel very spirited at the time."

Rufus had been present for some of that particular melodrama, partially by design. Not being more than acquainted with most of the involved parties, he had treated it as little more than a source of diversion to him. Not wholly benign diversion. "How did you feel?" he asked, as though paying attention now could compensate for his former detachment.

She spread her hands in a gesture of ambivalence. "It's hard to say. Everything was happening very fast. It was dark, and Valentine was furious and chasing me through a wood. He got me trapped against a tree or something and . . ." Breaking off, slightly breathless, she seemed to become aware of how quickly she was speaking. "I don't think he would have hurt me. But I do remember thinking he *could*, and that I would be able to do nothing to prevent it, and that, in one way or another, it was always going to be like that, so . . . well, I panicked and shot him."

"My own behaviour does not currently merit scrutiny," he murmured, "but there is perhaps an object lesson here about chasing women through dark woods. Truthfully, I think it was magnanimous in the extreme that you forgave Valentine for all that nonsense."

"On the contrary"—returning to cheerfulness with a visible effort, she grinned in a way that flashed the points of her canines—"I am bearing an eternal grudge. From novels, one would think it might be exciting to be chased around the country by a duke hell-bent on marrying you, but the reality leaves much to be desired."

"With all due respect, you seemed to be rather enjoying it at the time."

"Well, I *was* in my Heroine Era."

This was so typically Tarletonian: an idea that made sense only to Belle, delivered with absolute conviction. "What the fuck, dear heart, is a heroine era?"

"Oh, you know. A time of life characterised by hope and delusion equally."

"And what era are you in presently?"

"Probably my Still-Trying-to-Work-It-Out Era. My Eat-All-the-Cheese Era. My Entirely-Out-of-Fucks Era?"

"I may live in those, er, eras. But I shall aspire to a Heroine Era."

"You would make a marvellous heroine, Rufus," declared Belle. "Far better than I did."

"Alas." Rufus put his hand to his heart with a flourish. "I go in want of a hero."

"It is not a hero that defines a heroine."

He shrugged. "I would still like one."

"Then I'm sure a hero can be found."

"I have not succeeded thus far."

"Have you genuinely been looking?"

"Perhaps not," Rufus admitted. "I've more sort of been fucking anyone who looked at me with a passingly kind eye. Sometimes not even with that."

"Ah." Belle nodded sympathetically. "I have also been in that era."

"You know not everything has to be an era? Sometimes they're just a series of bad choices."

"Doesn't it give things a certain grandeur, though?"

He laughed a touch sardonically. "Nothing can give my sex life grandeur. Besides, if I am in any era at all, it is my Stuck-in-a-Carriage Era. Are we nearly there yet?"

"Nearly to Scotland?"

"Nearly to anywhere."

"No more than we were before."

Rufus slumped sideways like he'd taken a mortal wound. "God almighty."

"Perhaps," suggested Belle, otherwise unsympathetic, "we could play a game to pass the time more pleasantly?"

"Our resources are quite limited in that regard. 'I spy with my little eye something beginning with *C*.' Oh, let me guess. It's still the fucking carriage."

Tilting her head, Belle regarded him coolly. "Maybe I was wrong about you and Bonny. You are reminding me rather strongly of him right now."

"Except it's adorable when he does it."

"No, no." Belle sounded very certain. "It's annoying from both of you."

With an effort of will, Rufus returned to a reasonable approximation of a sitting position. While he felt no less wretched than he had mere moments ago, he had been recalled to his duties as a travelling companion. Certainly he was never going to be a good one—long journeys brought out the worst of him, too much time for regret and self-reflection—but he could probably avoid being so abysmally awful that Belle would throw the anvil at him at Gretna Green. "What would you like to play?"

"How about the way we used to entertain ourselves at boring balls?"

"By leaving? I'm not sure that's an option."

"No." She flicked impatient fingertips in his direction. "The . . . the game. You know, the *game*."

"You mean," he asked, "when we used to sit in a corner, watching the people who walked past, and deciding what they'd be like to sleep with?"

"Exactly."

"You know that game was quite wrong of us."

Another finger flick. "Of course I do. That's why it was so *fun*."

Rufus was tempted. Admittedly, he would probably have been tempted by a piece of fluff just then. "How would it even work in the middle of the countryside? Are we going to assess the sheep to see which are giving us bedroom eyes?"

"Admittedly, we can't rely on sheer numbers the way we usually would. But I have seen other travellers on the road. How about we simply divide them between us: the first we pass will be my potential partner, the next yours, and so on."

"I can't quite believe I'm agreeing to this," said Rufus. "But fine."

He was rewarded by a gleeful noise from Belle. And they both leaned forward so they could scrutinise the view for hypothetical lovers. Across the course of many minutes, they beheld nothing but grass, farmland, the occasional tree or knot of trees, at one point the shimmer of a lake upon the horizon. It was not, in all honesty, causing the journey to pass any quicker, but at least it was giving them something to do.

Finally, Belle spotted a figure in the distance.

"Look," she cried, "there is a person for me."

Rufus, whose eyesight was quite sharp, twitched a brow. "I wish you the happiest of liaisons."

A few minutes later, the carriage rolled past a stooped old man, eighty if he was a day, with a stick in one hand and a basket of cabbages in the other.

Rufus's brow twitched again.

"I have realised," Belle said, frowning, "that this game feels significantly less acceptable when it involves innocent members of the public going about their day rather than our richest, most influential acquaintances indulging their personal vanity."

"Interesting you should discover your social conscience when on the hook for a dalliance with an octogenarian."

The glance Belle directed at him was scathing before she returned her attention to the window and the elderly gentleman who was already falling into the distance. "I notice his strong gnarled hands and bright yet gentle eyes and find myself quite taken with him, for such qualities transcend time and class. Unfortunately, he has been married to his true love these past sixty years and therefore does not return my interest. He shares his recipe for cabbage stew instead."

"What a charming encounter for you both," murmured Rufus, oddly moved, in spite of himself.

"Indeed."

It was a little while before they passed a second traveller. Another man, perhaps making his way home like the first had been, except he was considerably younger, stripped to the waist and carrying a scythe with the nonchalance of long familiarity. The setting sun gleamed upon the ridges of his abdomen and the hard muscles of his shoulders, strewing gold through the abundant curls of his chest hair.

Rufus shrugged. "We fuck like wild rabbits and are equally satisfied by the experience."

"He's carrying an exceptionally large implement," Belle noted. "Maybe that implies inadequacy in other areas."

"Do not reflect your own vulgar tastes onto mine."

Her eyes widened in teasing outrage. "How dare you."

"It is only those of limited imagination and inflexible mind who assume the only satisfactory member is a sizeable one. Smaller varieties have their advantages too. Less demanding on the throat. Expressively mobile during one's more forceful thrusts."

"I . . ." Belle looked briefly lost for words, which was quite an accomplishment. "Our friendship is such an educational experience."

"Forgive me. I should have not spoken so indecorously."

"Oh no, please be as indecorous as you wish. While one may assume I am being sarcastic at least seventy-three percent of the time, I was sincere on this occasion. I have not previously given much consideration to the underappreciated pleasures of the more petite phallus. But that is because I am inclined to believe the bulk of consideration to phalluses is given by those already possessed of them. To the rest of us, they are no great matter."

"If you say so," returned Rufus, unconvinced. And then, glancing at the road ahead, "Look—someone approaches."

"Some two," said Belle. "Quick, we need fresh rules for twosomes."

"The one closest to the carriage is yours, the other mine."

"Agreed."

As they drew closer to what turned out to be a pair of ladies, Belle's expression grew distinctly smug. Both women had their beauties, but the one allocated to Belle was clearly more conventionally radiant—with a face straight from a portrait, and hair an even brighter gold than Belle's. Discreetly Rufus drew down the window sash that they might catch a little of the conversation.

". . . wildflowers," the beauty was saying, at sufficient intensity and volume to be heard with some clarity. "Can you believe it? They're just plants from the ground."

Her companion was shorter, less idealistically proportioned, and touched by several scatterings of freckles that were not to fashionable taste, but otherwise quite charming. "Are not all flowers plants from the ground?"

"Urgh," declared the beauty. "No wonder I have always found them so paltry a gift. Jewels would be so much better."

"Such a convention would also preclude all but the wealthiest paying court to you."

"Yes? And?"

Her friend sighed. "As a general rule, dearest, accepting expensive gifts is the province of ladies inclined to be liberal with their favours."

"That would not be a problem for me. I am illiberal by nature."

Somehow her companion did not comment on this. "I meant ladies who . . . work in . . . ladies who—"

The beauty waved a hand airily. "Oh, you lost me at *work*."

"Well," said Rufus.

The triumph that had blossomed briefly upon Belle's face was now distinctly wilted. She let out a little huff. "I am shallow enough to make the attempt. She re-iterates her distaste of labour of any kind, complains throughout, and neither of us are left with any great esteem for the other. You?"

"I come clean about preferring men exclusively, she is wholly understanding, and I strongly encourage her to reconsider her choice of intimates. We become the greatest of friends."

"How great?" demanded Belle, unexpectedly.

Rufus glanced at her in some confusion. "Six great? What are you even asking?"

"Is she as great a friend to you as . . . well. I am."

"Belle." He wasn't sure whether to laugh and decided not to. "Are you jealous of my fictional relationship with a young lady I have no knowledge of and shall likely never see again?"

"I don't know. Possibly? Now we are discussing the matter, it does not seem wholly reasonable of me."

There was something strange happening to Rufus's heart. He normally conceived it as hard and gnarled, like a peach pit. Now it was as soft as the peach itself. "I . . . I'm flattered, Bellflower. I do not think anyone has ever felt jealous over me in my entire life."

"It's a Tarleton trait, I'm afraid. We are possessive in our way. And I don't think it's necessarily something to be celebrated."

"Is wanting to possess something not a sign that you value it?"

"But also that you seek to control it. I have experienced enough of that for myself; I would never wish to do it to anyone else."

Impulsively, he reached for her hand. "I am to be your husband, Belle. Possess me a little. I shall tell you if it ever feels constricting."

"Well"—her look was typically ironic, but her colour was heightened—"you are a very lovely man to possess."

Now it was his turn to be flustered. "Ah yes. A veritable catch for anyone."

"Do you doubt it?" She gave one of those quizzical little head tilts of hers. "You are handsome—"

"Passable," he corrected her quickly.

"Kind," she offered.

"Hardly."

"Thoughtful."

"When?"

"Entertaining."

"Speaking of which"—it was the clumsiest of segues, but he could do no better—"should we not return to the game?"

Belle scowled. "I'm rather out of sorts with it. I did not think it was the sort of game it was possible to lose, but I am most assuredly losing at it."

"There, there," he said consolingly. "We are bound to encounter a morally reprehensible person for me sooner or later."

Belle was still scowling. "Then let's hope sooner. Your turn."

The next traveller they encountered seemed to be a blacksmith. He was stripped to the waist, his hammer resting casually against his shoulder. The setting sun gleamed upon the ridges of his abdomen and the hard muscles of his shoulders, strewing gold through the abundant curls of his chest hair.

Doing his best not to laugh, Rufus said, "We fuck like wild rabbits and are equally satisfied by the experience."

"Gah" was Belle's rejoinder. And, some minutes later, "I am being punished by the universe."

This wasn't helping Rufus's attempts to treat the situation with the gravity Belle clearly felt it deserved. "I think people are just proceeding with their lives. I don't think it's personal."

"Well, it feels personal," retorted Belle.

The carriage had slowed to negotiate a crossroads.

"The next person we encounter," she went on, "had better be . . ."

For some reason the carriage had drawn to a full halt.

". . . absolutely fucking delightful or—"

The muzzle of a pistol appeared at the window. Followed by the masked face of a highwayman. For a moment, his gaze seemed to waver between the two of them, before he announced somewhat querulously:

"Your money or your life?"

"Oh, for *fuck's* sake," said Belle.

Chapter 15

"Um," said the highwayman.

Rufus leaned forward before Belle did anything rash. From the way his hand trembled upon his weapon, this did not seem a particularly competent highwayman, which was all the more reason to be cautious. Guns were, to Rufus's mind, even more dangerous when in the possession of idiots.

"I'm sure we'd love to oblige you." He sounded composed at least. More composed than he felt, which took him slightly aback, as he was used to his composure in potentially deadly situations not being counterfeit. But then he was also used to not being in a potentially deadly situation with a reactive Tarleton. "The problem is, we are not over-endowed with valuables at present."

The pistol wobbled. "Um," said the highwayman. "I was not—that is . . . there are two of you?"

"As you see. We will not, however, do anything silly, will we, Belle?"

"Are you new?" Belle asked the highwayman.

He bristled. "*No.* I am a dangerous criminal."

"Of course you are," said Rufus hastily.

"There are ballads and broadsheets about me," insisted the highwayman. "About how dashing and daring I am."

Rufus nodded. "That's as may be. But the fact remains that we have travelled in haste and packed lightly to the point of non-existently. You may have noticed that I do not even possess a coat."

"And your companion?"

Belle gave an indignant squeak. "I have my pelisse. But if you think I will allow a footpad to remove my garments—"

"No no"—the highwayman seemed as concerned by this possibility as Belle—"I insist that you keep your clothes absolutely on. I more meant . . ." He glanced again at Rufus, an incomprehensible question in his eyes. "I did not expect—she would be here."

This was the strangest highwayman Rufus had ever encountered, although, admittedly, he was working from a sample size of zero. "That need not interfere with"—he made what he hoped was a conciliatory open-handed gesture, rather than a startling "Time to shoot me" gesture—"our business?"

"Well, if you're certain." The highwayman was worrying his lip, clearly in a state of some anxiety. "I suppose I can see why you might find it comforting in a way. To have a woman present. It might make things feel less . . . you know."

Rufus did not know. "I think I find my ease equally when travelling with men or women or those who are both or neither."

"How fortunate for you," returned the highwayman, a little waspishly.

"Look"—only the necessity of controlling the situation as best he could was preventing Rufus from rubbing his brow—"I'm not sure what's happening anymore. We don't have any valuables, so you can't rob us. And it would be a terrible idea to shoot us, so I strongly discourage you from doing that."

This return to business seemed to galvanise the highwayman. He leered into the carriage. "I wouldn't say you don't have *any* valuables."

"Absolutely not," said Belle and Rufus at the same time.

The leer lingered awkwardly on the highwayman's face, as though he had committed to it and now had no idea what to do with it. "A dastardly rogue I may be, but your lips are jewels fair enough for me."

"Are you intentionally speaking in verse?" asked Belle.

"What, no? I'm just . . . speaking. Can you stop interrupting? You're ruining the mood."

She blinked. "There's a mood? You're doing crime."

"To allow such a prize to slip between my fingers is the true crime here," declared the highwayman, with more determination than conviction. "A night in my arms and you may go, that is, both of you, can go free. Though there will no freedom sweeter than the passion I teach you when you give your lovely untouched body to me."

"Perhaps," began Rufus, hoping to defuse the situation before—

"Ew," cried Belle. "*No.*"

Rufus flinched. "Belle, he's got a gun. Let's . . . ah . . . discuss this calmly, shall we? My good man"—he turned to the stranger—"it's not really appropriate for you to go around coercing women to sleep with you, no matter how dashing you believe yourself to be or how convinced you are that they'll like it if they try it."

The highwayman was staring at him.

"Consent," explained Rufus, "is a vital part of—"

An intemperate gesture came perilously close to discharging the gun. "For God's sake, stop playing games with me. Not her. You."

"Oh." Rufus shrugged. "That's fine, then. You can do whatever you like with my lovely untouched body. How long do you need? Twenty minutes?"

"Um," said the highwayman.

"Ten?" suggested Rufus.

At which point Belle slammed her fist against the carriage seat—a gesture hindered by the padding, so it was mostly a soft *flump*. "No. This is not going to happen."

"My dear, don't give it a moment's thought."

"Of course I'm going to give it a moment's thought. I'm going to give it many moments' thought. If it is not acceptable for ladies to be coerced into sexual encounters, then it should not be acceptable for gentlemen either."

"I don't mind."

"Don't overwhelm me with your ardour or anything," muttered the highwayman.

Rufus glanced at him. "I'm sorry. Take me now, you scurrilous devil. Is that better?"

"A bit. But could you put a little more feeling into it?"

"Stop negotiating," yelled Belle. "You don't get to sleep with either of us."

The highwayman gave another ill-advised flounder with the gun. "He's consented."

"I have consented," agreed Rufus.

"I know." The look Belle cast his way was full of understanding. "And I do not mean to impede your decision-making, but I'm afraid you might have agreed out of apathy, and a lack of self-consideration, rather than genuine desire."

"He's just playing hard to get," put in the highwayman. "He'd better be playing hard to get, because this is already more bloody trouble than he's worth. Lord in heaven."

"Please let's not," began Rufus, reaching out a restraining hand.

But it was too late. Belle had already erupted.

"How dare you. How dare you speak of anyone like that, least of all him. Dashing rogue, my left arse cheek. You're . . . you're *disgusting*."

"What's happening?" asked the highwayman, visibly alarmed.

"You ought to be ashamed of yourself," Belle concluded.

And before Rufus could prevent her, she had thrust open the carriage door with sufficient force that the highwayman was sent reeling backwards, having taken a severe buffet to the face. It was an effective move and had, essentially, solved their problem. But, in typical Tarleton fashion, she had to take it too far, flinging herself bodily out of the carriage after him.

"Belle," Rufus tried again.

Momentum and sheer angry rabbit energy bowled her into the already disorientated highwayman. They fell to the ground in a tangle of flailing limbs, light slapping, and hair pulling.

"You . . . you . . ." Belle seemed to be trying to bite his nose. "You scoundrel. You reptile. You vile creepy-crawly. You belong under a log."

"Help," wailed the highwayman. "Please. She's murdering me. I'm being murdered."

Rufus regarded the wriggling pair, wondering whether he ought to climb down from the carriage and physically separate them. "Don't murder the highwayman, Belle. It will make life complicated for everyone."

"Aiieeee," added the highwayman, still apparently in the midst of being murdered.

"Besides"—Rufus kept his tone light—"the punishment for highway robbery is hanging."

The highwayman had managed to get a hand protectively over his face. "But I'm not robbing you."

"You tried."

"What? No, I—"

There was another flurry of movement as he attempted to cast Belle away, but she was clinging like an exceptionally furious limpet. And it was at that moment the gun, which Rufus had not realised was trapped between their bodies, discharged with a muffled bang.

Time seemed to slow and stop altogether, hanging over them like a moon.

And then Belle slumped forward.

"By God"—Rufus sprang from the carriage—"if you've hurt her, I *will* see you hanged."

"I didn't," protested the highwayman. "I mean, I didn't . . . I wasn't . . . it was an accident. God, is that blood. Is it mine? Am I dying? I feel faint."

"You are the worst highwayman in the history of larceny."

The highwayman made a sound of pure exasperation. "Well, obviously. I'm not a fucking highwayman, am I?"

"Then what on earth would possess you to start holding up travellers? Actually, never mind. You are the least of my concerns right now." As carefully as he could, Rufus drew Belle into his arms and turned her onto her back. Her face was very pale, her eyes closed. The words "Oh, please no" burst out of him involuntarily as he bent to check her breathing. Just when he was close enough for it to be as uncomfortable as possible were she not to be dead, her eyes popped open again.

"I think I've been shot," she said. "How exciting."

He let out a long, shaky breath. "Don't trifle with me, Bellflower. You could have been killed."

"I haven't, though, have I?"

Her gaze, he realised, was a little unfocused. And the sleeve of her pelisse was dark with blood. It was not the time to be scaring her or scolding her. "Not even a little bit. But I had better take a look at the wound regardless."

"I say." The highwayman was still dithering nearby. "I'm terribly sorry. I've never shot anyone before."

"You astound me," said Rufus.

The combination of the fight and the gun going off had startled the horses. Having settled them, the coachman passed the reins to the under-coachman and jumped down. "Is everything all right?"

"I've been shot," Belle said. "Isn't it exciting?"

The coachman did not look as though he found this exciting.

"What were you thinking"—Rufus glared up at him—"stopping the coach for this Bedlamite?"

"He said he was your friend. That you were expecting him."

"Why would we be expecting a highwayman?"

"I mean," said the coachman, "he's clearly not a highwayman, is he? Haven't seen a highwayman for some twenty years. And you do have some peculiar friends."

Through a mixture of tearing, peeling, and applying his teeth as carefully as he could, Rufus had managed to coax Belle's pelisse away from her arm. The sleeve of her dress was already soaked through, the blood vividly red in the fading light.

"I'm going to be naked by the time we reach Gretna Green," he muttered, dragging his shirt over his head and using several layers of folded fabric to try and stanch the wound.

The highwayman made a sound.

"I think"—Rufus glanced up again—"we'd better get her to the inn as quickly as possible."

"She's present," Belle insisted, although somewhat less forcefully than usual. "I'm not Valentine. I don't go around *fainting* just because I've been shot."

"Yes, yes. You're extremely mighty."

"Probably with some assistance, I'll even be able to make it to the carriage."

True to form, she was attempting to sit upright before anyone could stop her. Though, perhaps, both of them might have preferred if someone had, for she turned an even ghastlier shade of white and fell back against him.

"I'll carry you," he told her. "But you won't thank me for it."

"Everyone doubts my capacity for civility—oh, you bastard."

"I'm sorry."

He'd lifted her as gently as he could, but he must have jarred her arm regardless—and without direct pressure, the blood had begun to flow again, almost as quickly as before, splashing his wrist and speckling the road like an extremely ominous April shower. To his surprise, the highwayman darted forward, gathered up Rufus's shirt, and put his own hand over the wound. Even with the help of the highwayman and the coachman, it was a clumsy, uncomfortable shuffle to get Belle into the carriage, one she bore with stubborn equanimity. That was the thing about Tarletons: stubbing a toe was the end of the world, but when they were truly hurt, they got small and quiet, and that was worrying.

Eventually Belle was settled, her head in Rufus's lap, her colour still far from good, and the highwayman was peering into the carriage with a pleading look on his face.

"Um," he said.

"For fuck's sake"—Rufus was so far beyond the end of his tether that he wasn't sure the tether would ever be retrievable—"stop saying *um.*"

"Um," said the highwayman. "I mean. Um. I truly didn't mean to shoot your friend."

"That doesn't make me any happier that you did."

"I know, but . . . but. I can help? It will be easier to tend her between the two of us."

Rufus gave him an incredulous look. "Are you asking for a ride?"

"A little bit," admitted the highwayman. "I had a horse. A black horse, actually. Very . . . impressive and in keeping."

"And the stylishness of the horse is relevant because?"

"Because I just—it doesn't matter. In any case, it took fright when . . . the whole 'shooting your friend' thing happened. So I find myself slightly on the stranded side? And I don't know this part of the country very well."

"Why were you holding people up in it then?" asked Belle, the words little more than a whisper.

"I wasn't. It's . . . it's . . ." The highwayman heaved a forlorn sigh. "It's a long story."

"I don't care if it's a Homeric epic," snapped Rufus. "Fuck off."

The highwayman hung his head sadly.

Belle stirred very slightly. "Oh, let him come."

"He *shot* you."

"Not—not on purpose. Besides, hearing a long story will p-pass the time nicely, won't it? Since"—her voice was growing weaker—"I fear I might not be the best company j-just at present."

"I care about you being well, not your being entertaining."

"Also," added the highwayman hastily, "it's not a good story. It's entirely foolish and best not spoken of. You don't want to hear it. Forget I brought it up."

Belle shook her head, or rather tried to shake her head, but quickly seemed to discover it was a bad idea. "On the contrary, those are the sort of stories I like to hear best."

Chapter 16

Being shot had turned out to be profoundly unexciting. Belle might even have gone so far as to say it was tedious. It was inconvenient, and made one very weak, and it had clearly ruined both her dress and her pelisse. Moreover, and in spite of Rufus's best attempts to keep her braced, every sway and jolt of the carriage seemed to rattle through her, deep enough to reach her soul. The pain itself was troubling less for its intensity—though, when stirred up, it had moments of great intensity—than from the sense of anxiety it brought with it. The body had its own ways of knowing when something was very wrong, and this felt like nausea in her skin, a tangle of hot and cold and both and neither radiating from her arm and shoulder. Perhaps she should have followed Valentine's example and fainted. But she hated the idea of his being in the right about *anything*. And, besides, Rufus was looking so worried she didn't quite have the heart.

Instead, she tried to focus on their new companion. Now that he had removed his tricorne and mask, he was a rather ordinary young man. To be frank, he had seemed somewhat ordinary even with them. He was only an inch or so taller than Belle, slender and nervy, like a deer one twig snap from flight. His face was an expressive mishmash: wide mouth, narrow chin, button nose, slightly rounded cheeks, long-lashed hazel eyes into which his hair—a profusion of tight curls—was perpetually falling. After a moment, he drew a pair of glasses from the folds of his cloak and put them on.

Shifting on the carriage seat, Belle tried to find a more comfortable position and abruptly realised there wasn't one. That, in fact, *no movement whatsoever* was probably her best bet for neither screaming nor passing out. "I don't think," she said, mostly to keep her mind occupied, "that we've been properly introduced yet?"

"I don't think we have," agreed Rufus. "Miss Arabella Tarleton, this is the pissjester who shot you. Pissjester, this is Miss Arabella Tarleton."

"Um," said the pissjester, unhappily.

"I, meanwhile, am Sir Horley Comewithers."

"But call him Rufus," added Belle. "It suits him so much better, don't you think?"

The pissjester squirmed. "If I call him Rufus, will he stop calling me *pissjester*?"

"'But'"—Rufus mimicked Belle's tone—"'it suits him *so much better*.'"

"I think he must be concerned about me or something," Belle told the pissjester, wondering if that was true, and what it meant if it was. Rufus probably did not actually want her to die, but it would simplify his life a lot if she did. "He's not usually this rude. What's your name?"

"Gilead," offered the pissjester, after a moment. "Gilead Postlethwaite."

A shiver of mirth travelled through Rufus's body. "Are you sure you wouldn't prefer *pissjester*?"

The former pissjester drew himself up primly. "Gil is fine, thank you."

"Any connection to Postlethwaite's Rare Books?" asked Rufus, momentarily diverted from his hostility.

If Belle hadn't been convinced moving her mouth would end up hurting her shoulder, she would have smiled. While she knew Rufus had been making considerable efforts with her the past few days (his discomfort with long-distance travel aside) it was in moments like these that she felt closest to him. When she believed she knew him or might come to do so. There were shades of her London friend, yes, his quick mind, and his curiosity, the sharp tongue that had always delighted her, but they existed alongside the parts of himself he had long been hiding—his fears, and pains, and uncertainties. Despite his insistence that there was nothing of himself in the men, or the man, he had pretended to be, Belle thought the truth was likely more nuanced. He was not the exquisite accessory he had been in London, but nor was he the irredeemable ruin he claimed. He was both, and neither, and all the spaces between. She only hoped he would be able to believe it one day.

"Um," Gil was saying, a blush standing high on his cheeks, "yes. Please don't tell anyone."

One of Rufus's eyebrows lifted into a mocking arch. "That you're a bookseller?"

"No. That I"—the ex-highwayman gestured hopelessly at himself—"this. Any of this."

"Does *rare books* mean *porn*?" asked Belle.

Gil's blush over-spilled his cheeks, splashed over his brow, and rushed down his jaw. "Heavens, no."

They both stared at him.

He wilted. "Well, maybe a small amount of porn."

They kept staring.

"A medium to moderate amount of porn." He gave a kind of full-body twitch, as though he would have physically bolted had he not been stuck in a closed carriage. "It's not my fault. Etching seems to make humanity absolutely rampant, especially in Italy. And don't get me started on the books of hours."

"Please," murmured Rufus, "get started on the books of hours."

Gil dropped his voice to an awestruck whisper. "The illustrations those monks were drawing in the margins. I've seen things you people wouldn't believe."

"You are in danger of over-selling this."

"Knights," said Gil quickly, "in deadly combat with snails. Murderous rabbits performing deeds of extraordinary violence. Nuns plucking severed members from trees. A naked woman astride a flying phallus. A bird with the head of a man in its anus. A stag with the head of Jesus suspended between its antlers."

"Well"—Rufus seemed to be considering the matter—"at least Jesus wasn't up its anus."

"I'm sure," returned Gil, in rather hollow accents, "somewhere, in some book, he is."

The carriage rolled over a rut in the road that felt like a mountain, and Belle ground her teeth together lest she cry out. Or worse, whimper. Valentine had whimpered *a lot*, despite later maintaining he had borne his travails with dukely stoicism. Through sheer stubbornness, she was able to mostly control her vocalisations. The trembling, however, was another matter. It had started as little shivers running like ants across her body. Then begun to burrow deep until it was as though her very bones were trying to knock together.

"R-rufus," she asked, "is it especially cold in the carriage?"

He put his free hand against her brow—which, despite the chill, somehow felt repulsively clammy. All he said, however, was "Yes." And, to Gil, "Give her that damn cloak, will you?"

Gil immediately pulled it off and tucked it round her. It might have helped a little, but it was hard to tell when she was prey to so many conflicting sensations.

"Sorry," she whispered, "t-to take your damn cloak."

"Not at all," he returned. "It shouldn't have been necessary to ask."

She tried to gather her thoughts, which seemed to want to roll away from her in all directions. "Did you say you were a bookseller? Or did I imagine it?"

"No, no," he reassured her. "I am a bookseller."

"Then"—her thoughts continued rolling—"why are you dressed as a highwayman?"

Somehow, Gil was *still* blushing. "It's embarrassing."

"You may consider the explanation penance for having shot me."

"I also fear you may find it sordid or unsuitable. You see it concerns, um, the affairs of gentlemen."

He was so hopelessly teaseable that Belle could not help herself. She widened her eyes in faux naiveté. "Political matters? Business correspondence? That kind of thing?"

"No." He made a mortified little sound. "Affairs *between* gentlemen. Affairs of the heart and . . . and other . . . *areas*."

"Gentlemen?" gasped Belle. "With other gentlemen."

Gil looked about ready to fling himself from the moving vehicle. "Oh my God. I have spoken the unspeakable. Named the unnameable. I have sullied your maidenly innocence with my depravity."

It was Rufus in the end who took pity on him. "She's fucking with you. She knows full well what you mean. As do I, for I share your inclinations."

"You do? But"—Gil's gazed flicked rapidly from Belle to Rufus and back again—"I thought . . . are you not . . . ?"

"We're eloping," Belle explained.

"Even though he . . . ?"

She remembered, just in time, not to shrug. "I do not need his physical passion." Carefully turning her gaze up to Rufus, she added, "I like your company very much, though."

His smile was soft and effortless. "And I yours, dear heart." A pause, his eyes glinting in the gloom of the carriage. "About eighty-seven percent of the time."

"That is a good percentage," she declared. "Any more, and our life together would be dull. Any less and it would be frustrating."

Gil was still looking confused. "But if you are not corporeally compatible, will you both not miss the . . . um . . . carnal opportunities offered by the single state?"

"I don't see why marriage to each other," said Belle, "prevents either of us from enjoying whatever opportunities, carnal or otherwise, come our way."

"I suppose I had just taken it for granted that it should. Although"—and here Gil's expression grew rueful—"I am clearly the last person to claim insight into either carnality or opportunity."

Even with the distraction of conversation, Belle's head was beginning to swim. While there had initially been something almost reassuring about the pressure of Rufus's hands upon her, they had increasingly become the source of an ache, both itchy and numbing at once. She stirred fractiously beneath him, but he only steadied her and asked their companion, "Surely you didn't think holding up passersby was the ideal way to meet a partner?"

Gil made an impatient sound. "Of course not. I was holding up someone by pre-arrangement."

"Someone wanted you to rob them?" asked Belle.

"Not rob them. Menace them. Seduce them."

This was apparently too much for Rufus, who cut in with "This seems needlessly byzantine, my friend. Could you not have simply gone to the docks or a discreet establishment in Moorfields like the rest of us?"

"I have tried, *my friend*. I have encountered many a soldier, sailor, or candlestick maker willing to make use of me. But my preferences lie elsewhere."

"In menacing?"

Belle did not blame Rufus for his scepticism. But she thought he need not have poured all of it into his voice.

"Yes," returned Gil, clearly stung. "Is it so hard to believe?"

"Completely."

Gil drooped a little.

"Nonsense," said Belle. "I believe you could be very menacing."

Gil drooped more. "Now I just feel patronised."

"Maybe you could say *um* less?" suggested Rufus.

"Oh, you have feedback too?"

"A few notes."

"Wonderful. A performance review is just what my evening needs."

Rufus raised a brow. "I could shoot you, if you like?"

"Do let it go," said Belle, wishing she sounded, and for that matter felt, stronger. "He's sorry, and I'm going to be fine."

His hand pressed down painfully. "Of course, my dear. Absolutely fine."

Then:

"Belle? Belle?"

Her name tolled distantly. Like a bell, she thought with an internal giggle.

"Belle."

The darkness behind her eyelids was as soft as goose down. She was floating in it quite contentedly. At least until Rufus slapped her. She gazed up at him, betrayed. "What was that for?"

"Gil is about to continue his story"—his attention flicked sharply across the carriage—*"aren't you?"*

"Um . . . am I? I mean. Yes. Yes, I am."

"And you don't want to sleep through it, do you, dearest?"

"Maybe I could hear it later? I'm . . ." It was strange. She could have yawned, but even the effort of that felt beyond her just then. She just wanted to close her eyes again and be borne sweetly away. "Tired."

His lip curled. "How very feeble of you. I would have expected something like this from Valentine but not from—"

"I'm awake," she yelled. "I'm awake."

"Glad to hear it. Now, Gil, if you would be so good as to continue mortifying yourself for our entertainment?"

By way of answer, the bookseller took refuge in grumbling. "I don't know what more to tell you."

"At this juncture"—there was an odd tight note in Rufus's voice—"anything. Tell us how you came to mistake us for your pre-arranged menacing?

Or, for that matter, how one goes about pre-arranging a menacing in the first place."

"Classifieds."

"Do they allow you to advertise for that kind of thing in the newspaper?"

"Not in so many words. But there are ways of indicating that one may be searching for particular kinds of friends. And I fell into correspondence with another such gentleman." Gil gave a wistful sigh. "It was a very pleasant correspondence."

Another gently enquiring noise from Rufus. "Oh?"

"We spoke as frankly as was advisable—but still more frankly than I have ever spoken to anyone—of our desires and our difficulties in fulfilling them."

The world, temporarily confined as it was to a carriage with two other people in it, kept slipping away from Belle. She was doing her best to concentrate, so as not to seem impolite, or worse, an overly indulged milksop like Valentine, but voices ebbed and flowed around her, the speakers themselves smudging into shadows. She found she was glad, after all, of Rufus's hand. It was still uncomfortable. Yet it felt *tethering* too. She roused with an effort. "Your correspondent had a wish to be menaced, then?"

Gil's curls bounced as he nodded. "A passionate wish, yes. I should have known it was too good to be true."

"How so?"

"Your friend has the right of it, Miss Tarleton. Look at me. Who would possibly want to be menaced by"—a gesture of self-directed despair—"this?"

"Well," Belle offered. "If you inclined my way, I would."

Rufus snorted.

And she wished she was not so very . . . hazy, because this was something she felt strongly about. "I am in earnest. If I were to allow someone to menace me, it would have to be someone like you, Gil. Someone kind and considerate and gentle at heart. It would be foolish, I think, when seeking a menacing to put your trust in a more callous character."

"Why, Bellflower," drawled Rufus. "The areas of your expertise."

"I would not say I'm an expert," she returned. "But I have enjoyed an occasional menacing. Have you not?"

"When I am being menaced, I have rarely enjoyed the experience."

"Then you've been menaced wrong, hasn't he, Gil?"

This brought fresh pink to the bookseller's cheeks. "My own exposure to the subject has been strictly theoretical, I'm afraid. I had hoped to rectify that with my . . . my epistolarian friend, but you can see how well that went."

"He turned you down?" she asked.

"He didn't turn up at all." Pushing his glasses up onto his brow, Gil squeezed the bridge of his nose. "Anyone else would have drawn the obvious conclusion after two hours of waiting. Then I saw your coach approaching and . . . I suppose I was more ardent than I was sensible."

"It is always better," said Belle, ardently, "to be ardent than sensible."

Rufus clearly saw the matter otherwise. "The presence of two complete strangers, one of them a woman, did not discourage you?"

"I was a little thrown," conceded Gil. "But my correspondent did describe himself as a flame-haired, cat-eyed gentleman. And you, sir, are a flame-haired, cat-eyed gentleman."

"And my companion is chopped liver?"

"I don't know. I thought you might want her to watch or something."

Belle managed a woozy smile. "I applaud your spirit of adventure."

Rufus just rolled his eyes. "I think you're a fucking idiot."

There was a tense little pause.

"Believe me"—Gil's voice wobbled—"there is no reproach you can offer more damning than the ones I am heaping upon myself. I have acted beyond foolishly, I have endangered another person, I have brought shame upon the good name of Postlethwaite, and for nothing greater than the basest of desires to menace another gentleman. One who, in this case, probably didn't even exist. He was more likely an elderly lady or university student, seeking entertainment at my expense. I mean"—he hid his face behind an upraised forearm—"who else would write so fulsomely of their own taut buttocks?"

"No." God, Belle was tired, impossibly tired, but she did her best regardless. "You mustn't talk like this. And Rufus is . . . Rufus is jealous."

Gil glanced up, startled. "Of what? Look at him. He could menace any gentleman he chooses."

"Yes." Rufus's tone had gone silky with distaste. "What would I possibly be jealous of?"

"Because nobody has been a fucking idiot for you yet."

"That's . . . ," began Rufus.

But it was no use. Even his outrage—which she loved to provoke, especially through the simple application of truth—wasn't quite enough to hold her. Then again, she wasn't sure what would have been. She was spinning away like flower petals upon a spring breeze, released from a body grown stiff and sodden in Rufus's arms. It didn't, in all honesty, seem a wholly positive outcome. In general, she thought, bodies were to be remained in, and for as long as possible.

She had tried that, though. She had tried very hard. As she had tried so very hard at so many things. Things that other people took for granted. Claimed were easy, natural, normal.

It was nice, in a way, to have something of her own that was easy.

"Belle, you need to stay with me."

Why? she wondered. When he didn't want her to begin with?

Falling asleep had never been Belle's favourite. It was like looking into a well. Then plummeting into one.

This was not like that. It was up, nothing but up.

She scattered herself across the sky. And while it was dark, it was soft as velvet and full of the promise of stars.

Chapter 17

Someone was ruining Belle's life by pouring something horrible into her mouth. She spluttered and tried to turn her head away, to no avail.

"This will be easier"—Rufus loomed over her, looking frankly ghastly—"if you're drunk."

"I don't want to be—"

Drunk? Here? It felt very like the sort of situation where nothing was easy. And, in fact, everything was difficult. Difficult accelerating towards miserable.

"Tough. Drink. Damn you."

She half drank, half failed to drink, her throat and lips burning. "Where am I? What's . . ." A comical hiccough briefly interrupted both her words and her train of thought. "What's happening?"

"You're at an inn. And I'm about to sew up your arm."

Only one of those seemed good. "Why? Is it falling off?"

"No. Obviously not. Must you be so fucking dramatic?"

"I'm not being dramatic," she protested, offended and lightheaded at the same time. She was, at least, in less pain than she remembered. But that might have been because she was now mostly made of whisky. "Bunny had a bonn—no, wait. Bonny had a bunny . . ." She giggled suddenly. "That sounds funny. Anyway, he had a bunny that he cuddled so much the arm fell off. So I tried to sew it back on because I was a girl, and that's the sort of thing girls are supposed to be able to do, except it turns out sewing is hard, so I ended up re-attaching it the wrong way round."

Rufus was threading a needle, his fingers less steady than might have been preferable under the circumstances. "Bonny did what to a rabbit?"

"Not a real rabbit. A toy rabbit." A further thought occurred. "Wait a moment. I am a girl and I can't sew. You're not a girl. Can you sew?"

"I don't think skill with a needle is directly linked to gender, dear heart."

"Not what I asked."

"I was in the army," said Rufus, still not answering. "I had a uniform to maintain."

Belle didn't quite shriek. "A uniform is clothes. I'm not clothes."

"Someone hold her down, please."

It was Gil in the end who caught her weakly flailing hands in a surprisingly steady grip.

"Oh." Belle blinked up at him. "Hello, Gil. I wasn't sure if I dreamed you."

"Sadly not. This is all a true thing taking place in my life."

"And mine," she pointed out. She tried to catch Rufus's eye. "Is there not a doctor who could do this?"

"We sent for one, but we're running out of time."

"Out of time for what?"

"Out of time for you to have blood inside your body."

She watched him heating the needle in a nearby candle flame. "Do I really need blood, though?"

"Unfortunately, it's generally accounted a necessity for continued existence. I really am sorry about this, Belle." And then, to someone just beyond her blurry range of vision, "And I'm sorry about your kitchen table."

"I mean," said a woman's voice, low and laconic, "emergency surgery is what I keep it for."

Belle considered this, thoughts loose from alcohol and swimming disconnectedly around her brain. "It's not, is it? She's lying."

"She's being very accommodating. Now, er, be so good as to hold on to this wooden spoon."

"Wffmffteeef?"

"Mmm. Just bite down when you need to."

Belle made an incoherently concerned noise that turned into a guttural squawk as Rufus doused her exposed arm in what felt like several gallons of alcohol. This, it turned out, was even worse than having to drink it. She violently spat out the spoon. *"Ow."*

"Belle." Rufus heaved a sigh of abject despair.

"What?"

"Just do what someone else tells you. For once in your life. *Please.*"

This seemed unjust. "I do what people tell me."

"When?"

"There have been times."

"Name three."

There was a long silence.

"Why don't you think about it with this wooden spoon in your mouth?" suggested Rufus. "And then we can discuss how terribly wrong I am about everything afterwards?"

"I . . ." Something in Belle quailed, various fears, barely admitted to herself, coalescing onto the nearest available object. "I don't like the spoon. The spoon is scary."

Rufus sighed again. Fine tremors racked his whole body. "I know, dear heart, I know. But I need you to handle it for—"

"Mouthle it."

"Pardon?"

"Technically, you need me to mouthle it."

"Right." He curled his lips wanly. "Can you manage that for me?"

She pouted. "If I have to."

"You have to. I can't do . . . what I have to do if you're screaming and . . ." Again, that tragic sketch of a smile. "You don't want me to sew your arm on backwards, do you?"

It was then—far later than she would have done had she been sober and fully supplied with the recommended quantity of internal fluids—that she realised he was more upset by her pain than she was. With the closest a Tarleton could manage to meekness, she let him set the spoon between her lips, and was, in the end, glad of it, for she had sworn to herself, in that moment, she would not make a sound, and being able to grind her teeth into the soft wood meant that she did not.

Not a single cry. Nor a single whimper.

And Rufus worked quietly, and swiftly, his head bowed over her, the sweat caught in the furrows of his brow, pausing every now and again to steady his hands, dab away blood, or reheat the needle. Once to wipe his eyes.

She didn't, for all her oft-avowed pleasure in *I told you so*s, ponder specific occasions on which she had taken instruction. Mostly, she tried to think of things that made her happy. Her twin reading and being infuriating about it, covering the book in notes and inserting little pieces of paper to remember his favourite pages. The smug way Bonny gazed at Valentine and the wonder-struck way Valentine gazed back. The sound of rain drumming like fingertips on the leaves of her favourite oak tree. Orfeo's voice, soaring through impossible notes as effortless as a falcon in flight. And Peggy, of course. Her lost lover, her dear friend, who was never meant to stay, whose laughing she still missed, from times when it had been solely hers.

When next she surfaced, the pain was a steady—if unwelcome—companion, instead of a wild thing trying to claw its way through her skin. Her arm was tightly bandaged, and Rufus was washing his shaking, bloody hands in a basin. She meant to thank him and wanted to reassure him, but the world was wriggling away from her again. It didn't feel like last time. There was no swirling ascent to infinity. Just a ground-in fatigue that was familiar and wholly of the body, and she sank into it with unexpected gladness.

At some point, Rufus was carrying her. He seemed to be doing that a lot lately.

And then she was in a bed, with fresh-smelling sheets and soft pillows, and hopefully very few to no bugs of any kind. She wasn't sure if she was still drunk or utterly exhausted, but she had a vague memory of being encouraged—made—to drink water, which technically counted towards Rufus's list of Belle Doing What She'd Been Told. Mostly, she was content to drift and doze and dreamily watch the soft-footed to-and-fro of figures in her room, catching pieces of conversation like reflections from the corner of her eye. She thought a doctor came and went. And, sometime later, which might not have been much later at all, she opened her eyes to find Rufus standing by the fire, still shirtless and haggard, with Gil's highwayman cloak cast over his shoulders and Belle's blood matted in his hair.

"You should rest too," Gil was saying, which Belle agreed with.

"I don't know how I could."

"I think if you lie down, you'll find it comes easily to you."

"And what if she—"

"I can watch her."

Rufus pressed his brow against the mantel. "That's not your responsibility."

"I did shoot her? That surely makes me a little bit responsible." Gil gave a pointed cough. "Also, it's no hardship. She's been a lot nicer to me than you have."

"I didn't shoot you back. That makes me a lot nicer than you deserve."

There was a long silence. Or Belle fell asleep.

Gil had his hand on Rufus's arm. "You really care about her, don't you?"

"Arabella Tarleton?"

175

"No, some other woman whose bullet wound you just sewed up."

"She's a pain in my fucking arse."

With a huff of exasperation and an impatient motion, Rufus shook himself free, striding out of the room without another word.

And this, Belle supposed, was what you got for eavesdropping, even if it was unintentional. It was one of the laws of the universe, alongside a single man in possession of a good fortune always being in want of a wife or there only ever being one bed. Listening to conversations not meant for you inevitably subjected you to things you didn't want to hear. But she was too tired to be able to spend a lot of time delving into the recesses of her feelings. She was hurt, of course, yet it hardly seemed to matter. What she mainly was, was unsurprised. Being a pain in the arse seemed to be rather her inescapable destiny. To be fair, it was Bonny's, too, except he made it cute.

Not for the first time, she wondered how different life would be had her parents not died so suddenly. Her days of *blaming* them for that (and feeling guilty for blaming them) were behind her. Had passed with the night-long weeping fits and the months of numbness, where nothing in the world felt real, and she kept waiting to wake up and find everything put back to rights. Herself in her bed at home, Bonny beside her (for he always crept in), her father at his dressing table—for he had, she saw with an adult's eyes, always been vain—her mother in her sitting room, reading or sewing, both of them beloved in their ordinariness, safe to take for granted.

Bonny had learned to take other things for granted. She never had. She knew her aunt and uncle cared for them, but she also knew becoming the guardians of two grief-stricken children was something neither of them would have chosen. She knew Peggy had loved her once, and that this love, too, which she could not reciprocate, had become a burden. She knew Valentine wanted to do right by her, in recompense for past wrongs, but she also knew his ideal would have been to think of nothing but Bonny until the end of his days. For that matter, Bonny would probably have preferred to be living happily ever after with the duke of his dreams, and not worrying about his strange, unloveable, unloving sister. Orfeo, at least, had never concerned themself with her, or what others tended to perceive as her problems, but that was largely because they barely noticed she existed.

All of which meant it made sense that—in spite of his promise never to reproach her for their connection—she would be primarily an inconvenience to Rufus as well. She had tried not to be, and some of that inconvenience had been for his own good. Admittedly, that time she'd nearly let him get killed and eaten was not working in her favour. But when he hadn't been lamenting the travails of long-distance travel, he'd truly seemed happier the past few days. He wasn't trying to drink himself to death, at any rate. Did that not count for something?

Or maybe she was making excuses.

Maybe she'd been selfish again. Fucked everything up again. Dragged someone, yet again, into the Charybdis of her nonsense.

All because she was frightened of what could be taken from her next.

Of being inevitably and inescapably alone.

Chapter 18

Rufus made it into the corridor before his legs gave way under him, and he sank against the wall, knees pulled tight to his chest.

"You're supposed to be watching her," he snapped as Gil joined him a few minutes later.

"She's asleep. She's fine. You aren't."

"I'm not the one who got shot."

It was to Rufus's annoyance that his tired, whirling brain had taken this moment to recognise that Gil had a soft, mobile mouth. It was currently possessed of a too-knowing curve. "You seemed to take it harder than she did."

"I don't think it even occurred to her she was in danger."

"Oh, I think it did. She just didn't want to worry you."

Rufus could barely muster the energy to raise an eyebrow, so he twitched it instead. "You seem very taken with her, considering you nearly killed her. Maybe you should be eloping?"

"I would in a heartbeat, if she'd have me."

"Didn't think she was your type. Or are you flexible in your menacing?"

"Not at all." Lowering himself to the floor opposite, Gil crossed his legs neatly. "But that doesn't seem to be a problem for her. Are there many such women in the world?"

"Probably more than you'd think. Women who prefer other women. Women not interested in coitus. Women with better things to do than tolerate our bullshit."

"It had not before occurred to me to seek one."

A soft laugh worked its way up Rufus's throat. "You're unlikely to find another Arabella Tarleton."

"Well, I do not, in general, expect women to be interchangeable."

"No, but she's . . ." Rufus broke off, not sure what term would be appropriate. "You know, she's completely ruined my life?"

His companion offered a gently enquiring sound. "How so?"

"I mean, I've as good as jilted another lady. I'm likely disinherited. Her brother will probably never forgive me for running off with his sister. The brother's extremely rich, extremely powerful husband-in-everything-but-name will consequently condemn me also. And I had all these plans, Postlethwaite . . ."

"Plans?"

"Yes, I was going to be dutiful and decent, and as profoundly miserable as I deserve to be."

"And now that's off the table?"

"She makes it very difficult to be miserable."

"Monstrous of her."

"Isn't it?" Recollecting the indignity of being curled up against the skirting boards like a very large snail, Rufus extended his legs, his booted ankle brushing Gil's knee. "Especially considering I've loved her brother since I first laid eyes on him. It was in an inn, not so different from this one. He's very like her, but softer, and brighter, as though nothing sordid or cruel or debasing has ever touched him."

"Do you feel touched by those things?"

He asked too many questions, the damn bookseller. But Rufus was too exhausted, and too defenceless, to do anything other than answer. "Most of the time I feel touched *only* by those things."

"I'm truly sorry to hear that," said Gil, finally.

Rufus shrugged. "Strange words from a man whose primary interest lies in menacing."

"You realise you're only proving your lady correct."

"In what particular?"

"That you have not been properly menaced."

"Going to show me what I'm missing, are you?" The idea was not, in that instant, completely repugnant. He welcomed the idea of a body that was not bleeding, almost dying. Wanted something to overwhelm the memory of frayed skin and knotted thread. "It might be your only chance. I don't have much fight left in me."

"Good Lord." Gil sounded less than enthusiastic. "I said I had a wish to menace a man. Not molest him in a corridor." He stood, offering a hand to Rufus. "Come."

Rufus regarded the hand. "You would like to molest me somewhere else?"

"I would like to take you to bed."

"Doesn't seem very menacing, but I'm game."

"To sleep."

It took a moment for the meaning—for the rejection—to sink in. It was disconcerting, the way one could accumulate mountains of them, snowdrifts upon mountains of them, and yet they never failed to bite. Leave the memory of themselves behind. "You're unexpectedly choosy for someone attempting to arrange assignations by correspondence."

Gil's grip, as he hauled Rufus to his feet, was warm and sure. "Don't be nonsensical. You're quite one of the loveliest gentlemen I've ever laid eyes on."

"I?" said Rufus, dazedly, swaying slightly where he stood.

"Positively baroque. But if you're sincerely interested in me in return, I would at the very least like you to be awake."

"Fussy, fussy."

"And," Gil added, steering Rufus firmly into the room next to Belle's, "compos mentis enough not to regret it."

"If you think being in full control of my faculties is enough to stop me doing things I regret, you have either under- or over-estimated me quite considerably."

With a little push, Gil propelled him onto the bed. Rufus told himself he could have resisted, but he wasn't entirely sure what it was he would have been resisting. The second his body came into contact with something soft and supportive, his limbs turned to blancmange, and he folded onto the mattress in a boneless heap.

"Try to rest?" Gil suggested. "You were remarkable today."

He rolled his eyes. "I'm all to pieces, and I don't know why. I was in the army. I've stepped over the dying without looking back. Seen men blown apart. Bleed out."

"Did you care about any of them?"

"Experience has taught me not to make a habit of caring about anything."

Pulling the covers off the bed, Gil cast them over Rufus where he lay. "Well, you'll find it makes a difference."

"I think," said Rufus sleepily, "I preferred it when you couldn't say anything but *um*."

"I'd been played with, manipulated, stood up, attacked, and I'd recently shot someone. I was not at my best."

"And this is you at your best, is it?"

Gil seemed unperturbed by this transparent—indeed borderline Tarletonian—attempt to rankle him. "I would say this is me at my daily median. Me at my best seems to exist mostly in my head."

"At least he exists somewhere."

"Please. Your best self has been much in evidence today."

"Then your standards must be very low. I've not exactly been kind to you."

"I shot your fiancée. Kindness wasn't merited."

"Nevertheless, I was going out of my way to be unpleasant."

Leaning over him, Gil pushed a lock of hair away from his brow. "Beautiful people can get away with being a little unpleasant sometimes. Besides, I can see how you adore her."

Some very tragic part of Rufus's brain noticed the word *beautiful* and wanted to hold on to it like an urchin with a farthing. The rest of his brain, thankfully, possessed enough wherewithal to dismiss it, though this left his mouth disgorging words without supervision. "We've been engaged for less than a week. I wasn't prepared to lose her. For the idea that I *could*." He let out a sound, half mirth, half pain. "There's something about them, Belle and her damn brother. Stubbornness or naiveté, I've never worked it out. But it feels like the rules should be different for them, somehow."

"In what way?"

"Oh . . . you know, fairy-tale rules. The good end happily, the bad end unhappily, dragons are defeated, princes are kissed, love conquers all."

"And nobody," Gil finished for him, "gets their arm grazed by a stray bullet while grappling with a bookseller dressed as a highwayman?"

Rufus inclined his head in vague assent.

"You saved her. What more can you expect of yourself?"

"And the next time?"

"Perhaps she'll save you. Or she already has."

"Or I'm not worth the gamble she's taken on me and she'll regret our union, and the few people who've ever thought passingly well of me will hate me for it."

There was the slightest of pauses. "The brother again?"

"Mmm."

"You recognise, of course, that you cannot win the favour of one with the other?"

At that, Rufus actually laughed, and laughed unhindered. "Is that what you think is happening here? Don't be absurd. Bonny's never given me a second glance and never will."

Gil offered a crooked half smile. "You talk about him a lot."

"Unrequited love, I'm afraid, turns one tedious."

"I wouldn't know."

"You've never been in love?"

"I'm not in a rush to be."

"Too preoccupied with menacing?" Rufus asked, not sure whether he was trying to be teasing or derisory.

"For the moment."

"To be honest"—kicking off his boots, Rufus dragged himself into a more comfortable position on the bed—"I think it's mostly habit with me at this point. I probably wouldn't know who I was anymore if there wasn't someone to make me feel worthless."

Picking up the boots, Gil placed them neatly by the door. "Perhaps you could consider it?"

"Sorry," said Rufus with a touch of unearned irritation, "my head's a little fuzzy because I just had to sew up a woman's arm before she bled out on a kitchen table. Consider what?"

"Finding out who you are in the company of those who don't make you feel worthless."

"Well, I'm about to marry one. Though God knows what she sees in me."

"I think she sees someone who saved her life today."

"So what you're saying," returned Rufus, sulky with exhaustion, "is that I'll be a fantastic husband when she's in mortal danger."

"Yes"—Gil gave him the sort of look he thoroughly deserved—"that's exactly what I'm saying." But then his expression softened, and he went on treacherously, "You know, as part of your resolution to spend time with those who treat you well, you might also consider being a little kinder to yourself."

Rufus threw a sheltering hand across his eyes. "Maybe when I do something to merit it."

"I don't think you should have to earn—"

"For God's sake," Rufus snapped. "Arabella Tarleton has probably treated me better than anyone in my entire life, and I did nothing to protect her today."

"I do not know the lady as you do." Gil's voice was almost unbearably gentle. "But I get the sense she needs your friendship far more than she needs your protection."

"And I am getting the sense," said Rufus from beneath his arm, terrified that he might start weeping, "that you ought to fuck off."

"Then I'll be with Miss Tarleton."

"Wake me if anything changes. *Anything.*"

"I promise."

The door closed behind Gil with a click.

Despite his exhaustion, Rufus's thoughts swirled unhelpfully for long minutes. Strange how quickly you could grow accustomed to things. Even relatively inconsequential ones like sharing space. One would have thought, after long days in a carriage with Belle, he would want distance, not increased closeness. But she had awoken some brutal, terrifying hunger in him, and now he missed the certainty of her body tucked behind him, the tickle of her hair against his neck, the possessive, protective arm thrown across his waist. He missed her scent and her breath. He missed being held. He even missed the fairly extensive conversations she would have with herself sometimes while deeply asleep. The cold little feet she would plunge mercilessly between his knees as though she had the absolute right to his body heat.

Since Belle had been shot, he had been clinging to anger like driftwood. Gil's foolishness. Her recklessness. How this was all somehow typical of the Tarletons. Because . . . it was? But that was fading now, breaking apart between his fingers as he lay alone in the dark, in an unfamiliar room, the events of the day—the sound of the pistol, Belle growing colder and colder in his arms, her blood on his hands—spinning through his head in an endless, agonising waltz until all that remained was fear.

Something Extraordinary

Particularly useless fear, even by the standards of that specific emotion, because it couldn't change anything. It could only strike out of nowhere like a snake and fill him full of poison, for he could so easily have lost Belle today. A thought which might, not so very long ago, have felt in some dark way freeing, not that he would ever have wanted something quite so catastrophic to happen to her. Now, though, it just made him feel a kind of pre-emptive grief. For the possibility of a life he still could not truly picture, and would never have chosen, but which nevertheless gleamed richly with the promise of unimagined, undared contentment.

Chapter 19

Unlike Valentine—who, as had previously been established, was a damp lily—Belle felt she made a strong recovery. Part of it, of course, was she had only been grazed, whereas Valentine had needed a bullet dug out of his shoulder. Still, the fever and the whining, she was sure, had been entirely his own doing. She had been very weak for a couple of days, mostly from the blood loss, but she was soon able to sit in the front parlour, wrapped in shawls and blankets.

It was, all things considered, a very nice inn to be stranded at, being spacious, well kept, and situated on the outskirts of a village, which meant the clientele was lively and comfortable, instead of merely passing through in a state of resentful fatigue. They had been able to scrape together the means to pay for their stay from what was left of Belle's money, alongside a contribution from Gil. Rufus had been predictably quick to point out the irony that their would-be robber was now financing them, but Gil had pointed out back that, if he hadn't shot Belle and delayed them, they wouldn't have required financing.

"Aren't you needed in your bookshop, though?" Belle asked.

"My sister is looking after things." Gil went a little pink about the ears and nose. "She thinks I'm meeting with an eccentric collector in, um, Fort William. So I should not return too soon."

"You must have been envisioning *quite* the fuckfest," drawled Rufus.

Gil shrugged. "What can I say? Hope springs eternal."

"That is precisely the correct way for hope to spring." Belle turned her attention from Gil to Rufus. "You know, I increasingly think your problem is not so much that your figurative glass is half-empty; it's that you don't possess a glass at all."

"If one does not possess a glass, one can never be disappointed in the glass. Now"—he rose and moved briskly to Belle's side—"how about we stop critiquing my philosophical stance on the abstract concept of optimism and I check your stitches?"

As impatiently as she dared, since impulsive movements still caused her considerable pain, Belle extricated her arm. "What are you expecting to find?"

"Ideally, no gangrene. And my sutures to have spontaneously improved."

"Oh, they look fine."

"They do not look fine."

Dropping to one knee, he untied the makeshift sling he had made from the remains of his shirt and carefully began unwinding the bandages. "I'm so sorry, Belle."

"I like them." She squinted at her upper arm, which was currently rather a mess of knots and thread but carried—as far as she could tell—no signs of infection and would likely heal into an impressively jagged scar. "It will be piratical. Don't you think I shall look piratical, Gil?"

"Splendidly," he agreed. "Soon all the other young ladies will be jealous."

"And"—Rufus, bent over her wound, barely spared Gil a glance—"you may volunteer yourself to shoot them." His fingers moved with exquisite care over the stitches. "Is there any additional tenderness? I can't feel any swelling or heat."

"No additional tenderness," Belle told him. "I am quite well. How long are you going to persist with this?"

"Until I am absolutely certain you are out of danger."

"And I thought I was supposed to be the pain in the arse in this relationship."

His eyes flicked up to hers, his expression confused, even a little hurt. "Pardon?"

"Nothing." If she had been in a position to kick herself, she would have. She had no idea why that had slipped out. Perhaps it was his solicitousness in spite of his frustration with her that felt so unexpectedly hurtful. "Gil," she called out, by way of distraction.

"Yes?"

"If you're supposed to be visiting a fellow antiquarian, won't it be a little suss if you come back empty-handed?"

"Ah. Well." He smiled, with a kind of bashful approximation of guile. "I did actually think of that."

"A scheme," cried Belle, who was sincerely excited by schemes in general, but also eager to move the conversation past her earlier foolishness. "I do love a scheme."

Rufus gave her a look. "Who? You? Never."

"I wouldn't say it was a scheme," demurred Gil hastily, "so much as a mild degree of forethought. I happened to independently source a first edition of *Memoirs of a Woman of Pleasure* from 1749 that I can claim to have, um, purchased from my imaginary collector."

Belle gasped. "Wait. Does this mean you've been running about all this time with a naughty book tucked in your trousers?"

"Not in my trousers. Such treatment would be very bad for the book."

"Is that proscribed material?" While Rufus was still ostensibly engaged in settling Belle's arm back in its sling, it was obvious he was smirking. "Or are you just pleased to see me."

"Can we perhaps discuss the matter with some circumspection? I have no more wish to be prosecuted for possession of an illicit publication than I do for highway robbery."

"I have never read an illicit story," said Belle, with one of her most tragic sighs.

"How unfortunate for you."

She nodded. "Yes, it is such a shame I know no-one with access to any."

"I am not your . . . your textual panderer."

"But"—she pushed out her lower lip, letting her lashes fall low—"you shot me."

"Leave the poor man alone, Bellflower." Rising, Rufus dropped a kiss upon the top of her head and returned to his seat.

"Must I?"

"Yes. You cannot go around haranguing people for pornography."

"I mean, I *can*. I am just yet to be met with success."

Gil glanced between them, brow faintly furrowed. "Do you think I haven't noticed the way you take turns to harangue me? You are like two cats with a mouse."

"It is how we show love," said Belle, at the same time Rufus offered, "It is because we are terrible people."

Their eyes locked, Belle smiling first, then Rufus.

"Both," she suggested. "It can be both."

"Both," he agreed.

Gil laughed, shaking his head, as though unable to decide whether he was amused by them or exasperated by them, which was—in Belle's experience—pretty standard. "If I had a better book, Miss Tarleton, I would share it."

"Oh." Somehow this was even worse than not being allowed to read it. She'd been looking forward to boasting to Bonny about having got her hands on something naughty and forbidden, but what was the point if it turned out disappointing? "Why was it banned, then?"

"For the same reason most things are: fear and ignorance. In this case, I suspect it has something to do with the fact the book takes as axiomatic that women can be creatures of pleasure just as men can."

It was depressing the way time marched on, and nothing changed as much as you hoped it might. Or could. "And yet," she asked, "it is not worth reading?"

There was a pause, Gil biting his lip, obviously conflicted. "You may if you wish. It's not really my place to decide for you. Though try not to, you know, fold the pages back or spill beans over it. Very few copies of this book are still in circulation."

"Surely it will be unbanned sometime soon?"

"Surely," echoed Gil, though he did not sound very convinced on the matter.

"Well, the idea of a woman liking sex can't remain so very shocking, can it? I expect we can figure that out in, say, less than a hundred and fifty years."

"Oh please." Rufus swiped his hand disdainfully through the air, as though dismissing the decades to come. "A hundred and fifty years to concede that women are people? Give us two hundred and ten, and we will probably still be banning books and hating each other."

Belle turned to Gil in despair. "You see what I mean? Absolutely no glass to speak of."

"I fear his cynicism is not wholly without merit. But"—and here Gil raised an imaginary glass of his own—"I shall nevertheless join you in hoping for better from posterity."

As topics of conversations went, it was not one easily followed. Misliking the silence, as she was often wont to do, Belle was the first to speak up. "If you don't mind me asking, Gil, what do you find so objectionable in this particular book?"

"I wouldn't say I found *Fanny Hill* objectionable. It's more that . . ." His head drooped, curls falling forward into his eyes. "It makes me sad."

Belle blinked. "That seems a particularly damning indictment of an obscene text."

"Well, what is obscenity, really? Perhaps the work of someone like de Sade, which speaks less of pleasure than of contempt, and, even less forgivably, is tedious to read. But no, Cleland's work is mostly exuberant. And nothing but imaginative when it comes to terms for the, the . . ." Perhaps recalling where he was, and with whom he spoke, Gil turned a painful shade of scarlet and pointed a finger in a generally "downwards" direction.

"Dick?" offered Rufus, helpfully. "Cock? Rampant fuckstick? All-dissolving thunderbolt."

"Yes. *That*."

"When you say *imaginative*"—Belle's curiosity had now been thoroughly stirred—"do you mean more or less imaginative than *rampant fuckstick*?"

"I would say, more euphemistic? Plenipotentiary instrument? Stiff staring truncheon. Engine of love-assaults?"

"And yet somehow you do not relish this?"

"There's a scene near the end," said Rufus abruptly, "where the heroine witnesses two young men together and is so disgusted by the sight she passes out, lamenting afterwards that she was unable to bring them to the swift justice they so clearly deserved for engaging in such an unnatural and debasing act."

"Oh." Belle's interest waned with nauseating rapidity, leaving only guilt and discomfort behind. "Oh. Yes. I can see how the presence of such content would preclude relish."

"And this," Rufus went on, "from a narrator who, as far as I can recall, engages in all manner of acts with men and women, including group sex and flagellation. And yet two young men engaging in what is clearly a consensual and mutually pleasurable exchange are fit only for the most vicious scorn."

"It upset me when I read it," Gil admitted. "Because it is prettily described, and I found it stirring—I felt there was tenderness in it, with an exchange of kisses and the elder playing wantonly with the other's curls as he entered him. And then . . ."

His voice trailed away, and fresh silence fell between them.

"Perhaps"—it was Belle again who broke it—"the author felt he could not include it *unless* he was shown to condemn it after?"

Gil gave a faint smile. "It is *quite* the condemnation."

"I do not doubt it. But there were still choices he could have made that he did not, choices that could have supported a negative perspective rather than confusing it."

Both Gil and Rufus were staring at her.

"I'm not defending him," she went on quickly. "Merely pointing out he could have portrayed the encounter as predatory or . . . or worse. He could have excised any of the details that pleased you or portrayed their coitus as distressing or unpleasant."

Slumping back in his chair, Rufus uttered a despairing groan. "Not everything needs to be championed, Belle, nor should it be."

"I am not," she protested. "I am simply considering that there may have been complexities to the situation we are not privy to."

"Reactive abhorrence is simple by its very nature."

"Possibly." That was Gil. "But it's still an intriguing thought, Miss Tarleton. One I was myself too flustered and . . . and hurt, in the moment, to consider."

"You're as hopeless as each other," muttered Rufus.

"I don't think it is *we* who are hopeless," Belle retorted.

"Ridiculous, then." He paused, regarding them both with an expression Belle could not read. It seemed . . . searching, almost? Then he relented, his mouth softening. "Perhaps the publication of Cannon's *Ancient and Modern Pederasty* that very same year also had some impact."

Belle tilted her head enquiringly. "Cannon's what now?"

"It is, I believe," explained Gil, "a defence of the love that some men feel for other men, on the philosophical grounds that what exists in nature is right and just, and that there cannot therefore be such a thing as unnatural desire, because desire is itself entirely natural. But that is all I can tell you. I have only been able to find fragments of the work, for the writer and the printer were both arrested on charges of indecency, and all copies ordered destroyed."

"There may additionally be some passages celebrating the"—Rufus, who did not usually mince words, gave a light cough—"male passage. And its potent Cling."

Gil cast a doleful look at the ceiling. "Well, I wouldn't know."

"How unfortunate for you."

"Don't you mean the passage?" Belle piped up, having been pursuing a different thought.

Rufus turned towards her, startled. "I beg your pardon?"

"You said *male passage*, but we all have that passage, and I can assure you the cling is equally potent."

"You . . . you have had opportunity to . . ." Gil was reduced to flailing and blushing.

Taking pity on him, Belle nodded. "Oh yes. Like most such activities, it has little to do with whether a person has a cock or wears a dress or both or neither, and everything to do with what an individual enjoys. Or"—she smirked—"is receptive to."

Gil gave a small wail. "Why does it feel like everyone in the world has entered effortlessly into that which I crave so ardently?"

"No, no," Rufus reassured him, "not everyone in the world. Merely everyone in this room."

"Are you sure you want to marry this man?" Gil asked.

"Yes," Rufus answered for her, which was not the kind of thing Belle usually appreciated but on this very specific subject was willing to let go. "Yes she is. Moreover, I shall now demonstrate my regard for both of you by reminding my affianced that she needs to rest. That should, in turn, spare some of your blushes, Gil."

"His blushes are adorable," said Belle, "so I see no benefit in sparing them. Also, I'm not tired and I don't want to rest."

"So you claim. And then you fall asleep in the corner."

"I'd rather fall asleep in the corner. Being in bed by yourself and during the daytime is *boring*."

"Belle—"

"My corner, my choice."

"Belle—"

"If you pick me up, I shall scream and bite you."

"I wasn't going to." *Clearly* he had been going to. "But," he added, "for future reference, screaming and biting tend to be mutually exclusive."

"Your face," she told him haughtily, "is mutually exclusive."

"What does that even mean?"

"I . . . have no notion. It just sounded insulting." Unfortunately, Belle could feel herself beginning to flag. The only thing worse than someone trying to convince you to do something you didn't want to do was them being in the right about it. "Ten more minutes?" she pleaded, as though she was eight years old again, and not wanting to put out her candle at bedtime. "Let us do something entertaining for ten more minutes, and then I shall retire without further complaint."

Rufus's eyes narrowed suspiciously. "Define *entertaining*."

"Let's play a game."

"Oh, I love games," said Gil.

"We're aware," Rufus threw back.

"Let's play *the game*," Belle suggested.

Rufus whipped back to face her. "Belle, no. The last time we played *the game*, you got shot."

"And what is the likelihood of such a thing happening twice?"

"With you? About fifty-fifty."

"What is, um, *the game*?" asked Gil, glancing between them.

"It's the best game," Belle declared. "How it works is that the next person to pass before the door on their way to the taproom becomes one of our lovers hypothetically, and we must explain to the others how such an encounter would proceed and what would be the consequences."

Gil considered. "Do they get a say in the matter?"

"Well, no," Belle admitted. "But only because they are fictionalised versions of themselves."

He squirmed in his chair. "This feels as though it could have the potential to become a little hurtful."

"You'd think that," said Rufus wearily, "but so far its only victim has been Arabella herself."

"See." Her store of gestures was somewhat curtailed, so she tried to toss her hair with vindication. "It's perfectly safe. What happened last time was an inexplicable aberration, and this time there can be absolutely no such—"

Footsteps resounded in the hallway.

A young man flung into the room, hand upon the hilt of his sword.

"Sir Horley Comewithers?" His burning midnight blue gaze raked over each of them before settling upon Rufus. "You have defiled my sister, sir, and I will have satisfaction."

Chapter 20

A frozen silence descended upon the parlour. Rufus, who had been lounging in a wingback chair by the fireplace, continued lounging in a wingback chair by the fireplace. Crossing one leg over the other, he regarded the visitor placidly.

"Not today, thank you, Valour."

The stranger, who could only have been Miss Carswile's brother, was brought up short by this response. "W-wait. What?"

Rufus seemed to have become distracted by the speck of dust upon the cuff of his borrowed coat. "I have not defiled your sister. I wouldn't even know where to begin."

"I could give you some tips if you like?" Belle offered.

"That is very kind of you," returned Rufus politely. "But given my unshakeable proclivities, I prefer to restrict my defilements to brothers." His eyes flicked wickedly back to Mr. Carswile. "How about it? Can I interest you in a mortal sin or two?"

Belle watched the young man with interest. She had never seen anyone spontaneously combust before. His mouth dropped open, words falling out of it like apples in a windstorm. "You . . . you openly admit your . . . your . . . your . . ."

"If you can't say it," murmured Rufus, "you don't get to complain about it."

Mr. Carswile stilled, his face very pale and set. "I told Verity she should not debase herself entangling with a creature like you. I am not, however, pleased to be proven correct. How dare you jilt my sister, you piece of abject human filth. She is worth a hundred, no a thousand, of you."

"I will not dispute that."

"I dispute it," put in Belle. "No human being is worth any more or any less than any other."

"Then"—ignoring her completely, Mr. Carswile descended upon Rufus, sword drawn—"you will grant me satisfaction."

Gently, Rufus pushed the blade aside. His voice was equally gentle as he said, "I will not."

"I . . . beg your pardon?" Once again, Mr. Carswile was nonplussed. "What do you mean *you will not*."

"I mean precisely what I say: I will not."

"Then you are a coward, sir, as well as a deviant."

Rufus shrugged. "Indeed."

"Did you not hear me?" demanded Mr. Carswile. "I called you a coward."

"I did hear you call me that, yes."

A new commingling of rage and bewilderment twisted the young man's features. "Do you have no pride?"

"I think"—Rufus tilted his head back, better to meet the gaze of his interlocutor—"you have confused the question of whether I have pride, which I may not, with the question of whether I care what you say of me, which I certainly do not."

"This is a matter of honour. It concerns what all right-thinking men will say of you."

Lifting his hand delicately to his mouth, Rufus stifled a yawn. "As you are at such pains to point out, I am a lost cause to right-thinking men already."

"Damn it, you . . . you . . ."

197

"Degenerate?" Rufus offered. "Caudlemaker? Sodomite? Catamite?"

"Will you answer me or no?"

"I *have* answered you. Several times, actually."

"Will you," persisted Mr. Carswile, "meet me upon the field of honour?"

"No," said Rufus.

There was a long silence, broken only by Mr. Carswile's harsh breathing as he leaned over Rufus.

After a moment or two, Gil cleared his throat. "I don't mean to interrupt, but I'm a little confused. Is this some kind of theatrical performance?"

"In every sense but the actual. This"—Rufus indicated the man before him—"is Mr. Valour Carswile. He is the younger brother of Miss Verity Carswile, the lady I was engaged to before I ran away with Miss Tarleton here."

"I confess," said Gil, "I am no less confused. For a gentleman with such a marked partiality for gentlemen, you seem to be involved with a lot of ladies."

Rufus sighed. "Believe me, I am as baffled by this as you are."

"It makes perfect sense," added Belle, who was highly relieved she hadn't gone to bed. "In *context*." And then, to Rufus, "I think you had better fight him, you know. He has said some very nasty and untrue things about you."

"I am not fighting anyone. Let alone on so slight a pretext."

"Is it slight? He has impugned—"

"Nothing of significance. Though"—and here he inched away from Mr. Carswile—"he is cleaving a little close for comfort."

Mr. Carswile reared back, as though struck or kissed. "Am I to understand you are *declining*?"

"Your marked incapacity to comprehend the word *no* is beginning to seriously concern me, Valour. For the last fucking time, yes, I am declining. I will not fight you."

"Because you are a coward?"

"As you've said."

"And a villain?"

"Apparently."

"A man without honour."

"If you insist."

"And indeed no man at all."

Rufus's lips curled into the most contemptuous sneer Belle had ever seen them wear, and he had quite a line in contemptuous sneers when needed. "Why is it," he said musingly, "that the greatest insult my sex can muster is to exile one from it? Where lies the great virtue in being a man? What is the great shame in being other than one?"

"I am not here," exclaimed Mr. Carswile, pushed to new heights of fury, "to engage in sophistry with a . . . with a . . . with *you*."

"Are you sure you won't duel him?" asked Belle. "He's being very annoying."

"Bellflower"—there was a note of unusual gravity in Rufus's voice—"let us not treat instruments of death any more lightly than we already have upon this journey."

"Couldn't you just stab him or shoot him a little bit?"

"He is a callow youth. I am a moderately seasoned soldier. There is no good outcome for either of us if we meet in violence."

"What did you call me?" snapped Mr. Carswile.

"Nothing less true, nor more insulting than the things you have called me, my dear."

"It is astonishing to me that Wellington would *ever* honour someone like you."

"That's the thing." Rufus accompanied the words with a languid gesture. "On the battlefield, where you stick your prick matters a lot less than where you stick your sabre."

The young man drew himself to his full height, which was quite impressive, for he probably cut a fine figure when not infuriated beyond reason. "I will not stand for this. I cannot."

"Learn," suggested Rufus.

"And perhaps"—Gil spoke up unexpectedly—"consider that the things of which you are accusing Sir Horley here are fundamentally incompatible with each other."

"Who the hell are you?" Mr. Carswile rounded on the bookseller.

"Um, nobody. Um, a friend. Maybe? But . . . but *logically*, the sort of gentleman whose tastes incline him towards other gentlemen is not the sort of gentleman to imperil a lady's virtue."

"This isn't about *logic*. It is about honour. And decency."

Gil twitched nervously. "I feel those things should probably bear at least *some* relation to each other?"

"What you feel," cried Mr. Carswile, "is wholly irrelevant to me. And as for you"—he spun back to Rufus—"I am done with your prevarications." With that, he delivered a sharp slap to Rufus's cheek—a blow intended for insult as much as injury. "Now what have you to say for yourself?"

Rufus patted gingerly at his face. "Ow?"

Mr. Carswile struck him again, the sound of it unnaturally loud in that bright, ordinary room.

"Please do stop hitting me; there's a good fellow."

"I will stop hitting you," snarled Mr. Carswile, "when"—slap—"you"—slap—"give"—slap—"me"—slap—"satisf—"

He got no further. Rufus was out of the chair in one swift, sure movement, his hand closing around the young man's wrist as he levered it behind his back, the position sufficiently unforgiving as to wring a strangled yelp from his would-be assailant.

"I see you had the right of it as usual, Belle," Rufus remarked, not even out of breath. "He is *very* annoying."

Then he marched Mr. Carswile, whose resistance had been reduced solely to the vocal, out of the room.

"Oh my," said Gil, in the wake of their departure.

He was looking, Belle thought, even more flushed than usual. "Are you quite well?" she asked.

"Mostly. I mean, not really. That was . . . that was, um, really quite unreasonably attractive, wasn't it?"

"I certainly enjoyed it, though I'm sorry I didn't get to witness a proper duel. The last one I attended was an absolute bust."

"You have contrived to live an extraordinarily eventful life, Miss Tarleton."

She was not accustomed to thinking of her life in such terms; mostly she spent it chafing against its restrictions. Then again, perhaps everyone did, in their way. "I have done my best," she said aloud. "But it has not always brought me happiness."

"I hope that will change for you."

"I had hoped to change it for others also. For Rufus at least. Unfortunately, that, too, seems out of my power."

"He adores you."

"He feels entrapped by me."

"I think . . ." Gil's gaze drifted to the open doorway through which Rufus had propelled his captive. "I think he is a complicated man. And complicated men are not always the best judges of their own needs."

"And some men," said Belle archly, "need to be better judges of each other."

His eyes went wide. "Surely you can't mean—Miss Tarleton, he would never."

"Never what?"

"Allow it. Look upon me favourably."

To that, she delivered a huff of well-earned scorn. "Well. If that isn't the silliest thing I've heard today, and we just had someone in here shouting about manliness and iniquity."

She might have said more—or she might not; it was not, after all, her job to bridge the foolishness of her friends—but it was at this juncture that Rufus returned, slightly tousled but otherwise unharmed.

"Well, Bellflower," he said. "We may count this interlude as your ten minutes of entertainment."

"Oh, we may, may we?" It was a halfhearted protest at best, for Belle really was more than ready to retire.

"Come, dear heart."

He lifted her into his arms, blanket included, making her feel like the cosiest of all the fairy-tale princesses. As a general rule, she was not a fan of being picked up. Her male lovers often liked to, because she was small and dainty, and it seemed to fulfil some deep-seated desire they bore to be physically overpowering. With Rufus, though, she had decided she liked it. There was something . . . safe about it when it was him. It made her feel treasured. An illusion, of course, because you did not treasure what was forced upon you. But even the illusion she had not been able to bring herself to give up.

They had not made it three paces across the room before there came the rapid staccato of new footsteps in the corridor outside. And there was barely even time to exchange "What now?" glances before Miss Carswile, travelling cloak streaming behind her, raced through the door, threw herself to her knees, and cried out, "Please, I beg you, have mercy, do not kill my brother."

Chapter 21

Rufus was the first to break the slightly stunned silence. "What in God's name is going on today? Miss Carswile, nobody is killing your brother."

"Then"—she glanced up, her beautiful eyes wild—"where is he?"

"In the water trough in the stable yard, thinking about what he's done."

"Oh. *Oh.*" Miss Carswile sat back on her heels, one hand pressed to her heart as she tried to steady her breathing. "What a relief. He swore blind he would challenge you."

"I was not," Rufus told her, "particularly inclined to be challenged."

"Well. Thank you. That was very kind."

"I'm, um, sorry to interrupt again," said Gil. "But is *this* a theatrical performance?"

Rufus shook his head and bore Belle, who was looking pale and droopy, away to bed. As he got her settled, she reached out, curling her fingers weakly over his wrist.

"You will be careful, won't you?" she said.

"I always am."

Her fingers tightened. "You are absolutely *not.*"

"Miss Carswile cannot hurt me, Belle."

"Can't she?"

"I do not get the sense she wishes to."

"That doesn't stop people from doing so. Also," she went on urgently, "I have been thinking about it, and it was probably wrong of me to encourage you to duel Mr. Carswile."

"A Tarleton?" He lifted his brows. "Probably in the wrong?"

"It does happen," she admitted. "*Rarely.* But I was being selfish. I had not fully considered the consequences, nor how it would make you feel to bring harm to another person."

She had flustered him, as she had been doing all too often of late. In trafficking with Tarletons, one accepted that this kind of heedlessness was part of their charm. Indeed—baser considerations aside—it had been some element of what drew him to Bonny, for he had always seemed so very *free*, when Rufus felt anything but. The boundless care, however, offered with the same freedom, was unexpected. Or had perhaps simply gone unrecognised because it had always come from the sister rather than the brother. "Don't worry. I have no intention of duelling with anyone."

"We will bear whatever slights he casts upon your reputation together."

"That's very wifely of you," he said, smiling. "But since I introduced him to the water trough, I do not think Mr. Carswile will wish to speak widely of these events."

She gave a great yawn, unselfconscious as a cat. "Would that I could have seen his face."

"I will do an impression for you . . ."

"Will you?"

"After you've rested."

"Oh. Bribery, is it?"

"Yes." He leant down and put his lips to her brow. "Now fucking well go to sleep."

Returning to the parlour, he found only Miss and Mr. Carswile in situ. The latter was gratifyingly drenched and accompanied by the unmistakable aroma of horse.

"—will not apologise to that degenerate," he was saying, as he dripped onto the hearthrug.

Miss Carswile, having recovered much of her composure, had taken a seat upon the little sofa Gil had previously occupied. At his entrance, she addressed herself to Rufus. "Your companion has tactfully gone for a walk. And my brother will apparently not apologise to a degenerate."

"That is quite all right. The degenerate neither seeks nor desires an apology. You should, however, tender one to your sister."

The young man continued to drip, though now with a faint air of outrage. "On what grounds?"

"For putting her in fear for your life. And for doing your utmost to turn her into a subject for gossip and speculation."

"You did that when you cast her aside on the eve of your wedding."

Rufus sighed. "And duelling over it will help the situation how?"

"He's right," said Miss Carswile. "This was immeasurably foolish of you, Valour."

"What was I supposed to do?" Her brother's manner was slipping inexorably from righteousness to sullenness. "Let him discard you like yesterday's newspaper?"

She turned her too-sharp gaze upon him. "Are you concerned for my feelings or simply insulted by proxy?"

"I . . . I . . ."

"That's what I thought."

"Verity, I . . ."

Her self-control slipped a bare inch. "Oh, please just dry off and go back to Cambridge, Val. Though heaven knows what they're teaching you there because it doesn't seem to be common sense."

"It's ancient Greek," retorted Mr. Carswile, which was not perhaps the damning line he had intended upon which to make his exit.

Nevertheless, exit he did, leaving Rufus alone with his former fiancée for perhaps the first time. At least the first he could recall, since he had spent the months preceding their wedding in a state of mild to excessive inebriation. It had not, he would be the first to concede, been well done of him.

Miss Carswile was much as he remembered—a sharp-angled woman, slightly beyond what fashion deemed marriageable age. She had been described to him as handsome, but he had never quite been able to see it. There was, perhaps, too much about her that reminded him of his aunt. Austerity, pride, and cold watching eyes. Then again, he was hardly a connoisseur of female beauty. For most of their acquaintance, he had taken it for granted that what he mostly saw in Belle was the echo of Bonny.

"I suppose," he said aloud, "I owe you an apology."

Her lips, which were elegant more than they were generous, thinned. "I *suppose* you do."

She was not his aunt, he knew that, but some part of him reacted as though she was, with shrivelling shame and seething resentment. Pushing such sentiments aside, he offered with what dignity and sincerity he could muster, "I am sorry for breaking our engagement the way I did."

It was not, however, the right thing to say. The chill of her brilliant eyes intensified. "Is that why you think you owe me an apology?"

"Well"—he risked a light laugh—"not if you don't, my dear."

"Please," she said tightly, "can you at least *try* to give some consideration to my feelings?"

"I would if I knew what they were. Of course I can see you're annoyed with me, and I do not pretend it's anything other than justified."

"I'm so glad we agree on something."

"But"—he wished he could have steadied the words, wished he could have said them to his aunt, to any number of people, to the whole damn world—"I cannot . . . I will not . . . apologise for who I am."

"Do you think I am asking that from you?"

"Frankly, I have no idea what you're asking."

Abruptly she rose, taking a few swift turns about the room. "I am not upset at the ending of our engagement because we should never have been engaged in the first place."

"My aunt didn't leave me much choice."

"Oh, please." He had never heard such sharpness in her voice before. "Try being a woman for five minutes and then lecture me about choices."

"Try being a sodomite."

She paused at that. "Are we in opposition, then, Sir Horley?"

"What do you mean?"

"Does my wish to live a life of truth and dignity impinge upon your wish for the same?"

"I mean," he said, laughing, "if you think that's what I've been aiming for, you're drastically mistaken."

Her lip curled, and even Rufus could admit she was rather magnificent in her scorn. "Clearly it hasn't been. But running away with Miss Tarleton seems to have at least been honest."

"To be fair"—and this time the amusement was real, soft with affection—"she didn't give me much choice either."

"Could you not at least have spoken to me?"

"About eloping with another woman?"

"About any of it. At any point."

"Would you have listened?" he asked mildly. "You gave every impression of being entirely committed to the salvation of my mortal soul."

"Should I not have been?"

"With all due respect, ma'am, the condition of my soul is none of your business."

"And if you were walking along a mountain road and you met a stranger, dangling by their fingertips from the cliff edge, you would also consider that none of your business?"

He gazed at her in mingled frustration and confusion. "Of course not. I wouldn't just leave someone in harm's way if it lay in my power to help them."

"Well, that is how I feel"—her eyes were steady upon his, unflinching—"about those who have fallen from God's grace."

"And I've fallen from God's grace because I seek the love of men, not women?"

"You have fallen from God's grace because you deny yourself *all* love. Or so I thought."

"How nice to know I'm moving up in the Lord's estimation."

She just sighed and shook her head. "You have treated me with disregard verging on contempt, Sir Horley. The distaste you hold for my faith does not excuse that."

"I . . ." The fact of the matter was, she was right. He knew she was right. But there was a curdled bitterness inside him that made saying the necessary words feel almost impossible.

Her eyes searched his face. "Do you believe me so deserving of hurt?"

"Do you believe that of me?"

"I believe that of no-one." For a second so brief he wasn't sure he imagined it, her self-possession faltered again, and her hand crept to the crucifix she wore about her neck. "I did not agree to marry you to hurt you, Sir Horley."

"No, you agreed to marry me to save me from something I don't need saving from."

"You did not tell me otherwise. When your absurd friends kidnapped us, you insisted to them that they were wrong. That you wanted my help."

"At the time, I thought . . . I thought they *were* wrong. I thought I was worth no better."

There was a long silence. And then, "How dare you." Miss Carswile's voice trembled with suppressed rage. "You may not like me, and you may like yourself even less, but how dare you treat me like a *punishment*."

"For my aunt's purposes, you were."

Her hand came up. And froze, shaking in the space between them.

"Are you going to hit me?" enquired Sir Horley, with gentle interest. "Will this cheek do, or should I turn the other?"

To his horror, she did not. Instead, she dropped back onto the sofa and burst into tears.

Chapter 22

For someone who disliked sleeping, even at night when you were sup-posed to, Belle had been peacefully resting, her arm braced against a mound of pillows so she didn't accidentally jar it. Except then Rufus woke her up by muttering her name urgently and at increasing volume directly into her ear until she stirred.

"Whuzzerat?"

"I need your help," he said.

"Why?"

"Well, Miss Carswile is in the parlour . . ."

"Do we need to run away from her again?"

"No, she's crying."

Belle was suddenly a lot more awake. "Crying?"

"Yes. I think it's my fault."

"And what does that have to do with me?"

"Nothing." Rufus perched on the edge of the bed and put his head in his hands. "But I don't know what to do."

"The normal things you do when a woman is crying?"

"Which are?"

"Oh, for God's sake. Help me up."

Once she'd been helped up, Belle took a moment to smooth the creases from her dress—or at least try to smooth the creases from her dress—and coax some kind of order into her hair because she did not think she could face even a purportedly crying Miss Carswile without some kind of protection. The lady was intimidatingly beautiful and possessed things like virtue and maturity, which Belle had been a stranger to her entire life.

She knocked on the parlour door before entering, which meant she was met by the sight of Miss Carswile posed rather picturesquely upon the sofa, her face turned towards the window.

"Are you sure," she said, in a rather choked voice, having caught the reflection of Belle's entrance in the glass, "you want to marry that man?"

"You mean because he prefers other men?"

"I mean because he's horrible."

Belle took a few more steps into the room. "He's not that bad when you get to know him. I quite like him, actually. I like him very much."

"He is devoid of compassion or remorse."

"I think," Belle tried, "he's been very hurt."

"And that excuses him from the hurt he causes others?"

"Absolutely not. He's treated you abominably. Deep down he knows that."

Miss Carswile was still staring rigidly into the far distance. "It is the . . . the"—she paused, to give a rather unladylike sniff—"*cruellest* thing to be used as an instrument for someone else's suffering. Even more so when they would turn you on themselves."

"I know. And I'm so sorry that happened."

Another sniff from Miss Carswile before she finally turned away from the window. Her eyes were red-rimmed, though a fading sheen of tears only enhanced their lustre. She lifted her chin haughtily. "What are you doing here, Miss Tarleton?"

"Eloping with your former fiancé?"

To Belle's surprise, Miss Carswile's mouth softened with the faintest hint of amusement. "In this room?"

"I came to see if I could help?"

"How?" asked Miss Carswile, not entirely unreasonably.

"I don't know," Belle admitted. "Maybe I'm just trying to assuage my guilt for my own part in"—she gave a one-handed flail—"all this."

"You seem to be injured?"

"Oh yes. I got shot."

"You got shot?"

"Yes." Belle nodded eagerly.

"How?"

"With a gun."

"I had deduced as much. But in what context?"

"In the context of Gil—did you meet Gil—holding up our coach while pretending to be a highwayman because he thought we were someone else."

Miss Carswile seemed to be doing her very best to make sense of this. "Gil is a highwayman?"

"No, Gil is a bookseller."

"I see." Miss Carswile obviously did not see. "And this took place while you were running away with my husband-to-be, having failed to dissuade him from an alliance with me on the occasion you and your brother kidnapped us both?"

There was no good answer to this. "Yes?" said Belle.

A few fresh tears slipped down Miss Carswile's cheeks, and she bent forward over her knees to shield her face beneath a hand—still, somehow, contriving to look graceful. When Belle cried, she ended up compressed into an ugly ball of misery. Miss Carswile looked like a classical sculpture, a queen temporarily brought low.

"Are you," murmured the queen after a moment or two, "familiar with the work of William Paley?"

"Maybe?" lied Belle. "Rufus would be."

"Who is Rufus?"

"Sir Horley."

A distant expression, half-defeated, half-defiant, settled upon Miss Carswile's features. "You know, I'm just not going to ask."

"William Paley?" Belle prompted her.

"Oh yes. He wrote a book in which he uses examples of social and natural order, like a watch or a telescope or the workings of the human eye or the revolution of planetary bodies in our solar system, to argue for the existence of God."

Belle was not sure she had consented to a religious discussion, so she offered a wary "Mm-hmm."

"A device as intricate and harmonious as a watch does not occur by accident. It requires a watchmaker. Ergo a creation as intricate and harmonious as the world must also have a Creator."

The only reason Belle was tolerating this was because it appeared to have stopped Miss Carswile crying. That, and she was looking especially beautiful, her eyes alight with thought, her face animated by conviction. "And this is relevant how?"

"Because," returned Miss Carswile, "I think if William Paley had ever met you, he would not have written his book."

"Wait a minute." Belle wrinkled her nose, unsure whether to be insulted or delighted, and settled on a little bit of both. "Are you saying that I, ipso facto, represent an argument in favour of the non-existence of God?"

"Yes."

"Well . . ." Belle thought about it a little longer. "I suppose that's fair?" And then, having considered the issue even further, "At least you do not consider me notably on the side of the devil."

"I do not believe in the devil."

"How can you believe in God if not the devil?"

"I think it is we who put evil into the world and we who should take responsibility for it."

"What is evil, though? People like Rufus and me?"

Once again came that enticing hint of a smile hidden in Miss Carswile's otherwise severe mouth. "I think the worst that can be said of Sir Horley is that he is cowardly and inconsiderate, and not very good at apologising."

Belle tried to think of something useful to say but had, unfortunately, come unstuck. She had always been subject to the most terrible weakness for a sharp person turned soft. For those who kept their secrets in the flicker of an eyelash or the curve of their lips. It was probably because she had always feared she was obvious. "Would you like to come for a walk?" she blurted out.

"A walk?"

"Why not? It's not an orgy."

"Thank you for clarifying that."

"Sorry. I just meant—there's nothing untoward in two ladies going for a walk."

Miss Carswile lifted her brows into perfect little arches. "I suspect you have it in you to make most things untoward, Miss Tarleton."

"Thank you?" said Belle.

"Should you be walking, though? With your arm?"

"Well, I don't generally walk with my arms?"

"You know what I mean."

It was a rebuke delivered as a caress. It travelled down Belle's spine like the brush of a feather in a lover's hand. "I do get tired easily. But I also get bored easily. So it's a rough situation for me."

"Where are we to walk to?" asked Miss Carswile, evincing absolutely no sympathy for Belle's travails in convalescence.

"Perhaps a little way past the village? There's a bridge, I think, and a willow tree."

"Does it grow aslant a brook?"

"Aslant a stream. And I'm afraid fantastical garlands are off the menu until I've recovered."

"Probably best to keep them off the menu in perpetuity. They do not lead anywhere good."

Since Miss Carswile was still in travelling clothes—including a dark-green pelisse with military-style braiding down the front and at the shoulders that managed to be at once lavish and austere—Belle hurried to retrieve a wrap, and they left the inn together. Rufus was still hiding from the consequences of his actions, but at the back door they passed Gil, who immediately expressed concern for Belle's well-being.

"It's fine," she told him. "If I feel faint, Miss Carswile has promised to give me a piggyback."

"You're tempting me," began Miss Carswile auspiciously, "to leave you where you fall," she finished, less auspiciously.

Belle peeped up through her lashes. "Ah, but you won't. It would be *uncharitable*."

"Maybe I would be charitably creating opportunities for other people to do good in the world."

"Does that count?"

"I confess the theology is tenuous, but I'm willing to take the risk."

With Belle concluding it was probably best not to push her luck, they made their way through the village. It was a pretty place, mostly just a line of thatched cottages and a few businesses, creating a loose sense of a main street. The blacksmith had found his shirt, which Rufus might have found disappointing, but Belle was just glad to be outside and away from the same set of rooms for a bit. She had, true to form, perhaps over-estimated her strength and, also true to form, had no intention of admitting it. Partly out of pride. Mostly because she didn't want to be "kindly" escorted back to the inn barely five minutes after escaping it. When she stumbled, however, Miss Carswile merely took her good arm with a gallantry Belle had not experienced from a dress-wearing person in some time. It was the sort of thing liable to give her happy flutters.

It was already late afternoon, the light dripping as thick as honey from the eaves and gables of the cottages, glazing the cobbles beneath their feet with amber. And by the time—at Belle's reduced pace—they reached the bridge, the sun was setting in earnest, licking scarlet fire across the sleepy stream and the little bridge that spanned it.

"Oh my," said Miss Carswile, her gaze turned to the horizon, her profile transfigured to gleaming bronze.

Belle was watching Miss Carswile. "Are you feeling better about the watchmaker?"

"I honestly don't understand how anyone could behold a sight like this and not feel something."

"I feel plenty of things," Belle told her. "I'm just not sure any of them are God?"

"Perhaps God is simply the name some of us choose to give to those feelings?"

"Probably that's what led to the Crusades." It was Belle's very sweetest voice. "'What a lovely view,' they must have said; 'let's go kill some Saracens.'"

"Miss Tarleton, the English have been seizing land and committing mass murder without the inspiration of Christianity for centuries. I am not making excuses for the ills of the past, but the song is not the singer and vice versa." She turned to face Belle directly. "Did you really suggest a walk so we could debate my beliefs beneath the open skies?"

"No. But I can't help being curious about them."

"What is there to inspire your curiosity? The Church of England has been an established part of most people's lives since the sixteenth century. I think the more pertinent question here is how you managed to avoid it?"

"I didn't avoid it," Belle said. "My aunt and uncle made my twin and me go to church with them every Sunday. I just didn't think anyone saw it as more than a duty."

"I'm sure many do. But there is a difference between dutiful acceptance and active rejection."

Belle shrugged. "Society has many ways of rejecting me, and the church is nothing more than another of them."

"I will say, I do not often feel an equal part of it. But beyond what you might call the cultural . . . *business* of religion, I like the way faith itself makes me feel."

"Which is what?"

"That the world is worth putting good into." She paused, almost self-consciously. "That I'm . . . loved."

"Ah," said Belle.

Miss Carswile was eyeing her with concern. "Why do you look like a cat trying to bring up a fur ball? Do I seem naive to the point of disgusting?"

"No. Not at all. Just . . . love and I are on the outs. I'm not sure we've ever been on the ins."

"That sounds as though it could be a tale."

"That's the thing." Belle cast the thought from her like a pebble into the water below. "It's not. It's merely something that *is*."

"No terrible betrayal? No ill-starred suitor? No broken heart?"

"None. I am simply not made to love."

"Come." Miss Carswile took Belle's arm again. "Let us rest a moment. You are looking tired."

"I think," Belle protested, "I'm looking annoyed about love."

With typical determination, Miss Carswile drew her from the bridge and towards the willow tree that was indeed growing nearby. "You can be both. Perhaps you haven't met the right person yet. Isn't that what we're supposed to say to the lovelorn?"

"I've met several *right* people. It's me who's wrong."

Beneath the lavishly falling fronds of the tree, the light flickered green and gold, all the violence of the orange skies soothed away into softness. They found a spot between the spreading roots and sat down, Miss Carswile with her legs tucked demurely beneath her skirts, Belle in a moody hunch, with her knees pulled up and her ankles showing.

"Wrong for them?" asked Miss Carswile, curiously.

"Wrong in general. Wrong for love."

"I don't know what that means."

"Do you think I do?" snapped Belle, her voice too loud for the space, cutting harshly over the gentle splash of the stream and the whisper of the willow. And then, in response to Miss Carswile's startled look, relented. "All I know is that I do not . . . I cannot . . . fall in love. I have tried. I wish I could. But even the idea of it"—she repressed a shudder of discomfort—"makes me want to crawl out of my skin *and die*."

"That seems to me like a strong indication you should stop trying?" Belle stared at her blankly.

"Well," Miss Carswile went on hesitantly, "if something makes you uncomfortable, probably you shouldn't attempt to do it?"

"I shouldn't *love*?"

"Is it mandatory?"

"From the way everyone goes on about it, one would think so." Belle hugged herself a little tighter. "I do recognise this is probably just the inescapable reality of who I am. That does not change the fact that it is a difficult reality to accept."

"What makes it difficult?" Miss Carswile could sound surprisingly . . . tender when she wanted to.

It was disconcerting. Especially because Belle was at her most pricklesome and strange. "Because," she tried to explain, "something that comes naturally to me—may, in fact, be integral to me—is so very much the opposite of that to . . . well . . . practically everyone else. It's hard not to interpret that as a fault in oneself."

"For what it's worth," said Miss Carswile, "I do not think it is either unnatural or a fault."

"Is that so? Because even I have difficulty seeing how *incapacity to love* could be considered an advantage."

"I said I did not think it was a fault. I do not think it is an advantage either."

Probably it was an unfortunate quality to take offence when someone tried to reassure you. Unfortunately, it was an unfortunate quality Belle seemed to be stuck with. "How lovely."

"I think it is probably neutral, like most human qualities."

"Is it not"—Belle found herself abruptly voicing a long-held anxiety, one she had hesitated to put into words in front of others in case it gave them ideas—"the hallmark of a villain or a criminal?"

"Are you a villain or a criminal?"

"I am not a criminal. I'm sure some would call me a villain."

"You seem very concerned with what other people think."

"Well . . ." Belle muffled a sheepish laugh against her own knees. "However different I may be in some regards, I am sad and predictable in others, and I wish to be liked."

"Everyone is sad sometimes, but you are the least predictable person I have ever met."

That was slightly reassuring. Belle risked a peep at Miss Carswile. "Really?"

"The first time we encountered each other, you kidnapped me."

"Oh yes." It had all gone horribly wrong in the end, but the kidnapping part had been fun. Belle felt slightly less like crying. "I did do that."

"And," Miss Carswile added, with audible reluctance, "I like you."

Chapter 23

It was one of Belle's very dearest things to hear. She thought it would have been, even if she *had* been romantically inclined. From everything she'd read and witnessed, love seemed altogether random. It came upon people chaotically and uncontrollably and swept them away—an experience they seemed to take for granted was worth it, rather than terrifying and slightly demeaning, to be reduced to impulse and emotion. Of course, Belle was a creature of impulse and emotion herself, but they were *her* impulses, *her* emotions.

If she forced herself to think about love in a positive way, she wondered if perhaps it was like music: something that cut past words and thoughts and worldly complications and spoke directly to the heart. That was, as it happened, an aspect of music she appreciated. But the notion of a *person* doing it, a person who could have been anyone, circumventing her, like maggots in a wound? No. Just no. Besides, if *love* was an arbitrary parasite, *like* was a tough little wildflower, springing up, bright and resilient, wherever you allowed it to grow.

At least, that was the theory. That was what she told herself when she felt alone and set apart. But today she wasn't quite done with being her own worst enemy. "What is the use of liking me?"

Miss Carswile made a sound at the back of her throat, low and amused, not quite a laugh. "What is the use of liking anyone?"

"Someone else could . . . give more?"

"Miss Tarleton, the great love of my life is—and will likely always be—my sense of an infinitely good and infinitely beautiful divine being."

"That doesn't mean you can't or won't love a person, too, though."

"True. But it's certainly not a priority for me. And my point is more to do with the fact that there are as many ways of loving in the world as there are people in it. What does it matter that there is one love that is not your love?"

It was the first time Belle had spoken about this to someone without the conversation falling apart on her. Without becoming a knife that was being blithely twisted through her innards. Rufus, she knew, was broadly comfortable, broadly accepting. But she also knew that was in large part because he didn't *want* anything from her beyond friendship, and sometimes not even that. Bonny was still convinced she was broken. Peggy had been deeply, profoundly, hurt. "But," she muttered, "is that not the love against which all other loves are shadows?"

"Some may believe so. It is not what I believe."

"Yes yes"—Belle rolled her eyes—"because, to you, divine love is the only love."

"That is not what I said. I see our earthly loves, in whatever form they come, as fragments of divine love. That does not make them less than God's love. It makes them part of it. It's not as though Paul wrote to the Corinthians, 'And now abide faith, hope, love, these three; but the greatest of these is that fluttery sensation in your stomach.'"

And what if you're wrong? Belle wanted to ask. *What if you're wrong and the rest of the world is right. What if everything I am is never enough? What if the way I love always feels like less than it could or should be.* Except she recognised instinctively that those were not the kind of fears that could be answered in words. Or by another person. The conversation may not have been knife-shaped (yet), but it had still left her raw around the edges. She had neither intended nor expected to subject

Miss Carswile to quite so many of her truths, like a callow lad casting up his accounts after a night on the town.

"This would sound a lot better," she said aloud, and perhaps more sharply than was fair, "if you had not been attempting to cure a man of sodomy through marriage."

Miss Carswile, who had been reclining at her ease between the roots, sat forward with a startled little cough. "I beg your pardon?"

"Was that not the plan?"

"No," exclaimed Miss Carswile, looking only slightly less distressed than when she had thought Rufus was about to kill her brother. "Heavens, no. I've only recently learned what sodomy *is*. I thought it had something to do with a lack of hospitality towards visiting angels."

Turning her face away, Belle did her best to stifle a giggle. "As far as I know, Rufus is exceptionally considerate to any and all angels that cross his threshold. Did you really not know you were engaged to a man who . . . well. Likes men?"

"You have to remember that Sir Horley has spoken nothing to me beyond the barest civilities. Everything I know about him, I know from his aunt."

"And she struck you as a reasonable judge?"

"In fairness, no. But I also saw no reason to disbelieve her when she told me that her nephew wished to turn over a new leaf."

"A new leaf of . . . living a life to someone else's preferences, instead of his own?"

Miss Carswile frowned—something else she did elegantly, her exquisitely carved features shifting into an expression of concern, when Belle's face in anger crumpled like a discarded stocking. "That was not how it was presented to me. I understood that he was dissolute and selfish, that he had done shameful things in the past, but hoped to do better in future. She alluded to some corruptive influence upon her husband that had led to his death, but I assumed drinking or gambling dens or whatever else men do."

"And," asked Belle, no less bewildered, "you still thought it was a good idea to marry such a person?"

"Well, I'm sure there are worse people to marry. Sir Horley was always very courteous when we met and assured me of his intentions to change. I did not think it was my place either to judge or condemn."

"Oh," said Belle.

"Yes," returned Miss Carswile, sharp again herself. *"Oh."* Then she gave a rueful half smile. "It took me quite some time to learn that my husband-to-be's terrible misdeeds amounted to nothing more than what I assume to be mutually agreed-upon encounters with other men."

"There are many who do see that as a misdeed, though."

"Well, I am not one of them. I certainly see no scriptural precedent. Or rather, one can find a scriptural precedent for most things, and no things, so it behoves one to consider the matter of context, and to extricate what we think of as the Gospel—the message of God's love—from a very old book we call the Bible."

Belle eyed her with sudden suspicion. "Nobody ever spoke like this when I was attending church. Are you some kind of heretic?"

"Who knows?" Miss Carswile lifted her brows wickedly. "Perhaps I am."

"No, but are you?"

"I'm simply someone trying to live their life in accordance with precepts they believe in."

For a moment or two, Belle was silent, thinking. "What if there is a God, and God does actually hate people committing sodomy?"

"While I cannot answer for God"—Miss Carswile also seemed to be thinking—"I can try to tell you what I think about what God might think, if that will help?"

"Sounds complicated, but go on."

"Well, I think there's a lot of violence and pain and cruelty and need in the world—what's the matter? You're making fur-ball face again."

"This didn't go where I expected. I thought you were going to tell me something *nice*."

"All I'm trying to say is that the world is big and there's a lot going on in it, and, even for an omnipotent, omniscient, all-loving being, God is probably quite busy. I really can't imagine, if I were in God's position, I would give . . . let me see, how would you phrase it. A flying fuck where people consensually put their pricks."

"That's a good point," said Belle, pleased. "But then if God is omnipotent, omniscient, and all-loving, like you say, why *is* the world full of suffering?"

Miss Carswile gave the deepest of deep sighs. "Belle?"

"Yes."

"Read a book. Start with Epicurus."

Belle, however, was not interested in Epicurus. "You called me Belle."

"I did."

"And you said *fuck*."

"Indeed."

"And *prick*."

"Quite."

"I liked it a lot."

"Thank you."

The sun was lingering upon the lip of the horizon; their bower was full of a mossy dark.

"Can I ask you a question?" piped up Belle.

"If it is about the fundamentals of Christian thought, no."

"Why did you want to marry Rufus."

"I told you. His aunt—"

"No, no, no." Belle cut her off. "That's about Rufus. I'm asking about *you*."

For the first time in their admittedly limited acquaintance, Belle seemed to have taken Miss Carswile by surprise. "Ah," she said, a shadow upon her cheeks that might have been a blush. "It seemed a useful thing to do for someone else. A married woman has more freedom. And I confess, when I learned the true extent of the convenience upon which our union would be based, I found the notion of a man who would want very little from me in a . . . in a . . . *marital* context rather appealing."

"You have no interest in men?"

"Aesthetically? Sometimes. Emotionally, hardly. Have you met them? Also"—and here Miss Carswile's lips turned into their elusive smile—"much like the Lord, I am quite busy."

Very naturally indeed, Belle edged a tiny bit closer. "Before you re-approach the issue of matrimony, you should have some understanding of what even the most convenient husband might wish you to abandon."

"Should I now?" Miss Carswile turned her head so that they were breath to breath beneath the willow tree.

"Don't you think?"

"For your information, I am not a complete innocent. I regularly see to the business of my own satisfaction."

Belle tipped her face up, so her lips did everything but graze Miss Carswile's skin. "The fact you refer to it as *the business* isn't a good sign, Verity."

"I see I have become Verity."

"You started it."

"Are you trying to seduce me, Belle?"

Drawing back, Belle put her free hand to her heart. "What an outrageous suggestion. I am offering you an instructive opportunity, upon which to inform future decision-making. Also"—she let her false indignation dance away with the gathering fireflies—"it's different when it's with someone else. It feels different."

"You're"—again Verity's voice trembled with a touch of uncertainty—"you're injured."

"Please," Belle retorted. "It takes more than getting shot and nearly dying to dampen my ardour."

"Don't you need . . . ah . . . mobility?"

"Listen"—Belle smirked—"you are *not ready* for what I can do with two hands. This is a blessing."

"God." If it was a prayer, it was a profane one; resignation and amusement and curiosity. "You're completely shameless, aren't you?"

"When I need to be. Do you mind?"

"Quite the contrary. I find it annoying and . . . and alluring."

Trying not to jar her shoulder—fainting before she'd even got started was not her ideal way to embark upon an assignation—Belle eased herself into Verity's lap and found herself immediately steadied there by an arm about her waist. It was always so delightfully shocking, that first moment of true closeness, when you irrevocably broke the boundaries of discretion and civility. When you committed to the risk of intimacy.

"That's good to know," Belle told her. "Because I find you alluring too."

"What about annoying?"

"I'm shallow."

With Belle perched as she was, they were eye level. The darkness had swallowed the colour from Verity's eyes, but they gleamed with no less intensity. "Do you really?"

"Do I really what?"

"Think I'm"—Verity cleared her throat—"what you said."

"Hopelessly. I've thought so ever since I kidnapped you. Surely you've noticed? Subtlety does not run in my family."

"I'm not used to the idea of being perceived that way. I know I have the requisite number of limbs and features in proportion. I wear green out of vanity because I think it suits me—"

"It does."

"But *alluring* conjures something specific."

Leaning forward, Belle indulged herself in small, teasing motions. Gliding her cheek against Verity's. Nosing into the sweet silken curls that bobbed at her temples in defiance of her otherwise drawn-back hair. Pressing her closed lips to odd places: the tip of her nose and the edge of her jaw, the thought line between Verity's lovely brows. "Would you prefer me to admire the quantity of your limbs? Four is generally my favourite."

To Belle's surprise, Verity tipped back her head and laughed, full-throated and joyous. "Let's stick with *alluring*, shall we?"

"Are you sure? Because the symmetry of your cheekbones drives me *wild*."

"Belle . . ."

"And the geometry of your chin is positively Pythagorean."

"You mean triangular?"

"Such harmonious configur—"

Before she got any further, Verity's free hand caught her by the nape of her neck—a touch that when correctly applied could make Belle as weak as a kitten—and dragged their mouths together. It was a very Verity kiss: direct and determined, with a hidden softness at its heart. Belle yielded gladly, let herself be taken and explored, knowing that first kisses flourished best when allowed to find their own way. And, sure enough, curiosity became fervour and Belle met the fervour and then gentled it, for this was a dance with steps for every season and every inclination.

"Well," murmured Verity when breath demanded they part. "That is certainly not something I could experience alone."

Belle laughed, the taste of Verity still clinging to her lips. "Bonny and I used to practice on our hands."

"I beg your pardon?"

"We wanted to make sure we were good at it by the time we found someone to kiss us."

"Now I'm concerned. Is it possible to be bad?"

"I mean, kind of. But," Belle went on hastily, "you weren't. I promise."

"I have so little experience, I'm not even sure what *bad* would look like in this context?"

"Oh, you'd know. To be honest, I think it's more about a lack of connection, which is subjective, than a lack of demonstrable technique. But sometimes it's a lack of demonstrable technique. Bonny has names for them."

"Names for bad kisses?"

Belle nodded. "Windmill in a Hurricane, Stabby Stabby McStab Stab, that sort of thing."

"I can tell," said Verity, with a kind of doomed curiosity, "I'm going to regret asking, but I feel compelled to ask."

"You really want to know?"

"I really want to know."

"This is the kissing equivalent," Belle warned her, "of fruit of the Tree of Knowledge of Good and Evil."

"Tempt me?"

It was an invitation liable to turn anyone serpentine. But Belle was afflicted by the curse of honesty. "I think you're going to be regretful rather than tempted, but here goes. Windmill in a Hurricane is when they . . ."

And Belle stuck her tongue into Verity's mouth, thrashing it chaotically until they were both laughing too much to continue, and she was gently but firmly pushed away.

"That was horrendous," said Verity.

"And Stabby Stabby McStab Stab . . ."

"Oh no, don't you—"

Lunging forward, Belle began a relentless oral thrusting—which turned out to be more difficult than she had anticipated, partly because it was tiring but also because her victim was squirming vigorously enough to present a moving target.

"That was also horrendous," said Verity, having successfully repelled further attack. "You nearly got me in the *eye*."

"And then there's Not All the Water in the Rough Rude Sea, which—"

"I don't need further illumination."

"Are you sure? Because it's when they lick all around your mouth over and over and over again."

"There shall be no licking."

Belle rested her fingertips lightly against Verity's lips. "Maybe hold that thought."

"If you say so. This has been a harrowing education."

"I'll make it better," Belle promised. "Bonny also went through a stage of inventing kisses."

"Inventing them?"

"Yes. Giving them names and writing lavish descriptions of how they ought to be performed. He was planning to write a book of them."

"Did he run out of kisses?"

"More just out of steam. I cannot think of one project Bonny has embarked upon that he has completed, unless you count falling in love with a duke and living happily ever after. I suspect I'm the same. About the projects, I mean."

"I don't know." Verity offered her a rather provocative look. "You seem quite accomplished at getting what you want."

Belle grinned back. "I'm working on it. Now let me see if I can remember . . ." She brushed her mouth lightly against Verity's, right at the corner of her lips, first one side, then the other. "Twin Butterflies."

"I like that much better than A Ship Wrecked against the Rocks or whatever it was."

"Moonlight upon Still Waters." The next kiss Belle bestowed slowly, languorously, her tongue pressing inside only at the last to stroke the length of Verity's. "The Honeybee's Daydream." This was a series of soft sucking nibbles until, once again, Verity's lips parted for her, and Belle was darting playfully between them, withdrawing before the kiss had a chance to deepen. "It's all nonsense, of course," she concluded.

There was a flush standing out upon Verity's cheeks. Her mouth still looked like invitation. "Is it?"

"Yes." Insinuating her good arm about Verity's neck, Belle wriggled closer, pressing her words to Verity's mouth like a fresh set of kisses. "The only kiss that truly matters is a kiss from someone you really want to kiss and who really wants to kiss you back."

"Then we are on the verge of the most perfect kiss in the known universe," Verity returned, her usually measured tones still shaky.

Belle did not believe in perfect—she believed in a wide variety of very good things—but what followed came perilously close. It was the sort of kiss where time lost its meaning, where the world shed all its anxieties and obligations, leaving only two bodies pressed together, two mouths likewise, everything that wasn't the to-and-fro of breath and heat, rough and sweet, rendered as insubstantial as the moonlight that fell in hazy ripples through the willow branches. Verity's hair shed its fastenings entirely, perhaps abetted by Belle's fingers, and came down around them both in a curtain of shadow and silk.

"Debauchery suits you," Belle whispered.

They were lying together in the embrace of the tree roots, Verity ever so unravelled, with her mouth parted and glistening, her pelisse undone, and her harsh breath causing her breasts to swell deliciously against the otherwise modest neckline of her travelling dress. "I have always been concerned it might."

Dipping her head, Belle pressed her open mouth to the base of Verity's throat, just to feel the passion of her quickened pulse. She hesitated after, not wanting to move too quickly or transgress where she wasn't welcome, but there was no resistance in Verity's body. Just that trust and wonder and thrumming eagerness. A little lower, and Belle felt the cool press of metal against her lips: Verity's golden cross.

"This is . . ." She paused. "You are comfortable?"

"A well-planned day or a cup of tea in the rain makes me comfortable," returned Verity. "I don't think *comfortable* is what you're intending, is it?"

"I just mean, you're not going to regret this afterwards?"

"Why would I?"

Belle toyed with the cross. "God or guilt or something?"

There was a moment of silence. Then, "Belle?"

"Yes?"

"Do you want a theological debate or to fuck me? I don't think I have the capacity to handle both at the same time."

"I'd *definitely* rather fuck you."

"That," said Verity crisply, "was the correct answer."

"You will tell me, though, if I do or say anything that . . . that you don't like or feels like too much?"

"No, I shall endure it in martyred silence like St. Sebastian. What do you take me for?"

Surprised, Belle laughed. "You're very sarcastic when you're inflamed."

"Indeed. We are uncovering many facets of me today."

Belle produced her best rakish leer. "I can think of a few facets I'd like to uncover."

Which meant Verity was laughing her rich bold laugh as Belle drew down the bodice of her dress. And then that laughter dissolved into a breathy sigh as Belle kissed her way first across one breast and then the other, chasing little flurries of responsive goose pimples across the tender skin. It was hard, when confronted by such bounty, not to lament having one arm in a sling because Belle would have loved to fill her hands like a pirate with gold doubloons. In this, she had always feared she was a little . . . unimaginative. All bodies were unique and full of beauty. The line of a hip, whether rounded or angular, could be nice. The dip of a waist, especially from behind. But the fact remained, for Belle at least, you couldn't get much better than a boob. Ideally two.

And especially when they were as supple and sensitive as Verity's were turning out to be, her nipples tightening as Belle circled them with the pad of her thumb.

"'Thy two breasts,'" she murmured against them, "'are like two young roes that are twins, which feed among the lilies.'"

Verity arched her back in offering. "Oh, so you *have* read the Bible."

"The good bits, obviously. I can also do 'And before the throne there was a sea of glass like unto crystal: and in the midst of the throne, and round about the throne, were four beasts full of eyes before and behind,' but it doesn't seem quite as appropriate."

"Revelation and the Song of Songs. I should have guessed."

"Of course. The Song of Songs is racy as fuck. And Revelation is utterly gothic. Those are my two favourite things." She danced her fingertips up and down the tantalising dip between Verity's partially exposed breasts. "You have to remember, my brother and I grew up in Surrey. It was a great trial to us because Surrey is extraordinarily boring. We thought the end of the world as described in Revelation, with the rainbow throne and all the strange beasts appearing and the sea turning to blood, would have been an improvement."

Verity was gazing at her intently—desire commingling with amusement in her eyes and upon her mouth, alongside an unexpected fondness. "'Thou art all fair, my love,'" she said after a moment or two. "'There is no spot in thee.'"

And Belle found herself flustered, though she hardly knew why. Before she could examine the feeling, however, she was drawn into another series of kisses, deeper, if anything, than the last, as they clung to each other and entangled tongues, limbs, hair, their increasingly dishevelled garments. Belle's hand drifted naturally downwards, stroking through layers of fabric the long spare lines of Verity's body. There was something, still, of the sculptural about her, so lean and sharp and austere, but she was fire now, not stone. A fresh-made Galatea, animated by not the whims of a yearning Pygmalion, but her own desires and choices.

Hiking up Verity's skirt and petticoat, and burrowing beneath her chemise, Belle's questing fingers discovered worsted wool stockings tied with a simple ribbon garter. Pressing her face against her companion's neck, she muffled a moan. "You are *killing* me, Verity."

"Whatever's the matter?"

"Women in practical undergarments are my *greatest weakness*." Not counting breasts. And prim people unravelling.

Verity gave a little cough. "Well, had I known I was to be corrupted beneath a willow tree rather than saving my absurd brother from getting shot in the face, I would have worn something a little more enticing."

"No, no"—Belle traced the boundary where wool became flesh—"I am in earnest. It makes it extra . . . extra . . . *everything*."

She teased her way around the garter, pushing her way beneath it to stroke the pristine skin and causing the stocking to slip, liberating yet more skin, as smooth as the pages of a newly printed book. It was somehow an even greater provocation not to be able to see—Belle's eyes were on Verity's face, when they were not bent, along with her mouth, in service to her breasts—but instead to be discovering her, learning her, by touch alone. The slight roughness of her knee. The little valleys at the top of her thighs. The soft abundance of the hair that sheltered her quim. And, of course, all the lovely wet heat that awaited Belle's exploration.

Verity let out a stuttering breath. "Oh—*oh*."

Slipping delicately between her folds, Belle gathered Verity's arousal straight from the source and used it to slide her fingertips upwards to the place she knew could often bestow the greatest pleasure. "You're well?"

"Of course I'm not fucking *well*," Verity snarled. "This is wonderful. More." She seemed to recall herself. "If you please."

"In this context," Belle told her, "I respond equally well to commands and petitions."

Verity's head tipped back, exposing the shadow-washed column of her throat, the tips of her teeth exposed by her open mouth. "You . . ." Her voice came in fits and starts, as though she had half forgotten how to use it. "You . . . were . . . right."

"I often am. But in what particular?"

"It *is* different. There . . . like that." Her hand came down and wrapped around Belle's wrist, her grip close to bruising. "Don't stop."

"I wouldn't dare." Belle sank her teeth lightly into the top of Verity's left breast, earning a guttural sound. "You need not worry." She kissed the reddened spot. "I have you."

Belle stroked and circled, watching Verity all the time, partly for the pure gratification of it but mostly so she could gauge what motions and what pressure elicited the greatest response from her lover. She knew from her own body, and from past experience, that too much of anything here—except at the moment of crisis—could easily become too much. That the pleasure collected like dew upon a spider's web, not simply from one place, but from all places, inside and out.

At last, Verity's grasp slackened, and Belle shook her off, turning her hand so that she could press a finger, and then a second, into all that clinging heat while her thumb worked diligently above. She was cautious, at first, because not everyone appreciated penetration, but Verity tightened in welcome, a hard ripple travelling through her whole body. She looked gloriously feral there in the dark and dappled moonlight, with her hair coiled about her like snakes, and her hips bucking up to meet Belle's touch.

"Harder," she said. "Faster. And kiss me."

And Belle was only too happy to oblige on all three counts. Her arm was beginning to ache, but it was the best kind of ache, being the result of service to another's satisfaction. And when she lowered her head to be kissed, Verity caught her mouth like a lion, all teeth and exultant hunger. It was like this, not long after, that she came, her wild cry smothered against Belle's lips and her body a reckless wave, hands thrown above her head, fingers curled into claws.

Belle coaxed her through it, her thumb pressed right where it was needed, gentling as the shudders faded and Verity's breath steadied. They fell against each other, sticky and tousled, and for a while said nothing, chasing private stars.

"What about you?" asked Verity, at last, her breasts still agleam and her mouth swollen from that final kiss, one stocking rumpled about her ankle.

"What about me?"

"Is there anything I can—"

"Oh no. Not this time."

"That does not seem equitable."

"Sex isn't an accounts ledger." A great yawn racked Belle's whole body. Rufus would probably scold her if he knew this was her idea of convalescence. On the other hand, at least she wasn't bored. "Sometimes the giving is the gift, and that's enough."

Verity's fingers trailed up and down the side of her neck. "I'll trust you on that. But I would nevertheless value an opportunity to balance the books." Her hint of a smile glimmered on her mouth. "For the sake of my continued education."

"Well," Belle murmured, "if it's *educational*."

They fell silent again.

"You know," said Verity, somewhat abruptly. "You don't have to marry Sir Horley either."

Some of the lassitude fled Belle's limbs. "That's quite the non sequitur."

"We can claim I have been your companion the whole journey. Neither of our reputations need suffer."

"And what about Rufus?"

"Does he want to marry you?"

"Not really," Belle admitted. "Probably slightly more than he wanted to marry you—no offence."

"None taken. But that's a low bar, Belle."

"I have a fairly substantial dowry, and his aunt has probably already disinherited him."

"Because no gentleman has ever found gainful employment."

"I think," Belle said softly, "he needs a home. Something that he can believe will not abandon him. I think I need the same."

It was not a topic Belle wanted to be pressed further on, and to her relief, Verity did not press. "May I at least accompany you as far as Gretna Green?"

Belle's eyes flew to her companion's, but they offered very little clue as to her thinking. "Why?"

"For one thing, I'm more than halfway there already, having already chased you the length of the country. For another, it is not appropriate for a woman to be travelling alone with a gentleman to whom she is not yet wed."

"I just had my fingers up your quim and my tongue down your throat."

"That has no bearing on what society does and does not observe, and what society does and does not censure. Besides," Verity went on serenely, "if I come with you, should you change your mind about tying yourself to Sir Horley for the rest of your life, or his life, you still can."

Belle glowered. "How noble of you."

"As you yourself have observed several times"—the irony lay thick upon Verity's voice—"I am a deeply virtuous person. Also, this way we can continue to . . ." She sighed. "I am too post-coital for euphemism. This way we can continue to fuck each other. I assume your fiancé will have no objection?"

"It would be bizarre if he did."

"And you yourself have no objection?"

"To us fucking each other?"

"Indeed."

"As it happens," said Belle, settling her head more comfortably against Verity's breast. "None whatsoever."

Chapter 24

They arrived at Gretna Green in a better state than they'd set out for it. Belle's arm was still in a sling, but, apart from that, they made an almost respectable party. Never mind that the two ladies, who were acting as the guardians of each other's virtue, were undoubtedly fucking. The gentlemen, by contrast, despite also sharing a room due to limited means, took decorous turns with whatever bed they were provided. Rufus had no objections to any of these arrangements—he wanted Belle to have her freedom as much as she wanted the same for him—but he was surprised to miss the times when it had been just the two of them. Not, admittedly, the time when Belle had thrown a trifle at him or the time when an innkeeper had nearly made a pie out of him or all the times they had argued with each other over who was abducting whom and whose future, exactly, was being sacrificed by their union. He had, however, grown almost imperceptibly used to the idea that Belle was . . . *his*.

His friend. His companion. His partner. His priority.

And this was a stark reminder that she wasn't. Or rather, that neither of them belonged to the other. That Belle had other friends. That she would want, and should have, lovers. That she liked him, and she cared for him, but there was nothing particularly special in that. For all she sometimes pretended otherwise, she tended to like people—she even seemed to like his former fiancée, a woman with, as far as Rufus could tell, very few redeeming features. He was the misanthrope, concealing a general disinclination for humanity, or at least a fear that humanity would disincline him, behind a sharp tongue and the rudiments of sophistication. Not for the first time, he rebuked the version of himself who had lain beside Belle in the dark, insisting upon his right to live mournfully in the shadow of everything he'd never had. Those shadows still felt familiar—the closest thing to safety he had ever known—but how foolish to believe he *wanted* them. Especially now he had caught glimpses of, he hardly understood what, something else? Something he might truly want.

With their various disruptions, it had taken them almost a full tenday to reach the border—less fleeing, in the end, as was surely traditional for eloping lovers, so much as undertaking a leisurely journey from England to Scotland. The village itself was a small and unassuming one for the site of so much scandal, consisting of a few scattered houses, whitewashed and prettily thatched, a fairly modern church with a mediaeval window, a sizeable inn, and the blacksmith's, where Rufus understood hasty weddings typically took place.

After Gil and Miss Carswile had departed together to stretch their legs and secure lodgings, Rufus and Belle were, at last, left alone. It had only been a couple of days, but to Rufus it felt longer, and he found himself unaccountably lost for words. Shy, as he might once have been with a lover, had his world ever allowed for such a thing.

Finally, he managed to unstick his tongue. But all he produced was "You know, you don't have to do this."

Belle's look was unutterably weary, or maybe that was due to the fact she had clearly been too diverted to spend her nights sleeping. "Don't let's start all that up again."

"I'm not. But with Miss Carswile's intervention, you are no longer obliged to wed me because you feel you have no other choice."

"Realistically," she said, "I don't have other choices. If I were to marry a different man, he might make husbandly demands of me, physically and legally. If I were to commit my life to someone and our relationship was not recognised by the law, the chances are very high that this person would be looking for something from me that I am incapable of giving. Either way"—and here she lifted a shoulder in a rueful half shrug—"the outcome is fairly miserable for everyone involved."

"And you trust me not to make you miserable?"

The look she cast up at him was sharp and a little cool. "Do you trust me not to make *you* miserable?"

"Of course I do."

"You are fully resigned, then?"

"Belle, I . . ." He took refuge in a bewildered laugh. "I would not say *resigned*."

"But you'll go through with it? With me?"

He smiled, wondering if she was nervous and this was her way of concealing it. "Well, I could try my luck with Miss Carswile again. I doubt she'd have me, though."

"She has learned better."

Taking her hand, he raised it to his lips and kissed it. "So have I, dear heart. And as for Gil, I think even in Scotland the marriage laws are not so lax as to allow that."

Whatever cloud had temporarily over-shadowed Belle's mood seemed to be lifting. This time her glance was fully Tarletonian, which was to say sly and unlikely to take no for an answer. "I do not think our highwayman is on the lookout for a long-term prospect, do you?"

"I wouldn't know."

"Why not? Haven't you spent the last few nights with him?"

"You are aware that it is possible for two men to share a room without fucking each other?"

"Aware, yes. But disproved by the literature."

"Well"—Rufus gestured at himself—"here is your proof."

Belle looked legitimately appalled. "Not even a little bit?"

"What would a little bit of fucking look like?"

"I'm not sure. Maybe you would rub off against each other while pretending to be asleep and never mention it again. Or you would lie in the dark together, suffused with passion, and reduced to frantic self-pleasure, apart but perfectly in harmony, even to the rhythm of your breath and the spurtings of your issue."

"That sounded almost romantic until spurtings became involved."

Unfortunately, that was just the sort of thing Belle would pounce on, and pounce she did. "So you *are* looking for romance?"

"No, Belle, I am not looking for romance. I simply chose not to insert my dick into one of our fellow travellers on the way to what is essentially my wedding."

She looked genuinely stricken. "Oh, Rufus, I did not consider the matter in those terms. I'm afraid I have been inserting parts of myself into Verity, and having parts of Verity inserted into me, the whole way here."

"It's fine. I am not about to play the jealous husband with you."

"That would certainly be verging on hypocrisy," Belle agreed. "But I would not wish you to think I did not take our union seriously."

"It's fine," said Rufus again, crushingly aware that the fine-ness of one's *fine* diminished rather than increased with repetition.

"I also took it for granted that you and Gil would be entertaining yourselves."

"Even presupposing he entertains that kind of interest in me—"

"He does."

"Even," repeated Rufus firmly, "presupposing that, I do not think we are compatible."

"Because of the menacing?"

Not wanting to get into it, Rufus shrugged.

Tucking her arm through his, Belle suggested, "Shall we walk?"

"Aren't we getting married?"

"Unless one of us loses our nerve, but it can't hurt to do a little sightseeing, can it?"

Rufus glanced around the village. "What a lovely tree," he offered. "Which one?"

"Any of them. As far as I'm concerned, a tree is a tree."

"How can you say that? Trees are as distinct as people." They made their way past the small patch of grass that represented the village green. "When we had to move in with my aunt and uncle, I was adopted by an oak tree that grew in their grounds."

"I'm just going to say *mm-hmm*," said Rufus. "Because I have no idea what to make of that."

"There was a hollow between the roots big enough for me to crawl into. I felt so safe in there. Like it had seen so many days come and go, and still it stood. Do you know oaks can live for over a thousand years?"

"That sounds exhausting."

"For a tree or in general?"

"Both. One must not forget Tithonus."

Belle thought about this for a moment and then declared confidently, "It is probably different for trees. Six hundred years to a tree could be the equivalent of five and thirty to a human." She thought again. "I've also long believed the moral of Tithonus's story is not to forget to ask for eternal youth at the same time you ask for immortality."

"Both seem a bad idea to me."

"But you would remain perpetually fuckable."

"It is only the young, Bellflower, who believe youth a necessity for fuckability."

"Well," she tried again, "think of everything you could see and do."

"I am already struggling to find meaning within a life of average duration. Besides, what could be worse than everything and everyone around you changing while you remain the same?"

"Only physically."

"We are creatures inevitably shaped by our sense of mortality. I do not know if it is possible to lose that and remain human."

Her nose wrinkled. "This is a very depressing perspective, Rufus."

"Is it?" Pausing, he turned to face her. Their wanderings had led them away from the village towards the river Esk, which lay low and flat and silver beneath the horizon as it wound its way, as lazy as a snake, towards the Solway Firth. Turned enquiringly up to his, Belle's eyes were a storm-churned blue, not like Bonny's at all. "I'm beginning," he went on softly, "to find it quite the reverse."

She tilted her head. "Oh?"

"To be so flawed and frail and fleeting, and yet to throw ourselves onto the thorns of life regardless. To try in spite of the probability of failure. To hope in the face of despair. To love always beneath the shadow of loss. No"—he shrugged—"I think I would rather find someone worth growing old with than live eternally without them."

"For what's it worth," Belle told him, "I intend to be very good at being old."

It was such an absurd, undaunted, quintessentially Belle response that he laughed. "Do you?"

"Yes, I am going to complain about young people running and being too loud and also too quiet. And say things like *In my day* literally all the time."

"I am going to wear waistcoats at least twenty years out of fashion."

"I will take up an extremely unpleasant hobby—"

"Such as?"

"Collecting bezoar stones. And I will entrap people in endless conversations about them until they are dying inside and ready to chew their own arm off just to escape me."

Rufus considered for a moment. And then: "I am going to take up pipe smoking."

"Good." Belle nodded approvingly. "It must be enormous, for you are compensating for something."

"For your information, I am more than adequately compensated. But yes. I will also be sure to smoke only the most disgusting tobacco I can find."

"Of course. Guests must fear the house is burning down the moment you light up. And," declared Belle, "I want a pair of absolutely enormous slippers."

"I want a hat that smells of sheep and makes me look like a mushroom."

"I shall use a million tinctures the moment my hair starts to go grey and yet insist it is my natural colour."

"I will go bald and wear an unconvincing wig and yet insist it is my natural hair."

They fell silent, almost at the same time, their eyes intent upon each other.

"I think I like our future," said Belle softly.

The world was silent with them, the surface of the Esk lightly rumpled by a barely perceptible breeze, and the birds wheeling too high and free against the sky for their voices to be heard.

"What's your home like?" Rufus heard himself ask.

"Swallowfield?" Belle sounded oddly self-conscious. "I mean, it's not Blenheim or Chatsworth or anything."

"What a shame, because I was fully expecting a palace."

"Honestly, I can't remember very well. It's been such a long time since I've been there."

"That must be hard."

Stepping slightly away, Belle shifted her gaze back to the scenery. "I think it was easier for Bonny to stop caring. Even when we could have gone back, he handed running of the place over to Valentine."

"People deal with painful things in different ways."

"Of course they do," returned Belle, sharply. "Yet Bonny never considers that."

"It is not his strong suit." It was true, but the words still tasted slightly of betrayal in Rufus's mouth. Who he was betraying, though, he wasn't quite sure. Some part of himself, probably, more than Bonny.

"We should not roam too far," he added, for Belle was following the curve of the Esk. "You're still recovering your strength."

"I can go a little further. The views towards Cumberland and Port Carlisle on a clear day are said to be quite pleasing."

"As you prefer."

They went along awhile, neither of them speaking, or looking at each other. In the distance, Rufus thought he caught the gleam of the estuary, reflections of clouds caught upon the pale waters, and smudges of shadow from the Cumberland hills.

"I seem," said Belle, a little dreamily, "to recall we had a moat."

"A moat? Somehow that is the most and least surprising thing you could have told me about your family's home."

"Only a small moat. But it's only a small house. Apparently in mediaeval times there would have been a drawbridge, but now there's just a bridge. I wish we still had a drawbridge. Then we could pull it up when we saw someone arriving we didn't like."

"You don't think they might take that amiss?"

"They might, but what could they do about it?"

"That is a very good point." And because she seemed to want to talk about it, he asked, "It's a mediaeval building, then?"

"Bits of it? Though some is Tudor because it has black-and-white gables. There's a courtyard in the middle, although it's not a full one because the west range fell off. Years ago. Before Bonny and I were born."

"Well, one prefers a house with a little character."

Belle nodded eagerly. "I agree. I like places best when they're a little bit of everything. It's prettiest when the wisteria is in bloom and the north range is dripping with purple flowers. Sometimes we get swans on the moat. And in the summer the courtyard is in full bloom. Also we have three priest holes."

"Three?"

"Yes, one is in a privy. Apparently it leads into the mediaeval sewer system, but we were never allowed to investigate. Wasn't that so unfair?"

"On the contrary," said Rufus, trying his hardest not to laugh. "I think it only reflects well upon your parents that they did not encourage their children to climb into a mediaeval sewer."

"And we have several ghosts."

"No abode is complete without them."

"They're quite boring, though." Belle scowled into the distance, clearly taking the quality of her family's hauntings personally. "One of our ancestors murdered a priest in a fit of jealousy, believing the priest was being untoward, well, *toward* his wife. He was convinced he would be barred from heaven for such an act and built a church to try and restore himself to God's good graces, even going so far as to have himself buried beneath the flagstones of that very church. But it didn't work and now he hangs about the house, lamenting his lack of restraint. Which must be very uncomfortable for the *other* ghosts, all of whom are priests who were tortured and killed during a raid by priest hunters."

"Perhaps we can broker some kind of peaceful accord between the ghosts who are murdered priests and the ghost who murdered a priest."

Belle paused, visibly intrigued. "How would we do that?"

"I'm afraid I have not thought that far ahead. Sage and sea salt, probably."

"As long as we don't accidentally banish them."

"We will be nothing but respectful to otherworldly residents."

To his faint alarm, Belle was blinking rapidly. And the next thing he knew, she had thrown herself into his arms. "Oh, Rufus, I am *longing* to go home."

He held her tight, feeling a little prickly in the eye department himself. "Well," he said, when he was sure he could speak lightly, "let's get married and you shall."

Chapter 25

The ceremony took about five minutes and was carried out, as was traditional, in the blacksmith's shop over an anvil. Gil and Miss Carswile were their witnesses. Once Belle and Rufus had confirmed their names, their abodes, and that they were both single, acting of their own free will, and—theoretically—of sound mind, the blacksmith (or the *anvil priest* as he was locally known) filled out a marriage certificate, and pronounced them man and wife.

"I really don't see why more people don't get married this way," said Belle as they stepped back outside. "It's so much more convenient."

It was only when Miss Carswile was offering them both congratulations that any of it began to feel even a little bit real to Rufus.

He was married.

He had married Arabella Tarleton.

Whatever his life had looked like before, it had irrevocably changed. So had Belle's, even though she seemed utterly oblivious of the fact. For a moment or two, he was almost annoyed with her. After all, if you had wed someone, you at least wanted them to give some kind of mild damn about it.

But no, she was laughing with Gil and Miss Carswile, exactly as she had yesterday, and the day before that. Had she no qualms whatever? Not one single concern or shred of doubt? If that was the case, was it because she believed in him, or because he didn't matter? Was he simply the key to a future she wanted? Someone she liked, and did not object to, but ultimately as irrelevant to her as he had always been.

"Rufus?" She was standing before him, peering up at him, in mild apprehension. "Are you quite well?"

"I am," he lied. Because he did not know what the truth *was*, let alone how to tell it.

She smiled, in that enchanting/infuriating Tarleton way that usually augured some ill-conceived adventure, and, taking his hand, drew him slightly away from the others. "I have a wedding present for you."

"What? How? I'm afraid I—"

"Please don't be silly about it." She pressed a heavy iron key into his hand. "Here."

He stared at it in some confusion. "You have already decided we are to live apart?"

"Didn't I just tell you not to be silly? Miss Carswile managed to rent a night in one of the currently unoccupied cottages. It will not be luxurious, but it will afford more privacy than a room at the inn."

His confusion had not abated and had now been joined by distinct unease. "Are you intending to give the impression that you wish to murder me later?"

"I thought you might wish to spend the evening with Gil."

"For God's sake, Belle, I have already told you that he is not for me, nor I for him."

"That is not how you look at each other."

He tried a different tack. "This is my wedding night, and you are encouraging me into the arms of another man."

"Well," she pointed out remorselessly, "ours is not exactly a traditional wedding, is it? We should celebrate in our own way."

"And you intend to celebrate with Miss Carswile?"

"I'm intending to celebrate with a large meal, a hot bath, and a deep, long slumber. You are welcome to join me for two of those if you'd prefer."

"Do you believe I would feel cheated of a different kind of experience if I did?"

"I would hope not." Belle flashed him one of those slightly too perceptive looks that always took him by surprise. "I would hope I could trust you to make decisions to your benefit and to neither of our harm."

"Ah," he said, because he did not entirely trust himself that way. Not that he would ever do anything to hurt Belle. But he had lived with the conviction of his own worthlessness for almost as long as he could remember.

Reaching up, she put her palm against his cheek—a gesture he was sure he ought to have found patronising, instead of oddly reassuring. "I'm beginning to understand better why you wished to marry a woman you believed could not accept you. I think perhaps it freed you from having to accept yourself. But I will never be that woman to you, Rufus. Stay with me. Go to Gil. It is your choice. I just urge you to choose truly if you can."

"Is it not selfish of me to put the fulfilment of my basest instincts above you?"

"If I were in distress, if I was lonely, if I needed you, if I had some reason to ask you not to, then yes. But, as I've already said, I will be in the bath. With cheese, if available, and a book. I am looking forward to it."

"And you"—Rufus tried to assay the query with even a hint of dignity—"you sincerely believe that Gil would wish to . . . with me . . . tonight?"

She stared at him. "Obviously, you stupid man. Why are you in charge of everything again?"

"I'm not?"

"But your subspecies is. No wonder the price of corn currently outstrips the price of bread."

"I've also . . ." Discovering fresh new layers of embarrassment with every word he uttered, Rufus turned away, making a stagily thorough production of knocking the mud from his boots against the scraper by the blacksmith's door. "I've also never been menaced before, and I'm not sure how to . . . to do it properly."

Belle let out a long "ohhhhh" of a breath. "There's very little mystique to it," she said. "Make sure he uses oil and that you are fully aroused, as that will help you feel relaxed when the moment comes. And when it does, all you have to do is stay relaxed and bear down upon—"

"Belle. No."

"What?"

"I have taken both parts, thank you very much. I simply question my capacity to play the role Gil needs."

"Well." Belle pondered this new conundrum. "I think that is for you to work out together, though of course you should not do anything that makes you the wrong kind of uncomfortable, nor should he want you to."

"There is a right kind of uncomfortable?"

"Certainly. You will know it when you experience it."

He huffed out a mortified sigh. "I have never before considered myself unproven in this arena. And yet you make me feel practically virginal."

"How appropriate"—he could hear the mischief in her voice—"for your wedding night."

"It is very helpful of you," he said, "to mock me in my moments of weakness and uncertainty."

"You have married me," she reminded him, "so you are stuck with it." But then she joined him by the boot scraper, her hand resting lightly on his arm. "I wish I had answers for you, Rufus, but I barely have answers for me. All I can say is that when I'm not sure what to do for myself, I've sometimes been able to take solace in doing something for someone else."

"Very Christian of you."

"Very funny."

"Miss Carswile would approve."

"I've given her other things to approve of." Now it was her turn to address the boot scraper. "Do you remember when I was living with Bonny and Valentine? And I was so miserable and so desperate to fall in love?"

"I remember your wanting to fall in love. I don't think I realised you were miserable."

"You wouldn't have. I'm rarely miserable when I'm with you, even if I'm miserable the rest of the time. I had convinced myself that *if* I could fall in love somehow, it would prove I wasn't broken or monstrous or permanently maimed by the death of our parents."

"Bellflower . . ."

"Don't." Her tone was brisk and not to be brooked. "I was being absurd. I would have pursued that absurdity, though, if it had not been for Peggy."

"Did she talk some sense into you? She's good at that."

"No, she fell in love instead, and had an almighty crisis over it. I know she gives off a great impression of being so very sound, but she can drama with the best of us when it suits her."

"And how did that help you?"

"Well," Belle admitted, "it didn't. At least not directly. But I did realise that I cared more about Peggy's happiness than my own folly. And so *I* was the one, believe it or not, to talk sense into *her*. Which did end up making me feel better."

"I'm not sure how that corresponds to letting a tiny bookseller do as he will with me."

"You get to answer someone's most profound and cherished fantasy. That is a great gift and a great responsibility, and a rare opportunity."

"A rare opportunity to fuck up irredeemably, you mean."

Belle became brisk again, which Rufus was discovering could be quite reassuring in its own way. "You will not fuck up, as long as you remain honest, and do not forget that fulfilling a fantasy is *also* a kind of fantasy. You are not there as a sacrifice to someone else's desires."

"And . . . ah . . . if I do find myself obliged to be honest?"

"Yes?"

"How do I . . . do that?"

"How do you be honest?" repeated Belle, in horrified accents.

"In this context." For some reason, the clarification did not seem especially clarifying. "How do I communicate my honesty?"

"With your mouth, in human words, is traditional." Belle paused. "And by pre-arranged signal if you foresee your mouth being substantially occupied."

"Go back to the first bit. Can you give me some examples?"

"*Please can you not* or *Can we take a break* or *I'm feeling uncomfortable*?" suggested Belle, a vague air of distress still clinging to her. "I am half-afraid to ask, but I fear I must: How have you negotiated such matters in the past?"

Rufus waved a hand insouciantly. "I have not, for it has not been necessary." Once again, his attempt to salvage the situation was making things worse. "Don't look at me like that. Most of my . . . I hesitate to use the word *lovers*, have been extremely swift and utilitarian affairs. My longer-term prospects have had their own complications."

"Like your priest?"

Damn Arabella Tarleton—or Lady Comewithers, as she was now—and her damned habit of paying attention. "What the hell do you know about my priest?"

"One hears things. Occasionally from *you*."

"Then how about we dwell no further on my tendency to fall for unavailable men? I am merely pointing out that in either context, it was preferable, for my own purposes, not to offer anyone the opportunity to"—Rufus attempted another insouciant gesture and produced something absolutely not insouciant—"to disregard me."

"I hope," said Belle in a small, fierce voice, "in future you will feel differently."

"Beggars cannot be choosers."

"You are no beggar, Rufus. Go talk to Gil. If nothing else, he will prove me correct on that score."

His heart churned in turmoil, and he hardly knew why. "The lengths you will go to in order to be right are quite extraordinary."

She shrugged, unperturbed. "Verity and I will be taking supper in the Queen's Head if you decide to join us. She's leaving first thing tomorrow because her virtuousness extends to mornings."

"What a lucky escape we had from each other."

Belle dipped a curtsy. "Another example of my indisputable rightness."

She gave his elbow an encouraging squeeze and went to join Miss Carswile and Gil, who had been politely, if awkwardly, maintaining a conversation with each other. With a few words Belle successfully extricated Miss Carswile, and, arm in arm, the two ladies continued on to the inn. That left Gil, standing at the roadside, managing to look everywhere except at Rufus. As he crossed the way to join him, Rufus belatedly realised he had once again become the subject—or the victim—of Tarletonian shenanigans.

"So," he said.

"Hello," said Gil.

"So," said Rufus again.

"Indeed," agreed Gil.

Having just gone to considerable trouble to scrape his boots, Rufus scuffed his toe into the dirt. While his most recent conversation with Belle had covered a substantial amount of ground, it had not, however, addressed the topic of how to initiate sodomy in broad daylight with a relative stranger. Rufus, of course, had his own methods, but they belonged to alleyways and docksides, and required a different sort of stranger.

"I understand," he tried, "that you could potentially be interested in . . . that is, you could potentially see me as a . . . participant in a similar endeavour to that which you planned for your original correspondent."

Gil pushed his glasses up his nose, his brow furrowing as he waded mentally through the mire of whatever it was Rufus had tried to say to him. Eventually he seemed to come to some kind of conclusion. "I'm sorry, but are you asking if I would like to menace you?"

It was hard to tell if it was worse or better to have the issue bluntly out there like the consequences of an undone breechclout. "Assuming that was something you were amenable to."

"Amenable?"

"Not actively hostile to?"

"Rufus"—Gil met his gaze with astonishing ease and directness—"if I have left you in any doubt, I can only apologise. I thought I was being tremendously unsubtle on the subject."

Doubt that he was amenable? Doubt that he was hostile? One of those was extremely bad. And the other was, now he stood at the brink of it, terrifying. "Which subject?"

"The subject of menacing you. For I am long past amenable. I am *ardent*."

"Oh," said Rufus, swallowing. "Well, that's . . . nice."

"Does this mean you, too, could be amenable?"

For a second or two, Rufus had no idea how to answer, even though the answer was *yes*. Because the wrong kind of *yes* was an ugly, vulnerable, naked thing. Except then he remembered what Belle had told him about being someone's fantasy. Of the power and humility in it. And, most of all, the need to be honest.

He smiled what he had lately come to think of as his Rufus smile, the one Belle had drawn from him. But he flavoured it with one of the Sir Horleys he had been for a while—a shameless, confident rogue.

"With a little help," he murmured, "I could probably find my way to *ardent*."

And was rewarded when Gil's eyes lit up like stars.

Chapter 26

"How does this work, then?" asked Rufus, intending for the question to be casual rather than interrogative, though nerves unfortunately brought it closer to the latter.

They had repaired to the cottage, which as Belle had told them was clean and comfortable, though not luxurious. Gil was kneeling by the grate, lighting a fire with surprising nonchalance for a man with menacing on his mind. "I would hope, however we want it to."

"I may need something more specific. Remember I am new to this particular"—Rufus made a gesture he hoped was illustrative but was probably just vague—"particular dynamic."

"Well." Rising, Gil put his back to the newly kindled blaze, looking far less ridiculous in his highwayman cloak than Rufus remembered. "This is one of my hideaways that I've brought you to."

"This cottage?"

"Indeed. Who would suspect?"

"Ingenious."

"One does not evade the king's justice through dullardry, lordling."

"And, ah"—Rufus couldn't quite tell if he was too self-conscious to be enjoying himself or if that was, in a strange way, part of the fun—"why have you brought me here?"

"I would not have had to, had you surrendered the kiss I asked for."

Without quite meaning to, Rufus altered his stance, attempting hauteur. There was, in all honesty, a touch of Belle in it. Especially the lifted chin. "That was presumptuous of you, sir."

"If you think presumption the worst of my misdeeds, you are sheltered indeed."

Gil came a couple of steps closer, his bootheels striking hard upon the flagstone floor. It was a natural instinct to step back in return, but Rufus decided to hold his ground and found himself circled instead. It was . . . disconcerting, though not unpleasant, especially when Gil murmured in approving accents, "Just look at you, lordling. So fine and so proud. Such a prize."

"I am no man's prize."

"Tonight, you will be mine."

It seemed correct under the circumstances, when Gil was facing him again, to attempt to slap him. Thankfully he had telegraphed the blow with sufficient theatre that Gil caught his wrist. Rufus could easily have broken free, of course. But he didn't, just put up a façade of struggle. Let his breath grow harsh and his heart beat quicker with it.

"Spirited too," said Gil, laughing.

What would Belle say? "Unhand me, you brute."

Using his arm ostensibly for leverage, Gil bore him to the bed and fell upon him, where they tussled for a little before Rufus was—with his tacit consent—thoroughly pinned, Gil fully atop him, holding his arms stretched above his head. Gil looked different from this angle, wicked and glittering, his curls falling hither-thither in happy carnage. Stubbornly, Rufus turned his head away, fully expecting . . . wanting . . . to be kissed regardless.

Instead, Gil merely nuzzled at his throat. "I tire of these games."

For a moment, Rufus thought Gil meant the *other* game and that he had proven himself an unsatisfactory subject for menacing—a discovery that would have troubled him not a jot less than a day or two ago and now felt rather crushing. "Whatever do you mean?"

"I do not intend to make this easy for you, my jewel. This is, after all, your doing as much as it is mine."

"I am not the one who carried someone off," Rufus pointed out, once again pleased by how well his friendship with Arabella Comewithers née Tarleton had prepared him for this whole undertaking.

"You did, however, try to have me captured. Did you truly think me so easily tricked?"

"Oh, because you would have settled for a mere kiss?"

"A mere kiss is it?" repeated Gil, half-mocking, half-not. "You undervalue your pretty mouth."

That rang a little too true to suit the story, so Rufus pressed on: "And then you would have been on your way?"

"But of course. Even highwaymen have honour."

"What could a rogue like you possibly know of honour?"

"More I'll warrant than those of wealth and power who sequester their sons away from the world, deny them knowledge of themselves, and sell them to the highest bidder."

Or leave them with a relative like an unwanted parcel. "How dare you. I am a gentleman, as I was raised to be. I had the finest education."

"Did they teach you this?" Gil's free hand pressed between Rufus's legs, giving his cock—which had so far been gently intrigued by the proceedings—such a confident stroke that he went from partial to full hardness so fast it made him dizzy.

"Oh-*ohhh.*" His startled gasp was real. As was the way his spine arched. "I . . . suppose they didn't." And that was not, from a certain perspective, incorrect.

"There we are."

The satisfaction lay thick upon Gil's tone like diamonds in a duchess's tiara, and Rufus, still laid bare with arousal, found it strangely heady. He tried to remind himself that this was nothing more than the simple art of pleasing, but it felt good to please someone—and whether that was for him, or for who he was pretending to be, didn't seem to matter.

"No, my jewel," Gil went on, settling his palm upon Rufus's chest. "I think this is what you wanted all along."

"I wanted to be seized by a ruffian?"

"You wanted something real. Something not prescribed by society or morality, or even your own family." Gil dragged his lips along the line of Rufus's jaw. "Tell me I'm wrong, lordling, tell me you haven't lain awake at night longing for a man like me, and everything I can give to you and share with you."

It seemed an apposite time to . . . well. Rufus didn't want to think of it as a whimper. Issue a dignified noise of conflicted protest such as an unravelling young lord might in such a situation.

At which point Gil caught him firmly by the chin and forced their gazes to meet. "Tell me no, and I'll take you back to the carriage. You can continue your journey—and your life—as if this never happened."

Rufus blinked up at him, ardour undiminished, though he was shocked afresh by that careful commanding touch. How did nervy, mild-mannered Gil, with apparently no experience and an exhaustive collection of fantasies, have this in him? And how easy he made it to . . . trust, play along, succumb as Rufus as well as in performance.

"If you don't say no," Gil promise/warned, "I'm going to kiss you. Because you do need kissing, my jewel. You need kissing thoroughly."

"Please . . ." Deliberately avoiding anything that could be construed as a *no* without sacrificing the ambiguity of someone caught in a slow spiral of desire, Rufus attempted a fretful flicker of the eyelashes. "I . . ."

"Say no. Or I'll make you mine."

Needless to say, Rufus did not say no. And Gil kissed him in exactly the manner he had indicated he would. Not just thoroughly, but relentlessly, mercilessly even, treating Rufus's mouth as if it was indeed a prize to be claimed. He was unaccustomed to having quite so much control taken from him quite so peremptorily, but he had also never been kissed with that kind of all-consuming passion. Which was not to say there had not been passion, even if, as a general rule, an act as tame as kissing had not been the focus of it. This, though, was a *gothic* kiss, perhaps even a baroque kiss: extravagant, absurd, and unabashed, lips sealed tightly to his, and a tongue penetrating him with undeniable intent. It was breath-stealing, heart-fluttering, a kiss for skies streaked with lightning, and rain lashing upon the darkened moors. A kiss for howling wolves and highwaymen, for torn shirts and rearing stallions, for every improper, impossible fancy anyone had ever dared to dream.

It left Rufus hot and flustered, needy and wrecked, only lightly sure of his own name. And Gil appeared to be just getting started.

"You are over-dressed for the occasion," he purred, clearly having the time of his life.

"Um," said Rufus. "Yes."

For he did, in fact, feel over-dressed, languid and feverish at the same time. It was almost a relief to be stripped, which Gil did for him, resolutely resisting any attempt to offer aid. That became self-consciousness-inducing again, Rufus having long lost any expectation of or interest in having his body lingered over. But Gil wanted to linger, and Rufus must have been temporarily enthralled because he allowed it. There was very little play to it, in the end, Rufus trembling with a kind of raw, re-discovered modesty, and Gil touching him with a wonder that felt neither staged, nor to Rufus's whirling mind, deserved.

"You know"—Gil pushed him back upon the bed—"that there's no shame in this, my jewel."

Oh, but there could be. Taking refuge in his part, Rufus cast an arm across his face and the genuine flush upon his cheeks. "I've never been naked with another person before. Let alone another man."

Gil, who had shed his cloak but otherwise remained mostly dressed, climbed up next to Rufus, running his hands freely across his body—long, sweeping strokes, from his throat to the base of his cock, down his flanks and up his thighs, a strange pattern of heat followed by electric awareness, until he felt bright within his own skin, illuminated inside and out.

"You are exquisite," Gil whispered. "I named you *jewel*, for so you are."

It took everything Rufus possessed not to leap off the bed and out of the nearest window. *You flatter me, sir* sounded like his line. But all that came out of his mouth was a croaked "I . . . I'm not."

Gil only laughed. "I did not take you for a liar, m'lord. Look, here's ivory and opals . . ." His fingers—which were as neat and precise as the rest of him—traced the interior of Rufus's thighs. The bend of his elbow. The side of his neck. "Carnelian aplenty." Here, he combed back Rufus's hair where it had fallen, sweat-heavy, across his brow and played a little amongst the silky red-brown strands that lavishly covered his chest and abdomen. "Malachite, of course." Kisses now, one upon each eyelid. "And let us not forget these tempting rubies."

It was predictable but also exactly right. Gil took his mouth again, and Rufus lost himself again in the pulling heat and fearlessness of it, more than willing at this point to be overwhelmed and possessed, cherished and spoiled. For desire to crest within him, unhindered by concerns like dignity, pride, and self-protection, and flow out of him in yielded lips and parted legs, and urgent moans that breached the confines of their kiss like spilled wine, as inevitable as floodwater.

"I'll have to take your word for it," he managed, dazed once more, and breathless, when at last they broke apart. "Given your choice of profession, I'm sure you must be a connoisseur of precious things."

"I am," said Gil, sounding briefly more like Gil. Before he distracted Rufus by straddling him and bringing their faces close together. "So tell me, my jewel, with what yearnings have you tormented yourself when you imagined this?"

It was a question Rufus wasn't prepared for and would not have been prepared for in any case, since his experiences were governed by acts and opportunities, rather than invitation and exploration. But it was even more disconcerting at that precise moment because he had just about reconciled himself to giving the lead over to Gil. With further consideration, however—and it was a minor miracle he was capable of thought at all—he understood what Gil was doing. It was one thing to pretend at powerlessness, or to choose it, another to have it imposed upon you. More than that, Gil was not seeking to be merely indulged in his own desires. He wanted a partner, an equal participant. To ensure the fantasy that had begun as *his* could become *theirs*.

Gil had returned to stroking the hair upon Rufus's chest. He seemed to have taken rather a fancy to it. "Your secrets are safe with me. I promise."

Chapter 27

Given their respective roles, Rufus's hesitation made a certain degree of sense, and he bit his lip in an attempt to convey someone torn between shame and passion. In actual fact he was trying to decide what to say. Something he thought would gratify Gil and amuse himself. Something he might have welcomed . . . needed . . . ached for when he was younger.

He cast his arm across his face again. "I . . ."

"Yes?"

"I wish . . ." He allowed his breath to hitch. "I wish to know how to please a man."

Gil laughed, fond and mocking, and clearly satisfied by the answer. "Well, aren't you sweet beneath your finery?"

"You asked," retorted Rufus, pouting with well-kissed lips, and trying not to laugh as well. "And I told you."

"That you did. But you *are* pleasing me. Who would not be pleased by such spirit and beauty?"

Rufus covered Gil's hand with his own. "I want more. I want . . ."

"You want to touch me?" Gil's voice had grown a little ragged, and Rufus did not think he was acting. "You want to feel how I . . . how *pleased* I am with you."

"*Yes.*" It did not take much acting for Rufus to sound breathless either. And he bit his lip once more because he didn't think you could do too much of that kind of thing.

Wrapping his fingers around Rufus's wrist, Gil drew him down to his cock, which was definitely rigid beneath his breeches.

Rufus made a little sound of shock and curiosity. "Can I . . . can I see it?"

"Of course, sweeting. You may have of me whatever you covet."

"Jesus Christ," exclaimed Rufus, forgetting his part as Gil uncovered *his* part. "Do you need a coachman to drive that for you?"

Pushing himself onto his elbows, Gil peered down at his own body. "Um? Is everything all right?"

"What?" Rufus was staring. "Yes. Sorry. Just, how do you not fall over."

"Oh, you mean—well, yes, I did sometimes wonder if it was . . . excessively dimensioned. But it does seem on par with what is represented in the illustrations and etchings to which I have access."

"Yes, but that's porn, man. You're not supposed to have one that looks like porn."

"Is, um, is it a problem?"

"God no. Though next time you attempt to arrange anything by correspondence, you should make sure to mention this." Then he dropped, with very little effort, into a breathier, more awestruck register. "It's so big. And hard. Is that because of me?"

Gil gave a cough that might have been a laugh. "Indeed it is."

"May I touch it?"

All Gil managed in response to that was a nod. And Rufus trailed his fingers up the—far from inconsiderable—length of his cock, trying to strike the right balance between eagerness and nervousness. In any case, the technique mattered little, for Gil slumped back onto the bed, a strained groan forcing its way between his teeth.

"Am I hurting you?" asked Rufus, with innocent concern, making a tight fist about Gil's girth.

Another sweetly agonised sound from Gil. "N-no, my jewel."

"Oh, look"—Rufus pressed his thumb against the head—"you are making pearls of your own."

"Perhaps I should have surrendered to your father's guards, for I fear you're going to be the death of me."

Rufus was enjoying himself to an outrageous degree. "May I kiss it?"

"Huuuhhnnhhhh," said Gil.

Which was a yes in everything but name. So Rufus spent a happy handful of minutes festooning Gil's cock with entirely chaste kisses, while Gil panted into the rafters and curled his fingers into the bed-clothes and appeared to subject himself to all manner of anguish rather than rock his hips or demand more. At last, Rufus took pity on him and dropped onto his knees by the side of the bed.

"What about like this?"

Gil struggled into a sitting position, his cock flushed and painfully hard. Then he caught up a pillow and laid it down, something it flatly hadn't occurred to Rufus to do. Once he was re-positioned, Gil put his legs on either side of him and took Rufus's face between his cupped hands. The tenderness of the gesture was only slightly impeded by the monstrous member that stood between them like a sea serpent rising from the deep. "It's truly what you want?"

"Yes," said Rufus, gazing helplessly up at Gil, faintly mortified by his own awful sincerity. And then, trying to bridge the gap between truth and character, added, "T-teach me how?"

"Do whatever is comfortable."

"What if I don't mind if it's uncomfortable?"

"Then that's your choice, but I will be captivated regardless."

Something hot and shuddery was travelling through Rufus's skin at this half-real gentleness, leaving him abruptly more naked than his nakedness should have warranted. He knew how to suck a cock—had, in fact, sucked many with great efficiency—but he was feeling oddly as though he didn't, in fact, know how to suck a cock. "How will I know what you like?"

"Because"—Gil was smiling like Gil—"I'll make sure you know."

And Rufus did know because Gil gave of his reactions with unrestrained generosity. It was an abundance of praise, almost to the point of embarrassment, but secretly Rufus relished it all. Every harsh gasp and broken moan, and the words that came in an incoherent stream, telling him how good he was, and how beautiful, and how his mouth was hot and tight and perfect. Rufus was trapped somewhere between the past and the present that was yet neither of them, almost wanting to believe the fiction they were spinning around each other. He'd always liked this act, even those first times, when it had seemed inextricable from shame, and later when it was so often rushed or enacted with little consideration. Something to do with the power and the powerlessness, and the sheer, all-consuming physicality of it, for, as far as Rufus was concerned, a cock never felt hotter, harder, or more demanding than when it was in your mouth.

This was especially true of Gil's, which stretched him wide, left his jaw aching, and blotted out his senses until all that remained was salt and skin, his own abbreviated breath, and the intimate taste of Gil. It was its own kind of blissful, overwhelming and a little base—for he could feel the moisture slipping between his lips, wetting his chin and coating Gil's cock—but he felt free to be imperfect, to struggle and lose himself, because he was pleasing Gil, because there was nothing to rush for and no guilt awaiting either of them. And because, in some kinder world, it was the first time he'd done this.

Eventually he drew back, with a wet gasp, discovering his eyes were wet, too, and his own cock, leaking and throbbing between his legs. "Can you," he managed to get out, "can you . . . help me?"

"Like this?" asked Gil, somehow still functional, resting his hands lightly upon Rufus's head.

Rufus nodded and allowed himself to be guided into position. The touch was anchoring and delicately threatening, stripping away a further layer of control, which was exactly what Rufus needed and was a little frightened of needing. Sometimes brutality excited him—giving over his body could feel, paradoxically, like something he was taking for himself—but Gil's cock was brutality enough on its own, and Gil seemed to recognise this, as he did not force Rufus down upon it. Instead, his hands were mostly encouraging, easing Rufus past his natural limits until that punishing crown pushed into the deepest part of his throat. He had a split second to feel ridiculously proud he'd taken such a beast and then his airway was convulsing, Gil was drawing him back up, and he was left coughing and drooling on his knees. Except the discomfort and the indignity were nothing in that moment. Not compared to the giddy wash of triumph and pleasure.

"Again," he rasped.

"Is it not too much for you?"

"Yes." Impatiently, Rufus blinked his streaming eyes. "But I like it."

Gil gave a nervous laugh. "It might be too much for me."

"You don't want me to—"

"No, I do. But I . . . I shan't last."

Re-settling his pillow, Rufus moved in even closer, feeling almost sheltered by having Gil's thighs pressed tight against him. "I don't care," he said. "Give me everything."

And this time, as he pushed himself down, he did not hesitate. He took the girth and the length, and opened his throat, letting Gil fill him completely. Despite his best efforts to breathe through his nose, the lack of air made him instantly lightheaded—his body wanting to panic but having no way to express it, and instead whirling him away to some sparkle-filled wonderland where fear and pain were bright and beautiful and wholly his. He did not know how to move, impaled so devastatingly upon Gil's cock, his whole world reduced to it and overthrown by it, but then Gil took control for him. His motions were oh so gentle, barely thrusting, but even that was enough for fresh tears to spill down Rufus's cheeks. To make helpless cries bubble in his throat, reduced instead to threadbare moans and choked-off whimpers. He wasn't sure he'd ever been so utterly used without the expectation of contempt. And it was one of the purest things he'd ever experienced.

Suddenly, Gil's hands tightened in his hair. It was probably a breathless hallucination, but Rufus was sure he felt the pulsing of his cock. And when he came, which he did with a sweetly heedless "Oh God, oh Rufus," he was buried so deeply down Rufus's throat that it wasn't even necessary to swallow.

Afterwards, he pulled Rufus onto the bed, Rufus apparently having lost all control of his limbs, and held him with no diminution of conviction. He was saying things again, and Rufus was sure they were lovely, but he was still adrift, far away even from his own body, which was riven with a trembling that would not cease. He was conscious only of his well-fucked throat and un-fucked cock, the former flayed gloriously raw, the latter thrumming hotly with unanswered need. He went to give himself relief, the instinct as unquestioned as a man in the desert reaching for water, but Gil caught his wrist and prevented him.

He made a fretful questioning sound.

"Do you think I'm done with you yet, my jewel?"

He made another fretful questioning sound.

"Ten minutes and I'll be yours and you can be mine all over again."

Oh, to be in your early twenties. "Or," Rufus managed, his voice little more than a whisper, "you could use your hand right now."

Seeming to recognise the time for games had slipped quietly away from them, Gil dropped his highwayman persona. "If that's what you prefer. But I'd love to fuck you."

"In ten minutes?" It seemed, to Rufus's present state of mind, important to establish that.

"Five, if you keep looking at me like you'll die if I don't touch you."

"I could very well die."

Gil stroked the outside of Rufus's thigh, the touch falling somewhere between soothing and inflaming. "Did what we—did it rouse you so much?"

"No," snapped Rufus. "I'm exaggerating for my own entertainment."

"Sorry. I'm . . . flattered, that's all. It felt so very much *for* me I was worried I'd been selfish."

Somehow Rufus managed not to grind his teeth or sigh or shove Gil out of bed. "No, I . . . I like being able to give . . . something to others."

"What a wonder you are."

"Yes, yes. I'm a hero among men."

"But that makes it even more important that I don't neglect your pleasure now."

"I told you, I *got* my pleasure. Or rather, I will when you let me—" He made a more energetic attempt to reach his cock, and, on this occasion, Gil did not stop him.

Instead, he just turned those expressive brown eyes upon Rufus and said, "Please."

"What do you mean"—Rufus felt oddly agitated—"please?"

"I mean, please let me *give* you pleasure too."

"You want to fuck me that badly?"

Gil nodded.

"All right. Fine. But at least get your damn clothes off."

Chapter 28

Gil shucked his garments in less than thirty seconds, emerging from them like a selkie from its skin. He was slim and smooth, and a little too pale, perhaps due to a career spent poring over lost and forbidden books. But having his faced fucked seemed to have made Rufus sentimental because words like *lovely* and *exquisite* insinuated themselves into his mind. He was a man of contrasts was Gil, the dark and fair, awkward and resolute, endlessly soft of heart and relentlessly hard of cock. A beguiling cupbearer who would bend any persuadable god over his own throne.

"I hope," he said aloud, "you didn't think you needed to stay dressed to enact your menacing."

Gil shrugged, a little shyly. "Maybe. But I also liked the"—he indicated Rufus, then himself—"difference? Having you naked when I was not. Did you mind?"

"No."

"Oh. We'll need . . ." Crouching down, he rummaged through the pockets of his coat until he found a vial of what looked to be oil, holding it aloft with an "aha."

"Very prepared of you."

"Well, you probably wouldn't last long as a highwayman if you weren't thinking several steps ahead."

Gil put the vial on a nearby table and re-joined Rufus on the bed. He was already well on the way to tumescence, and his first act was to snake a hand between Rufus's thighs. Without the game between them, he found himself, unexpectedly, a little at a loss—his body, stirred almost past bearing, trapped behind his mind. After what could have been seconds or long minutes, Gil reached for the vial again. His touch was exquisitely cool and slick as silk when he caressed Rufus's cock.

"Are you with me?" he asked, his eyes flicking up to Rufus's face. "Is there something else I—"

"No. I'm sorry. No." He was not used to being noticed when he slid away, as long as the rest of him was there, giving or taking, pressing or yielding, depending on what the moment demanded. Truthfully, he did not always notice *himself* doing it. Back in his skin, he re-discovered the sweet, lingering pains of use and the deeper ache of unfulfilled arousal. "I . . . ," he began, more than a little horrified to discover he was speaking. "I do not mind to take this part. But the first time, it was not . . . I did not especially enjoy it."

Gil stilled above him.

"It was not intended to be . . . ," Rufus went on quickly, only to discover he did not know how to finish, ". . . that way. But I was young. Neither of us knew what we were doing. We were fearful of being caught. I, ah, I think of it sometimes when I do not mean to. It was a long time ago."

"Rufus . . ." His name on Gil's lips should not have meant anything. And yet it enfolded him. "Would you rather my mouth or my hand? I'd offer to trade places, but I get so little out of it."

"Then we certainly should not."

"It's not," Gil over-explained anxiously, "a *problem*. I'm just not responsive to it, as I understand others can be."

"That's probably a blessing." Reaching for Gil's cock, Rufus palmed the shaft lazily. "If you were responsive there and with all this, too, it might be the end of you."

"I can imagine worse ways to go."

"Better, I think, to live."

"I like this plan." Gil rolled on top of him and kissed him a little more tenderly than before. It was not usually the sort of thing he had much patience for, but Gil was as demanding in sweetness as he was in command, and Rufus was still not quite together. Not that this, skin all over skin and a cock burning like a brand against his hip and a tongue at play within him, was liable to aid that. "But what would you like?"

Rufus raised a knee to better encompass Gil, letting him settle naturally between his thighs, against the cradle of his pelvis. "This is fine."

"Perhaps you'd rather be ravished by a highwayman?"

It was honestly tempting, which was in itself slightly astounding, since a handful of days ago, he would have scoffed at the very notion. Except the alternative was, in its own way, equally astounding. "I think I'd rather be ravished by you."

Despite having recently stuck his cock as far down Rufus's throat as it could go without causing actual injury, Gil blushed. "I . . . I can do that."

"You know, you can still menace people as yourself."

Gil got that not-unhighwaymanly glinting look. "People?"

"Me. You can menace me."

Seconds ticked by, Gil doing nothing, and Rufus—impatient, aroused, and trying not to feel too exposed by all this—not appreciating Gil doing nothing. Then Gil bent down and scooped his cravat from the cottage floor, looping it between the slats of the headboard. Rufus's face must have done something because he said quickly, "Just hold the ends."

"You can—"

Gil shook his head. "No, I'm going to want your arms around me sometime soon. This is enough."

In truth, Rufus was relieved as he took hold of the linen. He felt safe with Gil in this context, more than he had felt safe with anyone for a long time, perhaps ever, and he was mindful of Belle's encouragement, to be generous with others and to himself, but his feelings were sufficiently complicated that he was glad to have the decision made for him and glad for that decision to have gone the way it did. He knew he hadn't *lied*. He would probably have found ways to enjoy being bound, at least with Gil. But the sensation of being stretched out, his hands occupied, was vulnerable enough, even when voluntary.

"I love how you look like this," murmured Gil.

"Frustrated?"

"Available. At my mercy. Like a wild thing, bespelled."

Turning his face into the side of his arm, Rufus muttered, "Oh, stop your nonsense."

"And"—gripping his chin, Gil forced his head back—"somewhat hard-used."

The shudder seemed to roll through Rufus's whole body, making him tighten his grip upon the cravat. "Use me more?"

"Not this time." Gil grinned, far too wickedly for a demure bookseller. "This is all for you."

And Rufus would surely have delivered some kind of retort about Gil getting something out of it, too, except Gil took the opportunity to press a slick finger into him, and every word Rufus possessed fluttered away like starlings in autumn. He knew his body well enough these days to easily accommodate intrusions to it, but this one, anchored by a cravat he clung to of his own volition and a string of prior choices—choices to give, to hope, to share, to trust—he felt deeply. He wasn't initially certain if it was a bad deeply or a good deeply, and then it became such a *very* good deeply that he threw back his head and canted his hips and all but begged for more.

Which Gil gave him, with one finger, two, one again, three, filling him and fucking him, teasingly, roughly, unpredictably, far beyond anything he thought he needed. He tried to protest—he was not, after all, the delicate flower he had fleetingly pretended to be—but other than a kiss pressed against the groove of his thigh, Gil ignored him.

That was when Rufus realised he was being spoiled. Petted and pleasured into a receptiveness he would have given of his own accord. The feeling this engendered was sharp and unfamiliar, perilously close to humiliation. It made him want words and clothes and walls and distance. Because it turned out that being given what you needed was one of the hardest things in the world to take.

But he would take it.

For Gil. And for himself. And for Arabella Tarleton, who saw him and had married him, and believed he deserved good things.

By the time Gil had replaced his fingers with the head of his cock, Rufus was halfway to ruined, his body in constant motion, sweat running in rivulets across his skin, hands locked tight upon Gil's cravat. The stretch of entry was intense to the point of violating, but he just melted into it, wanting that sense of fullness—of completion and connection—so profoundly that there was barely a struggle.

In many ways, the touch of pain made it better.

Made it real.

Because while not everything in life had to hurt, he thought the best things, the ones worth fighting for, should a little.

Once he was fully sheathed, Gil seemed to go to pieces somewhat himself, falling over Rufus's chest with a sound that could almost have been a sob. Releasing the cravat, and ignoring the prickling sting in his arms, Rufus embraced him, and, for long minutes, they stayed like that, breathless and entwined and locked together.

It did not, in the end, take much more to finish them both. A handful of only half-heard words. Some clumsy thrusts from Gil. Rufus's legs thrown about him. The messy collision of mouths that, in that moment, rapturous and straining and losing themselves, passed for the most perfect of kisses.

Rufus was hardly aware of his climax approaching until he was already in the throes of it. He was used to it being the goal, the point, the conclusion which rendered all that preceded it worthwhile (assuming, of course, that it did). This time it was something else entirely. It was triumph and annihilation and completion. It was stepping back from a tapestry to see the whole picture revealed at last and yet knowing the colour of every thread and the placement of every stitch.

For a long time after, he floated on the pleasure, a shipwrecked sailor cast upon the mildest seas. And Gil, still in his arms, still inside him, floated with him. In languid harmony their pulses slowed, their breaths softened, and Rufus told Gil to get that damn thing out of him before it split him asunder.

"I need to get better at that," said Gil, having settled back down, with his head upon Rufus's chest.

Currently, Rufus was engaged in the act of tracing idle curlicues upon his companion's arm, not the sort of impulse he was prone to experience, nor to be indulged in. "From my point of view, you're already extremely good at it."

"I mostly meant the . . . the ending sequence?"

"The what?"

Gil made an extremely peculiar gesture that Rufus interpreted as representing a dick going into an arsehole. "I had no notion how overwhelming it would feel, despite my best attempts to practice."

"You might need to explain that."

"Practice in general, not practice for you specifically."

"You still might need to explain that."

"Oh. Well. I created a sort of device?"

"A sort of device?"

"Yes, a sort of . . . tunnel? Out of leftover binding leather. Lined with silk. Which one could oil. Why are you laughing?"

"I'm not," lied Rufus. "I'm celebrating your ingenuity."

"With laughter?"

"Exactly."

"In any case," Gil went on placidly, "it was a meagre substitute for the reality."

Thrown off guard even by implied praise, Rufus did his best not to squirm. "Glad you, ah, enjoyed yourself."

"Oh, I *loved* it. You were so warm inside."

"I should hope so. Otherwise I would probably be dead."

Gil made a sound of lustful yearning. "And soft yet also strong. Smooth from the oil and *clenching*—"

"We really don't need to discuss my interior in quite this much detail."

"My apologies. But you do have a delectable interior."

"It would be a shame, wouldn't it," mused Rufus, "if someone was smothered by a pillow right about now?"

A comfortable silence fell between them, during which nobody's innards were subject to debate and nor was anyone murdered.

"In all seriousness, though," said Gil at last, dropping a neat kiss upon one of Rufus's nipples. "Thank you."

And there were a million facetious things Rufus could have replied, but he wasn't, in the end, capable of any of them. "No, Gil. Thank you."

"Come by the bookshop sometime?" Gil picked up his heavily creased cravat from where Rufus had discarded it and let it dance across his skin. "Perhaps we can explore this more thoroughly?"

Rufus's heart knocked hard and insistently. There was curiosity there, and desire, but fear also that could have been the right kind of fear. "I might not be able to, but I'm willing to try . . . with you."

"And if you have any friends . . . ?"

"You want me to bring them?"

"What?" Gil laughed, biting lightly at his shoulder. "No. How insatiable do you think I am?"

"Substantially insatiable."

"That's . . . not inaccurate," Gil admitted. "I would, however, still prefer to menace my gentlemen friends sequentially rather than simultaneously. And over and above that, I should like to know more than one person like me, without the need to rely upon correspondence."

"Understandable. But I should probably note at this juncture that I do not have a good history with friends myself."

"Your friends have been bad to you?"

"I have not been in the habit of seeking friendship. And I do not think I have always honoured it or recognised it."

"You have me. And Miss Tar—that is, Lady Comewithers."

"Yes," Rufus told the ceiling, inclined to blame the hearty fucking for the sudden onrush of emotion.

Gil tilted his head to better see Rufus's face. "Are you all right?"

"Mmm."

"Are you sure? You aren't regretting your—"

"No. God no."

"Then perhaps you're missing her?"

"I saw her only this afternoon."

There was a pause. "Rufus? Would you like me to get her for you?"

At that he sat up abruptly, drawing Gil with him. "I did warn you I did not treat my friends well. Forgive my . . . my unpleasant manners. I am happy to be with you. I would not throw you from my bed, only to replace you with—"

"Your wife?" Gil was laughing. "And your manners are far from unpleasant, believe me."

"I would not have you feel unwelcome."

"I do not. All things being equal, I would choose to stay but mostly—in candour—from the ulterior motive of hoping to have my way with you again in the morning."

"Then do stay. And you shall."

"Tempting, my jewel. Another time."

"Please don't feel—"

Gil was already pulling his clothes on. "I cannot linger. The king's men are tracking me."

"Gil. Stop."

It was enough, in fact, to make Gil stop. In shirt and breeches, he tumbled into Rufus's lap. "God, your sweetness."

"I am not fucking sweet," protested Rufus, horrified.

"You haven't hurt me. You've given me the night, well, the evening, of my life. I'm happy, I'm grateful, and I rather like the idea of slipping away as such characters do in the ballads."

"What happens to me?"

"I suppose you see your wife and then go home to wherever you live and come and visit me again sometime?"

"No, I mean . . . you stole away with this innocent lordling, deflowered and seduced him. How is he to return to his sheltered life now?"

Understanding flared in Gil's eyes. "Such thoughts definitely haunt you, but return you must. Awakened to desire as you are, you are still who you were raised to be, and duty beats strong within your breast."

"So that is my future? Convention and obedience, and the memory of a single night?"

"Not at all. Your husband—"

"My husband?"

"Yes indeed." Gil nodded eagerly. "Our story takes place in a world where such things are possible, common even. While it was a match arranged by your parents, for your family's betterment, you find your husband unexpectedly handsome, charming, and kind. He is immediately captivated by your beauty and spirit, and in the bedroom . . . well, far from being shocked by your passion, he is delighted by it. He treats you as his equal in every way, except when you wish otherwise behind closed doors, and very soon you are utterly in love. Bar a single incident where—on the very cusp of achieving everything you wish with each other—it feels as though you will break up, you live happily ever after."

"And yet," asked Rufus, "I still occasionally seek the company of my highwayman?"

"No, you have no need."

"But I thought you said—"

"Let me tell you something else about the highwayman."

Charmed, in spite of himself, Rufus reached out to try and tease some order back into Gil's curls. "Please do."

"He has an enemy."

"As of a few minutes ago, he had many."

"He has a *particular* enemy. One who has sworn personally to bring him to justice."

"A determined gentleman indeed."

"But"—Gil wagged a finger—"a talented rogue always has a plan. I have set a trap for this determined gentleman. He will find himself taken, bound, and entirely at my mercy."

Rufus's cock stirred curiously. "Surely you do not expect him to yield to a blackguard like you?"

"Perhaps"—Gil's smile was brilliant—"we shall find out."

Then he kissed Rufus one last time, hard and swift and certain, pulled on his boots, picked up his cloak, and vanished into the night without a backward glance.

Chapter 29

For long moments after he had departed, Rufus sat on the edge of the bed, letting his mind somersault freely through everything that had just happened, for he felt neither hollow nor sad nor sullied. And he was not, he reflected, accustomed to partings that were performed in care. That carried with them no sting of shame or disregard.

He did not think Belle would join him—she had a bath and cheese to think about—but for decency's sake he pulled on some garments and climbed beneath the covers. Had he been a fool to let Gil leave? Maybe. Maybe not. In some ways, it was a mercy to be alone with his thoughts and his churned-up feelings. No need to pretend or perform, for—as much as he liked Gil—there were still things he did not want to share.

And this was one of them. The terrible fragility of happiness.

He must have slept, dozed, closed his eyes for a minute because when next he stirred, Belle was doing her best to get under the bed-clothes without moving them—a physical impossibility if ever there was one.

"I'm so sorry," she whispered. "I was trying not to wake you."

"Belle" was the only answer he had for her.

Which she seemed to take as the invitation it was to dive into his arms, her unbound hair spilling over him, her face tucked against his neck. She smelled and felt so familiar he could have wept. Everything he had done with Gil had been wonderful—exactly as brutally overwhelming and unremittingly considerate as he had needed—but he needed this too. Even if he couldn't fully articulate the *this*.

He just knew it began and ended, belonged to and with Arabella Tarleton.

She plunged a freezing foot between his knees. "You are my favourite person to hug."

And you are mine. "Did you come all this way in your nightgown?"

"Yes. All this way. Across the street and down the road. Gil lent me his highwayman cloak."

"We must already be a scandal."

"This is Gretna Green. We are *tame*. The innkeeper was telling me about a lord who wanted to marry his . . . housekeeper, I think it was? Anyway, he came in disguise as a woman, and the family got into a huge fight in the street. How can some minor bedswapping hold a candle to that?"

She had a point. Say what you would about Belle, she always had a point. "I'm glad you're here," he said aloud.

"Are you sure? I was fully expecting you to spend the night with Gil."

"I . . . I wanted you. I like"—he attempted a gesture, but for such a tiny person, Belle had a way of pinning you down—"this. Though I suppose it will not be necessary when we are not living from inn to inn."

"Is necessity the only reason to do it?"

"Men who fuck their wives rarely sleep with them."

"Bonny and Valentine sleep together every night."

"Yes, but they *are* fucking."

"If there are rules here, they seem very inconsistent. Perhaps we should just abandon them and do what we please? In fact, perhaps that *should* be our rule."

"That we do as we please?"

He felt her nod.

"We are embarked on a very unusual marriage."

"It was always going to be." Her voice was a little muffled. "Better to embrace it, don't you think?"

The cottage was quiet but for the fading crackling of the fire Gil had lit earlier. Rufus twisted a lock of Belle's hair around his finger—so like her, in its fairy-tale abundance, and its ridiculous resilience, springing back into coils the second you let it go.

"When I was drunk"—the words came out of nowhere, but did not surprise him, for he often felt them lurking—"did I, by any chance, mention my uncle?"

Belle lifted her head briefly. "Oh yes," she said cheerfully. "You told me you murdered him."

"Once again I am compelled to ask: And you still thought it was a good idea to marry me?"

"Well, if you literally murdered him, I'm sure you had a good reason. But I assumed it was more that you blamed yourself for his death."

"I do."

"While I am not privy to the details, I do not feel I need them to assure you that you should not."

"It is not a matter for *shoulds* and *should nots*."

Her eyes sought his, softened by the firelight. "What do you mean?"

"That some things move beyond questions of what is right and what is wrong, and all that's left to navigate them is how you feel."

"What was your uncle like?"

He knew she had altered course as a kind of strategy. In that moment, however, he welcomed it, for he would not have been able to speak without her spur. "Not like my aunt. To be fair, she was somewhat different when he was alive. She was still hard and self-righteous, but I think he must have made her happy."

"I feel compelled to remind you that she cared less than nothing about your happiness."

"I did not intend to take him from her." He tried to state it calmly. A simple case of fact. But his entire self betrayed him, and it emerged as a desperate whisper, seeking an absolution it was not Belle's to grant.

"Of course you did not," she said firmly. "You were little more than a boy."

"I was not a boy. I was nearly a man grown."

"Then let us not lose sight of the *nearly*, shall we?"

"My aunt has always disliked me. I have never known why. When I came to discover my inclinations lay towards other men, it almost made it easier. It pointed to something specifically wrong with me. Something that deserved her ire."

Belle's fingers curled into him so fiercely that her nails pricked him.

"Irrespective of your nature, Rufus, I cannot fathom why she should take against you so violently. You were a baby when you came to her."

"I know." He lifted a shoulder in a supine approximation of a hug. "She has always told me she felt it from the very first, the stain of iniquity in me, the moment she beheld my hair as unrepentant as hellfire. Perhaps it was because I was only her child in name."

"There is no such thing as a child *only in name*. If a child is your child, they are your child."

"Dear heart, do you mean to draw blood?"

With a little *eep*, Belle pulled her hand away. "I'm so sorry. I am just so very unhappy with your aunt."

"I was not trying to . . ." Rufus broke off, scenes from the past swirling behind his eyes, muddy through a memory of tears. "It was not perversity or vengeance. My uncle treated me . . ." He broke off again. "I would once have called it *kindly*, but my definitions are shifting. He treated me decently. And I would have done damn near anything for the barest scrap of affection. I *did*, in fact."

The pillow, this time, took the brunt of Belle's reaction. Which was to say, she sat up and punched it soundly. Then laid herself back in his embrace. "It was unbelievably wrong of him to do that to you, Rufus. Unbelievably."

"He did not. He is not the villain of this story. His greatest crime was probably incompetence."

"I despise incompetence," retorted Belle. "I sometimes think it is worse than malice."

It was not a situation in which Rufus could ever have imagined laughing. But he laughed now.

"I mean it," she insisted. "At least when someone hurts you out of malice they've put some effort in. When someone hurts you because they didn't know better or because they didn't care enough—urgh. There should be a special circle of hell for such people, where they spend eternity giving themselves paper cuts." She paused, flushed and breathless. "Giving themselves paper cuts in the webbing between their thumb and their finger."

With an effort, Rufus controlled himself, and wiped his eyes of the tears that had sprung to them beneath the protection of mirth. "My uncle was simply a man who did not understand who he was. I almost pity him sometimes, living his whole life that way, content yet miserable, and never quite knowing why."

"I do not pity him in the slightest," said Belle, with neither hesitation nor mercy.

And Rufus kissed her brow, touched, in a strange way, by her conviction. It had not occurred to him that anger could have been something he deserved or was allowed to feel. Too late now, of course. The past had carved its grooves into him, and time had only deepened them. But here was Belle, absurd, irritating, relentlessly loyal Belle, and she was furious on his behalf. It poured over him like cool water, like rain on a summer evening. It could not cure him, it could not change him, but it eased his long-borne pains and washed him gently clean.

"In any case," he told her, "my aunt found out. He took his own life. And that was the end of it."

"It was the end of it for him. You have lived with it."

"I have certainly had the better bargain. Though I do wish I'd been able to see that sooner."

"I am sorry"—Belle threw herself protectively across him—"for everything that happened. For then and for after and for anything that has made you believe, even for a second, that you are not worthy of all the good things in the world."

"Oh, shush now," he whispered, abashed and overcome. "You do know, don't you, dear heart, that you are the only person who has ever truly seen an iota of good in me."

She was still clinging, despite the fact she probably couldn't have stopped a reasonably aggressive mouse. At last, though, she looked up. "I would love to take credit for that, truly I would. But it's really less to do with me and more to with the fact other people are so terribly, terribly *stupid*."

And, once again, somehow, impossibly, Rufus was laughing.

Chapter 30

While the journey to Gretna Green, with its many delays, had taken longer in terms of actual time, Belle found the trip to Swallowfield close to agonising. It was like the day before a celebration, if the celebration in question only came around once every fifteen years or so. As a married woman, however, she felt it behoved her to act with maturity and restraint, which meant she only expressed her impatience every three to four hours, rather than every one to two. Rufus, with no such qualms, remained a terrible traveller, restless and easily bored—although, with her judgement compromised by fondness, Belle found it rather charming. They were not, after all, bored of each other, Rufus even remarking that every couple probably ought to spend a few weeks in a box together, since if neither of them ended up murdering their spouse, that was a good test of compatibility.

Eventually, though, after six or seven million years, they had made it to Warwickshire, deciding to continue on to Swallowfield rather than spend another night at yet another inn. Belle had progressed from agonised anticipation to a kind of bewildered disbelief—she was going home, she was really going home—and she pressed her face to the carriage window, searching for anything she remembered. Did the landscape, with its twisting paths and crowding woods, seem more familiar to her than other landscapes they had passed through? Or did it just look like England? She thought she liked it more, perhaps. There were few things as magical as a forest at twilight, suspended between sunset and moonrise, mist and shadow, not quite gold and not quite silver, not quite dark and not quite light. But was this how her parents had died? A too-tight turn upon a too-rough road, on some rainy night, grown dark quicker than anyone expected?

Then Rufus, roused from whatever stupor the dragging hours had cast him into, leant across the carriage to touch her knee. "'Men have died from time to time, and worms have eaten them, but not for love.'"

As You Like It had never been one of Belle and Bonny's more pored-over plays, for it contained neither twins nor murder. "Pardon."

He flashed a smile at her. "I think this is the Forest of Arden, my Rosalind."

"If I am to be Rosalind, you would prefer me a Ganymede."

"I prefer you as nothing but who you are. Are you nervous?"

"No," she snapped. Then, "Maybe?"

"All will be well."

"That's a different play."

"It still has a happy ending."

They continued on in silence, down roads that seemed to narrow as the dark pulled tight around them. Belle's hopes jangled uncomfortably with a stirring sense of unease that she told herself was nothing more than natural anxiety over a long-delayed homecoming.

"I think," she said doubtfully, "this is our carriageway?"

Rufus, either oblivious to the brambles and weeds obscuring the way or deliberately ignoring them for her sake, gave a heartfelt groan. "Thank God. I am going to have the longest bath in the history of mankind, even ousting Valentine."

"I . . ." She paused, the thought catching up to her only as she spoke. "I don't know what I'll do?"

"Just so long as it isn't trying to sneak into a mediaeval sewer."

She snapped her fingers, striving for levity. "Dammit. That was exactly what I was planning."

"How about," suggested Rufus, "I have my interminable bath, you ask for supper to be brought upstairs, then we acquire some clean night-clothes from somewhere—"

"Oh, we would be living the dream."

"Wouldn't we? And then we read some more *Fanny Hill* until we run out of candle or fall asleep? We rise at whatever time we please and spend the whole of tomorrow in the daylight reintroducing you to your home."

Belle's heart smooshed with gratitude and a touch of guilt because she could not imagine anything more perfect. And Rufus could proba-bly imagine many, *many* things. "I would love that."

"Same. Experiencing that book with you has been one of the high-lights of this journey, dear heart."

Gil had left it amongst their things, and they had taken to reading a few chapters a night, with the rule being that the second person had to take over narrating the moment the first one laughed. "It was not having a trifle thrown at you?" asked Belle innocently.

"No."

"Or nearly being put in a pie?"

"These rural tourist attractions never live up to their reputation."

Belle laughed. "You know, I'm sure Gil didn't just *happen* to forget such a valuable text by accident."

"Clearly it was his contribution to our mental integrity over the course of the journey."

"*Clearly* it was his way of ensuring a visit from you."

To her delight, Rufus blushed. "That too."

Suddenly Belle caught a glimpse of a shape upon the horizon. With trembling fingers, she yanked down the carriage window and stuck her head out. "Is that it? Is that our house?"

"Probably, but"—Rufus yanked her back in—"but for the love of God, be careful. That tree nearly decapitated you."

Settling back into her place, Belle twitched and wriggled, trying to look ahead without further endangerment of life and limb. "It does seem a little more, well, fairy tale? Than I remembered."

"It might need cutting back a bit," Rufus agreed. "But it probably looks worse in the dark."

"*Worse?*"

"More overgrown."

"It does seem as though we ought to be able to see the house by now."

"It's always the same with these country manors. The approach lasts forever."

Belle narrowed her eyes. "You're lying to me."

"I'm reassuring you."

"By lying."

"I don't know enough about the area or your home to lie, Belle. I have some mild concerns. But that does not mean there is anything to be concerned about."

"I feel a little strange too," Belle admitted, glad to have been able to say it aloud. "I didn't think it would be like this. But then I also don't know what I was expecting. Or what it *should* be like."

She knew Rufus well enough by now to recognise his various selves—the playful friend, the protective companion, the audacious hedonist, the callous sophisticate, and the tender, shattered man beneath them—and she also knew he saw them as fractures through the truth of him. Instead of simply what they were, which was the truth itself. Right now, she was getting Practical Rufus, the one who had been honoured by Wellington and sewn up her arm before she died of blood loss. The one who dumped volatile young men into water troughs. "Given there was no opportunity to send news of our coming," he said, "it may simply be that the staff are unprepared. We may find the house partially closed up. You should be prepared for that."

"Yes, of course." She did her best to seem comforted. "You're right."

Twenty minutes later, they had disembarked the carriage, leaving it in the care of the coachman, and were standing at the far end of the bridge, looking up at a still and silent house.

"Partially closed up?" asked Belle.

Rufus, too, seemed at a loss. "Forgive me for what is probably a very silly question, but is this the correct place?"

"There's the moat." Belle pointed to the sluggish waters that flowed beneath and around them.

"Mmm," said Rufus.

She turned slowly upon the weed-choked gravel, familiarity and strangeness passing her back and forth between them like dogs wrestling over scraps. The stable block, which stood—much as she remembered—to the left, at least seemed relatively well kept. But the farm beyond it had fallen utterly into disrepair and stood as dark as the main house. Not sure what else to do, Belle stepped onto the bridge and walked briskly to the gatehouse, Rufus keeping easy pace with her. The Elizabethan oak door that admitted visitors to the gateway was not locked, but that had always been the case, for it had stood open all day and only ever been closed at night. What was wrong, so very wrong, was the quiet.

"Where is everyone?" Belle's voice was swallowed up by the surrounding stone.

This time, Rufus didn't even try to reassure her. "I don't know."

"What's happened to the courtyard?" It had run wild with neglect, what had once been a neat lawn now a field of waist-high grass, the surrounding paving pushed out of joint by dandelions and dock leaves. "There used to be flower beds here. Rufus, I—"

"Shh." He caught her in his arms before panic could take hold completely. "Perhaps maintaining the house was not a priority to the estate. There may well be an explanation for all this."

Old fears and old furies were rising up inside her. That crushing sense of powerlessness that came from the world changing without you and in terrible ways. From having no choice but to put your trust in people who didn't care for the same things you did. And for being utterly betrayed, even though you should have expected it. "He was supposed to take care of it. He promised. Valentine *promised*."

"He would not break his word."

"Everyone says that, but he does. He has broken his word to me."

"If you mean your engagement, I think you were equally responsible for that."

"Before. He promised me his friendship, and then he forgot all about us. But still"—she gave a bitter laugh—"I am only a woman, and so he remains an honourable man."

"Belle—"

She pulled out of Rufus's embrace, not quite able to bear it. "Please don't defend him. Not right now."

For a moment, she couldn't tell if he was going to try and argue with her, but then he just nodded. "Let's try to find someone we can talk to. There's a light in one of the rooms."

He was right, though that single distant glow, like a lost star, only made the house look more forlorn. Like some poor creature, half-blind, and run to ground. "The kitchen maybe?" she suggested.

She picked her way through the mess of the courtyard and pushed open the side door that led to the south-east range, which housed the servants' hall, as well as the kitchen, pantry, and scullery. There was, indeed, a candle burning in the kitchen, but Belle got no further than the threshold. Rufus shoved her behind him so hard and fast that she banged her elbow upon the doorframe, her view of the room entirely obscured by his body for several seconds. From the way his shoulders moved, he seemed to be grappling with something. And then came the resounding *clang* of an iron skillet landing heavily upon the floor.

"What," demanded Rufus, at his most imposing, "is the meaning of this?"

Chapter 31

From the interior of the kitchen, there came a scramble of motion and a woman's voice. "Begging your pardon, sir. We thought you was ne'er-do-wells."

"Do you get many ne'er-do-wells popping into your kitchen?"

"Can't be too careful." Whatever Rufus had done to cow the stranger, she was becoming progressively de-cowed with every passing moment. "And gentleman or no, that don't explain why you're creeping around someone else's house in the middle of the evening."

"Ah yes. The middle of the evening. A famously prime time for larceny."

There was a brief silence. Then, "You what?"

"We're not creeping," Belle protested, mostly to Rufus's back. "Or doing any larceny. This is my house."

"I very much doubt that," returned the now thoroughly cowless servant. "And if you don't turn right back around, I'll . . . I'll—Miss Arabella?"

Belle had finally managed to squeeze under Rufus's arm, still clutching at her elbow, because was there anywhere worse to take a blow? The room beyond him was dimly lit, the fire mostly embers, and the candle little more than a stub, but all in a rush she remembered. She remembered it full of light, pale as flax in the mornings, and saffron gold in the late afternoon, and the cream-painted panels, and the moulded crossbeams that turned the ceiling into a giant game of noughts and crosses. She remembered sheets drying before the grate on rainy days, and the big brass scales that sat upon the countertop, and the stoneware jars that were full of secrets, not all of them as delicious as Bonny found to his cost the day he snuck a spoonful of what turned out to be mustard powder, and the big table where you were allowed to sit if you were good and watch plums being chopped for jam or dough kneaded for bread or gravy stirred for dinner, and if you were very *very* good, Hannah might—

"Hannah?" cried Belle, rushing into the embrace of a stranger who was not a stranger. "Oh, Hannah, I can't believe you're still here."

"I can't believe you've come back, miss. We thought the place was done for."

Reluctantly, Belle made herself let go of Hannah. She and Bonny, in the way of children for whom *grown-up* was a single category, had always assumed the cook was old, but she must have been young. She was still young, in fact, although she looked tired, her soft brown hair streaked here and there with grey. "Who is *we*. And what's happened?"

"That's a long story, miss. It's—"

The back door opened, and a slim, slight, clean-shaven man of about Hannah's age rushed inside, wielding an honest-to-goodness pitchfork. "Whoever you are," he announced, "and whatever the fuck you're doing, if you don't—"

Stepping forward, Rufus neatly parted him from the pitchfork. "Why is everyone around here so violent? Is it something in the water? Or is it something I'm doing specifically?"

"You're breaking into our house is what you're doing." The newcomer squared up ill-advisedly to Rufus, a doomed David versus an elegant Goliath.

"Tom, no." Hannah put herself between Rufus and the man addressed as Tom. "Miss Arabella's come home. And this is—actually,

I don't have a clue who this is. But"—and here she turned back to Belle—"this is the *we*. We're all that's left."

"I don't think we've met before?" said Belle, peering at Tom hesitantly. "Maybe you weren't here when I was growing up?"

"Oh, he was, miss. He was just different then."

Tom cleared his throat. "I used to be your mother's maid. Did a shite job of it, I'm afraid to say. I think at the end she was keeping me on out of pity. I work in the stables now, and do what I can for the grounds, which isn't much. And"—his chin came up proudly—"if that's a problem for you, I'll pack my things right away."

"If Tom goes"—Hannah stepped to his side and put her arm through his—"I go."

"Would you say," asked Rufus of nobody in particular, "that a journey from assault to blackmail is a de-escalation or the reverse?"

"I'm not trying to force anything," protested Hannah. "Just stating a fact."

"I'm confused," said Belle, ignoring Rufus for now. In all honesty, he was not at his most helpful, perhaps because he hadn't liked someone trying to clonk her with a skillet, even if it was circumstantial attempted clonking. "Why would I have a problem with Tom taking care of the stables? I mean"—she glanced again at Tom—"are you bad at it? Do you eat the horses?"

Outrage flashed across his face. "No, I don't eat the horses."

"Well then." Belle shrugged. "Nothing else is my business, is it?"

"Some people might reckon it was, miss," offered Hannah, shifting uncomfortably, her fingers tightening on Tom.

"Well, they'd be wrong," said Belle, dismissing that particular matter. "And please don't think me ungrateful for the fact you stayed and for everything you've done, and continue to do, for my family, but what's happened to my house? Where are the rest of the servants?"

Hannah made a fretful sound, blowing air across her teeth. "Dismissed. It's him got sent down from London, miss."

"The one who was supposed to manage things?"

After a moment or two, clearly reluctant to gossip, she nodded. "It wasn't so bad at first. I mean, he was always a snooty fu—fellow, gave himself all sorts of airs. But he seemed to be doing right by the estate. And then . . ."

"Then," Belle prompted.

"Then he just sort of . . . stopped, miss."

"Stopped?"

Hannah nodded again. "The farm was the first to go. Then everyone except us. Things started falling apart, and we tried, we tried to talk to him, didn't we, Tom?"

"Did you take your skillet and pitchfork?" enquired Rufus.

"I'm so sorry." Belle sighed. "He gets like this when he's worried I've been, or could have been, hurt. Rufus, I'm fine. Hannah, Tom, this is my husband, Sir Horley Comewithers. Technically, I should be Lady Comewithers, but for the sake of my continued health, I would like to remain Miss Tarleton."

"Oh, I couldn't." Hannah seemed genuinely scandalised. "Not now you're a married woman."

"Mrs. Tarleton then."

"It's not done, Miss Tar—m'lady. What would your husband say?"

"Her husband says," murmured Rufus, "that my wife can call herself whatever she damn well pleases. And, if it comes to it, I am more than happy to be Mr. Tarleton within this household."

Belle spun round, startled, her emotions swimming far too close to the surface. "You . . . you would allow it?"

"Why not?" He cast up his hands in a gesture of resigned exasperation. "You have explained to me in some detail why my own name is appalling and needs to be taken away and burned. Besides, this is your house. Your family. Your history. I"—he got that nervy, defensive look that suggested incoming sincerity—"would be honoured to be a part of that."

"Then it's settled," declared Belle, intending to hold him so tightly later it would annoy him. She returned her attention to Hannah and Tom. "What happened when you tried to speak to . . . I don't think anyone ever told me his name?"

"Smith," said Tom, in the tone most people reserved for obscenity.

"Mr. Smith," added Hannah, as if this would somehow make it better. "And what happened was nothing very much at all. Just flat out ignored us, he did. Said it wasn't our business and not our place."

"And we reckon"—the words exploded out of Tom, despite Hannah's attempts to hold him back—"he's been thieving. It started small, candlesticks and what have you. But—"

"But we can't swear to it," Hannah interrupted. "Though we did think best to take some precautions, begging your pardon for the liberty, Miss Tar—Mrs. Tarleton."

From the corner of her eye, Belle could tell Rufus was trying very hard to check his amusement. "Precautions?" he asked.

"Yes." Hannah hung her head. "We took some of the valuables and we . . . we stashed them in one of the old priest holes."

"Which one?" Somehow Rufus was maintaining his composure.

"The . . . the one . . ."

"The one down the bog," explained Tom. "We thought Mr. High and Mighty wouldn't look there."

"And we was right," Hannah concluded, still looking downcast, but with a trace of satisfaction in her voice.

"Well, my dear"—Rufus put a hand upon Belle's shoulder—"it seems that you shall go to the ball."

Tom eyed him, as though he was genuinely concerned Rufus had lost his mind. "*Bog* means *toilet*."

"I don't know how to begin to thank you both," said Belle, thinking it best to steer the conversation away from sewers, mediaeval or otherwise. "While I'm horrified by what's happened here, I'm even more horrified at the thought of how things would have gone without you."

"We've done our best," Tom told her, his eyes anxious and earnest. "But it's not good. Nothing's been cared for. Not for years."

Belle was doing her best to remain stalwart. But the thought of all that time and neglect piling up like dust in this place that she'd loved for so long was almost enough to reduce her to tears.

"Then," said Rufus quietly, "we shall simply have to start caring ag—" His head turned sharply. Somewhere in the distance came the undeniable creak of a hinge and the muted thud of a door closing. This was followed by a splash. "What was that?"

Tom scowled. "Probably Mr. Smith making a break for it, the weasel."

"That's what he thinks." Rufus took a few swift steps across the kitchen. "Hannah, do you have such a thing as a knife?"

"I do." Opening a drawer, she produced a moderately sized one and passed it over.

"Ooh," said Belle, rallying somewhat. "Are you going to stab him?"

He spared her an exasperated glance and a "Belle, no" before striding out of the room. Somewhat confused by his actions, Hannah, Tom, and Belle exchanged a few glances of their own before hurrying out after him. By the time they caught up, he was already halfway across the bridge.

"Where are you going?" asked Belle, panting slightly, for Rufus had long legs, and she had the opposite. "What are you doing? You are aware he went the other way and is probably through the gardens and across the fields by now?"

"I'm aware. Tom"—Rufus threw the words over his shoulder—"can you help the coachman with the carriage? And apologies in advance for what I'm about to do to the rig."

Even in the face of extremely erratic behaviour from the household, Tom proved stalwart. "Of course, Mr. Tarleton."

"I should probably apologise to you too." This was addressed to one of the carriage horses, which Rufus had severed from the traces with a few swift cuts of the knife. "You've already had a hard day. Belle, take this, and no stabbing under any circumstances."

She took the knife carefully, and Rufus flung himself onto the horse's back. It did not seem wholly impressed by this behaviour, weaving where it stood and bucking slightly. Belle had been around Peggy long enough to recognise expert handling when she beheld it, and, sure enough, Rufus had calmed his steed within moments.

"Where is he likely to be heading?" he asked.

"He's been going to London on the regular lately," Hannah called up. "For all the good it's done him. He came back in a right state the other day, though he tried to hide it."

"So London?"

"In his shoes"—that was Tom—"especially considering they're soaking wet, I'd head to Lapworth first. South-west."

Rufus gave one swift nod to the bystanders, clicked his tongue to urge the horse into motion, and then they were gone in a flurry of kicked-up gravel, hoofbeats fading into the night.

"Gawd," exclaimed Hannah. "Bit dashing, your Mr. T, isn't he?"

And Belle could only agree.

For even though it was not what he wanted from life, Rufus was proving to be an exceptional husband. He was amusing, supportive, thoughtful, pleasing to look upon, and apparently more than capable of chasing down an errant steward at a moment's notice, not a quality she would have previously considered vital. It made her feel faintly guilty, not the steward specifically, just the amount in general he was doing for her, when—with her house about three rainstorms from falling into ruin—she had even less to give than she'd thought she had.

While she waited for Rufus to return, she left Tom to stable the remaining horses and returned to the kitchens with Hannah. There, too agitated to sit—even when offered a cup of tea—she took up the candle and began a steady exploration of the ground floor, Hannah trailing anxiously behind her, trying to prepare her for the worst.

"It won't be as you remember, miss."

"I know," Belle said. "I know. But I have to see."

Though perhaps she should have listened. With the rugs grown threadbare and the panelling dull, with what furniture remained covered in sheets and pushed out of the way, with portraits missing from the walls and books from the library shelves, the house felt like no place she could remember. No place anyone could ever have called home. Upstairs was even worse because the ivy—which was crawling unchecked up the exterior stonework—had got under the roof in what had once been Bonny and Belle's room, bringing part of the wall down with it. This in turn had let in the rain, rotting away much of the panelling, leaving black-and-green mould to bloom blotchily across the ceiling and wind through the exposed plaster, bringing with it the undisputable reek of decay.

Hannah tried to wrestle a tattered curtain across what was clearly an attempt to board up some of the worst of the damage. "I'm so sorry. We did what we could, but it was too late."

The worst of it was, Belle could barely remember the room or its contents, whatever it was that Hannah and Tom had tried to save for her. Their books maybe? Favoured childhood toys? Had they been writing their stories even then, or had they had no need in those days of imaginary places and fantastical adventures? She didn't know. She would never know. And how futile it was, this desperate grief for things so lost that even memory rejected them, like the sound of her mother's laughter, or the colour of her father's eyes.

"You've nothing to apologise for," she told Hannah, because now was not the time to bow or buckle or break. "You've done more than enough. More than I'm sure I deserve."

"Your family has always been good to us."

"Even so, I'm astonished you stayed."

Hannah's mouth turned down briefly. "I can't pretend it was only loyalty. It was some of that, mind. But Tom wasn't sure about his prospects elsewhere, and . . . well . . . Tom and me, we . . ."

"You're as married, as I understand."

"It used to get talked of. It probably still would if there was anybody left to talk. Either them as used to know Tom thinking it strange and them as don't calling me no better than I ought to be for taking up with a man I'm not wed to."

"Then maybe you should make an honest lad out of him."

Once again, she'd slightly shocked poor Hannah. "But is that right, miss?"

"It's never wrong, Hannah, to be with someone you care for."

From below came the clatter of hooves, and they rushed to the cracked window just in time to see Rufus dismounting from his sweat-flecked steed, dragging a struggling bundle from where it had been unceremoniously tossed across the horse, and then equally unceremoniously tossing it over his shoulder.

"Well, I'll be," cried Hannah. "That's him. That's Mr. Smith. I never thought I'd live to see the day."

"Live to see the day he got hauled about like a sack of potatoes?"

Hannah was grinning, a cat who had not only got the cream, but had secured access to the pantry. "Couldn't happen to a more deserving fellow."

By the time they returned to the kitchen, Rufus had just entered it and was casting a drenched, extremely dishevelled gentleman to the floor in front of the grate.

Belle glanced from Rufus to the stranger, who as well as his other indignities was sporting a swollen lip, a black eye, a bruise upon his brow, a long cut across his cheek, and another upon his chin. "What in God's name have you done?"

"He was like this when I found him." Only mildly winded, Rufus settled into a nearby chair.

"You"—the young man uncoiled like a snake—"are a fucking *madman*."

Rufus raised an eyebrow. "And you, my dear, are a fucking thief."

This earned a shrug, then an inadvertent wince as though the shrug had been more painful than the shrugger anticipated. "So turn me over to the magistrate."

The supercilious Mr. Smith was a lot younger than Belle had thought he would be—her age, perhaps, or a little older. He was tall and angular, with a long, pointed face and heavy-lidded eyes that probably contributed to his reputation for being up his own arse. The situation was not doing him any favours, but she would have been hard-pressed to imagine a less prepossessing villain. And yet here he was. The man who'd treated her home, her past, like a carcass to be stripped. She could barely stand to be in the same room as him.

"What happens when we turn him over?" she asked.

"Probably they hang him." Rufus shrugged. "Or ship him off to Australia so he can play with the rest of the cockroaches."

Belle looked again at Mr. Smith. His irises were the palest grey, like frost-encrusted glass, and seemed to reflect no emotion whatsoever. No guilt, no fear. Maybe—if she searched—deeply embedded bitterness and a kind of sullen resignation. "I can't think about this tonight," she said. "If only we had a dungeon we could lock him in."

"What about the brewery?" suggested Hannah, ever resourceful. "He's not getting out of there in a month of Sundays."

"Yes. Put him there." Exhaustion was beating at Belle like waves against a cliff. She could feel herself crumbling a pebble at a time. "And make sure he has a towel and a change of clothes. Some blankets for the night."

"How magnanimous of you"—Mr. Smith's sneer was both audible and visible—"to take such pains over my comfort in your improvised dungeon."

There were things Belle could have said. Probably should have said. But she was as done as could be. "Oh, fuck off," she told him instead.

Then she went upstairs to one of the rooms that did not have an enormous hole in the wall, thought fleetingly about removing the dust sheets from the bed, gave up before even trying, and simply threw herself down upon the mattress, where—with dust billowing around her—she burst into tears.

She was still crying when Rufus joined her, having presumably seen to the incarceration of Mr. Smith.

"Dear heart," he said, putting a hand upon her shoulder, for she refused to turn around or even straighten from her woe-struck curl. "Please. You'll make yourself ill."

Belle snuffled desolately. "I insist you call him out. And then murder him. Very very hard."

"While I'm sure he deserves it, I don't think we should be taking the law into our own hands."

"What use is the law to us?"

"Well, we are rich and upper class, so quite a lot."

"But *he's* a duke."

"Mr. Smith?"

"Valentine."

There was a pause. "Ah."

"He's ruined everything," Belle wailed. *"Everything."*

Rufus stroked her back soothingly. "He has land of his own to govern, more money than any reasonable person would know what to do with, and Bonny to distract him. He has been drastically inattentive, but none of this was intentional."

"You know," she said, reaching for fury because it was so much *easier* than pain, "that I find negligence worse than cruelty."

"Even so, I do not think my killing him will improve the situation for anyone."

"It would improve the situation for me."

"Yes, but Bonny would be very upset, and I would likely have to flee to the continent."

"I would flee with you."

"Not to undermine your display of devotion, but that would be absolutely the least you could fucking do after inciting me to shoot our friend who is literally a duke."

"Benedick was willing to kill Claudio for Beatrice."

"And it turned out best for everyone that he didn't go through with it. Besides"—nudging her into the middle of the bed, Rufus lay down next to her—"you're a free-thinking modern woman. If you want to murder Valentine, do it your damn self."

Belle flipped onto her side immediately. "May I?"

"That wasn't supposed to be encouragement." Implausibly, the sight of her repulsively swollen and tear-stained face seemed to make something in him soften. "We will fix this, Bellflower. And without recourse to random acts of violence against our nearest and dearest."

"Fix it how?" she asked, overcome by a fresh flood of tears.

"Well, as far as I understand it, the land is no longer mortgaged, so that is a quantifiable asset we possess. We also have your dowry and apparently a privy full of valuables, which we can sell if we need—"

The breath seized in Belle's throat. "No. We are not *selling* my family's things."

"Very well. We have a privy full of valuables we can use to make the place look attractive. And as yet we do not even know what happened to the money Smith has been taking from the estate. Perhaps some of it can be retrieved. And more importantly, we have each other, we have our resourcefulness and ingenuity, and we have time."

"I'm afraid"—Belle could barely speak through the sobs that choked her—"I feel neither resourceful nor ingenious. I just feel . . . I just feel so *sad*."

"As well you might. You've had a challenging day." With a now-familiar motion, he drew her into his arms. "This must be devastating. It is, however, nothing that cannot be undone. You will see that tomorrow, when you will also remember you are one of the strongest, bravest, kindest, most appallingly creative people I know."

She buried her face against his shoulder. "Oh, but Rufus, I have *lied* to you."

"You have never lied to me."

"I promised you a h-home. But it t-turns out I c-can't even give you that."

"Belle"—he gave her the tenderest of shakes—"now you're just being a goose. A home is not a place. Trust me, for I have never had one before."

She wanted to argue with him. To point out that this was utter sophistry. Because while you could make a grand case for home as an abstract concept if you wanted, a house with a partially collapsed roof, a stagnant moat, and rooms filled with dust and dark made for a terrible one. But she was too tired, and tears had rusted all her words to nothing.

So she lay next to him on an unmade bed, both of them still in their travelling clothes, weary and none too fragrant, taking what comfort she could simply from his presence. She was grateful to him for concealing whatever disappointment he felt, for not rebuking her, when she would not have blamed him if he had, but she was also terribly, terribly ashamed. Why did she never learn? Why did she always believe—or hope—she could help people? That, despite what she lacked, rejected, and recoiled from, there was still something in her that was good. She had been so sure she was doing right by Rufus. So sure that she could give him some of what he needed.

But all she'd done, in the end, was cost him the rest.

Chapter 32

Rufus was at the very least partially right, and Belle felt better about some things in the morning. Approximately the same for others. Worse for a few. In daylight, she could see the full extent of the disuse the property and the surrounding land had fallen into. But she could also see what was left of the house itself—its wood-panelled, higgledy-piggledy Tudor cosiness, the coloured glass windows in the somewhat hyperbolically named great hall, casting gem-bright shadows upon the floor, the fireplace in the drawing room with its ornately carved pilasters, where lions played amongst flowers—and catch whispers of the home she remembered. Echoes not wholly lost to time.

"I don't know where to begin," Belle admitted, hopeful and discouraged at once, as she sat on the edge of the table in the kitchen, munching bread and jam.

Apart from a little tired, Rufus looked no less resolute than he had the night before. "Probably with the man in the brewery?"

"I . . ." She swung her legs disconsolately. "I don't think I want to be responsible for a man's death." A pause. "Unless it's Valentine."

"Then he can be transported. He is not our problem, Bellflower. At least, not personally. He has certainly *caused* some problems."

"What if the money is gone?"

"Then we use what we have." His face darkened momentarily. "If push comes to shove, we can possibly petition my aunt to—"

"How about," suggested Belle, "we don't do that?"

"Valentine, then?"

"Under no circumstances."

"This situation at least partially arose due to his lack of oversight."

"That's as may be, but I am sick of my life being a trinket for him to disrupt and disregard as the mood takes him."

Rufus took up her hand, even though it was slightly sticky with jam, and kissed the knuckles with a courtly flourish. "Then fuck him too."

"I don't mean to make things difficult for us."

"Oh, please. What else was I doing with my life before I met you?"

It was true that he had been in the midst of making some very poor decisions, but could she not have found a way to reach him, to set him free of other people's nonsense, without permanently entangling him in her own? Unfortunately it was far too late now, and she did not think a round of mid-morning lamentation was fair to him, especially because he might feel obliged to comfort her, as he had last night.

"Very well," she said, hopping down from the counter. "Let's go talk to Mr. Smith."

❦

Mr. Smith, in breeches and shirtsleeves, with a blanket round his shoulders, was sitting on the floor of the brewhouse, which like the rest of Swallowfield stood sadly denuded of its former character and purpose. It was a windowless stone room with an arched ceiling and benches running down either side, which Belle remembered bearing barrels and bottle racks, alongside big, exciting jars full of bubbling liquid.

"Have you decided what to do with me yet?" Mr. Smith smirked up at them with what struck Belle as rather hollow defiance. While he wasn't soaked through with stale moat water today, he still looked terrible—his eyes shadowed and red-rimmed and his face lopsidedly swollen, dappled all over with dried blood.

"What happened to you?" asked Belle.

"Someone saw fit to hunt me down like a dog, and then I spent a night in an abandoned brewery—what do you think?"

"Before that. You've been beaten."

Mr. Smith made an attempt at a wide-eyed expression, but it just made him wince. "Have I?"

"This is getting us nowhere." Rufus was leaning casually in the doorway, arms folded. "Where's the money?"

"Gone."

"Gone where?"

"Wherever money goes when it is forcibly redistributed into the economy—small businesses, I assume, the pockets of particular individuals, criminal enterprises?"

Rufus quirked a brow. "Belle, we should inform the Sheriff of Nottingham immediately of this man's capture."

"But think of the Lady Marian," returned Belle, clutching her hands against her heart.

For the first time since they'd encountered him, a flicker of *something* crossed Mr. Smith's face. Discomfort, she thought, at being laughed at.

"You admit it, then?" Rufus pressed him, serious again. "That you've been stealing from the estate?"

Mr. Smith resumed his blank and sullen stare. "Would it serve me to deny it?"

"It would if you hadn't," Belle pointed out, wondering if he would even believe her, "and this was some kind of . . . awful misunderstanding."

"I for one"—that was Rufus—"often leap into moats and embark upon cross-country midnight sprints for all manner of innocent reasons."

There was a long silence. Mr. Smith's battered fingers twitched where they rested upon one upraised knee.

"A thief, then," murmured Rufus, "but not a liar."

Their prisoner only shrugged.

Belle watched him, perplexed. "Are you perhaps morally unwell in some way?"

"Am I what?"

"I don't know. Internally compromised and unable to tell right from wrong?"

"For God's sake"—an expression of irritation flashed over Mr. Smith's face—"I know it's wrong to steal. I just didn't care."

"Oh," said Belle. Then to Rufus, "I can't believe Valentine hired this man."

This seemed to rouse Mr. Smith from his carefully maintained apathy. "I have a double first from Cambridge and excellent references."

"Excellent references from criminals?"

"No, from Lord Mulbridge. I was his steward for a while."

"Until," suggested Belle, "you stole from him?"

"I did not steal from Lord Mulbridge."

"Just from me?"

Some complex emotion stirred in the wintry depths of Mr. Smith's eyes. Possibly shame. "I . . . I did not know I was stealing from you."

"Who did you think you were stealing from?"

"A duke."

"Belle." Rufus spoke up, anticipating her. "Irrespective of your feelings about Valentine, it is still not ethically permissible to steal from dukes."

Belle glanced over at him. "It does make a difference, though, doesn't it?"

"I'm not sure it does."

"It makes a difference to me," Belle declared. "And not because of Valentine. Because I would always wish to understand the *why* of something."

"I do not owe you explanations," muttered Mr. Smith.

"No"—Belle gave him a sharp little smile—"you owe me significant financial redress, but I don't think you're in a position to offer that."

"What does it matter what I say? You already know I'm guilty."

Belle regarded him with a touch of impatience. "Do you *want* to go to Australia? They have enormous spiders over there. Enormous spiders that can kill you."

There was a long silence.

"Ironically," said Rufus, "I find myself in agreement with our charming recidivist here. What can he possibly tell you?"

She shrugged. "That's up to him, isn't it?" She turned back to Mr. Smith. "Why did you do it, please?"

Another long silence. And then, beneath the crust of old blood and bruises, Mr. Smith's mouth twisted into something that was almost a smile. "'Wherefore should I stand in the plague of custom, and permit the curiosity of nations to deprive me, for that I am some twelve or fourteen moon-shines lag of a brother?'"

Rufus blinked. "So you're a bastard? Or a thwarted actor?"

"The former," returned Mr. Smith, his voice once again stripped of inflection.

"The circumstances of your birth, unfortunate though they may be, do not justify your crimes."

For a moment it seemed like Mr. Smith might fall back on scorn. But all he said was "I know." And, with visible reluctance, "I just wanted something of my own."

"You mean," Belle asked, "my things."

The shame surfaced again and was hastily banished. "A home, at some point. The possibility of a family. A life not lived in thankless service to my *betters*."

"We all live our lives in service to something or someone," Rufus said mildly.

"Some of us"—bitterness roughened Mr. Smith's voice—"get more choices about it."

"This is ridiculous," Belle announced, after some consideration.

"Indeed." Rufus pushed away from the doorframe. "Shall I fetch the magistrate?"

Belle startled. "What, no? I only meant, it's ridiculous trying to have a conversation with a man who looks like Rumpelstiltskin on a bad day. Is Hannah in the kitchen? Can we have some warm water and a soft cloth?"

"Of course."

But Mr. Smith, who had an air about him that, while not quite vanity, suggested a preference for precision, in both dress and person, had taken Belle's comments somewhat amiss. He levered himself upright against the wall, his disdainful gaze sweeping from Rufus to Belle and back again. "What manner of man are you to do the bidding of a woman?"

This only made Rufus laugh. "One who isn't a dick. Something you could learn from."

"I'm sorry," said Belle once he had departed. "I did not mean for my comment about your appearance to sound like criticism. Blood and filth is an unfortunate look for most people."

"Most people? Who does it become?"

"Triumphant pugilists? Fictional Vikings?"

Mr. Smith stared at her, curious—animated even—for perhaps the first time. "I . . . I was not prepared for you to have an answer for that."

"You should probably be prepared for me to have an answer for everything," Belle told him.

"I'm sure that will be very useful to me amongst the enormous killer spiders in Australia."

Belle sighed. "Mr. Smith, I think we would both prefer it if you didn't have to go to Australia."

"I would certainly prefer it," he admitted warily. "I don't know why you would."

"Perhaps because I know a little of what it is to feel overlooked and unfit for the world. For your choices to feel either constrained or irrelevant."

"But I *stole* from you."

Belle thought of the dusty rooms and the dark corridors, the collapsing roof, and the tangled courtyard. "I'm hoping you had a lapse in judgement."

"Honestly"—something wry crept into his voice—"I don't know what I had."

The door opened and Rufus returned, bearing a bowl of water, a couple of cloths thrown over his forearm. The former he placed on the floor, the latter he passed to Belle. "As requested, dear heart, and my masculinity remains unimperiled."

"Sit down, Mr. Smith." Belle knelt on the edge of the blanket and began wetting the cloth.

"I can tend to myself," said Mr. Smith, pressing himself against the wall as though he would have liked to tunnel through it.

"I'm sure you can. But I'm going to do it anyway because I'm a monster."

"There's no need."

"Listen"—Belle nudged him in the ankle—"you can't see yourself. Count that a blessing and let me work."

So Mr. Smith sat as directed and remained rigidly stoic as Belle did her best to clean him up. The face that emerged was still in a bad way but considerably easier to behold.

"At this point," Belle remarked, "you might as well tell us how this happened. Oh, was it the ghosts?"

Mr. Smith's good eye gave a slight twitch. "The ghosts?"

"Yes, the house is full of ghosts. At least one priest murderer, and several murdered priests. Maybe they took exception to your ransacking the place and beat you up."

"How could ghosts accomplish that? They're ghosts."

Belle dabbed carefully at his nose, relieved it was battered rather than broken. "Well, obviously they couldn't strike you in a conventional fashion. But they could throw furniture at you, drop things on your head, and trip you as you went downstairs. You know, general irate ghost behaviour."

"I'm sorry to disappoint you, but this is the work of mortal fists and boots."

"I *am* disappointed," Belle agreed. "What is the point of having ghosts if they do not rise up in defence of one's domicile?"

Something that could have been amusement warmed the almost translucent grey of his eyes to silver. "You must get your next steward to manage them better."

Belle glanced briefly at Rufus, to see how he was taking this, and was surprised by the way he was watching them both. Amused, but with a lightness beneath it. Almost a glow. She focused again on Mr. Smith, feeling . . . she hardly knew what. Pleased? Reassured? "So who did it, then?"

"I didn't catch their names. But they were employed by the gaming hell I'd gone to in an attempt to make my fortune with the money I'd taken."

"You intended to gamble your ill-gotten gains?" murmured Rufus. "Risky."

"I intended to restrict myself to vingt-un. If one is aware of what cards have been dealt, and what cards are yet to be played, it is possible to calculate the probabilities of success or failure, and make one's decisions to stand or otherwise on that basis."

Rufus made a sound of grudging interest. "Ingenious."

"I told you"—Mr. Smith cast him a look, at least as pained as it was proud—"I am."

As gently as she could, Belle began to clean his split lip. Once again, he neither flinched nor complained, but his breath was a little unsteady against her fingers. "It does not seem to have done you much good on this occasion."

"On the contrary, it worked too well. The house insisted I was cheating, reclaimed my winnings, as well as the money I'd brought with me, and delivered the lesson I am still wearing." Mr. Smith's control slipped a fraction, his shoulder slumping. "Since I could hardly seek redress for the loss of stolen funds taken from me by an illegal gaming establishment, there was nothing for me to do except come back here." And there again, in his words and in his manner, was that delicate trace of irony. "I had not counted on the sudden return of the actual owner."

"And to think," said Rufus, "you would have got away with it if not for—"

"I would never have got away with it," Mr. Smith finished for him. "It was a foolish, desperate plan."

"Let us not forget, illegal and immoral."

Mr. Smith sighed. "And against the natural order, if that is where your philosophy tends."

"It is not where *my* philosophy tends," said Belle. "I do not believe in natural order. But I have another question."

"You earlier claimed that you had an answer for everything. You did not say the same for questions."

That drew a laugh from Rufus. "Oh, it's both. With Belle, it's usually both."

"It seems to me"—Belle tried to choose her words carefully—"that you did not take this position with the intent of doing harm?"

She wasn't sure if Mr. Smith would reply. He'd been quite resistant to conversation earlier, though having her in close proximity to the wounds on his face seemed to have softened him slightly. Maybe just because he didn't trust she wouldn't poke him in the eye. Eventually he offered a single, reluctant "No."

"And you did not steal from your previous employers?"

"No."

"Then what changed?"

"Can we get on with having me transported now?"

"Is the truth so unconscionable?"

He shook his head. "No, but it belongs to me. I have lived my life in service to others, to be worthy of others. I will not give up what little I still possess of . . . of"—he made an abortive gesture of despair—"myself."

"I can understand that," said Belle, because she did. "I suppose that leaves you with a couple of choices, then."

"Hanging or transportation, I'm aware."

"I was thinking more—do you wish to stay or not?"

Rufus, who had resumed leaning against the doorframe, now pushed away violently from it. "You cannot be thinking of letting this man go?"

Belle shrugged. "What would be achieved by not doing that?"

"He's a thief."

"I think," she said hesitantly, "being a thief and having done some thievery might not necessarily be the same?"

"Our actions define us."

"Not always. Not in this case. It seems out of character for him. He has no history of it, nor has he expressed any intentions of continuing a life of crime."

"Or remorse," Rufus threw back. "He hasn't expressed any of that either."

Mr. Smith interrupted them with a soft, wretched noise, despite the fact Belle was no longer touching him. "It is not necessary to defend me."

"Well," she said, "you're doing a terrible job of defending yourself."

"I am not *trying* to," cried Mr. Smith, once again irritated to the point of an outburst. "When will you understand, I am not going to give you what you're looking for? I'm not going to explain myself or make excuses, I'm not going to grovel repentantly before your sanctimonious friend, and I'm not going to beg for leniency either. You cannot take any more from me. I will not let you."

Belle regarded him steadily. "I am not *asking* you for that. I am asking whether you wish to stay or go. If you go, I hope you will change course re: the criminality, and, in the light of your actions, I'm afraid I cannot offer you a reference. If you stay . . ."

"If I stay?" Mr. Smith repeated, looking rather stunned.

"If you stay," she finished, "I am in dire need of a steward, for my house appears to have suffered greatly in my absence, and I am given to understand you have a double first from Cambridge and an excellent testimonial from Lord Mulbridge."

Mr. Smith just stared.

"It will require a lot of work. This is not an easy job."

With what seemed to be a visible effort, he recovered some semblance of his former arrogance. "I do not need it to be an easy job."

"But please," Belle suggested, "try not to steal from me again? That would be embarrassing for both of us."

"I swear upon—" Mr. Smith broke off, apparently out of things to swear upon.

"Your honour?" suggested Rufus. "Your father's name?"

"Rufus," protested Belle.

"This is a mistake, Bellflower," he told her, gentling his tone.

"Then"—she rose, dusting off her skirts—"it's my mistake to make."

"It isn't," insisted Mr. Smith, surprising them both with his sudden vehemence. "I mean, it is your decision, but—it's not a mistake. I will make sure of it. On my life, I will."

Chapter 33

"I don't trust him," said Rufus, not entirely unsurprisingly.

Belle looked up from where she was drying her hair by the fire. "You don't trust anyone."

"Yes, but that's usually because I am a misguided cynic who finds it easier to spurn people than risk caring about them. On this occasion, however, young Mr. Smith has literally stolen from you."

"Which has left me a poor target for further theft."

It had been a strange and disorientating day, one Belle had mostly spent—when she had not been interrogating criminals in a disused brewhouse—re-discovering her own home, moving memories around like broken puzzle pieces, and trying not to become utterly over-whelmed by how much had changed, how much had been lost, how much would need to be done. That they should create a habitable space to sleep in had, in the end, been Rufus's suggestion, offered per-haps out of practical necessity, or because he saw, or sensed, the swirl of her mind and wanted to give her something to focus on. Between stripping dust sheets, sweeping, scrubbing, and salvaging what they could, it had taken them most of the afternoon and a good part of the evening, and they had still only partially succeeded.

Belle gestured around her. "Case in point."

"It's better than an inn."

With a bath still out of the question, Rufus was washing himself at a basin. Having completed this task, he wrapped a towel round his waist and tied it there. While it did not seem appropriate to behold her now only mostly naked, gentlemen-inclining husband with atavistic eyes, Belle hoped it was acceptable to admire him a little. After all, it would be a miserable fate indeed to be wed to someone you could not admire.

"What?" he asked, a hand upon his hip.

"I was appreciating you aesthetically."

"Oh God"—he actually rolled his eyes—"I suppose you've been talking to Gil."

"About your aesthetics? Yes, we write long letters to each other daily about how handsome you are."

He blushed, the pink of it slipping down his throat and across his chest, half losing itself beneath the silky red-gold hair there. "Shush."

"Does praise of this kind truly make you uncomfortable?"

"I'm not accustomed to it." A smile turned up the corner of his lips. "But I might secretly like hearing it."

"Even from me?"

"Especially from you."

Nevertheless, her uncertainties lingered. "You don't think it's strange without the possibility of—"

"No. I think it's different." He joined her by the fire, and then, because she had begun to braid her hair for bed, "Let me do that."

His fingers were deft at this, and she enjoyed his touch. There was something easy and light about it, a gentle kind of pleasure, as natural as a summer breeze.

"For what it's worth," he whispered, "I value your aesthetics as well."

"Because I look like my brother." She had meant it as a joke, but the words came out oddly flat.

"Because you look like you."

"What if I ate all the cheese?"

"You *do* eat all the cheese."

That made her laugh. "If I were a man," she told him, "I would want to menace you like Gil."

"If you were a man"—his eyes glinted wickedly in the firelight—"I might want to menace you."

"Perhaps we could menace each other."

He tied off the bottom of her braid in a bow far neater than she would have bothered with herself. "Whatever our circumstances, I am glad we would find our way to equity."

Of course, the thought crept up on her cruelly, if she were a man, she would be able to offer him what he truly wanted. Except no. Whatever shape her body took, she would still be *her*. Still a cold, lost stranger in the court of love. Always doomed to be somebody's compromise.

"Bellflower?" Rufus caught her attention again. "What's wrong?"

"Nothing," she said unconvincingly. And then, "I'm just a little tired."

"Let's have *Fanny Hill* another night, then."

Nodding, she slipped into bed, between the closest that could be managed to fresh sheets. It didn't feel quite real that this had once been her parents' room, still less real that it was now hers. Hers for the rest of her life.

"Forgive me." Rufus shed the towel and joined her. He always said this, despite the fact that she had grown quite used to him on their return from Scotland and had never been particularly perturbed by nakedness.

"There's nothing to forgive."

"It's a little vulgar."

She snuggled close, resting her head against the comfortable plateau where his shoulder met his upper arm. "Maybe I'm a vulgar person."

"Next time we run away together, do try to remember to pack some clothes for me."

"Next time we run away together, do try not to be terribly drunk at the outset."

"I shall have no cause to be."

"We've barely been married a fortnight," she said. "I'm sure I shall instil a bad habit or two in you before long."

"I highly doubt it."

She reared up slightly so she could peer directly into his face. "Do you think I need you to be perfect?"

"You've seen enough of me, figuratively as well as literally, for me to know that you do not. But for once in my life, I intend to make the best of things."

He had said as much on the road to Gretna Green. And, to give him his due, he had kept his word and never once made her believe that he resented her or was anything less than committed to their marriage, unconventional though it was. Nevertheless—and she knew this was more about her own feelings, rather than his behaviour—it still rankled, no it *hurt*, to be something someone else needed to make the best of.

She was feigning sleep when he spoke again. "I should probably head to London in the next few days."

"And leave all this?" she asked, striving to put aside her foolish melancholy. "How could you?"

"Trust me, I'll be eager to return. But, given the work ahead of us, we'll have need of your dowry, so I should set your affairs in order."

"Legally, they are your affairs now."

"Our affairs, then." He was silent for a moment. And then, with unusual awkwardness, "Arabella, I'm sorry to ask. But I shall have to . . . I shall have . . . that is, may I spend some of your money?"

"Please say it is on liquor and whores," she returned, still struggling, for her husband's sake, to be normal, and only mildly concerned that this was the sort of observation which apparently passed for it. "I shall feel entirely cheated if I do not have a husband who spends my fortune on liquor and whores."

"Then you must endure the disappointment, for I have no interest in liquor or whores. I do, however, have a strong interest in not having to beg my aunt for my possessions. And while I'm grateful you packed some necessities for me from Valentine's things—"

"Actually," Belle put in happily, "I stole them."

"You did what?"

"I stole them."

Rufus groaned. "Oh God, what have you done? Does Valentine strike you as a man who would countenance wanton use of his shaving brush?"

"No," said Belle, with no diminution of her joy. "And you know what would solve that problem?"

"Are you going to suggest I murder him?"

"If," Belle concluded, "you murdered him."

"Bellflower, are you going to spend the whole of our marriage trying to convince me to murder our friend?"

She gave this the consideration it was due. "Yes," she said, about two seconds later.

"Is your consent to buy myself some clothes contingent upon homicide?"

"Of course not." She pushed herself sharply to her elbows, peering down at him. "Get yourself whatever you need, whenever you need. The whole of Bond Street, if you like."

"I shall not require any part of Bond Street. I intend to pay a visit to that tailor of Peggy's."

"Are gentlemen *allowed* to wear anything but Weston?"

"We shall find out. I may well turn to dust in the first ballroom I enter."

"I hope you know"—only mildly distracted by this exchange, Belle was not quite ready to lie back down—"that you do not need my permission to spend money."

"I don't want you to feel taken advantage of."

"And I don't want you to feel like you have no power within your own marriage."

Putting an arm about her shoulders, he drew her back down onto his chest. "You are very good about that, dear heart."

"I am not your aunt, Rufus. I have no need to keep you beholden to me."

"I am, though," he murmured.

She knew he meant it sincerely, even kindly, but gratitude felt wrong. Unearned and uncomfortable. "Please don't. Even if the law offered me a choice in the matter, what's mine would be yours."

"I was not speaking in purely material terms."

That flustered her, though she didn't quite know why—if it was hope, or selfishness—so she rushed on as if he hadn't spoken. "And this house is your home, inasmuch as it is capable right now of being anyone's home."

He tsked, clearly finding her ridiculous. "Of course it's capable of being a home. We have a bed and a roof over our head, ghosts aplenty, and even a resident felon."

"Maybe," suggested Belle, suspecting that Rufus would come round to Mr. Smith, as he had to Gil, in his own time, "we could prioritise clearing one of the rooms for you."

"Are you tired of me already, Bellflower?"

"No," she said quickly, for she was not, and could not, imagine being so. "But it's important to have a space that feels truly your own. Not merely . . . on loan."

"It sounds like you're speaking from experience."

"The last time I wasn't a guest was in this very house."

"When you put it like that"—he spoke to the ceiling—"I have spent my whole life as a guest."

"No longer," said Belle. "I give you free rein, even knowing your taste in decor."

His gaze returned to her. "Pardon?"

"Bonny told me about your hunting lodge."

Rufus sighed. "That is *not* my taste."

"It was *your* hunting lodge."

"It was a hunting lodge my aunt permitted me to maintain. And I had it furnished that way to annoy those who needed annoying and shock those who needed shocking."

"Bonny was neither shocked nor annoyed."

"He wouldn't be. Are you aware"—amusement softened his voice— "that the little reprobate took a . . . well, a personal item from me? And this after I extended my hospitality to him and his damnable duke."

"Really?" Belle did her best to sound surprised out of loyalty to her twin. "That was very naughty of him. You should ask for it back."

"I think he knows I will not."

"Do you want me to?"

"Under no circumstances."

While Belle very much enjoyed failing to pick up on hints, she thought it best—for her own sake, if nothing else—to enquire no further into the nature or status of the personal item.

She was just circling sleep, half-soothed, half-anxious, when Rufus said, "Bellflower?"

"Mmm?"

"When I have a room of my own, does that bring an end to . . . to this."

She muffled a yawn against his shoulder. "To which?"

"This," he explained helpfully. And then, "Will I no longer be welcome here?"

Her eyes opened, though there was little to see beyond shadows and the haze of his chest, rising and falling with each steady breath.

"I look forward to this time with you," he went on. "The whole day, I look forward to it. Watching you comb out your hair. Holding you in my arms or being held. How it feels to talk in the dark as though we are our own world entire. The truth is, I might have grown"—he coughed—"accustomed. Is there any possibility you might also be . . . accustomed?"

"I am more than accustomed," she blurted out, delighted and abashed and wondering if she was dreaming. "I am"—self-consciousness abruptly dug its claws into her—"more than accustomed. And you will *always* be welcome here." She paused. "Unless I am fucking someone else."

He laughed, sounding relieved, or perhaps she imagined that too. "Thank you for clarifying. Under those circumstances, I will be more than content to sleep alone."

"You will miss me, though, won't you?" she asked, sounding—even to herself—greedy as Bonny, if not quite as shameless about it. "Just a little bit."

"Yes, dear heart." The night was soft around them. His voice full of indulgence: "Just a little bit."

Chapter 34

The following days, busy as they were, found their own rhythm. Rufus—accompanied, when he would permit it, by Mr. Smith—was mostly occupied with the estate itself. Unlike Belle, who had been educated, through nobody's fault but her own, haphazardly, he had been raised with the expectation of governance, proving himself, yet again, a superlatively useful husband. Best of all, though, he was a discursive one, more than willing to spend his evenings going through everything they were doing, and drawing out her own ideas, until Belle either understood or was too bored to care, as turned out to be the case, for example, with soil aeration. In return, she continued to give something she had not given so bounteously for a long time: her trust. Watched him sleeken beneath it like a well-pampered cat.

Her attempts to manage the household were, at best, a work in progress. But then so was the household. The previous housekeeper had left meticulous notes, which Belle spent her afternoons poring over, tracking expenditures over time, incomings, outgoings, everything that was required to keep even a relatively small manor house from falling apart at the seams or collapsing into its own equally small moat. While she had no natural head for figures, she soon discovered she did not precisely need one—there was no great mystery to neatly aligned columns of numbers; she just had to care enough to pay attention, and she had never before had motivation to care. This, however, was her house now, and it needed her. And, at some point, it would need flour. Coal. Fresh candles.

She could not tell if it was amusing or simply laughable that she had spent most of her life in pursuit of the right adventure, the one that would teach her who she was, or who she was supposed to be, and all she had truly been looking for was a way to come home. It was the most conventional of endings for someone who had once intended to be a heroine, but it felt hard-won nonetheless.

Deep in her notes and numbers, she was oblivious to the general tumult of the house, and it was not until Hannah stuck her head round the door to tell her she had a visitor that she even realised there'd been a knock on the door.

"A visitor?" she repeated, not having expected anyone.

Hannah nodded. "A clergyman."

"Urgh. Really?" Her heart sank. "Isn't that typical? I've barely been in residence a week. I suppose there's a church roof in need of repair, or he wants to lecture me on my womanly duties or something."

"No, no," Hannah told her. "It's not the local feller. He's actually quite decent. Wouldn't come sniffing around unless he was sure he'd be welcome."

"You mean, there's a strange clergyman on my doorstep?"

"In the hallway."

"I suppose you'd better send him up."

Sweeping her skirts in lieu of a curtsy, Hannah departed. That left Belle with a scant few minutes to discover just how unsuitable her environs were for entertaining. She had set herself up temporarily in the great hall, spreading her ledgers across an old oak dower chest that she was using as a table. But with the rest of the furniture still covered, and the walls bare of their paintings and the tapestries, it was a hollow room, a cold room, its flourishes—like the stained glass and the great Jacobean chimneypiece—reduced to mere relics of their former grandeur. She made a futile attempt to arrange the ledgers in a more orderly fashion, then rose, in the hope it would settle her nerves. There was an odd feeling to the whole situation, as though she had herself been caught naked.

The door opened for a second time, admitting her visitor. A little taller than average height, with no particularly striking characteristics, dressed sombrely in black as befit his profession, his appearance should probably have alleviated her anxieties. And yet it did not.

He came forward, his eyes darting quick as beetles here and there about the room before they settled upon her. "Lady Comewithers?"

Forcing her lips into a polite smile, she managed not to step back. "You have the advantage of me."

"It is true, then?" he asked, either unconcerned about any advantage he might possess or determined to retain it.

"Is what true?"

His eyes swept her as they had her surroundings, cool, glistening, and evaluative. "That he married."

"Why would you address me as Lady Comewithers if you were in doubt?"

"It was not for your fortune," he said, with another flick of his gaze.

Abstractly Belle rather admired his talent for ignoring her. In less abstract terms, she thought she might dislike him. "No," she agreed.

His lips, which were full and might—in a different face, at a different time, or had they belonged to a different person—have carried a certain sensuality, curled into an unchristian sneer. "Nor for your person."

She had been in error. She did not dislike him. She *despised* him. The truth was, he had the rudiments of a handsome man about him, but there was something about him that felt . . . stagnant. A pond at midsummer, viscous with algae. A fig, red raw and overripe, splitting from its skin. "Perhaps," she murmured, "we should forbear commenting on each other's persons."

Once again, he disregarded her. "I would see him."

She lifted her brows curiously. "Would you?"

"Madam"—now something thwarted stirred heavily in his eyes—"do not trifle with me. Where is he?"

On principle, she wanted to fight him over every word. But it would have achieved little. "Out." And then, instinctively apprehensive of riling him further, she hurried on. "I don't know exactly where. The south-west pasture, possibly."

He stepped past her to look through the window, his hands clasped behind him in that "I believe I own everything" fashion that certain gentlemen seemed to naturally gravitate towards.

"Why are you here?" she asked, when it became clear he had no intention of turning back.

For a long moment, he did not answer, and she began to wonder if he would say anything at all. "Is it not obvious."

"Why now, then?"

At last, she had his attention. "What do you mean?"

"Have you not had many previous opportunities to see—" She broke off abruptly. She would not share anything of Rufus with her visitor. "To see Sir Horley?"

"That is no business of yours."

Feeling a little more in control, Belle sat down on the edge of the chest she'd been working at, jauntily crossing one leg over the other. "As you wish."

As she had hoped, this seemed to spur her guest to further disclosure.

"I come," he said, "when it is significant. When he has need of me."

"Now *that* is assuredly not my business."

He stared at her.

She smirked.

"Spare me your vulgar insinuations. I have known him far longer than you have, and I know him far better than you ever will. Who do you think he will turn to, when this fancy passes, when you bore him or disgust him or demand too much of him?"

Belle let an insolent finger rest lightly against her jaw. "It was very good of you to travel all this way to insult me."

Silence lay between them, as thick as the dust motes pirouetting sapphire, jade, and gold in the light that streamed through the stained glass windows. "I warned you," said the visitor, his brows knit in an unbecoming frown, "not to trifle with me."

"Or what?" asked Belle curiously.

"You think me a provincial clergyman, perhaps? But I am a powerful man, an influential man—"

"Do *not*," Belle cut him off, "start that nonsense with me. I have had it up to here with men telling me how important they are."

"But"—a note of mild panic touched his voice—"I am. My patroness—"

"I don't want to hear about your fucking patroness. Besides, what would you tell her? That you don't like the wife of a man you have likely committed prosecutable acts upon but are too cowardly to be with?"

"It's . . . it's not like that. I have a *calling*."

"A calling to a safe, comfortable life, you mean." She snorted. "And, believe me, you do look very comfortable."

He drew in a sharp, outraged breath, and she waited, a little intrigued to see what he might say in a temper. To her disappointment, however, he seemed to calm, his mouth shaping itself into something malicious. "Do you think you can make him want you? Is that what this is about?"

With a hand pressed to her heart, she did her best to mime shocked distress. "Are you saying I can't?"

"He'll never love you, Lady Comewithers. He's not made that way. Your marriage is nothing but a sham, and that's all it will ever be."

"Here's the thing about my marriage." Setting both feet back on the floor, Belle leaned over her own knees. "If I had my way, Sir Horley would never trouble himself with you again. You're complacent, self-righteous, and hypocritical, and I'm very much getting the sense that you're dull in bed."

"How dare—"

"More to the point, I think you enjoy keeping him on the outskirts of your life. You get to look after your own well-being without ever having to think about his, knowing you can call him back for an illicit thrill whenever you chafe against your respectable life, knowing he'll come because he's the better man and—for whatever reason that is your own to keep—he cares about you."

Once again, it seemed like her visitor was mustering himself to speak.

And, once again, Belle did not give him the opportunity. "But," she went on, "fortunately for you, it is not up to me. Because—and here is the real truth of our marriage that you believe you have so incisively discerned—who Sir Horley chooses to love is none of my business. Who Sir Horley chooses to fuck is none of my business. Who Sir Horley chooses to forgive is none of my business. In other words, *you* are none of my business."

"Then—"

"Unless"—she whisked a palm through the air—"you are of a mind to become part of our lives, in which case there will be no more of"— her next gesture encompassed the whole of him—"*this*. Posturing and spite and selfishness. I will welcome you, whoever you are, for his sake, but make no mistake. I do not like you. I am not pleased with you. I am unimpressed by you. And so you enter our home as a rich man enters the kingdom of heaven, do you understand? On your fucking knees."

From the doorway came the sound of a single set of hands clapping. Rufus, in ill-fitting riding clothes borrowed from various members of the household, was propped against the frame, regarding them both with an unreadable expression. "Do you want him on his knees meta-phorically or literally?"

Belle gazed at him, unsure about how much he'd heard, and whether she owed him an apology. "I haven't decided yet. But probably—"

"Both?" he finished for her.

"I'm . . . ," she began.

But then his attention snapped to the visitor. "I thought I was never going to see you again, Asher."

A subtle change was stealing across the clergyman, and Belle was hard-pressed to pinpoint it. It was not that he had softened, exactly, or shed any of the worldly lacquer that she personally found so off-putting. But however he looked at Rufus—whatever he showed to Rufus—was clearly not something he shared with anyone else. She thought it might be the realest thing about him. "You must have known I'd come."

"Well, no," said Rufus. "That's why I just told you I thought I was never going to see you again. Do pay attention, darling."

"I . . ."

"Bellflower?" Rufus turned back to her. "This is Mr. Asher Andrews, one of my closest . . . what are we calling ourselves these days, Asher?"

"Friends," he offered, in a rather strangled voice.

Rufus simply shrugged. "Friends it is. Asher darling, my dear old *friend*, this is my wife, Arabella Tarleton, now Lady Comewithers. Rather peculiar of you not to introduce yourself. What were you thinking?"

"Of you," returned Asher, somewhat stricken and perhaps genuinely. "I was thinking of you. I didn't—"

Whatever Asher didn't, Rufus clearly had no time for. "My wife isn't wrong, you know. Your capacity to think about me has varied greatly down the years."

"I have always been there—"

"You have always been there at your convenience. When you've wanted something from me."

There was a pause. If Asher and Rufus had not been between her and the door, Belle would have tried to make a discreet exit, a thought she was very proud to have entertained, because it was surely evidence of great maturity that she was willing to miss out on what could be a very dramatic meeting between her husband and his lover.

Asher, too, seemed conscious of her presence. "Could we possibly continue this conversation somewhere else?"

"Why?" asked Rufus coldly. "So you can taunt me with nostalgia, remind me of everything you have chosen instead of me, and make me fresh promises you have no intention of keeping?"

Belle winced, though she was not quite certain for whom she winced.

"You have no right"—the anger was hot and bright in Asher's voice, and became him better than his placid superiority—"to throw my compromises in my face when you have made the exact same compromises."

Sauntering across the room, Rufus rested his hands on Asher's shoulders, looking up at him with an intensity of his own. "But you would never have chosen otherwise, would you, darling? First there was respectability and the acceptance of your peers. Then prosperity and stability, though you call that God. And let's not forget your wife."

Asher shivered slightly at the other man's touch but did not push him away. "Are you sincerely expecting me to believe that you would have given up those things for me?"

"I told you I would. Several times. I begged—"

"And yet here you are, married too."

"I can't decide," murmured Rufus, "whether I find it adorable or delusional that you think you have a right to be angry about that. But you are, aren't you? *That's* why you're here. Because you feel cheated that I did something with my life that wasn't about you."

Asher swallowed, a fish caught on the hook of truth. "You said you never wanted this."

"Oh, and you accept that, but none of my other professions?"

"I was concerned for you." Asher was frowning again. If nothing else, Belle thought he probably believed what he was saying. "At first I gave the reports no credence. Then I feared what could have happened, what pressure may have been applied to you, to make you go against something you have always stringently maintained."

This time, when Belle winced, it was for herself.

"Things change," said Rufus, shrugging lightly. Perhaps because he did not feel he owed Asher more than that. Or perhaps because Belle was right there, and he didn't think it was appropriate to say *Actually, my wife-to-be abducted me.*

"You don't," returned Asher, his eyes locked upon Rufus's. "This doesn't." And then, half pleading, half demanding, "You love me."

Rufus nodded wearily. "Yes."

At this, Asher's gaze slipped for a half second towards Belle.

"But," Rufus went on equally wearily, "I don't think that's a good thing. For either of us."

It took a moment for Asher to speak. Belle got the sense—had in fact had that sense ever since he had walked into the room—that he was not used to being checked or challenged or denied in any way. "Even for you," he declared finally, "this is nonsense."

"Is it nonsense? Well, it's my nonsense." Rufus's mouth twisted into something that could almost have been a smile. "Go home to your wife, Asher. Write a sermon. Beget a child."

At this, Asher jerked back as though Rufus had struck him. "You must know I've never laid a hand on her. I can't. I—"

"Ah"—Rufus's tone was mild, but his eyes were as desolate as ash—"the quickening of your blood brings you to me, as it has so many times before."

"You act as though it is an insult to admire you."

"No. Asher. *You* act as though it is an insult to admire me. Use your fucking hand." Rufus spun on his heel. "Belle, my dear? Mr. Andrews is leaving. Let us see him out."

She would not have stayed had it not been impossible to leave, and she would never have put herself between them without an explicit directive. That Rufus did not, in this moment, want to be alone with his former lover was not something she felt it was her place to speculate about. But it pleased her. Not the circumstances themselves, but the fact he was allowing her to protect him, as he had so often protected her.

The walk to the forecourt was silent and unpleasant, and Belle occupied herself for its duration by trying to imagine a set of circumstances in which it would be entirely natural for Asher Andrews to fall in the moat. Fortunately for everyone concerned, she was unable to do so.

Asher had another smoulderingly resentful glance for her as they approached his carriage, despite the fact she had paused at some distance from the pair.

"Is this to be it between us, then?" he asked Rufus, his voice pitched low, clearly hoping she would not overhear. "After all these years, and everything we have shared?"

Rufus stared at him, long and hard, like he was committing his face to memory. "Perhaps. For the foreseeable future, at least. I am tired of being your—" He broke off, laughing in that harsh mirthless way she had not heard for a while. "It's not even your second choice, is it? Your fourth or fifth."

"If you want soft words . . . if you want me to beg—"

"I . . ." Rufus hesitated, a bewildered, almost wondering quality touching his voice. "I . . . don't think I want anything from you, Asher."

"You will regret this." It sounded too sad to be much of a threat.

"My regrets hold soirées by moonlight. I can live with another."

Lunging forward, Asher caught Rufus in a fervent embrace, and kissed him. Even from her place by the bridge, Belle saw how the seconds stilled for them, the way they came together like stars colliding, all light and impossible fire. It was Rufus, in the end, who stepped deftly away, the kiss just another memory between them.

"I don't want . . . ," said Asher, raw and breathless. "I don't want to be without—"

Rufus was already halfway back to Belle. He barely turned. "Try not to dwell on it."

He did not touch her as Asher departed, but he stood close enough that she could feel the shape of him, familiar from so many nights sharing a bed, and the heat of him. Even the rise and fall of his breath.

Eventually they were reduced to watching an empty carriageway.

"Are you . . . are you well?" she asked tentatively.

He pulled her close with sudden urgency. "I don't know, Bellflower." Leaning over her, he pressed his face to her neck. "I didn't think it would be so hard."

"It's annoying, isn't it? When things are that way."

A muffled laugh. "Terribly annoying."

Gently, she ran her fingers through his hair. "I don't think I can tell you that you did the right thing, because only you can know that. But I admired you very much."

"You must think me quite the fool. He wasn't always like this."

"I believe it." She sought for something she could say that was neither untruthful nor disdainful. "He has the makings of a compelling man."

"Yes. But he has never been willing to suffer, for anything. I cannot blame him for that."

"Nobody should *have* to suffer," Belle said, still choosing her words carefully. "But fortifying yourself against it so assiduously can sometimes be its own kind of punishment."

"I'm not trying to punish him. Not when I . . . I feel as I do. Even if I didn't."

"I know," she said quickly. "I know. But this is between him and his conscience."

Rufus made a soft, pained sound, half-lost against her skin. "He's the closest thing to mine I've ever had. The closest thing to a lover, as my aunt was the closest thing to family. Now they are both gone, and I have nothing of my own. Not truly."

She wanted to tell him that he did. That he had her, and Swallowfield, for as long as he chose to call them his. But she would have been speaking for her own reassurance, hoping for him to look up, smile and agree. Which he would probably do, because he was kind, not necessarily because he believed her. He might never believe her. She, and her pile of Tudor chaos, might never be enough.

So she said nothing. Just held him quietly beneath the butter-bright sun. Let him feel everything he needed to feel. And wished she could give him something he could trust in.

Chapter 35

Despite Rufus's oft-expressed qualms, Mr. Smith proved as good as his word. Within the week, he had presented Belle with a detailed plan for the restoration of the estate, upon which—from the deep circles beneath his eyes—he had clearly worked all night, perhaps several nights. With Rufus's help, they refined it, prioritising the few remaining tenants, the farm, and the acquisition of essential servants only, someone to help Tom in the stables, a housekeeper, and a maid, so that Hannah could focus on her beloved kitchen. The house interior would be a longer-term project, but they could at least create some liveable spaces within it, and Mr. Smith had drawn up a list of reputable local craftsmen to help with the roof. The main problem, however, remained the ivy, since any repair work would be futile while it continued to dig itself into the masonry. Belle, of course, did not want it destroyed, but it was going to take a small army of gardeners to rein it in. In the end, it was Rufus who suggested they borrow some from Valentine—enough, at least, to wrestle the ivy, dredge the moat, and restore some semblance of order to the courtyard and kitchen garden.

"I hate this idea," Belle said, as she walked with Rufus to the stables.

"I know, dear heart. But it's our best option."

She also hated that it was their best option. "You must not be grateful. Not even a little bit."

Annoyingly, Rufus laughed. "How am I to do that? 'Valentine, may I have the assistance of some of your gardening staff, for I'm sure you are able to spare some? Oh, I can, how wonderful, now fuck you'?"

"Sounds good to me."

"You don't think that might perhaps induce him to rescind his gardeners?"

"Bonny would not allow him to."

"I would still prefer to deal with him in a broadly reasonable fashion, if you can live with that."

Belle considered the matter. "*Probably* I can live with it."

"If it helps," suggested Rufus, smiling, like any of this was *amusing*, "I will impress upon him very severely the consequences of his negligence."

"How severely?"

"I just told you: very severely."

"No, but *very* is such a subjective term. What you think of as *very* I might think of as *averagely*."

There was an expression she had noticed that Rufus got sometimes when they were talking. A certain crinkling around the eyes. A softness of the mouth. As though he was smiling with everything but his lips. Belle was not sure what to make of it. She just knew it was hers, somehow. In any case, he was wearing it now.

"How's this for a measure of severity?" he asked, contorting his face into an unconvincing glower.

"Disappointing."

"My words, then, will cut him as diamonds to glass."

"Will they, though?"

He sighed. "Bellflower, you will have to forgive Valentine at some point."

"I'm forgiving him *all the time*," she protested. "He just keeps on doing things that upset me."

"And your good opinion once lost is lost forever?"

Now it was her turn to sigh. "It's not that. It's more that I can like Valentine for how much he loves Bonny, and how happy he makes him, and dislike him for everything else at the same time."

"Would it not be easier to embrace the first and let go of the second?"

"Not at all." Her eyes widened. "You see, Rufus, something you have to understand about me is that I'm very talented at disliking people and can do it in all sorts of circumstances that others might find discouraging."

Laughing, he took her hand and kissed it—something else he did so often and so easily, she wondered if he even noticed anymore, or if it was an oddly charming habit to him. "I celebrate all your talents."

Tom was waiting for them in the forecourt, with a horse already saddled for Rufus.

"You will ride safely, won't you?" Belle said.

"I will," he promised. "I'll even wrap up warm while I do."

She leaned in and prodded his shoulder. "Well, forgive me for caring that you don't break your neck and die in a ditch."

Before he could answer—which she was sure he would do sarcastically—they spotted a horse and buggy coming along the carriageway towards them.

"After the ivy," Rufus remarked, watching the harried driver ducking and weaving through the branches, "we must do something about the road. It's a death trap."

"It could be a blessing in disguise. Think of how it will discourage unwanted visitors."

"What about wanted visitors?"

She wrinkled her nose. "*Are* there any visitors we want?"

"Yes. Our friends and lovers. The people we wish to work on the estate."

It felt strange . . . nice . . . strange . . . to hear him speak so readily and so nonchalantly of the future, when he had not wanted such a future with her at all.

At last, the cart rolled to a halt before them, and the driver—a no-nonsense, rough-set man—climbed down. He moved almost immediately to remove his cargo, which turned out to be a large basket from which slight movement and gentle snufflings emerged.

"Miss Tarleton?" he asked, arms full of basket.

Belle, who was a big fan of surprises, stepped forward. "Mrs. Yes. Is that for me?"

"Aye. Here's the note." Laying the basket at her feet with a muffled *oof*, the man produced a crumpled scrap of paper from the interior pocket of his coat.

"What is it?" Rufus was not a big fan of surprises, and thus his tone was suspicious.

Unfolding the page, Belle read it quickly. "It's from Uncle Wilbur. It says, 'Congratulations on your marriage. Wishing you every happiness.' And then an ink splodge and a coffee stain. He's not a wordy person."

"You mean"—Rufus eyed the now increasingly animated basket—"this is a wedding present?"

"I think so."

Crouching down, Belle tugged off the lid, peered inside, and burst into tears.

Behind her, Rufus made an appalled noise. "Oh my God, what's wrong? Did he send you something awful?"

"No," she sobbed, "he sent me something *beautiful*." She reached into the basket and drew out a glossy black piglet, who settled comfortably into her arms, its bright gaze darting about with eagerness and curiosity. "Look."

Rufus took a step back, apparently concerned he was going to be made to hold a pig. Which just went to show what he knew because Belle wasn't going to let just anyone cuddle her pig. Cuddling pigs was a privilege, not a right. "Yes," he said. "I am looking. That's a pig."

"Not just any pig. This is one of Boudica's children." She squeezed the little piglet tighter, though not in a way that would make it uncomfortable. "Boudica is my uncle's prize sow. She's the fattest pig in Surrey."

"Congratulations to her?"

"Very much congratulations to her. It is a great accomplishment. She is also very intelligent. Her favourite plays are Restoration comedies, especially the work of Aphra Behn."

"Are you sincerely telling me you spent your childhood reading Restoration comedies to a pig?"

"Of course not." Belle tossed her hair. "Boudica and I read lots of plays." Adjusting the piglet in her arms, where it seemed perfectly content to nestle, as long as it could see about it, she looked up at Rufus. "What are we going to call her?"

"Boudica Strikes Back? Revenge of Boudica? Boudica II: Candlelight Boogaloo."

These suggestions, Belle simply ignored as they deserved. "She needs her own identity, Rufus."

"Of course she does."

She narrowed her eyes at her husband. "I do not think you are taking our pig seriously."

"Our pig?" he repeated, his expression briefly unreadable. Then he came forward and tentatively reached out a hand to stroke the piglet's head. "Does it—does she like this?"

"Oh yes. Pigs are very affectionate. They don't always like being picked up, but I suspect she's a bit tired from her journey and overwhelmed by being somewhere new."

The man who had delivered her cleared his throat pointedly.

"I'm so sorry," cried Belle, recalled to her duties. "Thank you so much for coming all this way." She turned to Tom, who had been patiently standing by Rufus's horse during all the porcine excitement. "Can you take this gentleman to the kitchen, please, so he can rest and refresh himself? And ask Mr. Smith if there's anything we can give him for his trouble."

When Tom and the newcomer had departed for the house, Rufus resumed his cautious petting of the piglet. "Lady of the manor suits you."

For some reason, this left Belle oddly flustered. "Do you think so?"

"I do. Have you thought of a name for our pig yet?"

"It should be a noble name. A name for a warrior and a queen."

"Æthelflæd?" suggested Rufus.

And Belle smiled up at him giddily because Rufus's mind in action was a wonderful thing. "Oh, that's perfect." She gave Æthelflæd another squeeze. "Just like you, Æthelflæd. Do you like that? Æthelflæd?"

Æthelflæd definitely liked that.

"Look how pink her nose is," said Belle. "Isn't that just the loveliest thing?"

"Well"—it was Rufus's driest voice—"at least I need not worry about you lacking for companionship while I'm gone."

The truth was, Belle would miss him, but she was too embarrassed to say so in case it sounded clingy or gauche or wrong or presumptuous or too much or any number of things that were bad somehow. "When will you be back?"

"Three days? Five at most? Six if I visit any rare booksellers."

"I shall expect you in six then."

"Very well, then." He swung himself effortlessly onto the waiting horse. "Be good, Mrs. Tarleton."

"What, me?"

"Well, try to cause only a manageable amount of drama and chaos."

"I promise, Mr. Tarleton."

He paused for a moment, reins in hand, looking down at her. Again, something unreadable crossed his face. Not quite a frown. Ambiguously thoughtful. "I'll miss you," he said.

Before she had a chance to reply, he had urged his horse into motion and was away, leaving her somewhat confused and cuddling a pig.

Life at Swallowfield continued in its busy turbulent fashion, so Belle should not have felt Rufus's absence *too* keenly. It caught her mostly in the evenings, when she had grown accustomed to him simply being there, whether he was doing something with her or not. Her closest point of comparison was growing up with Bonny, when, despite their aunt and uncle's care, they had often felt as though they had only each other. Their world was limited and unsatisfying—contained too much pain—so they had created new worlds for themselves and taken it for granted they would always be together. That, of course, had been the silliness of lost and lonely children. They had needed to grow up, needed to expand their horizons. But Bonny had long ago stopped needing her. She was his twin; that bond was eternal and unbreakable. But Bonny took it for granted, the way people took their liver or their soul for granted. Belle, though she did not begrudge him that, still felt the loss.

Needless to say, her friendship with Rufus was very different from her relationship with her brother. But she realised she hadn't felt that sense of *certainty* with anyone since Bonny. Of being part of someone's life, rather than simply a part of their journey to somewhere, or someone, else. It scared her a little. Perhaps more than a little. Because while Rufus had been true to his word, and never spoken to her again of his need for romantic love, she could not forget that—although he was everything she wanted, and more—she was a compromise to him. Or worse, an obstacle.

Besides, even without Rufus to worry about, she knew it was when you got comfortable that life took things away from you.

It was upon the fourth day after his departure that Belle decided to start work on the library. Not, strictly speaking, a vital room, but knowing it was there, and all shut up and dusty, was a thorn in her heart. Compared even to Valentine's London residence, it was not very grand. It was, in fact, little more than a sitting room that had probably once been a bedroom. But it had a wide stone fireplace, which was perfect for winter evenings, and several sets of rectangular windows, which were perfect for summer afternoons, and several bookcases just waiting to be filled. There'd never, as far as she could remember, been a desk. And, indeed, after releasing the pieces of furniture from the sheets in which they were swaddled, she discovered them mostly shabby but functional: a set of mismatched chairs, a couple of them upholstered in faded tapestry, a mahogany armchair with scrollwork arms that had once been able to fit both Bonny and Belle, and a re-purposed drop leaf dining table, at which her father and mother had sat, working separately upon their correspondence. *A desk is a piece of furniture for one person,* her father had said, *and one person alone. A library is a space to be shared.* And, suddenly, for all its future promise, for all the memories contained within it, the room looked terribly bare and empty.

Once she had finished a furtive cry, Belle got to work. There were cleaning supplies aplenty stacked up in the old brewery, now it was no longer being used to incarcerate wayward stewards, and—in a series of trips—she was able to provide herself with buckets of water, bars of soap, and solutions of herb-infused vinegar, as well as various cloths and scrubbing brushes. Æthelflæd was very interested by this process and trotted to and fro with Belle, before she was encouraged to stay in the kitchen with Hannah, lest she accidentally put her snout in the lye.

Back in the study, Belle was briefly daunted by the scale of the task before her. In many ways, beginning was the hardest step because she had to pile all the furniture out of the way and re-cover it, and then roll up the rug in case it could be salvaged, all of which made the room look even less like a room than it had before she'd got involved. Probably if she had been more like Mr. Smith she would have made a plan or a list or something, and that would have helped her feel like she was acting with purpose and making progress. But she was a Tarleton, and Tarletons, for better or worse, just did things.

So she cleaned the windows, inside and out, cutting back the ivy she could reach and scrubbing the grime from the glass, until the light could sweep the room unhindered. For the most part, it simply illuminated everything that still needed to be done, but it was encouraging, too, revealing possibilities for the future in bright strips and dancing dust motes. It made Belle happy. And once, some hours later, the task was done, she flung all the windows wide, letting fresh light and fresh air claim the room anew.

Anyone else might have called it a day, but Belle was gliding like a pond-skater on accomplishment, and she decided to scrub the fireplace too. This required considerably more labour than the windows because soot and dirt had been allowed to build up, and she was increasingly convinced something (or several things) had made a home (or successive homes) in the chimney. Bats, she thought, from the colour and texture of the droppings. Possibly jackdaws at some point? And what had her life become that she was speculating so deeply about poo?

"Mrs. Tarleton?"

Coming disembodied from somewhere behind her, Mr. Smith's voice was both startling and unexpected. Her response was, therefore, a yip.

"What are you doing?" he asked.

She scuttled out backwards on her hands and knees. "Cleaning the fireplace?"

"You're not a maid."

"Well, no." Sitting back on her haunches, she wiped the sweat from her brow, realising belatedly she had probably just smeared herself with soot. "But we don't have a maid."

It had been some days since she'd seen Mr. Smith, for he'd been busy about the estate. As she had suspected, even with fading bruises on his face, he cut an intriguing figure, not dandyish but neat, with a hint of rigidly controlled sensuality in the cast of his features, suggesting a man in conflict with either his history or his nature. Clean and drawn severely back from his face, his hair was almost silver. His eyes paler still. "You still shouldn't—" he began.

"Shouldn't what? It's my house. I can do what I like."

"You're a lady. It's beneath you."

"I don't think honest work is beneath anyone. Though," Belle admitted, abruptly aware of how sweaty and dishevelled and tired she was, "I could do with a lot more practice at it. Is there something I can help you with?"

He tucked his hands behind his back, as though he were a schoolboy about to make a report to his housemaster. Then seemed confused because Belle was still kneeling in the grate like an urchin.

"Sit down?" she suggested.

This idea he apparently liked even less, eventually compromising on a kind of awkward half crouch that must have been murder on the thighs. "I came to update you on progress so far."

"Exciting."

"The family I"—he coughed—"I evicted are willing to return to the farm, at a reduced rate, of course, given the work ahead of them, and under more favourable terms, given the"—he coughed again—"damaged trust. They are good, reliable people. I did them a disservice and cast them into significant difficulties, and, even though it is less legally advantageous to us than it might be to find entirely new tenants, I still recommend—"

"Of course," said Belle. "This is absolutely the right thing to do."

Mr. Smith swallowed, his colour fluctuating briefly, and then fading away almost entirely until he looked positively grey. "I've also committed some of your remaining funds to improvement of the cottages, including those still under lease. That decision was, I will concede, primarily ethically driven, but once they're fit to live in, the properties will be a consistent source of income."

Belle nodded. "Once again, very good thinking, Mr. Smith."

"As for the south-east bedroom, I've engaged a stonemason and a roofer to come in once the ivy has been managed. They would both like to be your first port of call for similar issues and, should this be agreed, are willing to defer payment for their labour until next year, meaning you would need to cover the cost of materials only, at least for now."

"How wonderfully you have negotiated this, Mr. Smith. I agree without hesitation."

"The updated plans for the estate," he went on, almost as though Belle hadn't spoken at all, his eyes fixed distantly upon the chimneypiece behind her, "I've left in the moat room. I believe you'll find them comprehensive and cohesive."

"I'm sure I—"

"And that being so, I hereby tender my resignation, effective immediately."

Chapter 36

Belle's mouth dropped open. "Is this because I cleaned a fireplace?"

"No."

"Then why? Are you so soon regretting your decision to stay?"

Rising, with a faint wince, he moved restlessly to one of the windows. "It's not that, Mrs. Tarleton."

"I know you do not like to share yourself"—Belle rose, too, disappointed in spite of thinking she should probably have known better—"but I would appreciate it if you talked to me about this."

He half turned, his mouth rueful, and a little sad. "Still trying to understand me?"

"That's not a crime, you know."

"Unlike my own actions."

"Oh," she said impatiently, "I did not mean it like that. I just meant, I am not trying to entrap you or claim power over you. It is not so terrible a thing, Mr. Smith, to allow yourself to be known sometimes."

"A bastard is an embarrassment or a tool to be used. 'Knowing me'"—his long fingers traced quotation marks around the phrase—"has never been a factor before."

Pain rippled through her, like she was a puddle someone had stepped in. "I'm sorry for that," she told him, hoping he would trust her sincerity. "And I'm sorry I can't give you any of the things you said you wanted, like a house of your own, but there *are* things you can have here. Things that can be yours."

"Like what?" He was looking down at the courtyard now, and his voice was harsh.

"Friends? Family? Purpose? A home?"

His hand came up, bracing him against the casement, knuckles turning white. "I don't deserve that, though. I don't deserve any of that."

"Because you're a bastard?"

"Because"—and here came one of those outbursts, a ferociously self-controlled man, coming apart at the seams—"I fucking stole from you."

"And," said Belle, pressing her point with all the gentleness she could muster, but also all the determination, "I still don't know why."

An unsteady breath gusted out of him, half sigh, half sob. "Because nobody cared, Belle. Because nobody has ever cared. And"—he made a desperate attempt to regain his composure—"please forgive my presumption in addressing you by your given name."

"I don't mind. I like it, in fact. What do I call you?"

Twisting round, he stared at her as though he didn't understand the question.

"What's *your* given name," she asked.

"Oh. Ah. Francis?"

"Are you sure?"

"What do you mean, am I sure?"

"You didn't sound very sure."

He shook his head, exasperated, almost amused, and very lost. "It is Francis."

Feeling like a hunter in pursuit of the wildest, most impossible prey—a unicorn, perhaps—Belle crept closer to him. "Then what did you mean, Francis, when you said no-one cared?"

"As it sounds." The emotion was draining from his voice again, word by word. "My father is a proud man. So proud, not even his

345

bastard could elude his pride. He had me educated at Eton, then at Cambridge, separate, of course, from his legitimate sons, who went to Oxford. I've met him only once, as he took me from my home, took me from my mother, and left me at school. 'Be worthy of me,' he said."

"Oh, Francis." Having made it to his side, Belle let her head rest gently against his upper arm, and he did not shake her off.

"I have tried," he went on. "All my life I have tried. To be worthy of him. To be worthy of anyone. But it does not matter. I can strive and excel and succeed beyond whatever expectations are set for me. Devote myself to worthy causes. Live a life of moderation and exquisite virtue. It will never be enough. Nobody will ever care."

"And that is why you stole? Because you saw no merit anymore in being good?"

"It was the same pattern here. I worked hard, at first, and set about restoring the estate's fortunes. But the duke I thought had hired me never noticed. He never visited. Never answered a single letter. And when I started taking—stealing—he didn't notice that either."

"This duke," put in Belle, "is a notoriously oblivious man. I do not blame you for turning to iniquity in pure frustration. You are not the first person it has happened to."

He blinked down at her, his lashes pale and pretty, almost invisible unless in motion. "It was not the duke. It was everything. And, in a moment of despair, I decided that, since doing right had brought me nothing, I might as well try doing wrong. But I failed to take into account one thing."

"Which was?"

"That *I* cared," he said shakily. "I care about the kind of man I am. I do not want to be a thief. I do not want to exploit others. I do not want to be unworthy of trust. I do not—"

Going on tiptoes, Belle put all four fingers directly upon his lips, shocking him into silence. "You are none of those things, Francis. You felt alone. You made a mistake. You must forgive yourself."

He wrenched away from her. "I cannot. All these years knowing the world despised me, and all I have achieved is proving that correct."

"Oh, you have not." Belle stamped her foot. "If anyone is to despise you, surely that right lies with me? For I'm the person you stole from. And yet I do not."

"You should," he muttered.

"How could I? When you have had so much stacked against you, and no-one to take your part, or see what is true and precious in you, and yet here you are, this brilliant, thoughtful man with so much to offer and—"

"For the love of God, stop it. Please, I beg you. I cannot bear to hear this. You should not be defending me, Belle."

"You have done nothing indefensible."

"I am a thief. I should be punished, not rewarded and . . . and . . . indulged."

There was a long silence, Belle's mind whirling rapidly, as she tried to assemble the full picture of Mr. Francis Smith, the parts he had revealed to her, and the parts he had revealed inadvertently. Because she knew on her own account this welter of shame and guilt and help-lessness. Knew it far too well. "Is that why you're trying to leave?" she asked. "As punishment?"

One of his shoulders came up in a hopeless half shrug. "I don't know. Possibly."

"In which case," she announced, "I have a better solution."

"Oh?"

"Yes. Would you like me to spank you?"

The room filled up, floor to ceiling, with silence as thick as water. When Francis finally spoke, it was cautiously, rather than with outrage. "Would I like you to what?"

"Spank you. If you wish."

"Why would that be something I would wish?"

"Sometimes it can be quite cathartic."

His eyes sparked a muted challenge at her. "You sound as though you speak from experience."

"Oh yes. I have gone out of my way to experience as much as possible." She met his gaze calmly. "You have not said no."

"I fear I may have lost my mind."

"Why?"

"*Because* I have not said no."

She smiled at him then. "I do not know you well, Francis, but it is evident to me already that you are your own worst critic. I can see why you might consider, if not outright welcome, an opportunity to relieve yourself of that burden."

"I . . . ," he began, some combination of pride, need, and hope warring on his face.

"There are some rules, however," Belle continued, suspecting he would benefit from a lack of opportunity to second-guess himself.

"I did not realise it would be so complicated for you to"—a stark flush painted the arch of his cheekbones—"strike me."

"Spank you. It's not the same."

"If you say so."

"I do say so. Firstly, we must take care that this aspect of our relationship does not affect our day-to-day dealings. Do you think you can do that?"

He gave a swift nod.

"If at any point, you cannot, or I cannot, we will end this at once. You will always have a place here, irrespective of anything we do together."

Another nod.

"And you *must* tell me immediately if I do something or say something and it becomes too much."

He huffed out something that was almost a laugh. "I mean no disrespect, but you are . . . five foot four at most. Do you truly believe you are capable of being too much for me?"

How useful it was, sometimes, to be under-estimated. "Even so. For my peace of mind. Simply say 'No,' or 'Stop,' or anything equivalent, and we will pause. If there comes a time when you find you want to say 'No' and 'Stop' and *not* have us pause, then we can discuss that when it becomes relevant."

"You are speaking as though I am likely to"—he seemed uncertain how best to continue—"*allow* this to happen more than once?"

Belle produced her most innocent smile. "Best to cover all eventualities, don't you think?"

"I bow to your superior experience and agree to your terms."

"There's more."

"I can no longer tell," murmured Francis, "which aspects of this are the most absurd: that you want to do it in the first place, that I am willing to let you, or that you feel the need to discuss it in this much detail."

"None of that is absurd." And Belle gave such thoughts the dismissive hand wave they deserved. "My next rule is that this represents the end of your self-recrimination. Redress has been sought and given. That is the end of the matter."

"I . . ." Francis hesitated a moment. "I will do my best."

"That is also a rule. That you may be as honest with me as you care to, and can be, and I shall never chastise you for that. But that you must also do your best to accept what I'm giving you, in the way I choose to give it to you."

He made a gesture of bewildered indifference. "Fine."

"Good. Now please go get my gloves. They are on the table in the entrance hall."

For a long moment, he regarded her, his face set but conflict glittering in his eyes like tears. She waited, expecting a question, or perhaps a challenge, but then he turned and left the room, returning a few minutes later with her gloves.

"That was a test, wasn't it?" he asked, passing them to her.

"Yes."

"To see if I meant it when I said I'd follow your lead in this."

"Yes."

Again, his eyes were on hers, alive with whatever he was thinking, all traces of his previous sullenness gone. "I have miscalculated, haven't I?"

"In what way?"

"The depth of your understanding."

"Perhaps." Belle drew on her gloves, flexing her fingers until they were comfortable. "But I am not your opponent in this. Now be so kind as to bend over the window seat for me. You can rest on your forearms."

Finally Francis balked—though, Belle thought, not in deliberate rebellion. "I'm sorry. I . . . I don't think I can."

"I think you can," she said, encouraging but not pushing.

"It's too . . ."

There were a lot of words she knew that could have fit—*humiliating, exposing, frightening, overwhelming*—so she did not give any of them time to settle. "Try," she suggested. "And I will help."

His look was sceptical, to say the least, but he did, after a second or two of further hesitation, lower himself towards the window seat. The moment she could reach, Belle put a hand upon the back of his neck and urged him down the rest of the way, feeling how tension and acquiescence thrummed in strange harmony through his body.

"Well," he muttered. "This is assuredly the most mortifying thing that has ever happened to me."

"Shh." She stroked the nape of his neck lightly, this time rewarded by a long shudder of surprised pleasure. "You're doing this because you need punishment. I'm doing this because I care."

"Wait—what."

He half rose again, and she pushed him firmly back into place. "Because I care. Because I believe you infinitely more capable of good than its opposite. And because, if you need me to, I will hold you to that."

"Belle . . ."

"You promised me acceptance. You know how to stop this."

He stilled, closing his lips upon a thready, miserable sound.

Reluctantly, Belle lifted her hand from his neck. She wanted to keep soothing him, for him to feel close to her, but she was a sadly bimanual creature. As she drew down his breeches and drawers, he buried his face in his forearms yet offered no further protest.

"Ready?" she asked.

"Almost certainly not," he returned, a touch of dry humour in his voice. "But go ahead."

"Remember, you asked for punishment. So, this will not be pleasant."

"I think"—this time he sounded impatient—"I can handle a few—oh—oh God."

Her first strike, which echoed crisply through the room, was harder than she had originally intended. He had, however, made it necessary for her to make the point. Her next few slaps, delivered in a flurry before he could fully catch his breath, were gentler, though not by much. They were too sharp and swift to be much of a warm-up, and yet a warm-up they were, even if he was too inexperienced to recognise the mercy.

"I," he said, in the momentary break between her blows, "I—"

She returned her spare hand to the back of his neck. "Don't try to talk."

"Wh-what *do* I do?"

"Feel. Endure. Let go." She ran her palm lightly over his upraised flesh. His arse was not generous, exactly, but it was firm and leanly muscled, yielding just a little as she slapped it. "This becomes you."

"No," he protested. "It cannot."

She struck him again, increasing the intensity, keeping her palm and fingers flat. "You should probably learn not to argue with a woman when she's spanking you."

"Oh God." His shoulders hunched. "I'm sorry."

She hushed him again. "You're doing wonderfully."

"Please don't."

At that she paused. "You've had enough?"

"What? No. Not the—just the—I don't know—the things you say."

"That you're good?" Another blow, aimed at the tender undercurve of his buttocks. "That you're worthy?" A second, delivered to the same spot. "That I expect better things of you?" Now two to the opposite side and then more, alternating between. "That it matters what you do?"

The first true sound broke from his lips, a moan of surprised pain.

"It's fascinating, isn't it," said Belle, "the way the heat builds. I can feel it through my gloves too."

"Fu—fuck."

She set to work in earnest, covering his arse and the tops of his thighs with a rich red blanket. He was doing his best to remain still, because he wanted to obey, or he was stubborn, or he was clinging to misplaced notions of personal dignity. But occasionally, his resolve would falter, and he would toss his head back or stamp a foot in response to a particularly vicious blow. It was delightful. Everything about him was delightful. And she was delighting in being able to share this with him, the power and tenderness, and release of it.

"Belle"—his back bowed like a cat's, as though he wasn't sure if he was trying to get away from her or the opposite—"it . . . hurts."

She let her hand rest simply upon him, and even that inspired a low hiss. Definitely part cat, then. Apart from the fact a cat would surely be the one to deliver a spanking, were the option available. "I did mention that."

"When does it stop?"

"When you tell me to. Or when I feel you've had enough."

"When . . . when will that be?" He sounded adorably plaintive.

"I'm afraid that's for me to know, and you to find out."

"Did you not also mention s-something about catharsis?"

"I did."

"I would appreciate receiving some. Imminently would be appreciated."

"Oh, look at you." She pulled off her glove and dragged her nails across the glowing skin, and Francis actually *yowled*. "You poor boy. You think you have to fight the world. But right now, you're only fighting yourself."

The instant she drew back her hand, he arched half off the window seat. "Please—no. I . . . I can't."

Very carefully she put her arm to her side. "Francis? How about when you need to stop you say my full name? Arabella. Can you do that?"

He twisted his head to look at her, his eyes stormy with unshed tears, and his mouth slack, sweetly dazed. "What?"

"You keep telling me to stop when I don't think you want me to stop. Do you want me to stop?"

"N-no?" The word was vehement if slightly shocked. Perhaps he had not believed he was about to utter it. "I w-want . . . I d-don't know."

"Say *Arabella* and I stop," she repeated. "And know that I will be proud of you whether you say it or not, whatever you take for me today."

His expression cleared for a moment. Replaced by something naked and hungry. "Proud?"

And there it was: the moment she had been drawing him towards, pain of the heart laid bare beneath pain of the body. "Yes," she said, as she resumed spanking him, feeling the sting in her palm, even through gloves, the heat that flared between them, passed back and forth like a kiss. "Yes, I'm proud of you."

She struck him again, for even her lighter blows made him shudder now. "Nobody should feel invisible. But it's hard being visible as well."

"Surely this"—a moan broke his sentence apart—"can't be anything you'd wish to see."

"Your vulnerability? Your strength? Your truths? Your hurt?" She gave him an admonishing tap upon the deepest of the burgeoning bruises. "That's the most ridiculous thing you've said yet. This is beautiful. You are beautiful. And it's time for you to accept that."

"I can't . . . I—"

"It's not up to you." This time, she landed something far less forgiving than a tap. Francis made a shocked sound, half gasp, half howl, like he had no idea how to deal with the pain, as he half collapsed over the window seat. "You said you would accept whatever I gave, and I am giving you this."

"Belle—"

"You are not in control, Francis. You need to accept that too."

Despite having played upon both sides, she did not consider herself a particular aficionado of exchanges like these. Francis, though, she had trusted from the start, even when she'd had every reason not to. He was not like her, not exactly, but she understood him, his loneliness and restlessness, the self-recrimination, the fear of not mattering. So, while the thought that came upon her now was unexpected, perhaps somewhat audacious, it also clicked neatly into place. As if it, too, was finding its way home.

"You know," she went on conversationally, "I'm beginning to think it isn't quite right for you to call me Belle."

Somehow, even with a distant fear in his eyes, he managed to sneer at her, impressive man that he was. "Mrs. Tarleton."

"In this context"—she stroked him firmly, possessively even, and he took that more readily than her words—"try Daddy. I think it will suit us both."

He went rigid. "Absolutely not."

"Well," said Belle cheerfully, "let me know if you change your mind. Or use my full name to call a halt."

She went back to spanking him. They were light blows, but, by this stage, he reacted as though they were not, half trying to twist away and then impelled by his unfaltering sense of honour to steady himself for the next strike. It filled her heart to overflowing to see him like that, suffering and desperate, and almost ready to offer it all to her: the deepest, most wounded parts of him, given to her safekeeping, to be cherished until he could cherish them for himself.

"Please," he tried. And it came out half a sob.

"Please what?"

To that he responded with something like a scream, fury and fear caught within it, fighting each other like the feral beasts they were.

"Say it"—Belle put all the gentleness her hands had surrendered into her voice—"and I'll tell you when we'll stop."

"Fuck you."

She was lifting her hand for a harsher blow when—to her relief because she would not have pushed him much further—he dissolved into helpless weeping. With her free hand upon the back of his neck for reassurance, she crouched down beside him, and was unexpectedly touched when he turned his tear-streaked face towards her, almost as if by instinct. She put her lips to his ear. "Say it."

"Daddy," he whispered.

"Tell me you know that Daddy is proud of you."

"D-daddy's proud of me."

"Tell me you know that Daddy cares about you."

"Daddy cares about—about me."

"My precious, precious boy." Sweat had darkened his hair to tarnished pewter. She smoothed a lock from where it had fallen into his eyes. "If you can allow it, Daddy will never let you get lost again. Now"—she rose again—"twenty more and we're done."

His mouth twisted tragically. "But you said—"

"I said I would tell you when we're done."

"Please don't."

"Take them for Daddy. Show me just how good you can be."

He sobbed afresh, his hands curling and uncurling against the window seat. But all he said in the end was "Yes, Daddy."

He cried through all twenty of Belle's softest blows yet offered no resistance. Quite the opposite, in fact, his body limp and utterly surrendered, his responses coming less, she thought, from an extremity of pain than an inability to hold them back. Or, perhaps, a lack of desire to.

Afterwards, she sat on the floor, and he lay with his head in her lap, letting her stroke him and whisper to him—all the lovely things he needed to hear, and had been taught he did not deserve.

Eventually some shreds of coherence came back to him. "I . . . I still don't quite know what you just did to me."

"Oh," said Belle, "I spanked you? Didn't you notice?"

"Amusing." It was the voice of someone who did not find it amusing. Or rather, the voice of someone who secretly found it amusing and didn't want you to realise. Belle had been the recipient of that voice a lot in her life. "But I think I made quite the spectacle of myself."

"If by *spectacle* you mean *magnificent vista I would gladly witness on many occasions*, then yes."

"I suspect I meant *shameful display*."

"Oh, Francis." She let her head fall back against the base of the window seat with a clunk. "My hand cannot take spanking you again straightaway. Let us not invest shame where it does not need to be."

"But—"

She flicked his nose. "Listen to Daddy."

An immediate blush set his face afire. "You won't tell anyone about this, will you?"

"Of course not. But for the sake of privacy, not because either of us have done anything embarrassing. Although," Belle added quickly, "I should mention to my husband that our friendship has taken on a new dimension."

"Good God, Mr. Tarleton. I did not even think—"

"Don't worry. He will not mind."

"I would mind, in his place."

"You are different kinds of men with different kinds of . . . interests, shall we say."

He settled his head more comfortably against her leg, curling unselfconsciously into her. "I will take your word for it."

"A practice you would save yourself considerable discomfort if you adopted with such alacrity in future."

He was quiet a moment or two. "You speak as though you expect this to happen again."

"Don't you want it to?"

"Do you," he countered, "believe me in such severe need of correction?"

"You already know I don't. But I think you might wish to be reminded that you are seen and cared for. That Daddy is proud of you. And there to keep you on the straight and narrow."

"Perhaps . . ." He hid his face beneath his arm. "Perhaps that would be"—he swallowed—"needed, yes."

"It's a pleasure." Belle feathered her fingers through his hair, which fell between them as lightly as swansdown. "And an honour to have a little of your trust."

"More than a little," he whispered.

"Then I am more than honoured."

Rather than being reassured, as she had hoped, he seemed to find some new avenue of concern. "In which case, if we are to possibly continue with this, I have to confess something."

"I'm rapt."

"While you were—while that was happening, I was . . ." Finally, Francis looked at her. His blush had dissipated, but his eyes were anguished. "I entered a state of physical arousal."

Belle blinked, trying very hard not to laugh. "If you imagine I was unaware of that, you do your member a disservice."

"I have no idea what to say."

It was hard to tell if she had gratified or appalled him, so she did her best to explain. "Because you were looking for punishment and catharsis, I felt it would be taking advantage of you to introduce elements of seduction. Was that wrong?"

"I . . . ah . . ." He gave an adorable little cough. "I'm flattered that elements of seduction were even a matter for consideration. But I'm honestly bewildered as to *why* such a thing might happen at such a time. I was humiliated and in considerable pain."

"The body and the mind respond to all sorts of things."

"Surely those are bad things to be responding to. Especially in such a fashion."

"Maybe you were responding to a sense of safety or of being seen or of getting what you needed. Or maybe not. Maybe in the right context, when it's something you have chosen for yourself, you enjoy a little humiliation, or a little pain. Many people do."

"It did not *seem* like a little."

"Such matters are relative. But there is no harm in what you experienced. If you wish, we could explore it further in a different setting."

He pushed himself onto an elbow, his eyes seeking hers hopefully. "What do you mean?"

"Well"—she shrugged—"we have seen how you respond to pain and humiliation in the context of punishment. Perhaps we should also see how you respond to them in the context of pleasure?"

"Is that . . . is that . . . appropriate?"

"To whom?" she wondered, trying not to laugh at the question.

"Well"—he seemed to sense he was being ridiculous—"the matter of marriage vows."

"For one thing, I was married at Gretna Green, so we barely exchanged any. For another, I would be fascinated to hear the service that included a spanking exemption under *forsaking all others*."

"Belle." He gasped out her name, utterly flustered. Then began to laugh, though even that carried a tremor of astonishment. "The things you say."

"You are very lovely," she whispered, more charmed by him than she had realised she might be, "when you're shocked."

"Then I must often be very lovely in your presence."

"Am I such a source of consternation to you?"

"Yes," he said. "But I like it very much. I would rather not, however, be a source of consternation for your husband. He is a formidable man."

"Isn't he?" said Belle, proudly.

"I thought him little more than a fop."

"He is a fop *and* a formidable man."

"Then you understand why I would prefer not to draw his ire."

Intrigued, now the possibility of sensuality lay before them, Belle put her fingertips to the sculpted arch of his upper lip. "You will draw his ire only if you treat me badly."

"I would not treat you badly, Belle, for fear of yours."

And Belle lay back, pleased with his answer, anticipating what else she might find to be pleased with in future.

❦

She did not, as it happened, have to wait long to find out, for Francis came to her that very night. And she put him over her lap, crooning to him and caressing him, filling him afresh with only the gentlest pain, for a languorous couple of hours. There was nothing, on this occasion, for either of them to overcome. There was simply the joy of giving, and they both gave freely, generously, completely. He writhed and moaned, and shed some lovely tears for her, and let tenderness strip him of shame as severity had earlier. Eventually passion mastered them both, and he pressed her onto her back amidst the pillows, entering her with care, and fucking her with facility. Such facility, in fact, that Belle lost her sweetness, and they found their climaxes in ferocity instead, her legs flung around his waist, and his tongue deep in her mouth, teeth marks on his neck, and claw marks on his back, both of them breathless, feral with exhilaration and the unforeseen discovery of the other.

This time, when their bodies fell apart, it was Belle who lay with her head on Francis's chest, and he whose fingers idled in her hair.

"Well," he said, "I seem to be learning rather a lot about myself."

She twisted slightly so she could look at him. With his pale cheeks flushed and his fine hair hopelessly tangled, he was a study in exquisite debauchery. "I'm learning rather a lot about you too."

He laughed. "I hope it is more to your satisfaction than your initial impression."

"Oh"—she gave a luxurious stretch—"I am very satisfied, believe me, Francis."

"I . . . err. I truly had no notion I had it in me."

"Which part?"

"Any of it." The slyest of smiles flickered upon his lips.

"Someone," remarked Belle teasingly, "is proud of his performance."

He gave one of his sweetly awkward little coughs. "Not very seemly of me, is it?"

"Nonsense. One should always celebrate one's accomplishments."

"It's just I've always taken it for granted that I was not a particularly . . ." Momentarily at a loss, he cast his gaze to the ceiling. "Not a particularly corporeal person. Nor particularly skilled in the physical arena."

"But," protested Belle, wide-eyed, "you have a double first from Cambridge."

"They didn't cover this, Belle." Then he broke off with his second laugh in minutes, gratifying her with the unexpected generosity of his mirth. "Amusing."

Giggling but relenting, she went on. "I think you could apply your talents to whatever arena you chose, Francis."

"It never occurred to me to apply them to this one." He flipped her onto her back and covered her, kissing her deeply, still as much wonderment as surety in his touch. "But what of you?"

"I think you've already felt the application of my talents."

"No, I . . ." A fresh blush crept across his cheeks. "I mean, I would like to learn about you too."

"Oh." And, just like that, a chill settled over her. Because this was how it started. With *I want to know you*, until it became *why don't you love me*, and ended up *what's wrong with you*.

"Did I over-step?" asked Francis, drawing back immediately.

She shook her head. "No."

"Are you certain? I would not want you to think a few marks of favour and I have already forgotten my place."

"Francis"—she reached up to touch his cheek—"your place in this house is whatever you wish it to be. And this is about me, not about you."

"How so?"

"I . . ." The truth lay inside her, heavy and inevitable, needing to be spoken, and yet—in that moment—impossible to speak. So, like a craven, she fell back on a different truth. "I'm afraid I will prove a disappointment."

"Good God," he murmured, his breath warm against her neck. "I am hard-pressed to imagine anyone being disappointed in you."

"That's because, as we are discussing, you do not know me."

"And why you prefer that I don't?"

She swallowed. "It's complicated. But maybe."

To her surprise, he did not react with impatience or irritation. He did not even turn away from her. "Do you need me to leave?" he asked.

"Do you need to?" Oh yes, she was nothing but cowardice tonight.

"No," he told her simply. "I would like to stay."

"It will not change anything."

"On the contrary, it will make me extremely content to spend the night beside the lovely woman who has given me much and to whom, I think, I have given in return."

"Francis," she said, a little desperately, hoping against hope she would not embarrass herself by crying. "I can't . . . I don't . . . I'm so very tired of not being enough."

"There are few fears in the world I understand so well as that one." His hand found hers and twined their fingers together. "But I have wasted enough of my life lamenting what I do not have and would rather value what I do. Can you trust me on that? Just a little?"

She wanted to. She always wanted to. In the end, she managed a pathetic little nod, which Francis—perhaps out of kindness—seemed to accept. She knew she ought to tell him, but it seemed absurdly presumptuous to speak of love, even the impossibility of it, after a single encounter, no matter how mutually pleasing. Then again, if she said nothing, he might later believe himself deceived or led on in some way. And even if she could find some semi-reasonable way to raise the subject, whether it was now or on some other occasion, there was no guarantee of understanding. She could not count on everyone being like Miss Carswile. Indeed, until she had spent time with Miss Carswile, she would not have counted on *anyone* being like Miss Carswile. But that was the problem when someone was kind to you. It made it harder to bear when others were not.

And what a peculiar cruelty it was, a wasp sting from the world at large, to be someone who required *explanation*. It was this, in the end, the sheer weariness of it, that made her hold her tongue, while Francis drifted easily off to sleep beside her.

Chapter 37

Rufus returned from London with rope burns on his wrists, a promise of gardeners from Valentine, and—having stopped by the post office in Lapworth—a letter from Peggy, which, in the absence of a butler, he brought up to the library himself.

"What does it say?" he asked as Belle tore into it immediately.

She scanned the page, clicked her tongue, and passed it back. "Why don't you read it."

"'Dear Lady Comewithers'"—he smoothed the page—"then 'HAHAHAHAHAHAHAHA' for the whole sheet."

"Cross-written too." She hid a smile behind her hand. "Why are one's dearest friends always the absolute worst people?"

Flipping the page over, Rufus skimmed the continuing HAHAHAHAHAs. "Oh, wait, there's something in this corner. 'Congrats on wedd. bliss. Do me a favour & go see Orfeo at Lady F's. Good for them to have friendly faces. Can't get away. Kid won't sleep, won't stop wriggling, may well kill nanny if left alone or nanny may well kill self. Love P.'"

Belle threw her hands in the air. "Why are one's dearest friends always the absolute worst correspondents?"

"This coming from a lady whose letters all read 'This is a disaster come at once.' Or 'Cannot go on unless I have blue-ribboned shoes' or 'PLEASE HELP EMERGENCY.'" Rufus rotated the page. "There's a postscript. 'Increasingly convinc'd have birth'd small wolf. No complaints. 10/10. Love again P.'"

"She sounds so happy," Belle said, happy by association.

"She does," agreed Rufus, briefly crouching down to greet Æthelflæd, who had taken it upon herself to oversee the business of the house, including the coming and going of its residents. "And what about you, little one. Are you happy?"

"Me?" asked Belle.

"The pig. I assume if you were unhappy, I would know about it."

"Would I?"

"Know if you were unhappy?" Resting his hip against the dining table, currently piled high with papers, as well as some of the books that Tom had liberated from the privy, Rufus let his leg swing back and forth. "Again, I would assume so."

"Know if *you* were unhappy," Belle clarified, distantly aware she was probably being strange. But how could she not be when so much of what she had, right down to Swallowfield itself, came at cost to him?

"Yes indeed. I intend to be positively Tarletonian about it."

"You do?"

"Walking into rooms where you're sitting, so I can walk pointedly out of them again. Finding multiple doors to slam in the house. Chaises to cast myself upon. And you are in no way prepared for my collection of noises: woebegone sighs, irritated *tsk*s; even my breathing will communicate resignation and despair."

This sounded quite *specifically* familiar. "Was Bonny upset when you visited?"

"Something to do with a cerulean dressing gown? I think he and Valentine occasionally like to argue over nothing so they can indulge in all the pleasures of making up."

Belle wanted to ask how it felt for Rufus, seeing Bonny again, with Bonny perpetually oblivious and unendingly in love, and Rufus now married to Belle, of all people. Unfortunately, she was afraid of the answer. "Did he say anything about . . . you know . . ."

"Our marriage?"

She nodded.

"He's trying, Bellflower. He wants the best for both of us. He just can't quite understand why that might look like this."

She sighed, also perhaps paying slightly more attention to Æthelflæd than one small pig merited. "We don't all need a happy ending."

"Oh, we do." Rising from the table, Rufus crossed the room and stood before her, his hands resting lightly upon her hips. "It's just that not every happy ending has to look like Bonny's. In any case, apart from sparing me the occasional tragic glance, he was mostly too concerned with the catastrophe of the dressing gown to pay much heed to me."

"I'm sorry," she said, not quite sure what she was apologising for.

"About Bonaventure? Please. Having a world that begins and ends with Valentine is his modus operandi and always will be." He nudged the tip of her nose with his. "What would you like to do about Peggy's letter? Is it time for Mr. and Mrs. Tarleton to make their first public appearance?"

Belle thought about it. "In all honesty, I might be content to never go back to London again. But I owe Peggy approximately sixty-seven thousand and ninety-three favours—"

"Is that all?"

"And," she went on, ignoring his teasing, "I do love to hear Orfeo perform."

"As do I, even if the price one must pay is one of Lady Farrow's musical events."

She smiled up at him. "If nothing else, we have had a lot of practice in surviving tedious social occasions."

"We are practically experts at it."

"And," she added excitedly, "we can play the ga—"

He put his hand over her mouth. "Under no circumstances, Mrs. Tarleton."

⚜

Lady Farrow had learned precisely zero lessons from her previous endeavours in hosting musical evenings, or *soirées*, as she insisted upon calling them. She still provided uncomfortable chairs and insufficient refreshments, the guests still were somewhat unpleasant—Belle even thought she caught a glimpse of Orfeo's former patron, the Marquess de Montcorbier, amongst them—and the majority of the performances were still, if not actively painful, at least somewhat dreary. As upon the last occasion, Lady Farrow took several moments to passionately impress upon them the wonders of Art before introducing Orfeo. And, like last time, they entered without ceremony, dressed simply in sober black, and, accompanied only by some strings and a harpsichord, casually obliterated Belle with their voice.

She wasn't, as ever, quite sure what they were singing about, but it didn't matter because she felt it. The music was spare and bittersweet, and Orfeo, eschewing more flamboyant embellishments, soared instead through shades of pure, sharp longing that left Belle aching and breathless. There was a lightness, too, an airy expansiveness, a kind of freedom, but alongside it a sense of something not quite complete, suffering just a little.

Her eyes were burning, pressure building in her nose, but she would have stabbed herself with a chair before she shed tears in public. Was it any wonder she had briefly entertained the notion of trying to fall in love with them? Of course it had been a ridiculous plan. Even then she'd known love didn't work that way—that it wasn't something she could force upon herself or others—but listening to Orfeo sing was the closest she'd ever felt to what other people claimed to feel for each

366

other: an emotion of such strength and profundity it was capable of transfiguring your whole internal landscape.

Then it had occurred to her she just liked music.

And she didn't want her internal landscape transfigured. When the aria was done, Orfeo bowed into the hush, then departed to dazed and rapturous applause. Belle took a moment to blink the tears from her eyes.

"That was 'Vedrò con mio diletto,'" Rufus told her, "from Vivaldi's *Giustino*."

She tried to smile. Normally she appreciated opportunities to experience Orfeo's art. Tonight, however, it had prised her open, made her too aware of otherness and emptiness, and left her like that, an oyster without a pearl. "Is it about a tree?"

"Not this time. It's sung by the Emperor of Byzantium as he rides forth to battle a rebel army. He's thinking about his wife, and the opening lines are something like 'I will meet with joy the soul of my soul.'"

"Ah," said Belle, "but this is opera. Will he, in fact, meet with joy the soul of his soul? Or will he be immediately killed, or will she have proven false, or will most of his duets be with his closest male companion?"

Rufus laughed. "No, the imperial general turns out to be the villain and everyone ends up reconciled and/or married and/or punished as appropriate. There's a sea monster, though. And a bear. And a bit in a tomb with a ghost."

"I do like a sea monster," Belle admitted.

"Who doesn't?" He fell silent for a moment or two, looking down at her with that soft and particular look of his. "You do realise, my dear, that I am currently perpetrating the worst of all possible social sins."

"You are?"

"Indeed. I'm monopolising my wife." Taking her hand, Rufus bowed over it elegantly. "I should go and politely bore myself with others for a while."

"We could set a trend."

His eyes widened comically. "Of liking one's spouse? Bellflower, the world is not ready for such depravity."

With that, he vanished into the uncomfortable, underfed, and fractious guests. Before Belle had even had a moment to orientate herself, Lady Farrow—who must have been lurking, awaiting the opportunity—pounced on her.

"Buonasera," she cried, seizing Belle's arm and physically propelling her into a turn about the room. "Buonasera. Buonasera, Signora Comewithers."

"Good evening," returned Belle, a little startled, for she had never considered herself especially close to Lady Farrow, and here she was being treated as an intimate. "Thank you so much for another . . . unforgettable occasion."

Lady Farrow waved her thanks aside with a "Prego. It's my pleasure, my honour, as always, to be the humble vessel that delivers Art unto the world."

"Er," said Belle, already exhausted. "Yes." And then, with a desperate effort at civility, "How have you been, Lady Farrow?"

"I've been wonderful. Sto benissimo. Do you know, I've been learning Italian?"

"Really? I could never have guessed."

"Si si. La bella lingua. Il linguaggio dell'arte. Ci sono delle rane nel bagno."

"Are there?" asked Belle.

"Pardon?"

"Frogs?"

"Where?"

Over the years, Belle had just about learned the art of letting go. "It doesn't matter. It's lovely to see you so well."

"Oh, same, cara, same. Married life suits you, I think?"

"It might," Belle agreed.

"Isn't it wonderful"—Lady Farrow dropped her voice to a whisper as she leaned in close—"how much time one has when one is not obliged to fuck one's husband?"

This was not how Belle had seen this conversation going. Despite being rarely lost for words, she found herself stammering out something non-committal.

"I mean," Lady Farrow went on easily, "I assume you don't? Given what is said about his . . . *leanings*."

Belle frowned. "I don't think that's something it's right for me to talk about on his behalf."

"Oh. Oh God. Forgive me." Visibly mortified, Lady Farrow drew back. "But please don't misunderstand, I am fully supportive of men who dally with other men. I wish there were more such, in all honesty. It would save women a great deal of trouble."

"I mean, there are some women who might prefer to be with a man whose interests lay with them."

"No, of course. I still enjoy my husband's attentions myself, but sometimes . . . sometimes, is it not true that one wants to read a book?"

"That is indeed true," agreed Belle.

"Or not have to be interested in his poetry."

"Quite."

"Or just focus upon oneself." She took Belle's arm again. "I love Clement with all my heart, but Algy has been an absolute boon for our marriage."

"I'm very happy for you all."

If it had been up to Belle, she would have been extricating herself with some urgency, but Lady Farrow still had her in a social stranglehold and clearly had no intention of letting her go anytime soon. "Lady Comewithers?"

"Yes."

"Or Arabella; may I call you Arabella?"

Saying no did not seem as though it would achieve anything. "Yes, of course."

"May I ask you something?"

Saying no did not seem as though it was an option here either. "You may."

"It is on behalf of my husband, actually. My husband and Algy."

"Oh?"

"Yes. You see, of late Algy has taken rather a fancy to the notion of . . ." Lady Farrow broke off. "I'm not sure how to explain."

Some corner—possibly more than a corner—of Belle's mind was far away. In the home that was her own, watching its shape emerge daily from beneath a shroud of ivy, catching the echo of her husband's laughter, the occasional heated glance from her cold-eyed steward . . . "Directly," she said, "would be ideal."

Lady Farrow nodded. "Very well. Algy would like to be fucked from both ends."

As the seconds ticked by, the window in which it was possible to construct a reasonable answer was closing rapidly. "Good for him."

"And," Lady Farrow went on, apparently having exceeded the limits of her Italian, "I'm sure you're wondering what that has to do with you."

"The thought had crossed my mind."

"Well, you see, my husband, and Algy of course, thought perhaps that your husband might be . . . might be willing to oblige them."

"And it didn't occur to them to ask him?"

"They thought it might be better if it came from me. To you."

"So"—Belle reached for the most moderate tone she was capable of—"let me get this straight. You want me to ask my husband on behalf of your husband if he's interested in fucking one of your husband's lover's orifices while your husband fucks the other?"

"Mmm," said Lady Farrow. "Mm-hmm." And then, with a hopeful glance, "He's their first choice."

"How flattering for him."

"That was my idea," added Lady Farrow.

"That he should be their first choice?"

"No, that they should make a list, weigh up pros, cons, must-haves, no-thank-yous, attractiveness, compatibility, that kind of thing. After all, it must be someone they both desire. Someone trustworthy, communicative, understanding, and, one would hope, skilled."

What Belle had thought to be a piece of typical Farrovian whimsy was turning out to be fairly considered. She was—unexpectedly—impressed and pleased on Rufus's behalf that others would see in him what she saw herself. Or else she had lost whatever judgement she had ever possessed. "What an excellent wife you are, Lady Farrow," she said, wanting to share a compliment in return.

The other woman blushed. "Ah, thank you. I do try. So, would you mind putting this to your husband? I'm sure you'll know just how to do it. And, of course, if it is of no interest to him, they will both respect that completely."

"I can mention it to him." Probably Rufus would be amused. Maybe intrigued. He would certainly prefer it to either gentleman's poetry.

"Thank you." Lady Farrow kissed her, continental-style, on both cheeks. "They'll be delighted."

Belle was just about to make her excuses, there being few directions a conversation could go once double-ended fuckery had been introduced to it, when a thought occurred to her. "Ah, which . . . how . . . are matters to be arranged?"

Lady Farrow looked blank.

"Physically?"

Lady Farrow continued to look blank.

"In which part of Algy will Sir Horley partake?"

Lady Farrow's expression cleared. "Oh, they're both happy to accommodate his preferences, though—all things being equal—Clement would prefer to take Algy's mouth so he can watch his face. Ciao."

Chapter 38

Finally liberated from Lady Farrow, Belle skirted the edges of the guests, trying to calculate just how long she was required to stay to ensure leaving would not look rude. Rufus was on the other side of the room, clearly talking about opera, and she was in no humour to deal with people talking about opera, if she was ever in that humour. It was then that she spotted Roberta "Bob" Everley, Orfeo's secretary/manager/assistant, making a desultory assault on the refreshments. While they had not often crossed paths, the two women knew each other by name, sight, and reputation. Which was to say, Belle's reputation for being an impulsive fribble and Bob's reputation for relentless, even obnoxious, practicality.

In that moment, it felt like fate. After all, if there was anyone of whom she could ask questions she shouldn't be asking, it was probably Bob. Questions, for example, about Rufus's family. Questions he would never ask for himself that Belle was increasingly convinced he needed to.

Taking a deep breath, she sidled nonchalantly over, realising a little too late that it was impossible to sidle nonchalantly. Sidling was visibly chalant by its very nature. Thankfully Bob was still too involved with the refreshments to notice. "Is this capillaire?" she said, holding a glass of something straw-coloured and orange-scented to the light. "Orfeo isn't getting paid enough for this."

Belle was glad she had thus far eschewed the drinks. "But they are getting paid?"

"Handsomely. My point is, it's still not enough."

"Bob?" Having embarked upon what she knew was an ill-advisable course, Belle abruptly discovered there was no subtle way to proceed with it. So she went with unsubtle. "You know how you are generally accounted to know everything?"

"Yes."

"Is it possible to . . ." Suddenly Belle was feeling a lot more sympathetic to Lady Farrow's hesitant introduction of Algy's ends. "Is it possible to . . . find people."

It was testament to either Bob's job or Bob as a person that she received this question incuriously. "Find in what way? And what kind of people?"

"Just ordinary people kind of people? And find as in . . . locate?"

"You're not giving me much to go on. If they're peers, they'll be in *Debrett's*; if they're criminals, there's newspapers and trial records; if they're famous or notorious, word of mouth might be the answer; otherwise it's parish records, which aren't exactly anyone's idea of reliable. And you'd have to know which parish to go to."

"They're"—despite her determination to do this, Belle's heart was beating a rhythm of *terrible mistake, terrible mistake*—"my husband's family?"

"Who's your husband?" asked Bob. "What? Don't look at me like that. I'm not a *social* secretary. I can't be expected to keep track of the comings and goings of every friend of Orfeo's partner."

Bob was right. She *couldn't* be expected to keep track of that, but it was disconcerting to be reduced to the status of acquaintance—and flighty acquaintance at that—when Belle had once been fairly central to Peggy's world. On the other hand, maybe this was the perfect excuse to back away from something she shouldn't have started. "Oh," she said. "Never mind."

"Never mind who your husband is?"

"Never mind about any of it."

"But I'm mildly curious now," protested Bob. "Why are you trying to find someone else's family?"

"Aren't they technically my family on account of, you know, marriage and things?"

"Not really answering the question there, Arabella."

"I see you noticed that?"

"Nor there."

Belle sighed and then relented. "Sir Horley's parents left him with an aunt when he was very young. He feels they cast him off. I think it would help him to learn they did not. Hence my attempting to find them for him."

For long seconds, Bob was silent. "I suppose you already know," she said at last, "this is a terrible idea."

"Yes."

"I mean, what if they *have* cast him off?"

"I suppose"—Belle was cringing at herself—"I wouldn't tell him?"

"That's a terrible idea on top of a terrible idea. You'd be disregarding him twice over."

The part of Belle that had spent most of her life in pursuit of terrible ideas rallied. "But what about all the ways he keeps disregarding himself?"

"I've no notion what you're talking about."

Belle opened her mouth, then closed it again, for it didn't seem right to speak so intimately of Rufus to a relative stranger. Admittedly, it was an odd place to draw the line, considering all the ways she was going directly against his wishes, but both sets of actions were grounded in the same desire to take care of him. To prove to him he had a place in the world. That he'd always had one. Been loved. Been worthy. Maybe his blood family could give him that, since he could not accept it from her.

"I just want him to be happy," she said aloud.

Bob shrugged. "That's nice, but have you considered the possibility that you aren't responsible for his happiness?"

"We're married, though."

"Something I'm assuming he also agreed to."

Belle thought it best not to mention the whole abduction thing. "Mm-hmm."

"Then do what Orfeo and Peggy do: talk about stuff. It seems to work wonders for them. Might well work for others. Who knows?" Suddenly Bob paused, frowned. "Wait wait wait. Sir Horley? Did you say your husband was Sir Horley? As in, Sir Horley Comewithers?"

Belle's eyes widened. "Oh God. You know something?"

"I know lots of things."

"You know something about this—about *him*—specifically."

Bob let out a breath so long it became a groan at the end. "Look, it's not the sort of name you forget in a hurry. Isn't his father Rufus Comewithers? The one who married Ygraine? The artists' model?"

"That seems plausible," said Belle, who truly had no idea.

"I'm only telling you this," Bob went on briskly, "because it's practically common knowledge. We ran into them in Vienna, I think it was. Wait no. Florence, because she was posing for Thorvaldsen and his latest protégée—what was the fellow called again? Eckersberg. One to watch, I reckon."

While Belle's interest in Thorvaldsen and/or Eckersberg was not high at the best of times, it was currently less than zero. "Is there any way to reach them?"

"Eckersberg?"

"Sir Horley's family."

"You're really going through with this?"

"I will try my best," Belle promised, "to talk myself out of it."

Bob eyed her. "Why do I get the feeling you've never been talked out of anything in your entire life?"

"Most likely because it's true."

"Fine. The mess other people want to make of their lives isn't my business." Fishing a notebook from a reticule the size of a watermelon, Bob began scribbling something down. "This is the address of their hotel in Florence. They'll probably be there awhile. There's some kind of artist gathering out there, mostly Danes for whatever reason. Not that I'm suggesting the Danish need a reason to go to Florence. It's a beautiful city. Here."

Bob tore the page free and handed it to Belle, who took it dazedly. She was about to tender her thanks and, in all honesty, call it a night, when Bob abruptly addressed her once again.

"Hey. So, you know how I just did you a huge favour?"

Belle blinked. "Are we calling it huge?"

"It was definitely substantial."

"You wrote four lines on a piece of paper."

"Anyway"—Bob dismissed this tidily, probably an excellent quality in a secretary/assistant/manager—"would you mind popping in on Orfeo for me? They should be in attendance by now, and they're not."

A year ago, this would have been the opportunity of Belle's dreams. Now she wasn't sure if she had the kind of relationship with Orfeo that permitted popping in. "Are you sure? Are they all right?"

Bob wiggled her fingers, unconcerned. "Oh yes. They'll probably just be fussing with their hair. Or maybe they want their skirts fluffing or their corset fastening."

"And what makes you think I'm qualified to help with any of that?"

"Well"—Bob's eyes gave her a quick up-down—"you're a girl."

"Aren't you?"

"Yes," said Bob impatiently, "but the thing is, the thing about me, is I'm not like other girls."

Belle stared at her in confusion. "What does that even mean?"

"Oh, you know. I'm sharp-tongued and strong-willed. I'm interested in maths and science and things like that. I'm not beautiful, but my eyes are very striking."

"And you're under the impression that you're the only woman on the planet like that?"

"Name three others."

Belle pondered a moment. "Josephine Kablik, Mary Somerville, Caroline Herschel."

"Name three in this room."

Repressing a sigh, Belle scanned the guests. "Those two ladies who accompanied each other? One is an astronomer, the other the daughter of a famous naturalist who I believe has some experience in the field herself. The woman in the corner drinking perhaps a little heavily for the occasion is a writer, a reformer, and a reputed rakess. And the Scottish lady being rude to the Duke of Castlewell is a campaigner for the legalisation of trade unions. Oh and"—Belle gestured subtly with her fan—"those six ladies standing indiscreetly together? They are all members of a secret society who—"

"All right, all right," said Bob, looking a touch put out. "Now you're just showing off. But do go and get Orfeo for me, will you? There's a couple of people I need to talk to on their behalf."

At this point, Belle had little choice but to accede graciously. "Where do I find them?"

"Straight out the double doors, down the corridor, second on the left—there's a room set aside for them."

"And if they aren't feeling sociable?"

"That'd be a first. They love being adored. But just let me know and I'll make their excuses."

Resigned, and only mildly reluctant, Belle set out as Bob had directed. It did not seem, to her, like a good idea to interrupt a world-famous castrato at their toilette, but she assumed Bob knew what he was about. She would not have become indispensable to

Orfeo otherwise. It turned out that Bob's instincts were correct, though not necessarily for reasons she might have envisioned. Belle was about halfway along the corridor when she heard a crash, followed by a scream, followed by a lower-pitched oath.

Rushing towards the sound, Belle threw open the door to Orfeo's designated room and charged inside. Her first bewildered thought was that Orfeo wasn't there, for although the dressing table was covered in their powders and tinctures, they were not at it. But then came another muffled cry. The unmistakable thud and thump of bodies in motion or conflict. Turning, she beheld a chaise against the far wall, upon which a confusion of limbs flailed amidst piles of black velvet and the spilled ink of Orfeo's unbound hair. It took a moment for what she was seeing to resolve into something she recognised: Orfeo, half-dressed, struggling beneath a man Belle did not recognise. At least, Belle thought she did not recognise him. A broad back, in a well-tailored evening jacket, could have been almost anyone.

"Lasciami." Orfeo's voice cracked in fury and fear. "Vaffanculo."

Reacting, rather than thinking, Belle barrelled forward and leapt— all five foot and loose change of her—onto Orfeo's assailant.

"Stop it," she shrieked, pummelling away as best she could. "What are you doing? Leave them alone."

If nothing else, she had distracted the stranger, since even the most committed predator would have been hard-pressed to progress his ultimate goal with Belle screaming in his ear and whacking him in the head.

What came next was a kind of unintelligible physical anarchy, the man lurching in circles in an impotent effort to fling Belle off him, and Belle, finding herself ill-angled for punching, trying to poke his eyes out instead. Eventually, they crashed into a side table, sending both it and them flying, Belle colliding with the wall at a force sufficient to knock the breath from her body. It was enough to dislodge her, and she crumpled to the floor, limp as a pile of laundry.

Orfeo's attacker was breathing in heavy pants, a hand moving absently to smooth his thoroughly disarranged hair. And when he turned to confront her, Belle realised it was not, after all, a stranger but Orfeo's former patron, the Marquess de Montcorbier. For a second or two, she could only stare at him in comical disbelief. She didn't know him well, but her sense of him had always been of a composed, rather distant man, far more interested in art than the scandals and petty power plays of society at large. But there was little trace of elegance or refinement left to him now as he advanced on her, flushed and dishev-elled, the sweat glistening upon his brow, a set of sluggishly bleeding claw marks upon his cheek.

Pushing herself upright, Belle prepared to meet him, suddenly very aware of how tall even an average-sized man could look from the wrong angle. It was a bad moment to discover she had no idea what to do—how to even begin to contain someone when they were set upon violence—but she had little opportunity to make the attempt because he proved himself quicker, and more ruthless, than she, backhanding her across the face hard enough to send her reeling into the wall again. The sound came first, a crisp crack of skin to skin, then the shock, then the humiliating debilitation of it, her ears ringing and her eyes watering. The pain was almost an afterthought.

Her hand had flown instinctively to her jaw, which was not a help-ful place to have a hand when it seemed very likely that someone was about to strike you for a second time. She tried to brace herself, but mostly she was bracing herself against how helpless she felt, how small and uncertain.

His arm came up. Drew back.

And then he was being dragged away from her by Orfeo, who was clinging to him like a cat, and clearly had no more notion of how to fight than Belle did.

"Leave her alone," they cried, before the marquess shook them off, sending them spinning across the room.

They attempted to steady themselves but stumbled over their skirts, their shoulder catching the dressing table as they fell, bottles and vials falling with them, peppering the air with clatters and merry tinkles.

"Giovanni." The marquess's voice was coaxingly soft. Horribly reasonable, given the circumstances.

Orfeo scrabbled backwards across the carpet. "Stay away from me."

"There's no need for this."

"S-stop it." That was Belle, trying to speak, trying to reach them, but the whole world had turned to treacle around her. Or she was turning to treacle. Either way, she didn't like it.

"I said stay away."

Orfeo snatched up a pot of . . . Belle had no idea what . . . and hurled it at the marquess. It pinged harmlessly off his shoulder and bounced away into a corner.

"I always did adore your spirit, Giovanni." Somehow Belle knew the marquess was smiling.

"My"—another pot—"spirit"—a jar of ointment—"is"—a vial of rose water—"mine."

"And I will treasure it always," promised the marquess.

Belle started to crawl. Or she thought she did. Maybe she just lay on her face. Everything from the neck up—even her brain—was *throbbing*. She had church bells instead of a head, and monks were ringing them badly. Through her disorientated haze, she saw the marquess lunge at Orfeo, who snatched up yet another of their cosmetics to throw. As the little box spun through the air, the prettily painted lid broke free, dispensing a cloud of glittering rainbow powder that caught the marquess fully in the face.

"Jesus Christ." He staggered back, blinking frantically. "My eyes."

Orfeo and Belle rushed him in unison, bearing him to the ground, where he was capable of little more than writhing.

"We must secure him," Belle directed. Because this was an area in which novels had never let her down.

Without hesitation, Orfeo pulled up their skirts. Stripping off their stockings—which were black silk with silver clocks—they passed them to Belle.

"Oh," she said, still sore and shaken, but feeling better by the moment, "these are so pretty."

"Grazie."

The marquess did his best to resist as they secured his hands and feet, but with his eyes already swollen shut and the skin around them bright red beneath a scattering of rainbows, he was in no place to. Not one to leave anything to chance, Belle pulled tight the final knot and sat on him.

She and Orfeo gazed at each other across their fallen foe, jointly stunned, and more than a little worse for wear.

That was when Rufus and Lady Farrow burst into the room.

"What in God's name is going on?" demanded Rufus.

The marquess stirred and gasped out, "I think I'm blind."

"Lady Farrow." Orfeo rose gracefully, languidly, as if they entertained people in the wreckage of their receiving room all the time. "You really must show greater discrimination when it comes to your guests."

She glanced from Orfeo to Belle to the marquess and back again. "But . . . but . . . he's an Art lover."

"He is no lover," returned Orfeo, gesturing at themselves, the rips in their gown, and the finger marks upon their wrists, "of *this* art."

Lady Farrow's mouth fell open. The idea that someone could admire art and behave badly was clearly beyond her mind's power of reconciling. "He attacked you?"

"And may well have done worse if not for Miss Tarleton here."

"Belle." That was Rufus, falling to his knees before her, his fingers soft and cool beneath her chin. "What's happened to you?"

"Do I look dashing?" she asked, because the swelling at her jaw was limiting its range of motion.

"No, you look like you've been hit in the face."

Her eyes widened tragically.

"I mean, yes, you look like you've been hit in the face very dashingly. My poor darling."

"I'm fine," she assured him. "I'm gooth."

"I'm going to fucking kill him."

This was the final straw for Belle. "So you won't murther Valentine but you will murther the marqueth? That'th tho *unthair*."

Rufus's own face was doing something very strange, which Belle finally identified as trying not to laugh. "It would probably be best," he said gently, "for all our sakes if you didn't speak for a while."

"And I would prefer," Orfeo added, "that we dispense with talk of further violence. Could someone please see that"—they toed the marquess with a bare foot—"*this* is removed from my sight."

"Of course. Forgive me, Orfeo." Rufus rose, drawing Belle with him, only releasing her when he was sure she could stand unaided. Then he bent and dragged the marquess roughly upright by his bound hands. "Come. You and I are going to have a little talk."

"I do hope," murmured Orfeo, "that is not some masculine euphemism."

Belle sighed. "He'th not going to murther him. He'th curiouthly reluctant on that thcore. But he can be vocally devaththathing when he wanth to be."

"This is not something I would normally say to anyone"—Orfeo had a hand clasped lightly across their mouth as though they were trying very hard to contain laughter—"but you really should listen to your husband and be quiet a little while."

"But I'm fine," protested Belle. "I'm gooth."

Orfeo turned to their hostess. "Lady Farrow, might I trouble you to fetch Bob for me, and perhaps some ice for my friend."

"Of course," she cried, clasping her hands with the anguish of someone whose party has not gone as they had hoped. "I'm so sorry about all this."

"Giovanni." While the marquess was not strong enough to break Rufus's grip, he did manage to twist round in the doorway. "All those years, and I never asked a thing from you."

For long seconds, Orfeo made no reply. Even in bruises and tatters, they were magnificent, their hair streaming down their back and their eyes fiery with pride. It was only Belle, standing as close to Orfeo as she was, who felt them tremble. "And that gives you the right to take what you will?"

"No, but . . ." The marquess's face was such a mess it was hard to read his expression. But there was, for a moment, something sincerely sorrowful there. Even if it was also selfish. "I love you. I've always loved you."

Orfeo's lip curled. "You don't love me. You just want to have me. And"—their voice rose, ragged as a wild beast—"my name is fucking Orfeo." They flicked their fingers haughtily at Rufus. "Get him out of here."

It was only when the room was clear of everyone, and even the sound of footsteps had died away, that Orfeo came apart. Sinking to their knees upon the carpet, they covered their face with their hands and breathed like they were breaking. It was a grief so vast and private that Belle wondered if she'd been forgotten.

"Orfeo," she said softly, not quite daring to touch them. And then, trying to choose words that would not challenge her jaw: "It will be all right."

They glanced up at her, their fingers wet with the tears they'd shed in silence. "Ever since Peggy, I've sworn that no-one would make a trinket of me." Their voice was low and harsh, like nothing Belle was used to hearing from them. "Never again. She is worth more than the little I was taught to think of myself."

The door was flung open, and Bob raced in, hair springing free from its demurely fashionable chignon. "What's happening. Oh my God, emotions." Stopping dead, she stared at Belle and mouthed, "Do something."

"Orfeo," Belle tried again. "Thith . . . dammit. Thith ith not your fault. And Peggy will think no leth of you for it."

"It's what I was made to be." They wrapped their arms around themselves, growing smaller and smaller on the floor of Lady Farrow's drawing room. "There will always be those who will see me no other way."

"Then fuck them," suggested Belle. "Whatever thorrow there wath in your patht, you are your own perthon. Your own creathion. Nobody ith rethponthible for your thuchtheth but—"

A different noise drifted out from between Orfeo's fingers.

"Are you laugthing?" demanded Belle.

"I cannot help myself. No-one could. You sound ridiculous, cara."

"Well, tho do you," Belle retorted. "With everything that you're thaying right now."

Orfeo peeked up at her. "Probably you are correct. And I'm sorry for that."

"It'th all right." If nothing else, Belle prided herself on being magnanimous in victory. "You've had a thock."

"Indeed I have," Orfeo wheezed, "had a thock." A few fresh tears slipped from their eyes, but some of them, at least, seemed to be mirth. "I thought I was doing so much better. I hate that Nicholas has made me feel that I am not."

"He wath very, very in the wrong tonight."

"I know that. On some level I know that." They wiped their eyes and steadied their breathing. Threw the heavy weight of their hair back from their shoulders. Then stretched out a hand to Belle. "Thank you, Arabella. For this and for . . . earlier. I will soon be myself again."

"Of courth you will." She gave their hand an answering, reassuring squeeze.

"I just . . ." They broke off, with an embarrassed laugh.

"What?"

"Oh, it's foolishness. I just wish I could go home. I want to be with Peggy."

"Why can't you?"

They lifted a shoulder in a graceful shrug. "Commitments. We're sailing . . . not tomorrow but the day after, is that right, Bob?"

Still somewhat wary of the emotions happening in her vicinity, Bob nodded.

"I don't have time to get there and back and then to Dover."

Belle wrinkled her nose. "But don't you thet your own thchedule theth da—now?"

"Yes, but there are people expecting me. Hoping to see me."

"You're Orfeo," Bob put in. "They'll wait."

"You mean"—Orfeo gazed at her with eyes heartbreakingly full of hope—"I can go? I can see Peggy?"

Bob ran a tormented hand through her hair. "Bloody hell, yes. I mean, please don't go turning into one of those unreliable primos who can't keep two engagements together. But you're the boss. What you need, you get. You just have to tell me."

"We can do that? We can really do that?"

"Yes." Reaching into her vast reticule, Bob yanked out another notebook from a supply of many. "I'll stay put, get it handled; you go home, for as long as you like. When you're ready to tour again, drop me a note, and I'll take it from there."

Orfeo was on their feet in seconds, relief and excitement radiating from them with such undimmed fervour that Belle was almost a little envious. "You are, as ever, a wonder, Bob."

"I know," said Bob. "There'll be a carriage waiting for you, first thing in the morning."

"First thing in the—oh." Orfeo dimmed. "Of course. It must be well after ten."

"You know," Belle spoke into the silence, "my carriage"—well, technically Valentine's carriage, which Belle had refused to give back—"ith already here. Why don't I take you home?"

"It will be some hours' drive, Arabella."

"Tho? What elth would I be doing? Thleeping? Pah." To be fair, she would probably owe Valentine's coachman, who she had also refused to give back, a bonus. A significant bonus.

Orfeo looked genuinely torn.

"It's fine," Belle declared. "It's gooth."

"You really need to stop saying *gooth*," said Bob. "It's going to haunt my nightmares."

"But it *ith* gooth. I'd love to thee Peggy, who I haven't theen for ageth. And I can go home to my houth, where I'd much rather be than London, tomorrow."

"Well"—Orfeo was visibly struggling to contain their eagerness—"if you're sure."

Belle was sure.

Chapter 39

Between gathering Orfeo's things and conveying to Rufus where his wife was going, it took them about half an hour to get on the road, Belle clutching a pocket handkerchief full of ice which she had spent the early part of the journey holding against her jaw. Orfeo, dressed in the outfit they had performed in, with their hair hastily braided, cut a subdued figure, and they travelled, for the most part, in silence.

It was at about this juncture that Belle re-discovered her self-consciousness because, while she had always admired Orfeo from afar, she'd had little direct contact with them. Most likely they were disposed to think well of her, for Peggy's sake, but now that they didn't have the joint project of an attacker to overcome, she was slightly at a loss. Especially because, in the quiet, and with the address Bob had given her burning a hole in her reticule, her thoughts were churning and churning, growing rancid within her.

"I do not think," said Orfeo, at last, "that I have congratulated you on your marriage."

Belle's heart fluttered nervously. Yes, she had helped Orfeo defend themself. Yes, they were married to her best friend. But they were still *famous*. "Oh, well, technically we eloped, so there hasn't been much opportunity."

"Did you have a good elopement, then?"

She flexed her jaw, grateful the ice had relieved the swelling some, though she was going to have a spectacular bruise. "I think so. The weather was nice. The roads were mostly in good repair. Oh, and I got shot."

Orfeo's dark eyes widened. "You were shot?"

"Yes. By a bookseller pretending to be a highwayman."

"And now you have been hurt on my behalf also. What a life you lead."

"At least," she offered, not wanting them to feel guilty over what had happened, "it's not boring."

"Boring is not always such a terrible thing, Arabella."

It still made her slightly giddy that they knew her name. Even though it would have been extremely odd if they didn't, given their various connections. "Are you bored with Peggy?"

A smile broke upon their mouth like the dawn. "Blissfully. We go for long walks. Talk about the infinitesimal changes we have witnessed in our daughter. Peggy drinks a lot of tea. I have still not developed the habit."

"And then you depart to perform before emperors."

"Well"—they spread their hands wide, their nails polished silver, their voice full of private mirth—"why must things be *this* or *that*."

They both fell silent again after that, but it felt, to Belle, like a different silence. The silence of people who could, perhaps, become comfortable with each other. Not today, but in some not-too-distant future.

Normally Belle chose not to delve into the weeds of the romantic connections she witnessed around her. She could, if she thought about it hard enough, usually find her way to an abstract understanding of them. Bonny and Valentine, for example. Bonny loved Valentine because he was a duke who treated Bonny like a king. And Valentine loved Bonny because he was an idiot. Or rather, because everyone loved Bonny, on account of Bonny being irrefutably loveable. Regardless, it clearly worked for both of them, even though Belle would have thrown herself into a pit of spikes before she would have subjected herself to anything like it. With Peggy and Orfeo, though, she was struck by sudden clarity. Why someone who could have had anyone, who was celebrated and beloved and impossibly talented, would ultimately choose a life with Peggy. For Peggy was the steadiest person Belle knew. The warmest. The least likely to be dazzled by anything as insubstantial as starlight.

"Orfeo?" she said, their name clanging through the quiet like something she'd dropped.

"Yes, Arabella?"

"I think . . . I think . . . I might owe you an apology?"

"That seems unlikely."

Belle twisted her fingers in her lap. "You know last year? Do you remember me at all?"

"The tiny blonde with the hungry eyes—I remember you."

"I . . ." Why was it now so hard to speak of? Perhaps because at the time she'd not known enough to be ashamed. "I had this plan of falling in love with you."

"I'm flattered."

"No, you aren't," she said, refusing to accept the easy out. "Because all I saw was your voice and your beauty, and that is . . . that is not who you are."

The sound Orfeo uttered was part sigh, part groan, all exhaustion. "Cara, as we saw tonight, you are not the first to think and feel this way. You will not be the last."

"That does not make it any less wrong of me. I'm truly sorry, Orfeo." She addressed herself awkwardly to the floor, glad the interior of the coach concealed the worst of her blushes. "I will always love your art. But I also know you are more than that."

For long enough that Belle considered casting herself into the road and hoping to be eaten by wolves, Orfeo did not speak. "I think," they said finally, with some sweetly uncertain note in their voice that made Belle look up, "I may need to apologise as well."

"It seems unlikely," she returned, hoping to lighten the mood with a touch of her usual mischief.

Orfeo's fingers fluttered, in both acknowledgement and dismissal, though they remained serious. "I have not been fair to you. I have taken it for granted that you were like everyone else. But"—and here their head tilted inquisitively—"you're not, are you."

She wasn't quite sure how to reply to that, eventually settling on "I sometimes wish I was."

"Oh no," Orfeo told her. "Never wish that." Before Belle could frame a reply, they swapped to her side of the carriage, curling up beside her on the seat with the facility of someone who had spent a lot of their life travelling. "Do you mind?" they asked, putting their head in her lap.

"Um," said Belle, "no."

"Grazie. This has been a tiring day. You may stroke my hair if you wish. I very much enjoy it."

With that, Orfeo was asleep and Belle was stunned. Reaching out a disbelieving hand, she ran her fingers through Orfeo's tresses. Their hair was straight as arrows, soft as feathers, and, within the shadows of the carriage, the deepest of deep blacks. As Belle continued her caresses, growing bolder once she was sure of welcome, Orfeo's only response was something perilously close to a purr.

Slowly it dawned on her that they were giving her their trust. Showing her who they were when their voice was silent and the stage was dark.

⁓❧⁓

It was a little after midnight when they arrived at Hadwell Hall, the somewhat eccentric house Peggy had leased from its somewhat eccentric owner. Belle had visited a couple of times since Peggy had taken up residence and been shown—with great pride—the moody stuffed crocodile in the hall and the summerhouse shaped like a pineapple. Belle had not-so-privately thought it was shaped more like a boob, but Peggy had insisted upon pineapple, and disparaged the boobs Belle had witnessed if they reminded her so readily of pineapples, an exchange that had not, in the end, gone well for Peggy, since hers were some of the boobs Belle had witnessed.

Given how quickly they had departed London, it had not been possible to send word in advance, but Peggy was still awake, pacing around the entrance hall in breeches and a dressing gown, murmuring to the baby in her arms.

At their entrance, she cast them the sort of look you cast people when you have no energy to spare for anything. "Oh, hello," she said. "She won't sleep. She's supposed to sleep. The nanny says this can happen, but what if she never sleeps again? What if *I* never sleep again?"

"Aurrrghhh," contributed the baby. "Ehh—ehhhh—ehhhhhh."

Which caused Belle to regard it in horror.

Then Orfeo stepped forward, tension falling away from them like rainwater. "Mio principe."

Peggy froze, still hunched over the baby. "Orfeo?" Then, in an overspill of something Belle could only call joy, "Orfeo? Oh my God, Orfeo. I thought I wasn't going to see you for weeks."

"No, I . . . there was . . . I had to . . ."

"Belle"—overwhelmed as she was by the presence of her spouse, Peggy was still taking Belle's attendance largely for granted—"take my kid a sec."

"What?" cried Belle. "No, I've never—"

"Support her neck, don't drop her on the floor; it's not difficult."

Before Belle could issue further protests, a baby was being shoved at her—a baby she just about managed not to lose her grip on. Thankfully, this new experience of being left in the care of someone who had no idea what they were doing seemed of interest to Peggy and Orfeo's daughter. Her eyes widened as she peered into Belle's face, her cries softening into curious burbles.

Peggy and Orfeo, meanwhile, were in each other's arms, exchanging flurries of kisses and frantic little whispers. Then Peggy's gaze fell upon Orfeo's wrist. "What happened?" she asked, her fingers tracing the marks that someone else had left upon them.

Orfeo let out a slow breath. "It's . . . a story. I'm sorry, tesoro mio. It's why I'm here. Over and above wanting to see you, I needed to feel safe somewhere again."

"We're your family, Orfeo." Peggy pulled them into another fierce hug. "You can come here for any reason or no reason. You know that."

Bowing their head, Orfeo melted against Peggy, their hair falling forward to conceal their face. "It seems I may sometimes still need reminding."

Still holding Orfeo, Peggy swivelled towards Belle. "Sorry, Belle, I didn't see you there."

"I'm holding *your child*," Belle pointed out.

"And I haven't slept for thirty-six hours. Look"—she flapped her spare hand towards both Belle and the baby—"can you just take her for a while. Orfeo and I need to talk, and I . . . I need to close my eyes. Just for five minutes. Maybe slightly more than five minutes."

Belle gave an alarmed squeak. "You want me to—Peggy, I can't. I don't know anything about children. What do I do with it? What if I kill it?"

"Well, for starters, you don't refer to her as an *it*. Her name's Stella. But she also answers to Li'l Goblinface and Munchbunch and Poomageddon—don't ask—honestly, most things because she doesn't have any language skills yet. And you probably won't kill her. Babies are pretty hard to kill."

"Probably?" shrieked Belle.

"Yeuuuuuuurgh," offered the baby, abruptly—and not unreasonably— apprehensive, waggling her socked feet in a wholly terrifying fashion.

"Thanks," said Peggy. "Appreciate it."

Belle clung to Stella, then worried she was squeezing her too hard. "Peggy, please. This is a *life* we're trusting me with."

"Try to make her go to sleep. It'll be fine."

"How, though?"

"She's just a person, Belle. Well, the beginnings of a person. Go from there."

With that, Orfeo and Peggy disappeared upstairs, leaving Belle quite literally holding the baby.

"Um," she said, looking down at the bundle of gently flailing human in her arms. "Hello, Stella. Hello, little person."

Stella, still dubious, blinked up at her.

"Peggy wants you to go to sleep. Wouldn't that be nice? Going to sleep?"

"Auuuuuuurhhhhh." Stella did not feel going to sleep would be nice.

"That's all right; sometimes I don't want to go to sleep either. Oh, no no." She caught a tiny hand as it thunked against her jaw. "We don't punch Auntie Belle in the face tonight. You have to join the queue for that."

At this, Stella made a different sound: an utterly delirious trill that seemed to paint the whole world in the prettiest, brightest colours.

"Are you," asked Belle, "are you *laughing*?"

Stella made the sound again.

"Well," said Belle, helplessly enchanted. "I'm beginning to see why Peggy keeps you around."

All at once, Stella's face scrunched up like a fist, and she burst into fractious tears.

For some reason, Belle was less panic-stricken by this than she thought she might be. "Oh, you're quite the little drama, aren't you?" She gave Stella a gentle jiggle. "Is that better?"

Stella did seem to think it was better. Her tears vanished as quickly as they'd come as she bounced in Belle's arms.

"I can certainly tell my twin was involved in your production," remarked Belle. "You are going to be an absolute menace when you grow up."

"Yeh-yeh," declared Stella.

"No, you're right. Why wait until you're grown up. Start as you mean to go on."

The jiggling was already becoming yesterday's news with Stella. She gave a determined wriggle of her own that made Belle's heart plummet fearfully in case this was the moment when she inadvertently smashed Peggy's child on the floor. But no. Everything was fine.

"My, my," said Belle, still recovering, "you do not like to be bored, do you? I don't blame you. I don't like to be bored either. Is this why you won't go to sleep? Do you think you might miss something important?"

Stella gazed up at her, temporarily lulled by the rise and fall of Belle's voice.

"Well, you don't have to worry about that. Because you *are* the something important. Never let anyone convince you otherwise."

This was sterling advice and made Stella laugh again.

"I know," said Belle. "Let's go on a little explore, shall we? And we can look at all the things and—oh." She noticed a basket on one of the chairs, absolutely bristling with toys and blankets and other items she supposed necessary for the well-being of a small person. "Are these your friends? You'd better introduce me to every single one of them. Because that won't be exhausting at all, will it?"

So they made their way around the hall, Belle doing her best to distract Stella with whatever they came across—the fancy moulding around the fireplace, the wibble of their reflections in a set of silver candlesticks, a petal that had fallen from a jar full of roses—until even Stella's boundless inquisitiveness seemed to have run its course. Then Belle settled down in the big chair by the fire and went through the basket, waving various items in front of Stella's face and making them disappear again by holding them very slightly out of reach. In some respects, she thought, as Stella reacted in shocked delight to a rattle she'd seen two seconds ago, babies were a lot easier to deal with than their grown-up counterparts.

Eventually, to Belle's mild surprise—for Peggy had given her to understand such a thing was absolutely impossible—Stella slept, her favourite cuddly bumblebee in attendance, her whole fist clenched around Belle's little finger.

The hours ticked by, moving neither fast nor slow, but passing inevitably, bearing Belle with them, like waves drawing a lost sailor further and further out to sea. She was at once terribly content and terribly afraid because it had never before occurred to her that she might want this. That she—with her unmoved, unmoving heart—*could* want it. And not whimsically or impulsively, as she generally wanted things, but with the deep ache of waking to discover you'd bruised yourself in the night. This sad little pain that had been yours long before you'd noticed it.

❧

The nanny eventually disturbed Belle's listless slumber, drawing a still-quiet Stella from her stiff arms. Then Peggy, looking less tired than she had the night before, assuming a scale of human exhaustion that began at *weary* and ended at *dead*, brought her a cup of tea.

"Looks like my kid's still alive," she said.

Belle yawned, stretched, and then winced as a joint or two popped with a crack. "It was touch and go for a while."

"You got her to sleep."

"Yes, I banged her head against the wall. That seemed to do the trick."

One of Peggy's brows arched. "Funny."

"Sorry."

"I'm fucking with you. We joke about that stuff all the time. I think it's how we protect ourselves because I can't imagine anything worse than anything bad actually happening to Stella."

"She'll be fine." Belle shifted, found the shifting agonising, and wondered if she was going to be armchair-shaped for the rest of her life. "You said yourself that babies are hard to kill."

"Jesus, Belle, I was just trying to make you feel better."

Belle gaped, retrospectively appalled at her former ease.

"I'm fucking terrified," Peggy went on, "all the time. My mind is a constant litany of 'What if I drop her, what if she falls down the stairs, what if she falls out the window, what if she falls down a well, what if she gets eaten by a lion . . .'"

"I mean," Belle tried, "she hasn't died yet?"

Throwing herself into the chair opposite, Peggy extended her feet towards what remained of the fire, looking effortlessly louche for someone contemplating the demise of their offspring. "Suppose not. Thanks for, you know, taking care of Stella for me. The sleep I just had might have been the best sex of my life. God, I feel like a whole new person."

"How's Orfeo?"

"Better. Still in bed. Look, I"—Peggy leaned forward over her knees—"I hate that this happened to them and I wish it hadn't. But we're both grateful for the time together. Maybe it'll serve as a reminder that they can come home without needing someone to attack them first."

"I think that would be good," agreed Belle.

Peggy smirked. "Very gooth."

"Oh, stop it." Belle's pout was only about 30 percent counterfeit. "I was legitimately injured."

"I know, I'm sorry. You were heroic. But Orfeo's impression of you is the funniest shit I think I've ever seen."

"So," said Belle, "while I was down here taking care of your child for you, you were both upstairs laughing at me?"

Peggy nodded. "That's about the strength of it. Married couples. Can't trust us."

"Apparently not," returned Belle loftily.

"Though speaking of married folks"—Peggy's lazily shrewd gaze became energetically shrewd—"you and Sir Horley. Can't say I saw that one coming."

"To be fair, I'm not sure we did either."

"And it's all right . . . you know, with your . . ."

"My incapacity to love?" suggested Belle, hating to be the one thing the usually blunt Peggy felt uncomfortable talking about.

"It's what you want, though?"

Belle opened her mouth, intending to say yes. Because, in many ways, it could have been. "I don't know," she said instead. "Maybe I'm not very good at knowing what I want. Maybe that's been the problem all along."

"Or maybe," Peggy offered, in her brisk way, "it's not and you're fine."

It was hard to resist Peggy when she was set upon a course of making you feel better. Even if what that meant in practice was you gave up and agreed. Which was sort of what Belle did now. "Maybe."

"Anyway." Peggy's briskness tended to extend to her actions too. Done with sitting, talking, and Belle's nonsense, she stood. "Sir Horley's a good man. You'll figure it out. Are you staying for breakfast?"

And Belle said yes, because *not* staying for breakfast had never helped anyone. Though she might have been better off had she departed immediately, because, while Orfeo and Peggy did their best, they were too involved with each other to be good company. By the time she was back in the carriage, she was beginning to ask herself if she was actually going home, or if she'd just run out of places to leave. And whether letting herself become part of other people's compromises had only trapped her in one of her own.

Chapter 40

Scything, Rufus had discovered, was harder than it looked. Not quite trusting himself to take on the courtyard, he was in the kitchen garden, thrashing away inefficiently at the weeds that had not only run riot there, but were, in places, almost as tall as he was. Despite his lack of facility, and the fact he was soaking through his shirt beneath the mellow late summer sun, it was strangely enjoyable work. Swallowfield was not the sort of undertaking where action always led so directly to outcome, for it would probably take years for the estate to fully recover. That was not a thought that troubled him—he had time; he could imagine nowhere he would rather be—but it did mean he welcomed the simplicity of mowing grass and watching the grass he mowed get smaller as he mowed it.

However, he had made the choice to wed a Tarleton, which meant straightforward afternoons were not likely to be a regular feature of his life. He had just begun to find a rhythm, his arms growing accustomed to the flat sweeping motion of swinging the scythe, when Belle came racing, white-faced, towards him, her curls bouncing and her shawl flapping behind her. In some ways, it was almost a relief to find her in the grip of theatricality for, as much as he did not want her to have suffered some kind of upset, she had been oddly subdued since her return to London, while nevertheless insisting she was not. Her silences had made him realise how he had come to take her confidences for granted—to cherish them, even—but he did not think it would help the situation to make demands of her.

Therefore patience. And scything.

"Rufus," she cried. "I'm so sorry. I've done something terrible."

Since Belle and a sharp implement were unlikely to be a successful combination, he put the scythe aside. "What? Again. How could you."

"No, no"—she wheezed frantically—"I mean it. I've *really* done something terrible."

He had been about to suggest some of the potentially terrible things she could have done—committed bigamy, eaten a spider, taken out an advertisement for Valentine's murder—when he saw how truly distressed she was. Rather than merely dramatically distressed in the usual Tarletonian fashion. "Whatever it is," he said, determined to prove himself worthy of her faltering trust, "we shall handle it together."

"Not this. I . . . I've brought something to you, or upon you, that you may not want, and I . . . I meant to talk to you about, but I couldn't find the right time and now there's no opportunity—"

"Bellflower, you need to breathe, or you'll fall over. Have you volunteered me to fuck someone again?"

"I didn't volunteer you the last time," she cried. "That's unfair. You were *spontaneously invited*, and it had nothing to do with me."

"And I had a lovely time, so if the Farrows have been once again erotically inspired, I am more than happy to—"

She gave a little scream. "Rufus. It's not Lord Farrow. It's . . . me. Or rather, it's not me . . . it's . . . well, the truth is, I wrote to your family, and I was going to talk to you about it when they wrote back to see if you wanted . . . you wanted to . . . write to them and maybe you could forgive them . . . but now they're here. They're here right now. In the drawing room."

This was surprising news and, perhaps, secretly a little gratifying because Rufus had not imagined ever being forgiven. Let alone voluntarily visited. "My aunt is in the drawing room? Has she been struck by lightning?"

"Not your aunt." Belle gazed at him, stricken. "Your parents."

Two words that tumbled about him, heavy as masonry, robbed of all meaning.

"I wrote to them," Belle explained, slightly more coherently. "I thought they would write back. But they came straight here instead."

There was a distant ringing in Rufus's ears. His mouth tasted of salt and copper. "How did you find them?"

"It wasn't difficult. Your mother is quite famous."

"My mother is famous?"

"She's a model. And an artist in her own right."

"She's a model?" For some reason, the only words Rufus could grasp were ones placed immediately in front of him.

"Yes. Rufus, I'm so sorr—"

"And she's here," he asked.

"Yes. And your father."

"My father."

"Yes. Both your parents."

He sat down heavily amongst the weeds, unexpectedly comforted by the way the tall stems arched above him and around him, sheltering almost. His eyes drifted up to Belle in helpless anguish. "What have you done?"

"I don't know. I mean, I do know. But I didn't know they'd just turn up. Except maybe I should have known that because if I heard of my son for the first time in thirty years, I'd probably just turn up too."

Rufus put his head in his hands. The whole world drifted around him, flower petal fragments on a wayward breeze. The worst of it was, he was overcome, but he wasn't surprised. Part of him even wondered if he should have expected this. Seen it coming a mile away. "Why can't you ever listen? To anyone?"

"I do listen," Belle protested, and he heard the misery in her voice. "At least, I listen to you. It's just sometimes . . . sometimes you're misguided. I'm sorry but you are."

"That doesn't give you the right to make decisions for me."

Her foot came down in passionate dismay, mushing a buttercup. "Don't you think I know that?"

"If you do know that," he muttered, "your behaviour rarely bears it out."

"I'm not defending myself, Rufus. I can't. Because I did a bad thing, and there's no escaping it. I knew it would make you angry. Possibly make you hate me. But I did it anyway."

"You're right," he said flatly. "You are not defending yourself."

She knelt down beside him in the dirt, her eyes steady behind a sheen of held-back tears. "I know I'm in the wrong. But I thought the cost was worth it. I still do."

"That's not your calculus to perform."

"I'm not talking about the cost to you. I'm talking about the cost to me." She put her hand upon his wrist, her fingers chill as bone. "I promise you, I *do* listen. You've told me time and time again that you need a family. And your family has come all this way for you. They love you. They're desperate to see you."

He told himself he was furious at her. That he *should* be furious at her. She'd betrayed him, disregarded him, trampled all over him with her devastating good intentions. But he also recognised, in some distantly inaccessible way, that being angry at Belle felt safe when believing his family might ever have cared for him did not. In that moment, however, some piece of hope, no larger than an ant, broke free from the detritus of grief and fear and shame and proved itself stronger than any of them.

"Really?" he asked.

She nodded solemnly. "Yes. You should go to them."

Pushing himself to his feet, Rufus ran. He ran, barely even aware of drawing breath, and did not stop until he had reached the drawing room. Half falling through the door, he found within a man and woman, he seated, she restlessly pacing, both of them visibly exhausted from travel. For long, long moments, nothing happened. Nobody moved. Nobody spoke. The sweat stung the blisters upon Rufus's hands.

And then the woman—a statuesque beauty, her unbound hair the boldest, most familiar red—was standing before him, her eyes devouring him, as if they could never get their fill of looking. "Rufus." She turned to the man, who could have been any man except that he was not. "Rufus, he's my *son*."

⚜

It was a story told in tears, across hours, between embraces. It was not, in the end, the most important story, for that was not one story, but all the pieces of Rufus himself. Like the heroine of a fairy tale set an impossible task, Belle had gathered them from across the world and plucked them from the depths of his own heart, forgetting not one single speck of dust, and there he was in glittering mosaic. Whole not because of his parents, but for them.

His father had not been the only man to fall in love with his mother—she had been famous even then, beautiful, and scandalous—but he had been the one to marry her. It had cost him everything: his inheritance, his family, his position in society. And, for himself, he regretted none of it, but they had both feared for the child his new wife carried. Theirs seemed too precarious a life; unfair to make their son bear the consequences of choices made before he was born. His father's sister, now a very wealthy woman, had made promises, so many promises, so many convincing promises. She would raise the child as her own, give it every care, every blessing, every opportunity it could possibly need. Give it time to grow, she suggested, stable and safe, far from the shadow of gossip and disgrace. Let the child decide for itself. And so they agreed—no word from either of them until Rufus was eighteen years old. They were relatively poor in those days, living from hand to mouth, and friend to friend. It had all seemed for the best.

"But we missed you," Ygraine said. "Every day, we missed you. And every day we thought of you. We had to leave England because it hurt too much, knowing how close you were, and yet lost to us."

It had never occurred to either of them that Rufus's sister would not keep her word. That Rufus's eighteenth birthday would come and go, with no letters given over, no mention of the deal that was struck.

His father shrugged. "We thought you did not want to know us. We thought you were ashamed of us."

There had already been too much loss—they had already borne too much pain—for Rufus to tell them he had lived so much of his life convinced they were ashamed of him. Besides, these ancient ills felt far away as afternoon slipped into evening. Part of him, yes, but a fading part, as brittle as dry paper, when all about him, a life he had not known to hope for bloomed fearlessly amongst the weeds of the past.

❦

Had the house been even slightly ready for guests, Rufus would have begged his parents to stay. As it was, he begged them to return tomorrow, and need not have begged at all.

"Even if we talked all day and all night for the next ten thousand years," Ygraine said, as her husband helped her into the carriage, "I will still feel I have barely scraped the surface of everything we have to say."

Rufus, exhausted, hoarse from weeping, smiled at his mother. "You need to meet my wife. You'll like her."

Or they'd murder each other.

But probably not.

His father hugged him one last time—something else Rufus secretly thought he could not take his fill of even in ten thousand years—and then his parents were gone.

Or not gone.

Gone up the road.

Coming back.

As often as he wanted.

For several slow-passing minutes, he simply stood upon the forecourt, watching the now-empty carriageway winding between the trees, his own thoughts a mystery to him. While he had long maintained he would never reach out to his parents of his own volition, he had always on some level believed that knowing them would teach him how to know himself. But it had not. It had opened no doors, explained no riddles, taught no lessons. It had, in fact, changed nothing at all. Well, it had made him happy, though even that did not feel how he might once have imagined it would. Because, he realised with an odd jolt, he already was.

And he found himself wondering if this thing that he'd claimed he never wanted had simply come too late to matter. Except it wasn't that either. It did matter, it mattered very much. His heart was foolishly full with how much it mattered. So perhaps that was the difference. Being safe enough to brave the possibility of pain. And loved enough to be able to offer love. No longer lost within a life he didn't know how to live, tormented by needs he didn't understand how to fulfil, there was space, at last, for joy.

Turning, he made his way back across the bridge. Swallowfield was quiet, but not quiet as it had been upon their arrival. That had been a lonely quiet, a neglected quiet. This was a well-earned quiet. The quiet of a day well spent and a promising tomorrow.

Æthelflæd was nosing into the long grasses that continued to thrive in the still-untamed courtyard, gathering flowers for her pen, something he'd fully believed to be one of Belle's pig-favouring fantasies until he saw it with his own eyes. Pausing, he snapped off a stem of rosebay willow-herb, with its long-tongued purple flowers, and offered it to Æthelflæd. She was dubious at first but then she took it in her mouth and trotted off with it—though quite why she was so fussy about her own bedroom, he did not know, because she was a master at sneaking into theirs.

Belle was not in the kitchen. Nor in the great hall. He thought she might be with Mr. Smith, but he was in the moat room, reading a letter with such intensity that Rufus thought it best not to disturb him. Probably Belle would head down later and steal his candle until he promised to stop working. Except she was not in the library either.

Nor was she in the bedroom.

Had she gone for a walk? Was she in the bath? Down a mediaeval sewer?

Then he spotted the piece of paper on his pillow. He did not have a good feeling about it. Never in the history of the world had anyone left a note upon a pillow in a mood of contented optimism. Indeed, Asher had once left him such a missive. It had simply read *I can't do this*. Therefore, it was with his own mood of contented optimism dissipating around him that Rufus reached for the envelope and ripped it open.

> Dearest Rufus,
>
> I hope now you've met your parents, you can see you've always been loved. That you were always worthy of it. I want you to have the life you've always longed for. I want you to pursue the dreams you insisted were impossible. I want you to stop denying yourself what you need and what you deserve. I think you could do that here. Just not when I'm forever standing in the way.
>
> I believe you'll find your Bonny.
> Love always,
> Belle

Crumpling the sheet between his fingers, Rufus gave vent to a heartfelt "Oh, for fuck's sake."

At which point the door flew open with such force it crashed into the wood panelling. "What," demanded the normally placid Mr. Smith, "have you fucking done."

Rufus stared, hardly recognising him. "I haven't done anything."

"Then why has Bel—Mrs. Tarleton—left us?"

"You can call her Belle. I'm aware you're fucking. And I don't know."

"You must. Because it is for your sake she has gone."

"Jesus Christ." Rufus ran his hands through his hair. "I feel like I'm participating, without my consent, in one of those fairground games where you have to bash a rat in a sock."

Although he had regained his calm somewhat, Mr. Smith was now eyeing him as though he belonged in Bedlam. "What does bashing rats in socks have to do with driving your wife away?"

"Oh, I just meant . . . every time I think one aspect of my life is under control, something else goes wrong."

"I still don't think you should compare your wife to bashing rats in socks."

"You've *met* her. She's exactly like that." It was slowly beginning to dawn on Rufus that this wasn't helping the situation. "Look, what did she say to you?"

Mr. Smith's colour fluctuated slightly. "Some very kind things. But she also said she couldn't go on being selfish. That she'd taken your happiness from you, was liable to do the same to me, and therefore she was going to live in a villa in Italy."

Sinking onto the bed, Rufus continued doing violence to his own hair. "I mean, of course. 'Have a sensible conversation with your husband'"—he briefly let go of his hair in order to make a balancing motion—"'live in villa in Italy.' Trust a Tarleton to Tarleton. It is the one great constant of the universe."

"I don't understand," said Mr. Smith, still regarding him warily.

Rufus cast his mind to the conversation in the kitchen garden. He had been shocked and spoken, he would be the first to admit, intemperately, but he didn't think he'd said anything so terrible it would make his wife spontaneously run away from him. Or rather, this felt like an impulsive reaction to something much deeper. "Neither do I."

"I also don't understand why she wouldn't at least mention feeling like this."

It was unexpectedly reassuring to witness Mr. Smith's distress. While he'd given Rufus no reason to complain about his role in the household, Belle's affection for him had always seemed somewhat incomprehensible. Clearly, though, he cared for her deeply. And that, even beyond Swallowfield, was something he and Rufus had in common. "Because she's Belle?" he suggested.

"That's neither answer nor explanation." Mr. Smith began to pace the bedroom like a wolf separated from its pack. "What did we do? What did *I* do?"

"Did you quarrel?" asked Rufus, holding, somewhat unfairly, on to the vague hope he could blame Mr. Smith for Belle's disappearance.

"No." He shook his head. "She told me once she feared she would disappoint me in some regard, but I don't believe I have done anything to substantiate such a concern."

"That doesn't mean it's not real to her."

"Do you think I'm not aware of that?" retorted Mr. Smith, with a touch of his former sharpness. "I suppose I hoped that she would come to believe what I said at the time."

"Which was?"

"Not that it is any of your business, but that I desired nothing from her that she did not wish to give."

"It might not quite be a matter of *wishing*."

One of Mr. Smith's pale brows arched upwards. "Cryptic."

"It's not my place to speak for Belle."

"Given you have no idea what would cause her to abruptly flee her home, I'm not sure you're even qualified to."

Rufus rose, unsure if he was impressed or frustrated when Mr. Smith held his ground. "You forget your place, Mr. Smith."

"Well, you seem to have forgotten your wife."

"Are you in love with her?"

At that, Mr. Smith hesitated. "No," he said finally. "But before you accuse me of . . . of anything, Belle has given me no indication that she would welcome that from me."

"We can't always control how we feel."

"No," conceded Mr. Smith. "But what we have together"—and here a faint, oddly intriguing blush touched his cheeks—"works for both of us. Or so I thought until . . ." He broke off, his expression tormented enough to stir Rufus, reluctantly, to guilt.

"At ease, Mr. Smith. I'm sure you haven't done anything wrong."

Mr. Smith brandished his letter. "If I hadn't done anything wrong, would Belle be attempting to . . ." He paused, this time in confusion. "Does she even *have* a villa in Italy."

"No. No she does not."

There was a long silence, Rufus turning the page Belle had left him over and over in his hands, as though he might discover upon the paper some hitherto unnoticed message. The energetic surge of his initial frustration had already ebbed away, leaving only a kind of numbed bewilderment behind. To have regained one family and lost another in the space of an afternoon. It would have been comical if it had not been so devastating.

"If you will allow the question"—Mr. Smith's tone softened—"and if you are correct that I may not be responsible here, why would Belle say she has, what was it again, taken your happiness from you?"

"Honestly, I have no notion."

"Well, *has* Belle taken your happiness from you?"

"What? No." Rufus glared at him. "Of course not. She *is* my happiness."

"And you have, I assume, told her that?"

"I . . . well. I think so. I must have?"

The two men exchanged a series of looks, each increasing in gravity and alarm.

"Oh God," said Rufus. "Get Tom to saddle a horse. You're in charge of the house. Don't let anything happen to the damn pig."

Mr. Smith bristled. "I am quite capable of taking care of Æthelflæd."

"Do you have a double first in it?"

"Everyone is very aware"—Mr. Smith's tone was icy—"that when you're worried about Belle, you get very unpleasant to be around. May I remind you that, in this instance, the person who has apparently hurt her is you."

Rufus opened his mouth, intending to deliver the biting put-down this upstart steward deserved. Then realised he was completely correct. "If you had impetuously run off to live in an Italian villa," he asked instead, "where would you sail from?"

"Most probably I would start by crossing the Channel. So . . . Dover?"

"Wonderful." Flinging off his shirt, Rufus pulled on a slightly cleaner one. "I suppose I am going to Dover."

Chapter 41

Belle stood upon the deck of the packet boat that was to take her to Calais, trying to take comfort from the fact she had done the right thing for the people she cared about, instead of wallowing in deep, crushing misery. Unfortunately, the deep, crushing misery felt a lot stronger, and a lot realer, than the meagre solace afforded by righteousness. She wondered if she should keep to her cabin until the journey was underway, but she could not bear to deny herself one last look at England, since she would probably never see it again. Surely Italy would be beautiful, for it always sounded so in Mrs. Radcliffe's novels (and the likelihood of being abducted by a sinister nobleman seemed relatively low), but her heart already ached for the greys and greens of England.

With a sigh, she rested her elbows on the taffrail and let her gaze drift unseeing over the vibrant chaos of the port, through which a gentleman appeared to be ill-advisedly trying to ride a horse. It was fitting, from a certain perspective, that she would spend the rest of her days in an Italian villa—she assumed these would be readily available to all comers once she arrived in Milan or Venice—because, as it turned out, she was not the gothic heroine she had once pretended to be.

She had been the villain all along.

The sound of a commotion came from the gangway, but even that could not stir Belle from melancholy to curiosity.

It was followed by sharp, furious footsteps upon the deck, and she turned just in time to see Rufus descending upon her, his many-caped riding coat flapping at his heels like an irritable crow.

"Arabella Tarleton," he said, "you utter fucking ninnyhammer, I am going to fucking kill you."

For a moment she could only stare. Certainly his presence was a grave impediment to her very well-thought-out and necessary plan. Not an occasion for wild, uncontrollable joy. "Rufus?"

"No, your other husband."

"What are you doing here?"

He rolled his eyes. "I am bringing you home; what does it look like?"

"It looks like you're very annoyed at me."

"I'm not." He seemed to crumple all over. "I'm *devastated*, dear heart. As is your pretty Mr. Smith."

"Francis sent you?"

"No, I sent myself. I practically had to fight him for the privilege of retrieving you."

Belle may have been confused and upset and generally in an emotional tangle, but she was still inescapably herself. "There was a fight?"

"Yes, we ripped off each other's shirts and rolled about aesthetically in some mud."

"From your tone," she said dolefully, "I'm beginning to think you didn't rip off each other's shirts and roll around aesthetically in some mud."

"Sorry to disappoint you, Bellflower. But if you come home, he might well be persuadable."

The word *home* echoed inside her, as though she were a vast and empty cavern. "He's better off without me."

"That's not what he thinks."

"It may not be what he thinks *now*. But—"

"Enough." Closing the distance between them, he very gently put his gloved fingertips against her mouth. "Sometimes people know exactly what they want. Sometimes you should believe them when they tell you."

"I . . ." She felt the weakness of her own words, shaped as they were by trembling lips. "I just keep hurting people, Rufus. Often just by being who I am."

"I think," he said softly, "Mr. Smith has been far more hurt by your leaving than he is ever likely to be by your staying. But—and forgive my selfishness—enough of him for the moment. What did *I* do to make you feel you had to leave?"

She had been, even if she said so herself, extremely, or at least passably, brave, right until this moment. But suddenly, hopelessly, she started to cry. "N-nothing. You're so kind to me, and you make me s-so happy, but I'll n-never be able to forget what I've taken from you."

"Belle, Bellflower, no." His voice was low, and stricken, and urgent. "You have never taken from me. Only given. Even if on one occasion you gave me a whole trifle directly to the face."

This made her weep even harder. "Don't joke. Not now."

"I'm sorry."

"In any case"—she gave an aggressive gulp—"you have your parents. You have lovers who will treat you well. You h-haven't murdered Valentine, so I think you're probably still friends. You have everything you need to make you happy. To make you feel loved. To build the life you've always wanted. I'm not meant to be part of that."

"Not meant to be part of it?" he repeated. Between the sea and the open sky, his eyes were the brightest green she'd ever seen them. The precious green of growing things. "I would have nothing if not for you."

"You deserve it all. Don't let some misplaced sense of gratitude hold you back."

"Good God, Belle. How could you have this so wrong? Please don't leave me."

He sounded appallingly sincere. But Belle was fatally stubborn, often—she knew—to her own detriment. And, besides, people could be sincere, appallingly or otherwise, about all sorts of things. "You shouldn't be staying with me out of pity. Because you know I'm lonely and scared of being alone and unlikely to find anyone else."

He blinked, recoiling slightly. "Thank you, that's terribly insulting."

"Nooo," she wailed, wringing her hands. "I didn't mean it like that."

"Oh? Then what's the non-insulting way of telling someone you only believe they're with you on account of their standards being lower than the entire rest of the world?"

She felt like she was slowly dissolving into mulch. Worthless human mulch. "Rufus . . ."

"As you've witnessed, Belle, I have little pride. But even I think better of myself than that. Fuck, you *taught* me to."

"I'm sorry," she said, from the subterranean pit where her soul had fled. "I don't know what I'm saying."

"Well"—he huffed out a breath—"that makes two of us."

In a futile effort to force herself to coherence, she sniffed so violently that a passing sailor looked genuinely shocked. "You know I can't have . . . I don't want . . . the thing that everyone else does. But you do and you can have it. Or you could if it . . . if it wasn't for me."

"You aren't stopping me from having anything. Nor I you. Something else you taught me, by the way."

"What about your dream, though?"

He gazed at her in stark incomprehension. "Which dream?"

"The Bonny dream."

"Belle, I don't want to talk about your brother right now. I think I'm long past that fancy, as is right and proper, for he is a married man and so am I."

"Not . . ." She wiped her face on her sleeve. "Not literally Bonny. But everything Bonny represents. The one true love that is solely yours, and all-consuming, and lasts forever."

"What?" His hands flew out in a wild gesture. "Where are you getting this from?"

Now it was her turn to gaze in confusion. "It's what you told me," she said in what was definitely a calm, measured voice, whacking him on the shoulder for good measure.

"When?"

"About ninety million trillion times on the way to Gretna Green. You said marriage would steal your last hope of the kind of love you were looking for. I know we Tarletons have our ways, but I really . . . I really do"—her voice cracked—"I really do pay attention, Rufus, and I really do try. Back then, I thought you would come to see things as I did. Now I know how wrong of me it was to force that upon you. Also," she added, in an even smaller voice, "you told Gil I was a pain in the arse."

"You *are* a pain in the arse," he pointed out. "It doesn't make me adore you one jot less."

"You don't adore me. You tolerate me. You . . . you—"

"Don't you dare," he said, with such ferocity that it stopped her in her tracks, "tell me how I feel. And if you do, in fact, pay attention as you claim, then do me the honour of listening to me now."

She wasn't sure she'd ever heard him so impassioned. He had occasionally been earnest, of course, and sometimes unbearably unhappy, but mostly—even with his priest—he maintained a certain sardonic distance. This was new and somewhat disconcerting. On a different occasion, it might even have been gratifying. Nervously, she nodded.

"Then heed me when I say," he went on, with the same unusual fervour, "that I am not the same man who began that journey to Gretna Green with you. I am not the same man in many regards, but I like to think I have changed in one significant particular."

"Which is what?"

"Well . . ." He broke off, apparently struggling to articulate himself, either because of the intensity of the emotions involved or the complexity of what he was trying to communicate. "The fact of the matter is, there's something you need to understand about who I used to be, something mortifyingly and profoundly true, and while I wish it was otherwise, I'm afraid you're just going to have to find a way to accept it and live with it."

He was regarding her with such naked, pleading sincerity, and his words seemed to carry such deep significance for him, that Belle felt a little overwhelmed. Nevertheless she tipped her chin up valiantly. "Oh, Rufus, what is it?"

"This." He took a deep breath. "I was a fucking prickwit."

"P-pardon."

"I was a fucking prickwit. I didn't know what I was talking about. I didn't know what I wanted. I know now." Dropping to one knee upon the deck, he laid claim to her rather soggy hand. "It's you, by the way. I want you."

This was, without the shadow of a doubt, the *nicest* thing that anyone had ever said to Belle. That anyone had ever done for her. So much so, she half wondered if she was dreaming it. "Really?"

And it was testament to how deeply Rufus meant what he was saying that he didn't answer sarcastically. "Yes, really."

"But"—the words erupted out of her along with a fresh flood of tears—"what if . . . what if I might wish to have children?"

He barely reacted. "Then we'll have children?"

"How?"

"The usual way, I should imagine."

"Can you?" she asked.

"You are veering perilously close to insulting again, dear heart. I believe my virility is up to the task."

She squirmed. "No, I mean. With me."

"Admittedly, it's not something I'd find gratifying in the usual way," he said. "And I can't believe you're interrogating me about this on a public sailing ship. But I can think of few experiences I would cherish more than creating a life with you. Or many lives. As many as you decide you can handle."

"We shall hire people to help us handle the lives."

"Very sensible, Mrs. Tarleton."

"But also spend a lot of time with the lives ourselves. Nobody shall ever feel unwanted in our world."

To her surprise, Rufus seemed to be blinking back tears of his own. "Our world, Belle? God, I love the sound of that." He cleared his throat. "Though I should say, if the thought of me . . . if you would prefer someone else, I would be perfectly comfortable with that."

"You would raise someone else's child with me?"

He shrugged. "I'm not my aunt. Any child I raise will be my child, as I am my father's."

"Was that ever in doubt?"

"My aunt thought otherwise. It may be true. It may not. It does not matter. And it will not matter to me."

"I think I would still like it to be you," she said, feeling somehow bold and abashed at the same time.

"Then it shall be. Just"—seeming to forget all over again where they were, he wrapped his arms around his waist and pressed his brow against her hip—"don't ever do this to me again. You nearly broke my damn heart, and I'm not at all used to having one."

"I'm sorry." She truly meant the apology. But no sooner had she spoken than the happiness billowing inside her stirred her to mischief. "Though, you know, you're saying such wonderful things to me. That might tempt me to run away often."

"For fuck's sake, Belle"—his laughter was muffled but undeniable—"I can say this to you at home. Every day if you want. Every hour."

"Wouldn't that get tedious?"

"Not if it pleased you. Don't you understand, you ridiculous creature? I'd do anything for you. *Anything.*"

"You shouldn't," she tried. And then, "I don't—"

"Belle." He silenced her with nothing more than her name, sweet and perfect on his lips. "Whatever you think you need to say, on this occasion you don't. What you have done for me is immeasurable. I wish to do immeasurable things for you in return."

"But I haven't—"

"You saw me like no-one else has ever seen me. Fought for me like no-one else has ever fought for me. Cared for me like no-one else has ever cared for me. You've given me a life. You've given me a home. You've given me . . . a pig, apparently."

She tried to hold on to lightness. "No, how dare you; she's my pig."

"Fine. You keep your pig." When he smiled up at her, she saw his tears were flowing freely now. "You've given me hope. In myself, and in the world. You've taught me how to share that hope with others. You've made me happy beyond anything I could have imagined possible. You are my best friend and my most cherished companion. I have never had a dull day with you in it, and I don't think I ever will. I would choose you, Mrs. Tarleton, I would choose us, I would choose the life we are making together, over the phantasms I once called love."

"You don't have to choose. With me, you'll never have to choose."

He rose shakily but kept her hand. "I know that. When you fled, it was the only time you've ever tried to make me."

"I didn't realise," she admitted mournfully, "that was what I was doing."

"Then all the more reason to stay . . ." He paused, interrupting himself with an odd, self-conscious laugh. "To stay until you're bored."

She met his eyes, silly, flighty Arabella Tarleton steady for once. "I will never be bored with you, Rufus."

"Then stay forever."

Alexis Hall

Drawing her into his arms, he pulled her against his body, enfolding her completely, and held on so tightly that it squeezed every drop of fear from her. Banished every moment she had felt lacking or insufficient or broken or monstrous. She was just a person, like any other, flawed and messy and doing her best, as right for Rufus as he was for her.

It didn't even matter that, just at present, he smelled considerably of horse.

"I believe in this," he whispered. "I believe in you. This is the fairy tale. This is the happy ever—"

A horn blast broke the moment ignominiously.

"What the hell was that?" asked Rufus.

"Oh." Distracted, Belle had started rootling in her reticule for a handkerchief. "It's the boat departing for Calais."

He gave her arm a little shake. "Belle, we can't be on a boat to Calais. We have to go home. People are waiting for us."

"I mean, we can ask the captain to stop, but I doubt he will."

Something wicked flashed in Rufus's eyes. "Then we shall have to disembark."

"What? No—you can't—don't you dare—"

"Together, Mrs. Tarleton?" he asked.

She sighed, as though this was not secretly one of the best, most beautiful, and most exciting things that had ever happened to her. "If you insist, Mr. Tarleton."

Sweeping her into his arms, he leapt unhesitatingly over the gunwale. And, laughing, they plunged into the chill waters of the Channel.

ACKNOWLEDGMENTS

As a general rule, a book goes through multiple rounds of editing during the production process. In practice, this usually means the author works more closely with the developmental editor. For *Something Extraordinary*, however, I must offer my heartfelt gratitude to my brilliant copy editor, Bill Siever, and my equally superlative proofreader, Elyse Lyon. Their meticulous, considerate, dedicated editing not only improved this book immeasurably but restored my faith in it. Further thanks, as always, to my agent, my assistant, and my partner for putting up with me.

ABOUT THE AUTHOR

Alexis Hall has Bette Davis eyes.

He's determined to marry into money, as his grandfather drank half the family fortune and gambled the rest. He lives in a tumbledown mansion in a fictional county, and his valet doesn't even have a humorous name.

Keep up with Alexis and his latest endeavors by visiting his website at www.quicunquevult.com or subscribing to his newsletter at www.quicunquevult.com/contact. You can also find Alexis on Instagram (www.instagram.com/quicunquevult).